# Murder *at the* Mikvah

# Murder *at the* Mikvah

*Sarah Segal*

iUniverse, Inc.
New York   Bloomington

# Murder At The Mikvah

This is a work of fiction. All of the characters, names, incidents, organizations, and dialogue in this novel are either the products of the author's imagination or are used fictitiously.

iUniverse books may be ordered through booksellers or by contacting:

iUniverse
1663 Liberty Drive
Bloomington, IN 47403
www.iuniverse.com
1-800-Authors (1-800-288-4677)

ISBN: 978-0-595-53029-8 (pbk)
ISBN: 978-0-595-63083-7 (ebk)

Printed in the United States of America

iUniverse rev. date: 3/9/2009

*For Steve*

Authors Note:

Jews have been using water as a method of ritual purification for thousands of years. Translated, the Hebrew word *mikvah* means a "pool" or "gathering" of water. Mandated in the *Torah*, the Jewish Bible, male priests were required to immerse in a mikvah prior to entering the Holy Temple. The entire Jewish nation—men and women alike—did so before receiving the Torah at Mount Sinai.

Still today, immersion in a mikvah is considered an act of self-renewal and rebirth. For many men, it is customary to immerse prior to Yom Kippur, the holiest day of the Jewish year. Others opt to immerse each Friday, before the onset of the Sabbath, the day itself designated for renewal.

Oceans and rivers are natural mikvahs, though often impractical due to inclement weather and the fact that one must disrobe completely before immersing. Man-made mikvahs are more commonly used; but each must adhere to strict rabbinical oversight. A typical man-made indoor mikvah will be built into the ground, or otherwise be an integral part of the building in which it is constructed. Most likely it will resemble a miniature swimming pool, or *Jacuzzi*, with stairs leading down into a depth of between four and five feet of chlorinated water. Three or four people could stand comfortably in an average sized mikvah.

As part of the larger group of laws called *Taharat Hamishpachah,* —The Laws of Family Purity—married Jewish women are instructed to immerse monthly, at the cessation of each menstrual period. As part of the preparation process, a woman first bathes in an ordinary tub. It is important to note that soaking in bathwater *can never* substitute for ritual immersion in a mikvah; for it is only through a mikvah that a woman is cleansed *spiritually.*

There is extensive information available on the subject of ritual immersion. To learn more, I suggest the following books:

Abramov, Tehilla. *The Secret of Jewish Femininity; Insights into the Practice of Taharat Hamishpachah.* New York: Targum/Feldheim, 1988.

Kaplan, Aryeh. *Waters of Eden: The Mystery of the Mikvah.* New York: NCSY/Union of Orthodox Jewish Congregations of America, 1976.

# One

The wind was picking up and blowing papers off Father Herbert McCormick's desk. Earlier, before the dark clouds descended on Arden Station, he and Peter sat across from one another on two stiff leather chairs, as they did every weekday, while Peter sifted though the day's mail. Letters were read aloud and responded to, dictated by Father McCormick to Peter who typed them out at an impressive speed on a Macintosh computer, one of several items the rectory had inherited from St. Agassi High School. Most correspondence was from former parishioners, who, befitting of their ages, preferred the old fashioned method of communication—putting pen to paper—to e-mail or even the telephone. Typically, they were short, quick letters, written with perfect penmanship of their generation, describing the latest goings on: the upcoming church bake sale, the christening of a new grandchild. Then there were the obligatory sound bites, references to Father McCormick and St. Agassi Church, intended to prove unremitting allegiance to their former parish and it's aging priest. *The bake sales were always more profitable at St. Agassi, Father McCormick's sermons far more inspiring.*

One letter stood out today; it was from the Cardinal's office. Typed on impressive linen stationary and stamped with the official embossed seal of his office, a royal insignia of sorts, it provided the finalized relocation plans for Father Herbert McCormick of St. Agassi Parish. As Peter was aware, Father McCormick would soon be moving across country to Arizona. In just a few months time, the priest's new home would be Mt. Lemmon Village, an "active adult" community consisting of two hundred identical ranch style homes, each one surrounded by strategically placed palm trees, and a centrally located swimming pool and clubhouse.

Throughout his long career, Father McCormick had experienced periods where he was strongly opposed to church politics, most recently the church's less than stellar treatment of nuns and the heinous cover up of pedophile priests; but one opinion that he held constant was the impressive way in which the church cared for it's own. No detail was overlooked, no expense spared when it came to the retirement of those who had devoted their lives to God.

Peter dutifully moved from window to window, securing the rectory from the volatile conditions brewing outside. There was a storm advisory in effect until midnight, serious enough to interrupt *Wheel of Fortune* with a special announcement from the national weather service. A nor'easter the weatherman called it. Lydia had called, claiming to be worried—"What if they lost power?... What if a tree fell on the rectory?" She went on and on, but Peter didn't pay much attention to her. Lately that girl would find any excuse to call and pester him. Why couldn't she get it through her thick skull that he wasn't interested? He knew darn well it was his own fault for being nice to her, for giving in those few times.

He shook off the annoyance welling up inside him and headed up to the second floor. Well, hopefully there wouldn't be any thunder tonight. Samson could get a bit unnerved by loud noises. She had already spent the last hour barking at shadows. Peter often wondered how Samson would fare during the move to Arizona. He worried the noise and turbulence would traumatize the poor dog. Father McCormick had secured permission for her to sit in the passenger area of the plane, but still, it would be her first time flying.

As Peter struggled with one particularly stubborn second floor window, he looked out at the high school next door. The *former* high school, he corrected himself as a white car pulled into a parking spot under a tree—not too smart, considering the likelihood of a hefty branch smashing through it's windshield. A woman stepped out, grabbed her bag and headed for the back of the building. Peter gritted his teeth. This was the part that made his blood boil. Women had no business being out alone at night! He shook his head in disgust. No, it just wasn't safe, not with all the nut jobs running around. Heck, there were even monsters in the church! Of course, it went without saying that Father McCormick was one of the good guys; but still, there were more dirt balls dressed like priests than Peter cared to count. *You can't judge a book by it's cover*, his momma used to say. She used to say a lot of things. He never did pay much attention—all those sayings sounded so dumb at the time—and now he would give anything to remember just half of them.

Peter pushed down on the window with his right forearm. It finally gave way and he held it down while forcing the latch into place. He did a thorough check of the rest of the floor, finishing in his own room at the end of the corridor. Then, he grabbed his binoculars and returned to the hall window. The white car was gone and there was a black Lexus parked in the lot. He adjusted the lens. *It was the blond.* He recognized her from last month. And just like then, she had her face down in the steering wheel. *What the hell did she have to cry over?* Peter waited, expecting more cars to pull in, but none came. Maybe it would be a slow night because of the weather.

They always came one woman per car; Peter had been watching long enough to know they never carpooled. Every night for the past four months or so—ever since that rear part of the high school had been renovated—different women showed up, always after dark. A couple of them were regulars, the two old ones who showed up on the same nights week after week. *Must be in charge of whatever meeting went on down there.* At first, Peter thought of AA. But he'd gone to plenty of those in the old days to know that these women were no boozers. Besides, every week there were different faces. Alcohol rehab was not for dabblers. OA? Hell no. There were a couple of chubby ones, but not so many. *Most of them were actually pretty decent looking, all dressed up in their long skirts and all.* He felt his face flush and diverted his eyes for a second, ashamed of what his curiosity had almost led him to do more than once. He knew he shouldn't even be watching them like this. If Father knew what he'd been up to…

The truth was he *tried* not to look, but each night they came, as if taunting him, dressed as though they could be going to mass. *Hah! Jews in church!* Peter laughed out loud at the irony. The fact was that the Jews *would* be going to church. All eighteen acres that once belonged to the Catholic Church had been sold and now some kind of Jewish Center was being built. It was just a matter of time before he and Father McCormick would be forced out for good. Father McCormick would be off to the west coast, but Peter still hadn't figured out where he would go, and he had less than six months to come up with a plan. One option was to move on to another rectory, maybe another parochial school, but how likely was it that he would land a job when church facilities were being shut down all over? What was happening here was happening in cities and suburbs all across America. Mass attendance was down and according to Father McCormick, enrollment in Catholic schools was the lowest it had been since Vatican II. The whole religion getting sandbagged on account of those whack jobs calling themselves agents of God. Those scum of the earth were the reason the church had to pay multi-million dollar settlements; the real reason the church property on Trinity Lane had been sold.

Peter imagined there were others like him. Church custodians— *plant managers* as he preferred to call himself—all looking for work in what few remaining rectories there were. Peter swore he wouldn't trouble Father McCormick with his problems, so on the few occasions when the priest had asked, Peter had assured him that he'd be staying with family upstate. Lying was the least he could do. After all, Father was suffering too. Peter's blood boiled watching the man who had saved him from a life on the street being so callously tossed aside. Peter was actually thankful Father's vision was as bad as it was. The seventy-five year old should not have to bear witness to bulldozers pulverizing what remained of his home, his *life*. The chapel and rectory were the final phase of the takeover. Peter wondered if the Holy Spirit would stick around for a while, maybe save a few Jewish souls.

# Two

"Abba, Nehama's crying."

Rabbi Yehuda Orenstein was jolted from his sleep by the *tap tap tap* of a finger poking his arm. He opened his eyes and looked up; his nine-year-old daughter Rachel slowly came into focus. She stood on the side of the couch wearing a long white nightgown, a concerned expression on her face.

"What?... Oh, okay, Racheli... Where's Mommy?"

"I looked Abba. I couldn't find her anywhere."

Yehuda sat up and rubbed his eyes. After a minute or so, he was more fully awake and remembered that Hannah had gone to the *mikvah*. "It's all right Rachel... Mommy will be back soon," he told her, repositioning two small pillows that had been displaced while he slept. "Go back to bed; I'll take care of Nehama."

"Can I get a drink first?"

"Okay Racheli, but then, bed!" he told her, playfully wagging his finger.

She smiled back at him and padded off toward the kitchen.

Yehuda stood up and stretched. It was unlike him to fall asleep on *mikvah* night, but then again, with a newborn in the house, his share of the workload had increased substantially. Both he and Hannah were exhausted. Fortunately, Lauren, their babysitter, had been available 24/7 for the first month after Nehama's birth in September. But now Lauren was in class most days, leaving Yehuda no choice but to pick up the slack. This meant grocery shopping, preparing meals, supervising bath time, even doing a bit of laundry. Yehuda enjoyed the additional one on one time with his kids—helping Rachel with her homework, kicking the soccer ball with Eli—that being home more afforded him. It also gave him the opportunity to do the things so easily put off, like removing David's training wheels, and teaching the boys to cross the street by themselves. Nevertheless, he was starting to feel the familiar effects of having additional domestic responsibilities.

Whenever he and Hannah were blessed with a new baby, Yehuda was reminded of exactly how hard his wife worked to keep their home, *their lives* running smoothly. Somehow she made caring for a husband and five children look effortless. He didn't know how she managed it all: meals, school, tutoring, piano lessons, sports, doctor's appointments. All this in addition to hosting their weekly Shabbat guests, teaching women's classes at the center, *and* her volunteer work throughout the community. Each day, Yehuda thought of his wife during his morning prayers when he thanked God for, among other things, not creating him as a slave or a woman. These words were offensive to feminists and most secular Jewish women—as were a handful of other traditions— who often cited them in their argument that Orthodox Judaism was repressive to women. Taken at face value without fully understanding the meaning behind the traditions, Yehuda could see how they would reach such conclusions. He and his wife often addressed the issue in their classes, teaching that in Judaism, women were actually considered to be spiritually *superior* to men. When a man thanked God for not being born a woman, he was essentially thanking God for the obligation to perform more *mitzvahs*. Each mitzvah brought a person closer to God. Being spiritually inferior, men needed to perform many more, including an array of "time bound" mitzvahs from which women were excluded. God in his infinite wisdom realized that men needed to work harder than their female counterparts just to stay on track.

On a more personal level, Yehuda was thankful that God didn't make him a woman because, quite frankly, he doubted he (or most men in his opinion), could handle it. Besides the physical discomfort of pregnancy and childbirth, there were the never-ending responsibilities of running the home, which extended far beyond cooking and cleaning. The Jewish home was considered a living *beis hamikdash* or temple, in which the spirit of God, *the Shechina,* resided. The Jewish woman was charged with protecting and maintaining that spiritual presence. According to Jewish belief, the holiest thing a person could do was to bring God and spirituality into the physical world, and women were given the opportunity to infuse Godliness into the world through all aspects of domesticity, raising the mundane events of daily life to the most elevated heights of the heavens.

Yehuda heard Nehama cry out from upstairs.

*What time is it anyway?*

He looked at his watch; his eyes popped at what he saw.

12:07.

*Oh my God.*

"Abba, Nehama's still crying!"

"Ok, Racheli, I'm coming right now…" As Yehuda bounded up the steps toward the baby's room he went over the evening's events in his mind. *Hannah left the house at 9:45. She called home a little after 10:00… more than two hours ago.*

Visibly shaken, Yehuda reached into Nehama's crib and picked up the tear drenched infant. Pulling her close to him, he kissed her face and rubbed her back. "Poor Hummi... she's sopping wet! ..."

"Abba? Is something the matter?" Rachel stood in the nursery doorway, blocking the light from the hall.

"No, no... Nehama needs a change, that's all." He looked down at Rachel's pink bunny slippers; one of the ears was missing. "Did you have your drink?"

"Yes Abba."

"Good," he said, trying to keep his voice steady. "Rachel, please go check and see if there are any messages on the answering machine."

A cordless phone had been sitting right next to him while he slept on the couch. Though almost certain he would have heard it ring, it was possible that he had been in too deep a sleep. He swung around to the changing table and gently lowered the baby onto the pad. His eyes darted around—*diapers stacked in neat piles, creams lotions, powder*—Hannah kept everything so organized.

Rachel returned to the room. "No messages Abba." She looked at him, as if willing him to explain, but he didn't.

"Where are the..."

"Here Abba." Rachel cautiously approached the table and pulled three wipes from the container that her father's eyes had somehow missed.

"Oh... I didn't see them," he said, avoiding her eyes. He extended his hand toward one of the piles of diapers.

"Abba, why is your hand shaking?"

But Yehuda's mind was racing and he didn't hear her. He grabbed a diaper, inadvertently knocking a few onto the floor. He gently lifted Nehama's legs with his other hand and wrapped the diaper around her bottom.

"Abba?"

Yehuda tried to appear calm as he accepted the fresh pajamas Rachel was offering. "Rachel, I need you to sit with the baby for a minute while I make a phone call."

Rachel nodded obediently and leaned over to collect the fallen diapers. After stacking them neatly on the changing table, she sat down on the rocker. Yehuda placed Nehama gently into her sister's waiting arms. Rachel snapped the baby's pajama closures and began rocking slowly back and forth. Not surprising, Nehama's eyes started fluttering immediately. Rachel was very skilled at taking care of babies. With three younger brothers, she had had many years of practice helping her mom. By the age of five, Rachel could hold and carry an infant; by age seven, she was changing diapers and helping with their baths. Rachel knew that as the oldest, she was *expected* to help with her younger siblings, and fortunately, she enjoyed doing it. A few of the girls at school didn't. Rachel's friend Leah hated it more than anything else. Rachel could understand why. Usually Leah wasn't allowed to play after school because she had to help with her brothers and sisters. On a recent half day, Rachel offered to go over to Leah's house to help. She thought the two of them could help Leah's mom and have fun too. But Leah's mom had said things like, "Rachel, I bet *you're* a big help to your mommy" and "Leah, see how *Rachel* likes to play with the babies?" So in the end, Rachel didn't feel like she had helped her friend at all.

"Nehama's asleep, Abba!" Rachel looked up proudly, but saw that her father was already half way down the hall. She watched him round the corner and disappear down the stairs. She took a deep breath and gazed lovingly at her sleeping sister, her pink lips parted ever so slightly, breathing gently. *What was Nehama dreaming? Did babies even have dreams?* Whether they did or didn't, babies were lucky to be spared from worrying. Rachel felt a hard lump in her throat. Something was wrong and she suspected it had something to do with her mother. It wasn't like her to be out this late. Besides, the only other time she had felt this way or had seen her Abba so frazzled was when her mother was rushed to the emergency room four months ago, at the beginning of the summer. Rachel had never seen her father *daven* so fervently. Body swaying, he pleaded in Hebrew for God to save his wife and unborn child: *R'foanynu Hashem, v'nayrofay, hoshi-aynu v'nivshay-o, kis'hilosaynu oto, v'ha-alay r'fu-o-sh'laymo l'chol makosaynu, ki ayl melech rofay ne-emon v'rachamon oto. Boruch ata Hashem, rofay cholay amo yisro-ayl.*

"God heard," her father told her days later, after the danger had passed. "God hears all our prayers, especially heartfelt ones," he added.

Her mother was discharged with strict orders to stay in bed. Dr. Blynne explained that this was necessary so the baby wouldn't get any funny ideas about showing up early again.

Yehuda paced around the kitchen, his mind racing. He had just called both Hannah's cell phone and the mikvah line but there was no answer at either, just recordings. He checked his watch again. *12:19.*

*There must have been an accident.*

He grabbed the phone off the kitchen counter and dialed.

"911 emergency. This is Marie. Please state your emergency."

"Yes, hello. This is Yehuda Orenstein. I live at 62 Willow Lane. My wife isn't home… I mean she should be home by now… She went to the *mik*… uh… she went to an appointment and should have been back by eleven, and she's not."

"Sir, you say your wife was supposed to be home just a little over an hour ago. Is this what you are telling me?"

"Yes…"

Marie cleared her throat. "Mr. Orenstein, have you considered the possibility that she might just be running late?"

"No…" Yehuda stammered. "You don't understand. I'm a rabbi and…"

"Oh, pardon me. *Rabbi* Orenstein."

"…No… That's okay… It's just that we have five kids… We have a *newborn*… Something's not right. She should be home by now."

"All right Rabbi Orenstein, try to relax for me and I'll do my best to assist you."

"Okay…" Yehuda took a deep breath. "Thank you."

"Now what time did your wife, uh, what did you say her first name is?"

"Hannah."

"What time did Hannah leave your home this evening?"

"About 9:45, maybe 9:50."

"You're sure?"

"Positive."

"Where was her appointment? Do you have a street address?"

"526 Trinity Lane."

"526 Trinity?"

"Yes."

"Your wife went to church?"

"No!… No… The church is next door… Hannah went to *526 Trinity*, the old high school."

"St. Agassi High School is next door. Right. Thank you for that clarification. But wasn't that building turned into a community center or something?"

"It's going to be a Jewish Recreation Center… but right now it's in the middle of renovation."

"You're saying the former Catholic high school is currently under construction?"

"Yes."

"Rabbi, could you tell me why your wife had an appointment at a building under construction?"

"No… she had an appointment at the *mikvah*. It's in the one area of the building that's already finished. I'm sorry I wasn't clear."

"I'm not familiar with the term *mikvah*."

"The *mikvah*… it's a ritual bath… it looks like a small swimming pool… used for centuries by Jews…"

"A small swimming pool?"

"Yes, basically Jews believe in immersing in the *mikvah* water to remove spiritual impurities." *Did he really have to get into this now?*

"Oh, a religious thing, kind of like baptism. Okay. So, who was her appointment with at this pool?"

"The attendant… the *mikvah* attendant… Hannah was immersing tonight."

"And who would that be? Do you happen to know the attendant's name?"

Yehuda thought for a second. "Tonight would have been Tova Katz, I think."

*I should have called Tova.*

"Have you tried contacting this Tova Katz or the pool, er, *mikvah* area itself?"

"I called the mikvah; there was no answer. But I didn't try Tova… I guess I should do that…"

"Wait; Rabbi, before you hang up, I want to check with the police and fire departments to see if they responded to any accidents in the last few hours."

"Thank you, I would appreciate that."

"Please hold."

Yehuda pulled open Hannah's bill drawer. Tucking the phone under his chin, he shuffled papers around searching for her phone book. *Why hadn't he thought of this before?*

"Hello, Rabbi Orenstein, are you there?"

Yehuda nearly dropped the phone. "Yes. Yes, I'm here."

"It looks like it's been a pretty busy night... lots of fallen trees, wires down, that sort of thing. Surprisingly, no injuries as a result of the storm. However, I did learn that there were two unrelated emergencies called in tonight."

Yehuda held his breath.

"The good news is that neither appeared to involve your wife. The first was a drunk driver slamming into a parked car. The second was a ninety year old woman who took a nasty fall down a flight of steps."

Yehuda exhaled, relieved. There was no accident. Hannah was probably fine. "Thank you for your help. I'm sure I'll find her."

"I'd be happy to send a patrol officer to the location, Rabbi..."

"No, that won't be necessary."

"All right then. Will you be needing further assistance this evening, Rabbi Orenstein?"

"No... I'm sure everything's fine." *Please God.*

"Have a good night then."

"Same to you. Thank you... was it *Marie?*"

"Yes."

"Thank you Marie."

Yehuda placed the phone down and flipped through Hannah's pocket-sized phone book until he reached the "J-K-L" pages. He picked up the phone and punched in the number for Tova Katz. Possible scenarios raced through his head as the phone rang. *Maybe Tova needed help with something at the mikvah. Maybe Tova was feeling ill and needed*

14

*a ride home.* Hannah was thoughtful like that, but it wasn't like her not to call home and tell him what she was up to. Besides, he had just spoken to her around 10:15 and she hadn't mentioned anything about being late. Maybe it was a last minute change in plans. Was it possible that she knew he'd be asleep and didn't want to disturb him? He felt a surge of panic rising once again in his chest. He had not been in favor of opening up the new mikvah while construction was still going on, but he stood in direct opposition to the women of the community who were eager to use the new, modern facility. *Besides, the construction workers aren't around after dark when we use the building,* Hannah had said, assuring him it was safe.

"Hello?... Hello?" A man's agitated voice answered.

"Saul?"

"Yes; who is this?"

"Saul, it's Yehuda. Yehuda Orenstein."

"Yehuda?" Saul's tone softened. "I didn't recognize your voice... What's the matter? Is something wrong?"

Yehuda ignored the question. "Saul, is Tova with you?"

"No; she's not home."

"Tova didn't come home tonight?" Yehuda demanded.

"Yehuda, listen... Tova *did* come home, for about twenty minutes, to make a couple of calls and pack. Esti went into labor tonight, around nine. Tova drove out to New York to be with her; I spoke to her about an hour ago. We have a new granddaughter!"

"Mazel Tov..." Yehuda said, but the words were flat.

"Thanks..."

"Did Hannah go with her?"

"What? Now that's an odd question, Yehuda. Why would *Hannah* go with Tova to see my daughter and grandbaby?"

"I don't know..." Yehuda rubbed his forehead and took a deep breath. "No; of course she wouldn't have any reason to." He took a minute to regroup. "Saul, did she... did Tova work at the mikvah tonight?" His voice was calmer, but strained.

"Yes, but then we got the call from Esti, so she left early. Like I just told you, Esti had her baby tonight."

"The *mikvah* closed early then?"

"No, you know; they call a substitute... I think Tova called Estelle Ginsberg. What's going on Yehuda? You don't sound like yourself."

"Saul, I need Estelle's number. It's an emergency."

"Sure. No problem. Hold on a second."

Yehuda looked at his watch.

*12:39*

"I'm back. Here it is..."

Yehuda scribbled the number on a blank page in the phone book. "Thanks."

"Yehuda, tell me what's happening. You sound pretty upset."

"I am. Hannah never came home tonight... Look, Saul, I have to go... I have to call Estelle."

"Yehuda, wait," Saul said quickly. "Keep me posted... I'll be up for a while now anyway."

"I will Saul. Listen, I'm sorry for waking you..."

Yehuda dialed Estelle's number and listened to it ring and ring. A recording came on of an elderly woman speaking slowly. "*Hello, this is Estelle Ginsberg. I'm sorry I am not available to take your call at the moment...*"

Yehuda hung up and hit the redial button.

Again the recording. "*Hello, this is Estelle Ginsberg. I'm sorry I am not available to take your call...*"

He waited for the beep then blurted his message in as calm a voice as possible. "Estelle, it's Yehuda Orenstein calling. I understand

16

you may have worked at the *mikvah* this evening… it's uh, Monday, October 24th… please forgive me if I am waking you, but my wife did not come home and, well, I'm trying to find her. Please call me as soon as possible… call any time tonight. Thank you."

He hung up and scrolled down the recent calls list until he reached Lauren Donnelly, their babysitter's number. He hit the "dial" button and listened, expecting her to pick up any second. *"Hi, This is Lauren, leave a message!…"*

*What was going on tonight?* Yehuda didn't understand. Lauren was a light sleeper. How could she sleep through a ringing phone?

Yehuda called Saul Katz back.

"Yehuda is that you?"

He got right to the point. "Estelle didn't answer."

"Oh…"

"Saul, I need a favor…"

"Anything."

"Can you come over and stay with my kids? Lauren… my babysitter… didn't answer… something's not right. I have to find Hannah."

After ten years working as a 911 operator, Marie Pierce was adept at evaluating the urgency of every call, the credibility of each caller. She had learned to trust her instincts, and her gut was telling her that something was not right with the rabbi's wife. She hadn't realized it until just now, but *something* was going on at the old high school. Not wasting another second, she picked up the phone and called police dispatch.

# Three

The local Jewish community was thriving. Hoards of families were moving to Arden Station, in most cases, giving up acreage and forgoing privacy for the benefit of living within walking distance of a synagogue, a requirement for the observant, as driving was prohibited on the Sabbath and other holidays. Enrollment in Jewish day schools was on the rise as well. The two local schools, which had for years struggled to stay afloat, were suddenly experiencing an influx of interest and financial support. The *mikvah*, a cornerstone of any Jewish community and considered to be of greater spiritual importance than the synagogue itself, had been recently replaced by a new, larger facility. Modern features and aesthetics were now available to the hundreds of local Jewish women who observed the family purity laws of their ancestors, as well as to those women who were discovering the beauty of the mikvah for the first time.

Rabbi Yehuda Orenstein was honored to play a small part in the larger shift taking place around the world. People were returning to and rediscovering their Jewish heritage. This trend was referred to as the *Bal*

*Teshuva* movement. For the past five years, the rabbi had watched in utter amazement as interest in his Jewish learning center quadrupled. He liked to joke that people showed up to his classes for the food, specifically, the chocolate *bobka* his wife Hannah ordered from a well known Brooklyn bakery. But the truth was that the rabbi had earned a reputation as a knowledgeable and mesmerizing speaker. From members of the orthodox community to those with limited religious backgrounds, people were uplifted, moved, genuinely inspired by the relevance of his subject matter. One of his more popular talks addressed the common misconception that to embrace a Jewish lifestyle required relinquishing enjoyment of the physical world.

*God wants us to be happy. He wants us to enjoy and embrace the pleasures of this magnificent world He created for us! There is nothing inherently wrong with having money, a beautiful home, material things, if these are the blessings that Hashem—God—in His infinite wisdom has bestowed on you. But the question we must ask is why? Why am I blessed in this particular way? Why me? We must consider: how will I use my gifts? What should I do? What do you think the CREATOR would want you to do? This is your opportunity to make a "Kiddush Hashem"—a sanctification of God's name. Each one of us has the opportunity to honor God through the physical. It is our nature to think about God when things go wrong. Why me? We get angry at God. We DEMAND an explanation from him as if we are entitled to a seamless existence. We're not. Be it poor health, loss of a job, or, God forbid, an untimely death…we shout to the heavens, WHY GOD, WHY? God encourages our questions. He wants us to think, to challenge him. But most importantly he wants a relationship with us. We must not forget to pose those same two words: "why me?" when life is GRAND! When things are working out just right for us. When life is sweet! Talk to him, acknowledge your father in heaven when life is good! Recognize that He is entrusting you with good health, material wealth, extraordinary wisdom, unique talents... whatever they happen to be... they are His gifts to you. Three steps: thank Him... ask why... and infuse them with Godliness!*

Sadly, Yehuda recognized a spiritual void in most people. The preoccupation with *acquiring*—newer, bigger, better—he knew was just a flawed attempt to fill a nagging feeling that "something was missing." His goal was to show them that it was *God* they needed, and that religion and the physical world were not mutually exclusive. Yehuda realized that people weren't so quick to overhaul their lifestyles, and he wouldn't ask them to. What he *would* do was plant some seeds, nurture them with Torah and watch them grow.

And now, average class attendance had grown from a single digit to an impressive forty students. People of all ages and backgrounds flocked to the center. Yehuda was welcoming singles, young couples, families, empty nesters, all seeking a greater understanding of their religion. The older ones sometimes came at the urging of a son or daughter who had been making changes in their own life. Somehow they all managed to cram themselves, with surprisingly few complaints, into the small, five hundred square foot renovated flower shop that housed the Arden Station Jewish Learning Center since its inception eight years ago. Back then it was more than enough space, but with the rabbi's increasing popularity, they were quickly outgrowing it.

As an orthodox Jew, Rabbi Orenstein believed with total conviction that the Jewish Bible—the *Torah*—was the direct word of God. Throughout history, neither a single word, nor a single *letter* of the Torah was deleted, added or altered in any way. Torah scribes were meticulous with their craft, often taking years to finish one handwritten scroll. The *Torah* was God's gift to his people. By accepting this gift, the Jewish people had entered into an unbreakable covenant with Him. Translated, the Hebrew word "Torah" meant instructions. *Instructions for living*. If we were committed to building a meaningful life and reaching our highest potential, God was providing the blueprints. Mystical elements could be found in the Torah as well. Time was stacked, patterns were cyclical, behaviors repeated. There were hidden lessons to be learned; timeless truths to be grasped, embraced, and applied to our daily lives. But the common belief in more modern sects of Judaism was that the Torah at best was 'inspired" by God. Some held that God didn't have much, if anything at all, to do with the stories authored in the Torah. Ultimately, removing God from the picture allowed for a looser interpretation and application of its laws. Re-constructionist, reform and conservative Jews as a rule were more assimilated in secular society.

No matter what their differences with regard to its *authorship,* there was a general consensus among Jews that Moses had received the Torah at Mount Sinai following the exodus of the Israelites from Egypt. Each year, Jews around the world celebrated Passover, *Pesach* to commemorate that period of history when God freed their ancestors after two hundred years of slavery. For eight days, it was forbidden for a Jew to own or consume *hamatz*—bread or any product containing a leavening agent. The *Matzah* that was eaten instead resembled the flat bread eaten by the Israelites who, in their haste to depart, had no time for their bread to rise. Flat bread represented humility and trust in God. For the first two nights of *Pesach,* a special *seder* dinner was served, and the story of the *Exodus* told. Generations came together and read from the *Hagadah.* It was tradition for the youngest child at the table to recite the *four questions* asking, *why is this night different from all other nights?* On this night they would learn, perhaps for the first time, that "…this is what your Lord did for you… you were once a slave and now you are free." Holding the children's attention during the *seder* required a bit of ingenuity. The *Pesach* meal lasted hours, often extending into the wee hours of the next morning. Parents were encouraged to engage their children by relaying the historical facts of the exodus in the most vibrant, exciting and creative way possible. This was often achieved by emphasizing the ten plagues inflicted upon the Egyptians: blood, vermin, lice, beasts, boils, frogs, cattle disease, darkness, and finally the killing of the firstborn. It was not unusual to see plastic frogs springing across the table or to be poked by small fingers, wagging fabric puppets of lice or vermin. Sometimes the men and boys wore themed head coverings; *yarmulkes* of blood and darkness and death.

# Four

Weeknight patrols were usually quiet. By 9:00 PM, most Arden Station businesses were closed, kids were home studying or in bed, their parents glued to the TV or computer. And other than the occasional workaholic driving home after another fourteen-hour day in the city, there were relatively few cars on the road.

Tonight might have been different had the storm continued to rage. But by 11:00 PM, the torrential rain had stopped and the wind had all but died. Crews were out cleaning up the downed trees and repairing power lines. Railroad supervisors estimated it would be another hour or two before the main lines into the city reopened, but foresaw no delays for the morning rush hour. The bottom line for Officers John Collins and Robert Sedgwick was that it was shaping up to be just another night of business as usual.

The two were just pulling into the *Wawa* on Jenkins Street when the call came in from dispatch: *possible foul play at St. Agassi High School.*

*Juveniles* John thought immediately. At sixty-two, and with over thirty-five years on the force, he had seen plenty of teenage delinquents.

Arden Station had some wealthy areas and kids with enough unsupervised time and plenty of money to get into trouble. Then again, St. Agassi was a construction site. Plenty of valuable pickings for young and old alike.

John turned to his partner. "Looks like our donut break will have to wait tonight buddy."

Robert Sedgwick was a rookie who had been on the force for less than a year. Fresh out of the police academy, twenty-five year old Robert had not anticipated that his days would be spent issuing driving citations and filling out vehicular accident reports. The closest he had come to making a single arrest was warning a couple of drunk college kids about public lewdness, specifically that urinating behind a dumpster was *not* okay. As far as Robert could tell, beyond breaking up rich kid keg parties, there was not much excitement in Arden Station. This he would never admit to his girlfriend, who had gotten it into her head that he put his life at risk each day on the job. She was so terrified he'd be killed in the line of duty that she nagged at him constantly, reminding him that as long as he worked in such a dangerous profession, she would never consider marrying him. *How could she bring children into this world knowing they would be raised fatherless by their widowed mother?* This was reason enough for Robert to keep up the ruse, since marrying her was the furthest thing from his mind. The stress of the job, his girlfriend thought, was also the reason Robert spent so much time in front of the television, mindlessly watching cartoons and infomercials. The real explanation was simpler; with all his shift changes, Robert could hardly sleep. It was the policy for all the rookies: one month working days, the next working nights. It was enough to mess a guy up. On the flip side, they always paired rookies with more seasoned cops—guys who had been on the force for at least five years—and Robert had been lucky enough to get partnered up with John. But why John Collins, who had the most seniority in the department, would *willingly* work such lame hours—well, that, in the spirit of one of Robert's favorite channels—the *game show network*—was the twenty-five thousand dollar question.

"I said, it looks like our donut break will have to wait tonight," John said again. Apparently Robert had zoned out there for a minute.

"Roger that *Sergeant*," Robert said, sitting up and straightening his hat. "No donut break at twenty-three hundred hours."

John smirked at him before pulling out of the WaWa lot. He was fond of Robert, but the kid could be something of a smart ass sometimes. "Just *John*, all right? No *Sergeant*, no *Captain*, no *Detective*, got it?"

Robert laughed, all the while studying his partner. At 6'2" and solidly built, John was a living reminder that at one time, law enforcement had physical standards. Actually, with those Paul Newman blue eyes, prominent nose and strong chin, John looked more like a classic Hollywood actor than a cop. Minus the graying hair and about twenty years, he'd have made a perfect leading man. But regardless of his star qualities, John had chosen a career in law enforcement. It was no secret that he had moved up the ranks of the force. Rumor had it that he had once turned down the superintendent's position, choosing instead to remain in investigations. *So why take a demotion from investigations and go back to patrolling?* Robert guessed that his partner was sick of being cooped up in an office all day. Or maybe he was afraid of computers. A lot of older people were intimidated by the new technology. Robert had a hell of a time convincing his own old-fashioned mother to start using e-mail. She finally relented after the last postage stamp rate increase. Robert sometimes wondered if his partner was being pressured into retirement; maybe John had been given an ultimatum: *patrol or retire*. But there were other old timers on the force, and *they* hadn't made any changes. Whatever the reason, Robert would never ask. He knew John was a private person who didn't like talking about himself. John could be a bit odd at times. Robert couldn't forget the time he offered to drop off a jacket John had left behind at the station, but John wouldn't hear of it. "I don't like mixing personal and professional," he said. *Jeez!* All Robert wanted to do was swing by the guy's house! What was the big deal? For such a tough guy, John could be touchy about certain subjects too, including retirement. *The day I quit being a cop is the day I die,* was his response when Robert had once made a joke about his age. Robert later learned from one of the guys that John had gotten a taste of retirement a few years back. He had gotten sick or something, taken a leave of absence. Robert didn't know much about it except that it was around that time that John left investigations and went back on patrol.

John rolled the police car onto Barnes Avenue. They were only a mile or so from St. Agassi High School.

"This call... you know, it's probably for the best," John said with a straight face before casting his glance downward toward Robert's stomach. "You, my friend, don't need anymore *Twinkies* tonight."

"I'll have you know that this is rock solid!" Robert said. He thrust his chest out and patted his stomach proudly, like an expectant mother. Robert had packed on nearly ten pounds in about the same number of weeks, and was used to the nightly ribbing from his partner.

"Oh, yeah; that's all muscle!" John laughed. "Whatever you say, buddy. Whatever you say!"

# Five

St. Agassi Catholic High School was originally housed in the eighteenth century fieldstone mansion of Mr. Augustine Sinclair, who in 1911, died and bequeathed his entire eighteen-acre estate to the Catholic Church. With minimal construction, the gothic style residence was seamlessly converted into a boy's high school. Daily mass was held in the St. Agassi chapel a short distance away. Built in 1913, the chapel adjoined a modest size rectory, converted from Mr. Sinclair's original carriage house. Beginning in the late 1960's, girls were admitted to St. Agassi High; and in 1975 the school underwent a multi-million dollar expansion, quadrupling its size and increasing its capacity from 200 to 500 students. Thanks to the successful building campaign, state of the art facilities were added including a multi-media library, temperature controlled classrooms, atrium style lunch area, and an Olympic-sized indoor pool. The school continued to thrive. Yearly tuition was high, but necessary in order to attract the best teachers with bigger salaries and generous benefits. Prospective students had to navigate their way through a series of admissions tests; those not scoring in the higher percentiles were wait listed. It didn't matter. They were willing to wait as long as necessary, since St. Agassi graduates were known to go on to a disproportionate number of Ivy League colleges.

It was in the early 1990's that St Agassi High School began to lose fiscal footing, marked by the death of several key contributors and a steady decline in the number of yearly applicants. The demographics of Arden Station were changing. Simply put, the town was no longer predominantly Catholic. Members of other faiths were flocking to the area and establishing their own communities and places of worship. Intermarriage rates were on the rise and a significant number of younger Catholics were joining less rigid churches and questioning long held beliefs such as the necessity of a Catholic education. Besides, why should they send their children to St. Agassi, when the local public schools were ranked in the top ten nationwide for academic achievement? There were a large number of non-denominational private schools to choose from as well, which were equally, if not more, impressive. In 1995, after several years of struggle, St. Agassi High School graduated its final class—a meager nineteen students—before closing its doors forever.

Over the course of the next few years, several well-meaning but fruitless attempts were made to reopen the school, before the entire tract of church property along Trinity Road was quietly sold in 1999. The local newspaper broke the story within a week, claming that the sale had been to a private real estate developer. After several years of sitting idle, the high school it seemed, would be undergoing yet another transformation. This immediately stirred up speculation as to what the developer planned to do with the land. The rumors ranged from the building of twenty-six upscale homes, to the construction of a high-end shopping square, to the least favored possibility: leasing the property to the township to be used for additional school bus parking. Understandably, residents in the surrounding area were the most concerned. The fate of those eighteen acres would have a major financial impact on their own properties.

A year after the sale, word got out that it was in fact a private *individual* who had purchased the property, a Jewish philanthropist named David Tuttle whose wife had died of breast cancer shortly after giving birth to their fourth child. As a memorial to his wife, Tuttle intended to build a Jewish Life Center. He envisioned a place where families and individuals of all ages could come together to enjoy an array of activities—sports and games, educational classes, Jewish cultural celebrations, world class lectures—in a beautiful environment. The plans for the center were impressive: media rooms, a theater style auditorium, indoor track, health club, indoor and outdoor swimming pools, tennis courts, plus acres of outdoor fields for sports and playground equipment.

Not long after Tuttle's plans were made public, there were murmurings throughout the region questioning the decision of the church to sell the land to a Jewish interest group. In private circles people debated whether or not the church actually knew who the buyer was, and if they had known for what purpose the land would be used. These debates became more public, eventually making their way to the local newspaper. One anonymous letter to the editor argued that the church had been swindled and should demand a reversal of sale. He reasoned that because David Tuttle had used the name of one of his corporate entities to buy the land, the transaction had taken place under false pretenses. The church had been duped, he argued, thereby rendering the sale invalid. The situation worsened when a rumor spread that Tuttle planned to demolish the church and rectory. Anti-Semitic threats were made at a local synagogue, resulting in the cancellation of religious classes and services while the premises were thoroughly checked out by a bomb sniffing canine unit borrowed from Philadelphia County. A few days later, the Catholic High School was vandalized—windows shattered, obscenities spray-painted on the building. Both incidents were quickly traced to a group of unruly teenagers who had no interest in the ongoing debate, but had simply seized the opportunity to wreak havoc.

Meanwhile, David Tuttle countered the negative publicity by taking out large ads in the paper calling for mutual respect and open dialogue between religious groups. He stated his hope that the new Jewish Life Center would benefit the entire community, as membership was not restricted to those of the Jewish faith. Tuttle aligned himself with church officials who reassured local parishioners on several points, foremost that the sale was legitimate and equitable to both parties. The public was assured that demolishing buildings once used for religious purposes was not a sin against the church or Jesus Christ, and most importantly, that each of St. Agassi's precious church relics had been safely transplanted to other local and regional parishes.

The more vocal concerns were from older parishioners, many who had been with Father McCormick for over forty years. Why couldn't the high school be converted, they argued, while the church and rectory remained intact? Church leaders were sympathetic. They understood how attached some people became to their local parish and priest. Demolishing St. Agassi would be like destroying a piece of their personal history. But as emotionally wrenching as it was, the church had no choice. The fact remained that not only had parochial school enrollment dropped sharply, but mass attendance had as well. Fewer families were joining parishes and the Catholic Church was feeling the financial strain. Throughout the entire Philadelphia region, there was no viable alternative but to close schools and merge parishes. On a positive note, David Tuttle saw no reason why their beloved parish priest couldn't remain in the rectory until demolition began on the church.

Originally slated for that spring, the entire building project came to a screeching halt following the events of September 11th. It was a time of national mourning, but to the quiet delight of his loyal followers, it meant that Father McCormick would be sticking around a bit longer.

# Six

There was a snapping of fallen branches as John turned the police car into the high school parking lot, immediately spotting a backhoe, which looked as though it had been abandoned in mid scoop. There was one other vehicle in the lot: a blue minivan, parked directly under a tall streetlight. Robert called in the plate number while John stepped out of the car and began surveying the 15 ft. chain link fence enclosing the main building. Looking beyond the *no trespassing* and *danger* signs, John fixed his eyes on the impressive looking stone structure of the former high school. In some ways it was as if no time had passed since his own children had attended St. Agassi. Behind the scaffolding, the building looked relatively unchanged, better even. John knew that the historical society had something to do with this fact. The original stone had been repointed to preserve St. Agassi's original beauty—huge gray blocks flecked with mica, famously quarried over a century ago from a neighboring county. A towering stone archway sheltered two solid oak doors with large brass handles. This entrance had once opened into a vestibule leading to the administrative offices, but John recalled that most students used the side doors near the gymnasium, a more direct route from the bus circle to the lockers and classrooms. In his mind's eye, John could still see his three daughters scooting through those very doors, their backpacks flailing behind them. John shook his head in amazement. *Where had the time gone?* He and Patty had made the best decision of their lives sending their kids to St. Agassi. In a town where it was typical to see sixteen year olds driving new *BMW*'s and wearing *Gucci*, the ethical teachings and structure of St. Agassi helped keep their feet planted securely on the ground. Each of his daughters had chosen paths for themselves that made them happy and him proud. Liz, the eldest, was a nutritionist with twin girls. Francine, pregnant with her fifth child, taught creative writing in the Chicago public schools; and Paige, the youngest and most idealistic, was building homes in Sri Lanka.

John turned and gazed across the empty field where St. Agassi Church stood, raised on a slight incline. The grass had been matted down from decades of absorbing the parking overflow of churchgoers. During its more vital years, Father McCormick's Sunday mass was attended by upwards of four hundred people, a sharp contrast to the parish as it stood now, barren and dark. Next door, a single light shone from the second floor of the rectory, probably Father McCormick's room, John figured. The single light looked so *lonely*. He tried to remember when he had last seen the priest. For that first year after Jay's death, there were frequent visits, but once John returned to work, their weekly meetings had ceased, and communication was all but reduced to holiday cards and an occasional phone call. John felt a sense of shame as he stared at the lonely rectory. After all the support Father McCormick had given him! How could he have let so much time pass? He made a mental note to call the priest in the morning, maybe even invite him to dinner.

Patty, for one, would be pleased he had thought of it; she'd been on his case to call Father McCormick for a while now.

Within a minute, a crackly radio transmission identified ownership of the minivan to Yehuda & Hanna Orenstein of 62 Willow Lane. John requested backup and the two officers got to work, panning the scaffolding with their flashlights, tracing the outlines of each window. There were no visible signs of a forced entry. Marie, the 911 operator, had told the dispatcher that according to the caller, a part of the building was in use, which meant there had to be public access *somewhere*. Somehow the driver of that van had gotten inside.

John glanced down as something caught the corner of his eye. The blacktop was broken up in places—probably from the construction— with pockets of rain puddles. Then he saw it. A worn leather strap that looked like it had come off of a pair of binoculars. Suddenly there was a gust of wind, followed by a clang—the sound of metal on metal—coming from the side of the building. With a gloved hand, John carefully pocketed the strap and motioned to Robert. The two took off, quickly discovering the source of the noise: a construction gate slightly ajar with a padlock dangling loosely from a long flat hinge. *Access.* Fortunately the moon was full, because in contrast to the brightness of the parking lot, the side of the building was pitifully lit by a couple of industrial lights, each temporarily affixed to metal piping along the brick wall.

The two men proceeded cautiously through the gate and along the blacktop. A second construction fence ran parallel to the walkway, dividing it from several old tennis and basketball courts sitting at the bottom of a steep hill. For years, this had been a favorite sledding spot of local kids. Extending well beyond the courts was a vast open space. John remembered it had once hosted grassy fields for baseball, football and soccer. After years of neglect, it was now covered with random patches of dirt and weeds. Several hundred feet away, a row of 40-foot evergreens lined the outermost edge of the field, creating a natural separation of church property from what was once a sprawling private estate, but had more recently been sold and subdivided into ten residential lots—*Trinity Lane Estates*, the development was formally named; though informally, it was known simply as *The Estates*. Through some breaks in the trees, John noted that the entire street of homes had lost power. A few candles flickered on windowsills, but the others were pitch black. Now that the worst of the storm was over, most people had probably called it a night and turned in.

The two men continued down the path. Muddied with footprints, it led the way toward a bright red awning, which looked perky and out of place given the austerity of such an old building. Robert reached the door first. As expected, it was locked; but even after a few calculated body slams, it wouldn't budge. He ran back to the car to retrieve a crowbar from the trunk. In the distance, the sound of approaching sirens filled the air.

"That's our backup," he said, jogging up the path. He began working the crowbar into the hinge of the door.

"Even with that thing, it's gonna' take about ten good kicks," John said calmly. "Make sure you hit the lock dead center."

Robert dropped the crowbar and took a few steps back. He turned to his side, brought his leg up and gave a quick snap toward the door.

"Hit it with your heel of your foot—always the heel," John instructed. "Remember, you want to hit it dead center!"

Robert took a deep breath, pulled his leg back and gave it another kick, this time hitting the lock head on.

"That's it! Keep at it, just like that."

By the fifth kick, Robert was drenched in sweat, but the lock was noticeably weakened.

"Now use the bar to pry her open," John told him. "We'll be in there in thirty seconds."

He gripped his pistol with two hands, prepared to meet whatever was beyond the entrance. Robert grabbed the crowbar and wedged it between the door and the lock. He gave it one last kick and the door flew open. He flipped the crowbar to his left hand, and pulled out his gun with his right.

A small gust of wind pushed a pile of dry leaves behind the two men as they bounded into the room, weapons held in outstretched arms.

"Police! Freeze!"

There was no response, but they knew better than to let their guard down as they took a look around. The large open space resembled an upscale medical office and they stood on a white marble floor in what appeared to be the reception area. A circular desk was on the right, adjacent to a waiting room containing four upholstered chairs, a glass coffee table and a built in bookshelf filled with neatly shelved hard covers. The walls were cream colored with hand painted faux vines.

"Call an ambulance!"

Robert had dropped behind the desk where an elderly woman lay motionless on her stomach, an overturned wire basket on the floor next to her. Blood dripped from a deep gash on the back of her head. Shards from the crystal vase that had hit her were scattered about the floor next to a small pair of binoculars.

"No pulse," Robert said weakly. He noted the woman's comfort shoes; they were tan with laces, the exact pair his grandma Betty started wearing last year after her knee surgery. Was that a tear he felt on his lip, or was his nose running? He looked away from the body and willed himself to focus on three tiny white tubes that had evidently spilled from the basket. *Dead Sea Mineral Exfoliant*. This was Robert's first dead body and he was beginning to feel dizzy. *Do not pass out,* he told himself. The last thing he needed was to hear it later from the guys down at the station.

*Do not pass out. Focus on the lotion.*

There were some foreign letters printed on the tubes above the English—*Hebrew,* Robert figured, relieved to be feeling stronger by the second.

The sounds of feet running up the pavement meant that backup had arrived.

"Ambulance is thirty seconds behind us," one of the backup officers announced. "And we have four men surrounding the building."

The paramedics flew in and began attending to the woman.

"You all right there partner?" John asked, patting Robert on the shoulder. He took note of the binoculars and lotion samples, glad that his partner had the wherewithal not to touch anything.

Robert removed his hat and wiped some sweat from his brow. "Yeah, fine man. I'm good."

"Good, because chances are the perp's still here," John said. "You're sure you can do this?"

"Just lead the way," Robert said, flipping his hat on.

The hallway runner was soiled with mud. There were six closed doors along the walls—three on the left directly across from three on the right. In a less tense situation, Robert might have done his Scooby Doo impersonation, the one that drove his girlfriend nuts.

"You take the right; I'll go left," John said, gesturing with his chin.

Hand squarely on his holster, Robert tipped open the first door. It was a large bathroom with a separate tub and shower, toilet and sink. A Granite countertop was covered with an array of neatly placed women's toiletries—makeup remover, Q-tips, toothpaste, floss, tweezers, comb, nail clippers. A wrap around mirror extended from the counter to the ceiling. Robert briefly caught his reflection and cringed. His eyes were bloodshot and he looked frazzled. But who wouldn't be after discovering a dead woman? He slid open the tinted shower door—cobalt blue tiles with white edging. Inside were a few bottles of shampoo, soft soap and a mesh sponge. To the right of the shower, three terrycloth robes hung loosely on wood hangers; next to them, a shelf held a neat stack of white towels and washcloths. *Must be some kind of spa for women,* Robert thought. Women loved this shit, especially his girlfriend. With all her talk about facials and massages, this was her kind of place. It looked like someone had poured some serious money into this place, too. Robert checked the cabinet under the sink—just ordinary rolls of toilet paper and boxes of tissues—then backed out of the room.

"Full bathroom?" John asked, nearly bumping into him.

"Yeah, how'd you know?"

"Because that's what all five of the other rooms are, and they're practically identical."

Then they heard it—a low moan coming from the far end of the building. Without hesitating, and with John leading the way, they bolted toward the source of the sound. Rounding the corner, they stopped at the side of a closed door.

"Police Officers! Identify yourself!"

*Silence*

Robert reached for the door handle and slowly turned it. It was unlocked.

John took his position along the wall on the opposite side of the door.

"On the count of three," Robert whispered, his hand still on the turned knob.

John nodded.

"One... two... THREE!"

Robert shoved the door open and bounded into the room. Gun extended, he was nearly overcome by the harsh smells of urine and chlorine.

"FREEZE!"

John scanned the room. Approximately twenty-five square feet in diameter, the floor and walls were completely tiled in blue and white. A square pool was in the center. It had seven tiled steps leading down into the what appeared to be between four and five feet of water. A sturdy metal railing ran alongside it for support.

"Freeze!" John yelled again. He pointed his gun toward a hunched male figure on the floor. The man sat on his knees less than a foot from the top step of the pool, his body arched over a motionless woman, who lay naked with her legs spread and feet dangling into the water. The man shook uncontrollably and his chest heaved.

"Williams, Patterson!" Robert shouted. "Get in here!" He looked with disgust at the man who wore no shirt or shoes. Drenched jeans hung loosely at his hips revealing striped boxer shorts. Even with four officers now crowding the room, the man continued to be unresponsive. It wasn't until John grabbed the man's arm, that he appeared to even notice he had company. He flinched and looked at John with an expression of pure rage. Instantly, he jerked away and turned back to the woman, wrapping his arms possessively around her, clinging to her like a child might cling to a toy he didn't want to share.

"Get up!"

John yanked the man to his feet with such force that even Robert was startled. The man was short, about 5'7", and barely reached John's shoulders. His dark hair was damp and disheveled and he had some acne scarring on his right cheek. Judging from the look of agony on his face, it was likely John had dislocated his arm. But John continued to manhandle him, shoving him face first against the wall. It was then that he noticed the brown feces oozing from the bottom of the man's jeans. John gagged and nearly vomited at the sight—the man had relieved himself in his pants.

Robert took a step back from the commotion and his pulse quickened as something in the water caught his eye. It was a white shape sprawled out at the bottom of the pool. *Oh God.*

"It's a robe," Robert said, hand to chest, settling himself. "Just a white bathrobe."

John must have loosened his grip while watching Robert, because within an instant, the man had pushed himself off the wall, and with a quick jerk of his head, leaned down, opened his mouth and bit John squarely on the arm.

"Son of a bitch!" John barked. He slammed the man back against the wall and pulled his wrists together behind him. The man howled in pain as John handcuffed him. But within seconds he stopped struggling and his screams turned to sobs. Drool trickled from the corner of his mouth. He said nothing as John read him his rights and handed him off with a shove to one of the officers.

Still shaking his head in disbelief, John peeled back his sleeve to assess the damage. In all his years on the force, he had never seen a guy shit his pants. In an alley? Yes. In a dumpster? Sure. But never in his own pants! And it was true that John had sustained plenty of dog bites all right, but this was his first human bite.

*Guy's an animal* he thought. *A God damn animal.*

John kneeled down and studied the woman as the paramedics attended to her. She was in her late thirties, he estimated, young enough to be his daughter. Her hair was wet and tangled, and he felt the paternal urge to tuck it behind her ear. She wore nothing—no clothes, no jewelry, not even a hint of makeup. Her body was beautiful he thought. She was a mommy; that he was certain of. She wasn't overweight, but had that lovely softness in the middle that came only from bearing children. It was only when one of the other cops returned with a white bath towel and placed it gently over her torso, that it occurred to John that he should avert his eyes.

"She has a slight pulse," the paramedic announced without looking up. "That's better than the other one."

Detective Ron Smith Jr. arrived with a team of crime scene techs. They cordoned off the area and got down to work. The district attorney arrived on the scene in record time. Given the nature of the crime, he wanted to keep things quiet.

The two women were taken away on stretchers. It would later be known throughout the community that although they had worked tirelessly on Estelle Ginsberg en route to Senecca Hospital, the eighty-two year old woman was pronounced dead on arrival.

# Seven

Yehuda grabbed his keys before heading outside to wait for Saul. It wouldn't be long since the Katz's lived only a few miles away, not far from the kids' school. Yehuda paced nervously on the front porch. The quicker Saul got here, the sooner he could go and find Hannah.

As a result of the storm that had blown through Arden Station, Willow Lane was littered with fallen branches and several rubber lids, flipped from their respective garbage pails. It was still cold, but now startlingly quiet, a respite from Yehuda's own racing thoughts. He sat on a weathered teak bench—a gift left behind by the former owners—and gazed up at the sky. The full moon appeared larger and closer than it had four hours ago when he walked home from the center. Hannah always noticed and appreciated simple pleasures like this. "Thank you God, for this beautiful full moon," she would say, as if God had painted a special nighttime scene exclusively for her.

Yehuda smiled as he recalled the first years of their marriage when they had lived in Jerusalem. The leisurely strolls through the ancient stone walkways of the Old City. The daily prayers at the Western

Wall—Yehuda on the men's side, Hannah on the women's. He and Hannah would often sit on one of the nearby benches, mesmerized by the grandeur of what remained of the Holy Temple. Sometimes they would remain there for hours quietly witnessing the awe on tourists' faces, especially those who were visiting the holy site for the first time. People from all walks of life came—religious and secular, rabbis and taxi drivers, mothers and soldiers—some with tears in their eyes, all with yearnings and secrets. Many brought messages—prayers scribbled on tiny scraps of paper—to be tucked into the stone cracks of the wall. The sun would set and they would marvel at the uniqueness of the night sky. Residents and tourists experienced it the same way—in Israel, God felt closer somehow. But it was Hannah who described it so poetically: *up in the heavens, the almighty watches over his children, hidden just out of view, behind a thin veil of star flecked indigo.*

When was the last time they took a walk together, just he and Hannah? When had they last eaten a meal alone? Yehuda couldn't remember. Sure, they were the busy parents of five young children, but that was no excuse. Had he neglected his wife? How could he have taken her for granted, his beloved Hannah? What a hypocrite he was! Teaching his students how to have more fulfilling marriages, how to be better husbands and wives. Counseling couples on the importance of being attentive to one another. His heart ached with remorse. If God was speaking to him, he was doing it through a megaphone.

Yehuda took a deep breath, collecting himself. As soon as all this drama was over, things would be different! He would make some serious changes, starting with a reduction in his class load at the center. He would get home earlier each evening. The family would eat dinner together more often. He and Hannah would have date nights again. Maybe they would go away for a couple of days—just the two of them. His mother could stay with the kids. Yes, everything would be fine. There was a logical explanation to all this. He and Hannah would be laughing about it tomorrow.

Crackling sounds of gravel under tires jolted Yehuda from his private thoughts, and he looked up to see the headlights of a car turn onto his street. He raced down to the curb, expecting to greet Saul's black Lincoln Town Car. But it was a police vehicle that was approaching. Yehuda's heart skipped a beat as it pulled into the driveway and two officers stepped out. The driver stood solemnly at the side of the vehicle, holding his hat in his hands, as his partner swaggered, hands on his hips, toward Yehuda.

"Rabbi Orenstein…?"

*Oh God.*

Yehuda instinctively backed away. He felt weak, like the blood had suddenly been drained out of him.

"I'm Officer Clark…" the officer began, but was interrupted by the light honk of Saul's horn as he pulled in front of the house.

"Yehuda? What's going on?" Saul shouted through the lowered car window.

"Rabbi, could I have a word with you privately?" the officer continued, ignoring Saul. Yehuda's head spun.

*Oh God.*

Saul ran up the lawn. "Yehuda?"

The officer turned to Saul. "Excuse me sir, but I need to speak privately to…"

Yehuda waved his hands. He didn't know if he could muster the strength to speak, and was a bit surprised to hear his own words. "It's all right… Saul… is my friend. He can stay."

The officer nodded. "Rabbi Orenstein," he said, "there's been an accident. Your wife has been taken to Senecca Hospital."

Saul put his arm around Yehuda's shoulders steadying him.

# Eight

It was less than a ten-minute drive to Senecca hospital, yet felt like hours to Yehuda who sat like a caged animal behind the metal bars separating the front and back seats of the police car. He was desperate for information, but the two officers remained relatively quiet throughout the trip. Occasionally one would respond to a radio transmission, or mutter something in passing to his partner, but neither spoke a word to him, not once turning a head toward the bearded rabbi in the back seat. It was as though they had forgotten he was there altogether. In all fairness, Yehuda reminded himself, how many times had these guys had a rabbi in their car? Maybe they were intimidated by him, like others were intimidated by *them*. Gun or no gun, uniforms created lines of separation.

Back at the house, Officer Clark had been vague. The confirmed facts, he said, were that Hannah had been discovered unconscious in the renovated section of the old high school—she was breathing, but unconscious. She had either taken a nasty fall or been pushed, they said. Neither he nor his partner had spoken to the responding officers,

Clark said, so they had no further details at this time. With this last statement, Yehuda thought the officer sounded like he was reciting a well-rehearsed script. Saul had been the one to ask about Estelle. Yehuda, thinking only of Hannah, had completely forgotten that someone else had been at mikvah. They could only release information to the immediate family was what Officer Clark had told them. Yehuda couldn't help but notice that he looked down at the ground when he said it.

The police car continued to move swiftly through the streets of Arden Station. Few vehicles were on the road, making lights and sirens necessary only when they plowed, nonstop through the few intersections along the way. The steady movement was almost meditative and Yehuda's thoughts drifted to a lecture he attended recently. *Secular law vs. Jewish law.* In his mind's eye he saw the white bearded rabbi from Monsey take the stage. Nearly ninety years old, the man was still sharp as a tack. The discussion turned to traffic lights: *Secular governments were permitted to have systems in place to maintain order. Traffic lights ensured that there would be no gridlock, no question of who proceeded when. But at night, when there was virtually no traffic on the road, the question was, would a civilian vehicle need to wait at a red light? The Halacha, Jewish law, seemed to indicate that they would not; rather, treating traffic lights like stop signs would suffice. The catch being that if a cop was waiting behind the bushes somewhere, Jewish law would be of no help since secular fines in a secular country still had to be paid...*

It was a coping skill Yehuda had developed as a child. Easing his mind away from troubling personal thoughts and onto intellectual subjects was like turning to a channel that required his complete attention, and for him, as simple as pushing a button on a TV remote.

The car made a sharp left onto Edgeton, passing the field where Eli played soccer last year. A crew was repairing fallen power lines that lay draped across one of the bleacher stands. He thought of Eli, David and Yitzi sleeping soundly in their beds. Yehuda was relieved that he didn't have to worry about his children right now; they were in good hands. "Don't worry about a thing," Saul had assured him, "I can stay as long as you need me to."

Rachel would tend to Nehama, and the boys would probably sleep through the night. By the time they woke up in the morning, Yehuda thought, he and Hannah would be home. Everything would be back to normal.

*Please God let everything go back to normal.*

Yehuda felt a lump in his throat as he recalled the fear in Rachel's eyes when he hugged her goodbye. Who was he kidding trying to appear calm? She probably recognized the same demeanor in him that he had had just a few months ago when they almost lost Nehama. Chances were she would be up all night waiting for him, worrying. What did he think, that she hadn't noticed the police car with its silent spinning lights? The serious mannered officers? Right now his precious daughter was suffering just as much as he was.

The car made another left and the lights of Senecca hospital came into view. Yehuda remembered the last time he had driven up this road. Unlike today, the occasion had been a happy one: it was the morning of September 5th, just two weeks before the high holidays, and he had come to retrieve his wife and new baby daughter. Rachel was ecstatic the day Nehama was born. She was beginning to believe she would never have a sister, not after David, Eli, and Yitzi had burst, one after the other, into her life. Every one of his children was a miracle from God, Yehuda thought, smiling to himself, each with their own unique temperament. He loved watching them grow and become more of who they were meant to be. Rachel, the little mommy, was a natural caregiver, intuitive, loving and patient. Eli was their builder, always wanting to put objects together and understand the mechanics of how things worked. David, the quiet one, was happy tagging along with his big brother, or equally content sitting and reading for hours and hours. Lovable, huggable Yitzi was always smiling, and was, as Lauren called him, the Orenstein family *Gund*. *Who would Nehama become?* he wondered. God willing they would have many years to find out, many more years of family togetherness. It was a blessing that his children were close and got along well with one another, much better than *he* and his own sister had. Admittedly, things with Sunny *had* improved after his parents divorce. That's when the two of them understood on some unspoken level that they needed to stick together. Sink or swim. Things were different in the home Yehuda made with Hannah. His children had stability and two parents who would *always* be together.

# Nine

A man in a white lab coat met Yehuda at the emergency room door. He was older, about sixty or so, with a thick head of white hair, tall, but about thirty pounds overweight with a double chin. The photo on his hospital ID tag showed a younger and much slimmer looking version of himself under the words *B. Anthony Jarvis, M.D., Director of Emergency Services.*

The doctor grabbed a clipboard from an intake area and led Yehuda down a long corridor. They passed patients on stretchers—most in street clothes, some in quite a bit of pain—and finally entered a small dimly lit room. The pale blue walls were accented by framed watercolor paintings, free style swirls in muted shades of pink, yellow and orange. Tranquil, wordless music floated in through flat speakers on the ceiling, and tall leafy plants in ceramic pots softened the room's corner spaces.

Yehuda sat down on a stiff black armchair, the lack of cushioning striking him as odd in a room obviously designed with relaxation in mind. Doctor Jarvis took a seat across from him on a soft yellow couch. Hannah, he said, had just come out of surgery and was resting comfortably in the intensive care unit. He would take Yehuda to see her after they attended to some hospital business. Dr. Jarvis then handed Yehuda a clipboard with several medical forms attached. Yehuda patted his jacket pocket in search of a pen. It was empty. He stood up and checked his pants. Also empty. It dawned on him that he must have left everything on the bench outside his home—keys, cell phone, wallet. Normally this discovery would be disconcerting to him, but now he felt only a pang of annoyance at not having something to write with. Getting through the paperwork quickly would bring him one step closer to seeing Hannah. The doctor reached into his lab coat and pulled out a pen just as his beeper went off. He stood up and checked the number. "Rabbi Orenstein, if you'll excuse me. I need to step out for a moment." He handed him the pen before asking, "Can I bring you back something? Coffee, water, something to eat, perhaps?"

The offer made Yehuda realize he was quite thirsty. "Water would be nice. Thank you."

Yehuda returned to his seat and flipped through the papers in front of him. *Insurance Information. Pre-Admission. Medical History. Privacy Statement.* His head was spinning; he couldn't do this right now. Even if he *could* think straight, his insurance card was at home in his wallet, and there was no way he was going call the house; he had disturbed Saul enough for one night. He placed the clipboard on the table in front of him, and leaned over, hugging his arms around his stomach like he was going to be sick. His body felt weak. Maybe he was dehydrated. In the distance, he could hear the sound of approaching sirens. Curious, he walked over to a large double window draped in a heavy lavender curtain. He poked his head, childlike, through the middle divide of the fabric as if peeking at something he wasn't supposed to see. Here the light of the room was completely blocked out. He inhaled deeply and felt a wave of calm pour over his body.

Yehuda had a sudden sense of deja vu at that moment. It was strange; he hadn't thought of it in a long, long time, but now, the memory was so precise, the pictures so vivid...

He was eleven when his mom had surprised him and his eight-year-old sister Sunny with a trip to Disney World. They would be staying at one of the most beautiful hotels she said—*The Polynesian*—and it would be just the three of them. Their father had things he had to take care of at home.

Neither Yehuda nor his sister had ever been on a plane before. Prior to takeoff, the pretty stewardess gave each of them a wing pin and even took them up to the cockpit to meet the pilot. Yehuda clutched his pack of *Razzles* as the plane took off and ascended high above the clouds. His friend Douglas had been only half right about the chewing gum—it unpopped only one of his ears.

Disney World, Yehuda thought, was the most magical place he had ever seen. Each day was jam-packed with rides, shows, parades and of course the nightly fireworks. He was having the time of his life, until the second to last day that is, when his mom decided to break the news to them. Years later, Yehuda would thank her for having the wherewithal not to ruin the *entire* vacation. Even after all these years, the events of that morning remained etched perfectly in his memory: He and Sunny were dressed in their shorts and t-shirts, ready to go down for breakfast. Their mom was taking longer than unusual in the bathroom so he and his sister passed the time by leaping back and forth, in tandem, between the two double beds. When their mom finally emerged, she looked angry. There were crease lines along her forehead, and her lips were pursed tight like she was trying to hold in her fury. At first Yehuda thought they had been too loud, or that she was mad at the mess they had made of the beds, but when he examined her face more closely, he noted that it wasn't anger he saw, but despair. Her eyes were puffy and her makeup smeared. At home, she never wore makeup, but all this week she had been trying out different colors on her eyes and mouth. Now there were streaks of blue running from the outer corner of her left eye all the way down her cheek. It wasn't until she gripped a wad of tissues that Yehuda realized the makeup wasn't supposed to look like that. With a crumbled ball of tissues in her fist, she motioned for them to sit down. Yehuda and Sunny looked at each other, not knowing what to expect. Sunny's arms were crossed defensively, but her bottom lip trembled the way it always did when she was scared, but trying not to cry. Their mom took a deep breath and finally spoke. There was something difficult she needed to tell them. There was no easy way to do this, she said, so she would just go ahead and say it. She swallowed and licked her lips. She and their dad had split up. There would be a divorce and the three of them would not be returning home to New Mexico. That's when it occurred to Yehuda. Why had they flown across the entire country when Disneyland on the *west coast* was so much closer?

Everything would be okay, their mom assured them, wiping her eyes and forming her mouth into a strange, contorted smile. There were some special people they would be meeting soon.

How could this be happening? Yehuda stared at the red lipstick smear on his mom's front tooth. It was all messed up. Seconds ago it was perfect and now she had gone and messed it up! Somehow she was still blathering on, telling them some nonsense about this trip being some kind of "kick off" to all the new and exciting changes in their lives. Yehuda was stunned. What had his mom just said? A kick off? Like this was some kind of game? Who was she kidding? Games were supposed to be fun.

Yehuda stayed behind in the room while his mom and Sunny went down to the Coral Isle coffee shop. Most likely his mom would sip a glass of orange juice while Sunny proceeded to eat a full breakfast of cereal, eggs, potatoes and toast. Sunny had an unusually hearty appetite that was oddly unaffected by emotional turmoil. Yehuda on the other hand lost his appetite completely when he was upset, so his mom knew he was being truthful when he said he couldn't eat a *crumb* right now. Couldn't eat a *crumb of a crumb*. He might even be sick; suddenly he had begun to feel nauseous. Maybe their mom would give in and let Sunny order bacon today. At home she served strictly vegetarian meals, but all this week she had eased up, permitting the kids to eat burgers, hot dogs, and barbecued chicken. They had even eaten poi at the luau on the beach their second night, and neither he nor Sunny had gotten a stomachache like their mom predicted.

Yehuda lay on his bed—he had enjoyed having such a big bed all to himself—and stared up at the crackly stucco ceiling. It still looked like someone had done a sloppy job painting it, but his mom said, no, it was supposed to look like that. He listened to the steady flow of sounds outside the room—babies crying, doors slamming—and felt pangs of jealousy each time he heard shrills of laughter and the patter of little feet pass through the hallway. He was certain they were evidence of happy, intact families beginning another perfect day at the Magic Kingdom.

Suddenly, a thought occurred to him. Excited, he jumped up, ran over to the dresser and scooped up a handful of change from a glass ashtray. He would call his dad! Maybe this was all a mistake! Maybe his mom misunderstood. His dad would clear up the confusion and everything would be back to normal. He shoved the fist of change into his pocket, grabbed the extra room key and slipped out. Downstairs in the lobby, he jogged past a cluster of wheelchairs toward the phone booth area. There weren't any phones available so he would have to wait. Businessmen with long sideburns and name badges milled around in leisure suits puffing on cigarettes. Yehuda knew there were a couple of conventions going on in the hotel. He turned around at the sound of a parrot squawking from a high perch, one of many exotic birds enhancing the hotel's island theme. Then he looked back at the wheelchairs. Children his age and younger were sitting in them and most appeared to have some kind of limb deformity. One girl's right arm stopped at the elbow. Another was missing one hand and one foot. Others with bodies seemingly intact, had limited or no use of their arms or legs. Some of the wheelchairs were equipped with ventilators or other medical equipment; the kids sitting in them had flat facial expressions. Yehuda felt sorry for them, but more annoyed with the adults hovering around them. What were they doing bringing their kids to a place like this? *Do any of them even know where they are? Do they know what's going on?* The parents were selfish, Yehuda thought, trying to make themselves feel better—purge their own guilt—after creating such sick children in the first place.

"Damn shame is what it is."

Yehuda looked up. One of the conventioneers stood there, taking a long drawl of his cigarette. "Thalidomide is what done that to those kids," he said, tilting his chin. Smoke funneled out of his nostrils. "Some say it's God's will. I say God has nothing to do with it. It's man's arrogance thinking he knows better."

Yehuda looked again at the kids, not having a clue what the man was talking about, or whether or not a response was expected. Fortunately, at that moment, a phone became available. Yehuda nodded politely at the man, then tucked himself into the booth, pulling the hinged door closed behind him. He stretched up on his toes and shoved every coin he had into the slot, quickly dialed, and held his breath as it rang.

"Hellooo…"

"Uh… Larry?"

Yehuda always felt funny calling his dad by his first name, but what choice did he have? Whenever he said "Dad" his father ignored him. Sometimes he stared at him like he was speaking Martian. *You watch,* his dad told his mom who made it clear that she was opposed to such a thing, *they'll grow up faster if you stop coddling them.*

"Ira?"

"Uh huh."

"Where's Judy?" He sounded more annoyed than concerned.

"She's eating breakfast with Sunny," Yehuda said, realizing his father was not used to handling the affairs of his children. Their mom was the one who managed every detail of his and Sunny's lives.

"Then what's the problem?"

Outside the booth, there were shrills of bursting excitement followed by applause. Yehuda turned to see Goofy and Minnie Mouse pop out from behind some tropical plants. Both characters were dressed in island attire: Minnie in a grass skirt, Goofy in a flowery Hawaiian shirt. The kids' faces lit up as Minnie and Goofy handed out flower lays. A couple of the kids were so excited they looked as though they might jump out of their skins.

"I said, what's the problem, Ira?"

"I…" Yehuda was beginning to regret making this call.

"You what?"

There was a sound of a woman giggling in the background. It sounded like Marigold, his mom's friend. "Uh, Mom told us that you…"

His dad said something in a hushed tone to the woman, then spoke directly into the phone. "I can barely hear you Ira!… Speak up! What did your mom tell you?"

Minnie was dancing the hula with four performers from the nightly luau show.

Yehuda swallowed and tried to speak louder. "Mom said we... she said we weren't coming home."

"That's right." He said it like he was confirming directions. *That's right, make a left at the corner. You can't miss it.*

"So is it... is it true?"

Now Goofy was down on one knee, strumming a ukulele, in a serenade to one of the wheelchair bound girls. She squealed with joy as her dad snapped a couple of photos.

"I'm afraid that's the way it has to be."

"I..."

"Look, life's complicated Ira. When you get older, you'll understand... People grow apart. It's just the way it is. We only live once... We owe it to ourselves to be happy."

Yehuda cupped his mouth, trying to hold in the wail that was inching it's way past the lump in his throat. There was no way he would let his dad hear him cry.

"Be a good boy and help your mother."

Then there was a click and the sound of a dial tone.

Dazed, Yehuda returned back to the room. His mom and Sunny were still at breakfast, but the maid had come and gone, leaving washcloths folded into animal shapes near the bathroom sink. He pulled off his sneakers and hurled them against the wall, narrowly missing the mirror. Then he threw himself on the bed and sobbed like a baby into the bedspread. So it was true. They wouldn't be returning home. But then, where *would* they go? How would they live? His mom didn't even have a job. How would they buy food? Yehuda's mind drifted to the image of Minnie Mouse dancing the hula in the lobby. If only they could stay right here at the Polynesian. Everyone was friendly, and the Hawaiian women were so pretty, especially the way they tucked those big flowers in their hair. His mom was just as pretty, so maybe she could get a job as one of the performers! She would have to dye her hair black, but that wouldn't be a big deal now that she was using all that other makeup stuff. Yehuda rolled over and sighed; he knew she would never go for it. But that didn't mean *he* couldn't. Maybe he could find somewhere to hide in the park! It shouldn't be that difficult since the place was so massive. He even heard a rumor that there were underground tunnels. And earlier in the year he had read a book about a boy and his sister hiding in the Metropolitan Museum of Art in New York.

*Could children survive on their own at Disney World?* Maybe it *was* possible, though this would need to be a solo operation. There was no way he could bring Sunny along. Yehuda rolled over and covered his eyes. Who was he kidding? It would never happen.

*Be a good boy and help your mother.*

Even without his father's directive, Yehuda knew he couldn't abandon his mom; she needed him, and although she would never admit it, Sunny needed him too. Whether he liked it or not, he was the man of the family now. Besides, if he lived here at Disney World, he would miss them too much.

Yehuda wiped his eyes with his palms. He turned on his side to grab a tissue and studied the long flowered drapery pulled tightly along the windows. He suddenly had the urge to wrap himself in it. If he were lucky, it would swallow him up and send him off to another dimension, like the twilight zone. In an alternate universe he might transform into Captain Marvel or Spiderman; then he could solve *any* problem. Yehuda got down on the carpet and crawled to the far corner of the room. Out of view behind a small table and two chairs, he sandwiched his eighty-pound body between two thick layers of fabric. Feeling as secure as a newborn swaddled in a receiving blanket, Yehuda waited in complete darkness for the transformation to begin. A burst of cool air from a vent dramatically blew the curtain back a few inches.

*Was something happening?* At the sudden flash of sunlight, he examined his hands, and patted himself down hoping something would to be different. But, as expected, he remained completely unchanged. There was no such thing as magic. Not for him, not for those sick kids in wheelchairs. Even the magic kingdom wasn't really magic. It was all just one big lie. Mickey and Minnie were really just people in costumes. The exhibits were covered in wallpaper, powered by human hands. Yehuda closed his eyes; they were heavy from crying. He drifted off to sleep, exhausted.

Yehuda hid himself so well that upon their return from breakfast, his mom panicked and called hotel security. Sunny burst into tears, overwhelmed by both the news of the divorce and the concern in her mother's voice. Judith insisted to the hotel authorities that something must have happened. *It wasn't like Ira to wander off by himself. Someone must have taken him! Besides, his sneakers were here! He wouldn't have left without his shoes!* She and Sunny waited in the room while a massive search of the hotel grounds was conducted. His mother paced back and forth wondering if her eleven-year-old son had been kidnapped. All the while Yehuda lay perfectly still, slipping in and out of a light, almost hallucinatory sleep. Even if he had wanted to, he couldn't muster the strength to call out.

Two hours later, the search was called off after Sunny heard a low grumble coming from the corner. Yehuda's empty stomach had blown his cover. His mom pulled back the curtains to find her Ira curled up asleep on the floor. To his astonishment, there was no punishment. Instead, his mother hugged him tightly against her chest, drenching his cheeks with her tears.

The three of them spent the rest of the day at the hotel swimming pool, a spectacular grotto-like structure, encased in stonework with flowing waterfalls and slides. His mother must have known that the water was exactly what he needed; he felt lighter, like the weight of his problems had washed right off him. Before long, he made some friends and together they spent the next several hours splashing around as pirates. The boys even included Sunny, casting her in the role as the stow-away. For a while, Yehuda was able to forget about his parents divorce. But, every so often, he would catch a glimpse of his mom watching from the water's edge, and the uncertainty of what lay ahead for the three of them sent a shiver down his spine. His mom looked glamorous in a two-piece red bathing suit that tied halter style around her neck. Large dark sunglasses covered half her face, so he couldn't tell what kind of state she was in, or even if she was crying. When she noticed him looking at her, she would sit up, tuck her knees in, smile and blow kisses. Theatrically she'd catch the ones he blew back, even leaping off her lounge at times to chase the ones that got away.

Two days later, they checked out of the hotel, piled into a rented station wagon and drove six hours to Fort Lauderdale, where Yehuda and Sunny met their maternal grandparents for the first time. Harvey and Sylvia Orenstein, a kind looking couple, lived in a terracotta ranch style home with a tiny patch of sod, which they jokingly referred to as the "south lawn". They were waiting expectantly on folding chairs, and at the sight of the station wagon jumped up, and ran over with wide grins and open arms. Sylvia tattooed Sunny in lipstick kisses while Harvey hoisted a reluctant Yehuda up in the air. Before long, it was obvious that the kids were exhausted after such a long trip. Harvey ushered them inside while Sylvia stayed behind with Judith to speak to her privately. Their belongings, she told her daughter, had arrived safe and sound, a few days before. Sylvia had unpacked everything and set up two of the home's three bedrooms. If it was all right with her, Judy and Sunny would share one room and Yehuda would have the other to himself.

Living in Florida was very different from living in New Mexico. The temperature was the same, but somehow, Yehuda found himself sweating constantly, even when he wasn't running around. There were alligators instead of snakes in Florida, and palm trees instead of cactus.

Days, then weeks, then months went by without word from their father.

"Maybe he doesn't know where we are!" a concerned Sunny told her brother one night while stuffing her face with Jiffypop.

"Maybe," Yehuda replied, lying for his sister's benefit. Sunny's hearing wasn't as sharp as Yehuda's; she hadn't heard the whispered conversations between their mom and grandparents. Nor did she know that mail had come from their father's divorce lawyer—papers their mother needed to sign—proof that he knew their address! The fact was, their father could visit any time he felt like it; but simply chose not to. Maybe once he stopped being mad at their mother, he would call. Yehuda often tried to guess what caused his parents divorce. Initially he thought his mother must have done something wrong, even though he couldn't fathom what it could be. Everyone loved his mother, adults and kids alike. Judy was someone who always had *time*. Time to pitch in and lend a hand, time to help a new mother, time to cook a healthy meal for her family, time to teach in the communal school.

Yehuda admitted to himself that as far back as he could remember, there had always been something not quite right between his parents. Most of the time, it was as though his parents were living separate lives, hers with the kids, his without. Sadly, when Yehuda recalled his earliest childhood memories, more often than not, they excluded his father altogether. His dad was always running around, moving so fast, coming and going. It was like he could only stand to be in the house with them for a few hours at a time—except when his mom's friend

Marigold was around, that is. Then he had all the time in the world to sit and visit. Yehuda knew it was Marigold who inspired the name Sunny. "Marigold is such a groovy girl," his dad had said to his mom, "maybe our *Sunflower* will be the same way." It was funny when he thought about it. Despite the fact that his parents chose to live on a commune, they had always managed to maintain a conservative streak. But it was meeting Marigold that changed all that—at least for his father.

Most nights Yehuda lay awake, sometimes crying softly into his pillow. Other times, he finger sketched an image of his father onto an invisible canvas above his bed, willing himself to remember details: His dad's long nose, his high forehead, the ponytail he had begun to wear in the past year. Yehuda didn't have a single photo of his dad (oddly he had plenty of Polaroid's showing he and his mom and Sunny), but he wasn't about to be a traitor and ask his mother for one. Yehuda struggled to hear his dad's voice in his head, but the more time passed, the less he was able to succeed.

*Be a good boy...*

That fall, Yehuda and Sunny were enrolled in a Florida public school, which took some getting used to after being home schooled for their entire lives. Having to sit still for thirty to forty-minute increments seemed as pointless to Yehuda, as the amount of memorization he was required to do. He told his mother these things, but she had her own pressures and he didn't want to burden her. Newly enrolled in law school, she would spend hours in the law library after her classes, occasionally arriving home in time to join everyone for a late dinner. Sometimes Yehuda would wake from a nightmare at two or three in the morning, get out of bed and discover his mom surrounded by books at the kitchen table.

Though Yehuda never said it, the thing he hated more than

anything about his new school was his feeling of isolation. His sister made friends easily and before long there were knocks on the door for Sunny to come play tetherball at Sharon's or ride bikes with Linda and Nancy. Yehuda wasn't particularly shy by nature, but suddenly he felt different—like those sick kids at Disney World—like he was missing a limb.

After school each day, their grandpop met them at the bus stop two blocks away. "The walk is good for my heart," Harvey would say. On the way home, he'd ask how their day was. Yehuda's responses were grunts of two or three words, while Sunny could be counted on to engage him with longer and more engrossing stories. But Harvey wouldn't give up on Yehuda. In time, he was able to coax his grandson out of his shell. Although he could be loud at times (mostly because his hearing was poor and he refused to wear a hearing aid), Harvey Orenstein was generous and kind, and shared Ira's love of history.

One afternoon Harvey lugged out a big box of albums, and naturally, Yehuda assumed they were more family photos. Ever since they moved in, Harvey had spent a good deal of time showing off his massive photo collection. But this time, Harvey winked at him while making a dramatic show of opening the first one. About twenty individual stamps were set into tiny paper edges on each page. Yehuda leaned in to take a closer look. *France 1851, Poland, 1910…* Yehuda turned the pages quickly now, saying things like "Look at this one grandpop!" and "I never heard of this country!" Yehuda stopped at a gold page, which stood out from the others.

"Why is the paper different?" he asked.

Harvey grazed the page gently with his fingertips. "Those are from 1948, the year the State of Israel was born. Your great grandfather— my father—was the first in our family to actually *touch* the Western Wall…"

"What's the Western Wall?" Yehuda asked innocently.

Later that night, Yehuda overheard an argument between his grandpop and his mom.

"How could you not give them a religious identity?" his grandpop demanded. "How could they not even know they are Jews!"

# Ten

Yehuda pressed his face against the pane of dark glass, peering out to a winding cement sidewalk in front of the hospital. The coolness on his cheek felt nice, the next best thing to actually stepping outside for some fresh air. The room where he now stood was at one end of a long stretched out horseshoe. At the other end, was the entrance to the Senecca hospital emergency room and the automatic doors through which he had entered just a little while ago.

*How much time had actually passed?*

The sliding doors opened and closed dutifully as people hustled in—varying degrees of concern and panic in their eyes—and hospital staff in scrubs and white clogs snuck out for a quick cigarette break. A white haired man hobbled in, favoring one leg while being supported by a much younger man. *His son?* Yehuda would never know what it was like to help an ailing father. He had given up the fantasy of his own father being a part of his life years ago.

Now the full moon caught Yehuda's attention. There it was, still shining brightly as it had all night. Yehuda felt offended at its boldness, that it could be so unaffected by the tragedy unfolding in his life. How was it possible for the sun to rise tomorrow, as it most certainly would, as if nothing had changed? Yehuda stepped back and gazed at his shadowed reflection in the window. The image reminded him of overnight camp, when his counselor, Herschel Gold held a flashlight against his chin and shone the light up his face. His distorted appearance was perfect for telling scary legends of "Cropsy" the lunatic farmer who roamed the campgrounds after midnight. Herschel Gold was a third year yeshiva student when Yehuda met him, and well on his way to becoming a rabbi like his father and grandfather before him. It was Herschel who became something of a big brother and mentor to Yehuda, ultimately encouraging him to become a rabbi himself. Yehuda wondered what Herschel would say now. He always had a knack for finding the right words, even for the most horrendous of situations. Always compassionate, yet never trivializing matters with "what God does is always for the best..." At this moment, Yehuda would punch any guy, black hat or not, who offered such trite words of wisdom.

"Rabbi Orenstein?"

Dr. Jarvis had returned.

Yehuda jumped. "Right here," he said, awkwardly pushing the curtain to the side as he stepped back into the room. He squinted and covered his eyes from the sudden brightness. Dr. Jarvis didn't even blink, carrying on as if he saw grown men pop out from behind drawn curtains every day. He handed Yehuda a cup of water and then picked up the clipboard and flipped through the forms.

"I don't mean to sound insensitive, Rabbi," he said, his mouth turned downward, "but we do need these forms completed ASAP." The doctor sighed and held up a hand. "No. Scratch that. Never mind the forms right now. So be it if the hospital administration gets on my case. It won't be the first time." He motioned for Yehuda to sit down. "It's much more important that we talk about your wife." He waited while Yehuda drank his entire cup of water in one swig before continuing.

"Rabbi Orenstein, as you know, your wife endured a period of asphyxiation—lack of oxygen to the brain. I can't tell you for sure how long she was underwater…"

Yehuda's eyes popped. "Hannah was underwater?"

"Yes… the police told me," Dr. Jarvis stammered, obviously caught off guard. "I assumed you had spoken with them."

"I did speak to them, but they… they didn't say anything about this!" Yehuda jumped out of his seat and began pacing, his right hand nervously adjusting his yarmulke on the top of his head. "I want to see my wife… now!"

Dr. Jarvis held up a hand. "Rabbi, please, calm down. I understand how traumatic this all is. I assure you, I will take you up to her in a few minutes. She is still being settled in after surgery. It could be highly disruptive to her to barge in at this time. The important thing for you to know is that she is in stable condition." He tugged on his black stethoscope, as he spoke. Yehuda wondered if he was nervous, maybe hiding something. He couldn't believe how paranoid he had become; first the cops, now the doctors. Did he honestly believe they were intentionally withholding information from him? He sat back down and put his hands into his face. He looked up at Dr. Jarvis. "Tell me what they told you," he said. "I want to know everything!"

Ten minutes later, Yehuda and Dr. Jarvis were riding the elevator to the second floor. They wound around a series of short corridors and made their way through a domed glass skywalk connecting the two main buildings of the hospital. All the while, medical personnel in blue scrubs or white lab coats bustled past them, carrying charts and cups of coffee. Occasionally one would give an acknowledging nod to Dr. Jarvis, followed by a curious "once over" of the orthodox rabbi keeping pace beside him. Yehuda caught sight of his reflection in a large window and saw that one of his tzi tzi's strings was hanging out of his shirt. Usually he was impeccably dressed, but tonight he was a mess. Over and over in his mind, he replayed Dr. Jarvis's words: *They found Hannah unconscious… breathing was labored… water in the lungs… bruised body… fractured skull.* Then: *Swelling in the frontal lobe. Surgery.* He must have been mumbling out loud because Dr. Jarvis glanced at him, a concerned look on his face.

They stopped at a circular reception desk in front of two large doors. *Intensive Care* read the plate affixed to the wall, *General Access Prohibited.* A short Indian doctor holding a clipboard was talking to one of the nurses behind the desk. When he saw the two men, he ended his conversation and approached them.

"Rabbi Orenstein," Dr. Jarvis said, "I'd like you to meet Dr. Patel. He's the neurosurgeon I spoke of earlier. Dr. Patel is a pioneer in the field of TBI, traumatic brain injury. We're privileged to have him here at Senecca."

Dr. Patel nodded politely, and then turned to Yehuda. "I am happy to meet you Rabbi Orenstein," he said, speaking with a strong Hindi accent. He extended his arm, but Yehuda just stared at him, thinking that Dr. Patel looked as though he had been buffed and polished. His black hair was parted neatly on the far left side and had a sheen to it that made Yehuda think of the word "henna".

*Henna.*

*Hannah.*

Yehuda felt like he was floating.

"Rabbi?"

The whites of Dr. Patel's eyes looked like they had been professionally whitened, like teeth. An image of Hannah brushing Yitzi's teeth with a *Bob the Builder* toothbrush popped into Yehuda's head.

"Rabbi Orenstein?"

"Uh… yes… I'm sorry." He shook the doctor's hand.

"I am happy to meet you Rabbi Orenstein," Dr. Patel said again, this time glancing over at Dr. Jarvis, a questioning look on his face.

"You are my wife's doctor?" Yehuda asked, not the least bit interested in formalities.

"Yes, that is correct. I am overseeing the care of Mrs. Orenstein. I suspect you are very eager to see her."

"I am."

"Before we do that, have you had a chance to eat or drink something? You look a bit pale."

Yehuda waved him off. "I'm fine, just tired." *Exhausted*

Dr. Patel bowed slightly. He reminded Yehuda of Ram Dass, the Indian servant in *A little Princess*. It had been Sunny's favorite movie when they were kids. They had something in common; just like the poor little princess who was reunited with her thought-to-be-dead father, Sunny too dreamed of her father coming home.

"Very well. Rabbi, I will have to ask at this time that if you are in possession of a cell phone, you turn it off before we step through those doors. And may I ask sir, if you have any electrical implants such as a pace maker?"

"No, none. No pace maker; no cell phone either."

"Very good." He nodded to the nurse behind the desk. She pushed a small button to allow them entry.

"Rabbi Orenstein…"

Yehuda turned around, just then realizing that Doctor Jarvis would not be continuing on with them. "I wish you the very best," he said. "And please, don't hesitate to contact me if there is anything I can do for you—anything at all."

"Mrs. Orenstein is in room 246," Dr. Patel said, gently patting Yehuda on the back. Yehuda turned and followed him down the hall, his heart pounding so hard that he could feel the throbbing pulse in his neck.

# Eleven

Hannah lay peacefully on her back, covered by a white blanket with the top portion of her head wrapped in a thick bandage. Thin breathing tubes hung from her nose. The corners of her mouth turned up ever so slightly—suggesting just a hint of a smile—and her chest raised and lowered rhythmically. Had it not been for the wall of machines—computers flashing numbers and wave patterns across their monitors—and the IV bag steadily releasing small drips of liquid into her veins, one might have reasonably assumed she was enjoying a blissful nap.

Yehuda rushed to her side. "Oh my God, Hannah!" He took her hand and held it against his cheek.

"She has been comatose since her arrival," Dr. Patel said.

Yehuda swept a gentle hand across a small patch of his wife's cheek, the only area not bandaged.

"Can she hear me? Does she know I'm here?"

Dr. Patel shook his head and approached the bed. "No, in this state, it is unlikely that any words would register, although there are differing medical opinions on that."

Yehuda stood, but his eyes remained locked on his wife.

"Mrs. Orenstein scored a seven on the Glasgow Coma Scale, and the CT scan has confirmed a blunt head trauma. The force of her skull against the concrete wall has…"-

"The bandages…" Yehuda interrupted.

"Yes," Dr. Patel said, stepping closer. "Her frontal lobe was bruised from the impact."

*Bruised.* Bruised made it sound as if this was no different than Yitzi falling off his tricycle or Rachel twisting her ankle.

"When will she wake up?" Yehuda asked, heading off the images of Hannah being attacked that now seeped so readily into his head.

Dr. Patel, who had been prepared to go into a long discourse on the different types of head injuries, took a few seconds to regroup. "We cannot say."

Yehuda rephrased the question. "I mean in general…on average… how long?"

Dr. Patel shook his head. "I'm very sorry, Rabbi Orenstein, but we have no way of knowing."

"What? But how can that be?" Yehuda made no attempt to hide his annoyance. "You *must* be able to give an estimate… a day, two days, a week?"

Somehow, knowing when Hannah would awaken seemed like vital information—as if being able to put it on the calendar like an upcoming birthday would make everything that led up to it more tolerable. Yet, Yehuda knew this notion was absurd. As Dr. Jarvis had explained earlier, this was likely to be the beginning of a long and arduous recovery. From this vantage point, there was no celebration to count down to. At the same time, Yehuda wasn't ready to hear the doctor spew out a list of everything that could be wrong with his wife.

"Or even longer," Dr. Patel said. "Rabbi Orenstein, as cruel as it may sound, we have no choice but to wait."

Yehuda nervously adjusted his yarmulke. Patience was never one of his strong suits. "What exactly are you saying?"

"I'm saying that we have no accurate way of predicting the duration your wife—or any individual—will remain in this state. But Mrs. Orenstein's pupils *are* reacting normally to light—an excellent sign— and the surgery to reduce the brain swelling went better than expected. Now all we can do is hope and pray that she does, indeed awaken."

*Pray.* Now that *was* one of Yehuda's strong suits, though he couldn't help but wonder about all the prayers he had said already. What about the three times a day—for the past twenty years—chest pounding entreaties to God asking for health and longevity? Didn't those count? Didn't God care? Yehuda's shoulders dropped in surrender. His head hurt and he rubbed his temples, feeling immediately remorseful for his ingratitude. After all, God had blessed him with a beautiful family. God had listened to his prayers when they nearly lost Nehama. He of all people should remember there were no guarantees in life. Yes, God always heard, but sometimes the answer was *no*. Yehuda had to heed his own advice, words he had said to others more times than he could recall: *Trust in the Almighty's wisdom. What God does is always for the best.* To Dr. Patel's surprise, Yehuda suddenly burst into laughter. There it was, that trite piece of advice he didn't want to hear. But he couldn't very well punch his own lights out now could he? As quick as it had come, Yehuda's smile fell away, and his eyes welled with tears.

"Rabbi Orenstein?"

Yehuda rubbed his eyes and didn't look at the doctor. "You're saying there's a chance that she…" He could barely get the words out. Fortunately Dr. Patel cut him off and he didn't have to try.

"Yes, I'm afraid so."

"What are the chances?"

Dr. Patel sighed. "Fifty-fifty."

Yehuda kneeled back down next to Hannah and buried his face in his hands.

*Oh God, give me strength.*

"Rabbi Orenstein," the doctor said softly, "Senecca's trauma center is considered a level four facility—the most highly equipped. Your wife is in the very best hands. Our team will be monitoring her progress closely, especially during this first week."

"This first week?"

"Yes," Dr. Patel said gently. "Over the next seven days, we want to watch for signs of secondary injury, which could adversely affect her prognosis."

"*Secondary injury*? What is secondary injury?"

"It's not quite what it sounds like. Secondary injury can occur as a result of the body's reaction to the initial trauma—for example, tissue damage, infection, electrolyte disturbances, ischemia."

"Ischemia?"

Dr. Patel nodded. "Yes. Ischemia is inadequate blood flow. It can result from any number of situations…"

Yehuda was sorry he had asked. He held up his hand to stop the doctor. "My head is pounding and I'm not sure how much I'm capable of retaining right now…"

"Yes, of course." Dr. Patel said. "We'll have plenty of time to discuss all of this tomorrow. Just know that we will be doing everything we can to prevent further damage."

Yehuda collapsed onto a chair in the corner of the room. It was a recliner. He wondered how many people had slept here, not knowing if their loved one would live or die. Whether he liked it or not, he was now part of that private club.

*Further damage.*

Yehuda sat up. Something had suddenly occurred to him. "Dr. Patel, when you say *prevent further damage...* Does that mean that my wife already has... is she..." He swallowed. "Is my Hannah brain damaged?"

The doctor nodded slowly. He was used to repeating himself to overwhelmed loved ones. "There was damage to your wife's frontal lobe and possibly the temporal lobe as well." Dr. Patel said. "The left temporal lobe controls speech, writing, all areas of language processing."

Dr. Patel's voice faded as a flash of images burst into Yehuda's head: *Hannah laughing at his jokes. Singing at the Sabbath table. Reading to the children, Teaching her women's classes.* God used utterances to create the world. He had separated man from animal by endowing him with the gift of speech. Yehuda was certain Hannah's world would be irreparably altered without it.

"So, yes; technically, we must say that your wife's brain has been damaged, though the extent and severity of that damage have yet to be determined."

Yehuda took a deep breath. "Dr. Jarvis called brain injury a 'life long deficit'."

Dr. Patel nodded. "Yes; that may be true. But remember Rabbi Orenstein, our physical therapists are highly qualified. There are many encouraging cases. Individuals who have suffered even more severe trauma than your wife." He waited for a response from Yehuda, a glimmer of acceptance, even. But before he could get it, a young nurse poked her head in the door.

"Dr. Patel?" She acknowledged Yehuda with a slight nod and then turned back to the doctor. "Excuse me for interrupting, Dr. Patel; but Mr. Harmon's wife would like to speak with you."

Dr. Patel glanced at his watch. "Yes, of course. I'll be right there."

He turned to Yehuda. "Brain Injury may indeed be a lifelong deficit, but recovery doesn't end. The human brain is extremely resilient."

Yehuda looked down at his hands.

"Well, I will leave you now, so that you may have some time alone with your wife," Dr. Patel said. He bowed his head and started toward the door. Grabbing the handle, he turned around to face Yehuda one last time.

"Rabbi Orenstein?"

Yehuda looked up.

"We'll do everything we can."

# Twelve

Patty Collins lay on her back, tucked snugly under the white down comforter, her right leg lined smack up against her husband's like two pretzel rods. But while her closed eyes fluttered in a contented dream state, sleep once again eluded John. He stared up at the shadows on the bedroom ceiling and saw images—distorted shapes—that caused the hairs on his arms to bristle. They were products of his own mind, long serpent-like figures laying in wait between gilded squares. Symbolic, his therapist told him, of feeling out of control. John had had plenty of time to make these connections with Dr. Hendricks while on personal leave from his job; but though the weekly appointments had ended long ago, John remained haunted.

He turned and looked at the clock on the nightstand.

*5:27AM*

Despite his physical exhaustion, there was no way he'd be getting to sleep any time soon, not while the scene at the old high school kept replaying over and over in his mind: One dead, one barely alive—a rabbi's wife of all people! And there was something about the man they took into custody. He looked familiar somehow. But as much as he'd been trying, John could not place him.

It was pointless to just lay there staring at the ceiling, so John quietly slipped out of bed, pulled on his robe, and headed down the back stairs. The house was so old that it was next to impossible to move soundlessly, though he knew the few creaks of the hardwood floor wouldn't wake his wife, who had slept through countless nights of his insomnia. In the kitchen, John poured some milk into a small saucepan to heat on the stove. According to his nutritionist daughter Liz, tryptophan was a natural relaxant. While it heated, John studied the bite on his arm. It looked worse than it actually was, the doctor on call had assured him. Nonetheless, John had spent over an hour at the hospital while a dentist took photos and made an impression of the bite with vinyl polysiloxane. Then there was the obligatory saliva swab. John would just have to sit tight and pray the son of a bitch didn't have an infectious disease. Within a minute, the milk began to bubble. John poured it into a mug, added a tablespoon of sugar, and headed for the chess room. Just off the main library, it was a cozy, circular room with dark wood paneling and stained glass windows. A round, claw foot table stood elegantly in the center of the floor. A white marble chessboard rested on top; it's shiny pieces waiting at perfect attention. Four high backed chairs rounded out the perimeter of the room, each with it's own side table, reading lamp, and ashtray.

John sat down in one of the chairs and brought the mug of milk to his lips, momentarily focused on the pronounced sounds of his sipping and swallowing. Patty's father had installed special wall insulation rendering the chess room virtually soundproof, so the only movements one could hear were their own. John had always been fond of this room, and ever since Jay's death he'd been spending more and more time alone here. To John, it offered a womb-like reprieve from a crazy, out-of-control world.

John looked up at the framed oil painting of his father in law—Bertram in his riding gear, tan breeches and black boots, a pensive look on his face. What a shame John had never known the man. By the time he and Patty met in 1966, Bertram Randolph had already been deceased several years. John thought back to that sweltering June day when his life veered off course. Although it was over forty years ago, it felt like yesterday. While on duty in Center City John was summoned to the scene of a hit and run near Lit Brothers department store, where he was to interview several of the witnesses, including Patricia Randolph, a first year nursing student at Hanneman University. Dressed pristinely in a white blouse and pink skirt, Patricia appeared unusually agitated, alternating between wringing her small hands nervously and staring at her watch. John suspected that she was under the influence of some narcotic. But when he moved closer to peer into her eyes, she stepped back, surprised. "If you'll please excuse my odd behavior Officer Collins," she said, "it's just that I'm late for something… an event with my mother." She looked at her watch for the tenth time in five minutes. "If there is any way at all we could speed this up…"

Though average height, Patricia's petite bone structure made her 5'4" frame appear two inches shorter. She had big brown button eyes with long black eye lashes, a cute little nose, and a tiny pink-lipsticked mouth. Patricia was blond with the same pixie style Doris Day wore in *The Thrill of it All*. Though smitten before he finished interviewing her, what hooked John was the way she called him "Officer Collins". Something in her voice made him forget for a brief moment that he had four brothers with the exact same title.

Before long, Patty was spending each Sunday with John's family in their modest twin home on Passyunk Avenue. Swept up in the excitement of young love, it never occurred to John to wonder why he hadn't been invited to Patty's family home in the suburbs. He knew only that Patty's mother was a widow, and that she lived in Arden Station. For John, this was enough information; after all he was interested in Patty, not her family.

John proposed six months later, slipping a tiny pear shaped diamond on her finger.

"Well?" he asked. "Will you have me as your husband?"

She wrapped her arms around him. "I'll give you my answer on Sunday after you come home and meet mother," she said.

That Sunday, after church, John arrived at Patty's apartment wearing a brown suit and striped tie.

"Nervous?" she asked, looking down at his freshly polished shoes.

"Not in the least," he said, giving her a quick peck on the cheek, "just excited to finally meet your mother."

Patty got into his car, immediately noticing the wrapped bouquet on the back seat. "Uh oh," she said, slapping her cheeks dramatically. "Mother *hates* carnations!"

John's eyes widened. He looked at his watch. "What time is she expecting us? Maybe we can stop off at Murphy's and pick up something else." He yanked a handkerchief out of his jacket pocket and dabbed the tiny beads of perspiration that had appeared on his forehead.

Patty covered her mouth and burst out laughing. For such a big, strong man, he was carrying on like a flustered schoolboy. He just looked at her, bewildered.

"Relax! *I'm kidding…* Mother loves carnations!" She gave him a playful poke on the arm. "And you say you're not nervous, huh?"

Twenty miles west of the city, Patty directed John down a road marked *private drive.* It was lined on both sides with tall fur trees, marking the edge of what was otherwise dense, overgrown woods. After driving about a half a mile, the road dead-ended at a twelve-foot high gate with a large "W" etched tastefully into the wrought iron design. Patty leaned across John's lap—ignoring his stunned expression—to announce herself into the intercom. The gate opened slowly and she motioned for him to drive on. Speechless, John pulled the car around a small bend, his jaw dropping when the sprawling fieldstone mansion came into view. John's head spun as he tried to make sense of what he was seeing. He knew that Patty had been brought up well. She had attended an exclusive private school for girls and was always immaculately dressed and well mannered. But she was so down to earth, and got along so well with his family, that never in a million years would he have associated her with the mansion that lay before them.

The housekeeper, Mrs. Booth, informed them that Mrs. Randolph was resting, and suggested that Patty give John a tour. "Windmere," Patty told him, was built in 1910 and had been in the Randolph family for generations. Patty's great, great grandfather had made his fortune in lumber and spared no expense in building the estate, using an array of materials—everything from rock and brick, to crystal, marble, and quartz. The latest technological advances had been incorporated into the original design of the home, amenities not common for that time period, including indoor plumbing and a central intercom system. The residence totaled over 10,000 square feet, she said, had twenty-six rooms and six working fireplaces. After all these years, the original wood floors of cherry, oak, and mahogany were in pristine condition. Patty pointed out several magnificent stained glass windows including a ten-foot stained glass skylight on the second story. It looked celestial, John thought, and he couldn't help but compare it to St. Mary's cathedral in the city.

Patty and John made their way outdoors, passing through the

manicured lawn toward the gardens where Patty pointed out the chef's garden of rosemary, chicory, dill, basil and parsley. Next, she showed him the topiary maze where she played as a child. "It seemed so big to me then, like I could be lost forever…" She took his hand in hers and led him to a bench tucked behind some rose bushes, where they sat quietly for several minutes, his arm wrapped protectively around her shoulders. After a minute she sat up and pointed toward several old carriage houses and weathered barns in the distance. After her father's death, Patty said, his beloved horses, *Lucky* and *Misty* had been sold. Her mother couldn't bear to keep them; the memories were too painful. Patty continued to stare into the distance, lost in thought. Then she turned to John with serious eyes. Did he remember the day they met? Did he recall how agitated she was while he was interviewing her near the accident? Patty now seemed eager to explain: Despite all the pomp and circumstance of his lifestyle, her father was a pretty regular guy. He loved sports and had agreed to become one of the major financiers of a new Philadelphia sports arena. That hot day back in June—the day of the hit and run—happened to be the same day construction was beginning on the *Philadelphia Spectrum*. Patty had been on her way to meet her mother at the groundbreaking ceremony. She made it just in time for the ribbon cutting, but during the dedication speeches, Margaret Randolph was suddenly overcome by the heat and fainted. She was admitted to Pennsylvania hospital for observation, where the doctors determined that she had suffered her first full-blown panic attack. Through wet eyes, Patty described Margaret's ongoing battle with anxiety and depression, an uphill struggle that would not let up until her death twelve years later. After hearing this, John braced himself for a difficult encounter with Patty's mother, anticipating a needy, overbearing woman. But to his relief, Margaret Randolph was weary but welcoming. She was sedated, but lucid, and seemed genuinely pleased to meet him. She already knew a good deal about him, Margaret told him over tea and scones, since her daughter had spoken almost of nothing else for the past three months; but was there something else perhaps? Margaret smiled up at him and then at her daughter. "People are always much more complex than they appear," she said. "Before my husband died, I was a happy, carefree woman…" Margaret's voice trailed off. "But look at me now…" She shook her head and took a sip of her tea. "But enough about me. Let's talk about you. Tell me, what brings a big strong police officer like you to his knees?"

At the time, John had thought it an odd question to be asked; he brushed it off, not really understanding what she was asking, not yet realizing that we all have it. The thing that brings us down. All the way to our knees.

John set his mug down and stared up at the portrait of Bertram Randolph. It was one of several oil paintings a local artist had done of Patty's family when she was a teenager. John's favorite, hands down was the one of Patty and her dog, Duke. *Duke*. When he first learned the retriever's name, he was taken aback. The name sounded so regal. That's when it hit him. The woman he planned to spend the rest of his life with was a millionaire's daughter! Patty didn't understand why it bothered him. She insisted that her father had simply named the dog after John Wayne, the movie actor.

John remembered how difficult those first few years of marriage had been. Complete culture shock. So often, he wondered if he was good enough for her. He would never admit this to Patty, but even now, after nearly forty years, he *still* wondered if her father would have approved of her marrying a commoner from South Philly. Though how bad could Bertram Randolph have been? After all he was a die-hard sports fan! John tried to imagine Patty's father as the regular guy she claimed he was—a regular guy who just happened to be worth millions.

John thought the two of them would have shared a mutual respect. They might have even been buddies—shooting pool, drinking beer. At the very least, Bertram would have been relieved that Patty married a man who wasn't after her money—a man who not only loved her, but could protect her as well. John smiled, thinking of the private joke he and Patty shared when they were first married: She was his beauty; he was her brawn.

John's gaze passed over the marble chessboard. Bertram had been an aficionado of the game. Patty played a bit, but the girls were more interested in dance and drama. Then, of course, there was Jay who learned to play after he moved in with them. *All those nights when Patty would find the two of them in here at all hours.* John shook his head, willing himself not to think about Jay. For the life of him, John had never understood how his brother Tony could have thrown his oldest boy out like garbage. All because the kid didn't want to be a cop! John didn't have a son of his own, but if he did, he would have been *relieved* not to have to worry about the boy's safety! Apparently, Tony didn't see it that way. To him, it was a disgrace, the end of the civilized world. His kid refusing to go to the police academy? Not under his roof!

"I want to be an artist," Jay told John and Patty the night he showed up on their doorstep in the pouring rain without a jacket. His father had called him a *homo* and thrown him out of the house before dinner. Jay had just enough money for train fare to Arden Station.

"I'm not gay, Uncle John, I just like art."

Of course they took him in. And gladly paid for art school too.

Tony was the only one of John's brothers—the only member of John's entire *family*—who still spoke to him after he married Patty, and now he was furious. How dare they interfere in his kid's life! Just because John married into money didn't make him a God damn king!

Tony made it clear the only way he would take his kid back was if he gave up his art and enrolled in the police academy. But it didn't take a genius to see that Jay had talent, and it wasn't firing a gun. Just two years after graduation, Jay was commissioned by the city to sculpt a piece for the grand hallway of the Academy of Music, an unheard of opportunity for someone so young.

John ran his hand along the bite on his arm. Life threw us plenty of curveballs, but sometimes they felt like pianos being hurled from tenth story windows.

When the call came in, John's initial reaction was disbelief. Sure, Jay lived in New York City, but he didn't work anywhere near downtown Manhattan, so it had to be a mistake! Besides, Collins was a common last name. Patty would just keep calling his apartment, his cell phone. Things were chaotic in the city; it was just a matter of time before Jay would call.

Father McCormick called just days after remains of the twenty-three year old's body were identified among the wreckage at ground zero; but it would be weeks before John agreed to speak to him. In the very beginning, while his emotions were so raw, the last thing John wanted was to hear from the priest that Jay was in a better place or part of a larger plan. Dying on 9/11 had secured Jay a permanent place in the history books, but for those left to mourn his passing, dying publicly in this way—as one of thousands—had somehow diluted the loss, shortchanging them of their right to grieve selfishly.

It would be another two months before the mystery would be solved by the wife of a Tower One executive. Jay was there that morning to see her husband, Lilly Waxman told John when they met for coffee at a small Princeton diner. She had seen one of Jay's pieces—an abstract wind sculpture—at an exhibit in the village. She fell in love with it instantly and talked her husband into buying it for their house in the Hamptons. Jay, it seemed, did not want to inconvenience him, and offered to meet her husband at his office. "If only they had met at Jay's studio," she said, remorse in her voice. "My husband, and your son would be..." Her voice trailed off. She didn't finish her sentence and John didn't correct her.

On the drive home it occurred to him: he was carrying on as though he had lost a son. But Jay *wasn't* his son; he was Tony's! Maybe Tony was right. John shouldn't have interfered in the boy's life. What if instead of taking Jay in the night he showed up on their doorstep, he had sent him home? If Jay had been a cop in Philly, chances were good he'd be alive today.

*Because of me, Jay's dead.*

John fingered a rook from the chessboard. But it *wasn't* his fault Tony never made amends with Jay before he died—something Tony evidently regretted based on the surge in his binge drinking. Last John heard, Tony was in rehab again… Yep, life was like a giant chess game. We all believed we were in control of our lives; we liked to think we had the last say. But there were more powerful forces out there. Something else controlling our moves, a queen to our lowly pawn.

# Thirteen

Estelle Ginsberg was buried on Wednesday morning. The Litman Funeral Home was filled to capacity, each seat occupied by someone who had known Estelle, or had been affected by her tireless community work. Estelle's brother Morton, a frail man in his early eighties slowly ascended the steps to the podium. With a trembling hand, he pulled a thin pair of reading glasses and a folded piece of paper from his jacket pocket. He smoothed the paper out on the shtender, and addressed the sea of mourners in front of him. Speaking in what sounded like an Eastern European accent, he began.

"My sister, Estelle was a wonderful woman. She was a wife and mother. She was my sister, but she was also a mother to me. Many of you know about my sister and me that we survived the holocaust. Our parents, our two brothers… they were not so lucky."

He pulled a handkerchief out of his pocket and blew his nose.

"We were in Auschwitz, Estelle and I. She kept me alive. I was older, but I was weak. She was the strong one. She was healthy…." Morton paused to wipe his tears and collect himself. "My sister… she subjected herself to humiliation… demeaning, unspeakable acts, so that I would live. So that

I was given extra rations or clean socks, or an extra blanket. She did these things because she knew I would not survive if she did not. My sister was a wife and a mother. Because of what she suffered at the hand of the Nazis, she could not have her own children, so she took in a child that needed a home. Avi had what they call Down syndrome. His mother and father had six children already to feed. They could not take care of one more, especially one like Avi. My sister cared for him and loved him like he was her own. Estelle loved all children no matter what problems they had. Avi's heart also was not right. He had two surgeries, but still his heart could not be fixed. Avi died when he was ten years old. My sister was heartbroken, but always she made the choice in life never to despair. She gave all her time to others—children and adults. She helped many. She was trusted. My sister understood the dangers of *loshon hora*, improper speech. Never would she speak badly of another. Everyone loved my sister. How could they not? Always there was a smile on her face; always she spoke a kind word. She loved every minute of her life. I will shock you when I say that I believe she also loved her time in Auschwitz. I say this because she had *purpose*. Always did she find meaning in her life, as a prisoner in Poland during the war and also here, in our great country, living in freedom. My sister, she lost so much. Her wonderful husband passed away six years ago. During his illness, Estelle took care of him, never once did she complain. Never was she bitter. I know my sister. She would not want us to be angry or sad. She would tell us *God is good. God makes no mistakes. Everything he does, serves a higher purpose.* She would say we are created in his image. Everything we do must be also for a greater purpose. My sister would want us to remember the way of her life, not the way of her death."

# Fourteen

Elise didn't bother checking the caller ID before she picked up the phone. She had been expecting this call, polishing off her second glass of wine to calm her nerves.

"What's going on, doll?" her father asked in his usual enthusiastic tone.

Elise inhaled deeply to steady her voice. If she were to respond honestly to his question, the words out of her mouth would be an incoherent jumble, something like, "it was horrible... the mikvah... a woman is dead." Eventually she would calm down and attempt to convey the enormity of an entire community attending the funeral of a holocaust survivor. Naturally, he would want details about the crime and she would tell that there weren't many yet. But, she would say in her most assuring voice, there was no reason for concern; they already had him. The man who killed Estelle was in police custody.

*As if that would satisfy him.*

Elise knew better. One *iota* of news of a murder in Arden Station and her father would be on the next plane to the states. A knight in shining armor coming to rescue her, no matter that she had a husband named Evan to protect her. Maybe it was because she kept her maiden name—Danzig—that her father still felt so responsible for her. Elise had planned to become a Henner, really she had, but at the last minute, on the day of her wedding, during the signing of the ketuba, she just couldn't do it. Somehow, it felt too much like she was abandoning him.

In truth, her father had always been overly protective. Elise understood it to some degree now that she was a parent herself. She worried all the time about her own three kids—about their health, safety, happiness. At least she had Evan to co-parent with, to lean on for support. Her father, to the contrary, had been utterly alone.

"Elise?"

"Oh… fine, Dad; everything's fine… "

She was thankful the conversation was taking place over the phone. Had she been face to face with him, he would for sure know she was lying; he was *that* adept at reading her. But what else could she expect? After all, Lewis Danzig had been a clinical psychiatrist for over forty years. It was his job to read people! During the course of his long career, Lewis had also held posts at Boston Memorial and Harvard Medical School, but he was best known for his work in the area of posttraumatic stress. His research had been published in *The American Journal of Psychiatry, The International Journal of Mental Health*, and *The Journal of Child & Family Studies,* as well as countless other publications. His most acclaimed studies involved the use of cognitive reconditioning protocols in PTSD and three months earlier, he had been tapped by the U.S. military to work with army M.D.'s. It was all top secret; he couldn't talk much about it, could only tell Elise he was presently on an army base in Germany.

"And how's the peanut gallery doing?" Lewis asked, as usual, redirecting the conversation away from himself. "Everyone doing well in school? Elise?... Elise are you there?"

"What?... Sorry Dad... Becca! Stop pulling on my sleeve! I'll put you on in a minute..."

Lewis chuckled. "Elise, put Becca on. I want to talk to my granddaughter."

"...Becca, here... talk to Pop-Pop."

Elise went to check the oven. It was burger and fries night; the meal was easy to prepare, and was a virtual guarantee she wouldn't hear any whining from the kids. Her father had cooked plenty of meals like this for her when she was growing up. Some of Elise's fondest memories were of sitting at the kitchen table doing her homework while her father wrapped hot dogs in slices of fatty bacon and American cheese—*Texas Tommy's* he called them—and deep fried thick slices of Vidalia onions in peanut oil—his own homemade predecessor of the Houlihan's onion loaf. On snow days—and there were plenty of them in Boston—he made French onion soup with gooey provolone cheese and slabs of thick bread to keep her warm. Sometimes Elise was saddened by the fact that her children would never experience the pleasure of eating the very same comfort foods—the foods she equated with security and love. Now that they kept kosher, Texas Tommy's were off the menu, as were lazy trips to Burger King or a quick ride downtown for an authentic Philly cheese steak.

"Give the phone to your brother," Elise instructed Becca.

Becca reluctantly handed Ben the phone.

"Done!" the three-year-old announced, losing interest after less than a minute.

"I'm back Dad."

"Is there something on your mind, Elise?" Lewis asked, his tone serious.

Elise took a deep breath. Damn! Was he picking up something in her voice? No, she couldn't do it. She could *not* tell him about Estelle's death or Hannah's hospitalization just yet. It was too soon; she was still trying to wrap her head around the facts herself. From what little she knew, the attack had been completely random. The man they held in custody was a complete stranger to the two women. But that was no surprise; what were the chances that women like Estelle Ginsberg and Hannah Orenstein had *enemies*? Estelle was a helpless old woman, a holocaust survivor; Hannah was the mother of five, the wife of a rabbi. But what troubled Elise more than anything was that she too had been at the mikvah that night. *It could have been me. Just a few hours difference and it would have been.* She shivered at this next thought: *was the killer there the whole time, hiding? Watching her? Waiting to strike?*

How could she possibly tell any of this to her father? That he had come close to burying his only child? Well, fortunately she had some time. He wasn't due back in the states for another week.

"No, there's nothing on my mind, Dad," she said, clearing her throat and trying to keep her voice steady. "Well, Sam's getting his braces on in a few days." She pulled the bottle of chardonnay out of the fridge, "but other than that, there's really nothing exciting to report."

# Fifteen

"Hello?"

Lauren had been in a deep sleep when the phone rang. She rolled over and squinted at the clock on her nightstand. *9:47AM.*

"Lauren?"

The voice on the phone was faint, shaky. Lauren threw her blankets off and sat at the edge of her bed. "Rachel? Is that you? What's the matter? Is everything okay?"

There was sniffling, followed by a loud "No!"

Lauren willed herself to wake up. What day was it anyway? *Thursday.*

"Rachel…Why aren't you in school?"

Rachel's breathing was unsteady. "Lauren, how come… How come you didn't come yesterday or the day before?"

Lauren walked to the window and pulled up the blinds, blinking as the morning light flooded the room. "I'm sorry Rachel, but I won't be…"

"Why aren't you here *now!*" Rachel demanded.

Lauren sighed. She understood how confused Rachel must be with her suddenly not showing up. After all, she had been at the Orenstein's home practically every day for the past four months.

"Rachel honey, I know this is hard for you, but everything will be okay."

Rachel began sobbing. There was a thud as the phone dropped followed by a shuffling of shoes on the wood floor.

A male's voice came on. "Hello? Hello, who is this?"

"Yehuda?"

"Oh… Lauren! I didn't realize it was you." He sounded relieved.

"Rachel called me. I uh… I'm sure this must be difficult for her."

"It is."

Lauren gulped. This was not easy, even over the phone. "For whatever it's worth, I'm sorry about everything, and I feel terrible for the children, especially Rachel. She sounds pretty upset."

"She is… We all are. How… how did you find out?"

"What?"

"How did you find out about Hannah?"

Lauren didn't answer.

"You just said you knew."

"I…"

"Lauren?"

"Yes… I'm here."

"Lauren, Hannah's been admitted to Senecca Hospital."

"Hannah's in the hospital?" Lauren's hand flew over her mouth and the words came out muffled.

"Yes...there was an incident… Monday night…"

*Monday night.* Lauren swallowed. "An *incident?*"

Yehuda lowered his voice. "The boys are here so I can't talk freely…"

"Oh."

"…But I'm glad Rachel called you."

"You are?"

"Yes. I need you."

Lauren felt a lump of emotion form in her throat. "You… You *do?*"

"Could you come and stay with us for a few days? The kids really need family right now."

*But I'm not family*

Lauren bit her lip. "I don't think it's a good idea for me to be in your home right now." *Or ever.*

"What? Why not?" Yehuda asked.

"Uh, it's just… Maybe you should speak to Hannah first."

"Lauren," Yehuda began slowly, "why would I need to speak to Hannah? You've been with us for over six months. You're part of our family."

Lauren couldn't believe it. Did he just say what she thought he said? After the episode with Hannah Monday night, Lauren did not expect to see or hear from Yehuda again, and now, here he was, not only speaking to her, but also asking for her help, inviting her back into his home. Talking to her as though nothing had changed.

"I just think you should speak to Hannah," Lauren said again.

"That's not possible," Yehuda said, his voice cracking, "because Hannah's *unconscious.*"

Lauren heard the sound of a baby's wail in the background. Unconscious? Hannah was *unconscious?* Oh God, that explained everything. *He didn't know.*

"Hold on Lauren, I'll be right back."

*Correction,* Lauren reminded herself. He didn't know *yet.* It was only a matter of time before Hannah woke up and told him everything. Lauren's heart pounded at the thought. Maybe she should confess to him now, over the phone, it was better than doing it face to face. There was no way she'd be able to look him in the eye when he found out that she wasn't the person he thought she was. That he had been duped. That they had all been. Lauren's head spun. She couldn't think straight. What should she do? Just blurt it out to Yehuda right now? *Coffee.* She needed coffee to think.

"I'm back," Yehuda said seconds later.

"Uh, is Nehama okay?" Lauren walked to the kitchen and scooped a tablespoon of Folgers into her mug, then filled it with instant hot water.

"Honestly, no. We had to put her on formula…"

It dawned on Lauren that Hannah had been exclusively nursing Nehama. Supermom Hannah had nursed all *five* of her children.

"Wow. I'm sorry. That must be so hard," Lauren said, stirring her coffee. She struggled to sound empathetic, even as her mind raced ahead of his words to figure out what to do.

"It's been hard on all of us," Yehuda said solemnly.

"I can't imagine what you're going through." Lauren paused to take a gulp of her drink. This was her chance. If she was going to do it, she had to do it *now*. "Yehuda, there's something I need to tell you…"

She cleared her throat, preparing to blurt out the words, but he cut her off. "Lauren, I'm sorry, Yitzi needs me. I have to hang up. Can you come? It would be such a relief to have you here."

Lauren swallowed. "But I… uh… okay, sure. Whatever I can do… but you understand I have to bring Rosie with me."

"That's fine. Yitzi will be thrilled," Yehuda said.

"You're sure?"

"Yes, I'm sure!"

He sounded frustrated. But of course he would sound that way. He had more pressing matters than her indecisiveness to deal with right now. Now that she thought about it, maybe it was better that she *didn't* burden him with details of the other night. It would just be one more thing for him to think about. Besides, right now he needed her help.

"Give me an hour or two," Lauren said. "I'll be over as soon as I can."

No sooner had Lauren set the phone down that her own trembling hands sent it flying off the counter. It crashed to the floor, somehow managing to land as a single intact unit. She bent down to retrieve it, and felt a chill rush through her body. What she wouldn't give to be able to crawl back into bed and hide under her blankets! Lauren covered her eyes and groaned out loud. Ugh! Why had she said *yes* to Yehuda, when the right thing to do—the ethical thing to do—would have been to say *no*! She wouldn't be in this mess to begin with if she hadn't answered the damn phone! What was the point of having caller ID if you didn't use it? She went back to her bedroom and quickly changed into a pair of jeans and the heaviest sweater she had, a white cable-knit her *ex* didn't seem to miss. Still cold, she wrapped a throw blanket around her shoulders and began surveying her apartment. She had no classes today or tomorrow, but the errands she planned on doing, the vacuuming, the piles of laundry would all have to wait. The Orenstein kids needed her. *Yehuda* needed her! She was doing this for them. What happened between her and Hannah was not important right now.

She pulled a duffle bag out of her closet and tossed it on the bed. Rosie sat upright on the bed like a bowling pin and watched intently as Lauren moved back and forth between the closet and her dresser, making her selections: underwear, pajamas, jeans, T-shirts, a couple of sweaters and a suit for Shabbat. She went to the bathroom and grabbed her makeup bag and a handful of toiletries. Rosie jumped down and followed Lauren out of the room, eyeing her suspiciously as she emptied the litter box, removed the liner, and slipped it into large clean trash bag. It was when Lauren retrieved the cat's travel cage from a tall shelf in the hall closet that Rosie gave a little chirp and high tailed it under the bed.

"Relax, Rosie! We're not going to the vet!"

Lauren dropped to the floor. Splayed out on her stomach, she strained to see the cat. Wide-eyed with a fresh coat of dust, the orange tabby was cowering in the farthest, darkest corner of the bed. There was no way Lauren could reach her like this. She pulled herself up, zippered her duffle bag and carried it to the front door. She slipped into her coat and grabbed her keys from the hook. Minutes later she had loaded her car and returned to the apartment. To her chagrin, Rosie was still hiding. Lauren went into the kitchen and loudly poured some cat food into a plastic container. Sure enough, Rosie came bounding into the room, nose held high, sniffing the air. Lauren scooped her up before she could take off again, and dropped her into the travel cage.

# Sixteen

It was unbelievable how much had changed for Lauren in the past six months. She had gone from a public relations job that often stretched the definition of *ethical* to working for a rabbi, the ultimate personification of decency. Hannah Orenstein called it "hashgacha pratis", *divine providence.* "There are no accidents," she liked to say.

Right. As if it was pre-ordained in the heavens that Lauren would baby sit the Orenstein kids. *Hashgacha pratis.* Such nonsense! It was all Lauren could do not to laugh in Hannah's face.

Personally, Lauren preferred to think that God had more pressing issues to deal with, like terminally sick children or crazed, genocidal terrorists. No, there definitely was nothing extraordinary involved with the linking of Lauren's and the rabbi's worlds. In fact, it had all begun with nothing more than a simple promotional flyer.

Normally immune to the vast amounts of marketing materials cheapening the appearance of her otherwise well kept building (posters taped up around the wall of mailboxes, advertisements for shows and lectures, free newspapers and coupons), the title on this particular posting caught Lauren's eye: *Honor Thy Mother and Father, a Jewish perspective*. The sad truth was that ever since Lauren quit her job, her parents had refused to speak to her. It was as if they were taking it as a personal affront, mourning the loss of her fancy title.

*Assistant Director of Marketing.*

Honestly, she shouldn't have been surprised that a mere four words on a business card were all it took to impress them. After all, Lyle and Shira Donnelly had always emphasized appearances. "If they like you, they'll buy from you," was her father's credo. As a teenager, he had honed his skills hustling T-shirts on the strip in Las Vegas. By age twenty, he had sold everything from cemetery plots to pet health insurance before settling on car sales. At thirty-three, he bought his first of three Honda dealerships outside of San Diego.

Lauren had been calling daily, asking to speak to her mother, but still nothing had changed.

"Your mother isn't feeling well. She can't handle any of your problems right now, Lauren!"

Her father's words stung, but she knew there was more. Shira Donnelly believed Lauren was punishment from God. *Shira's crime?* Marrying outside the Jewish faith. Apparently God didn't feel that being disowned by her entire extended family was enough punishment for one woman.

"Why did you go and leave such a good job anyway?" her father demanded, as if at the ripe old age of twenty-six, she had committed career suicide. "Well, the only advice I can give you is *watch your money!*" he snorted. "It's not like you'll ever have a man to support you!"

Maybe this was it. Maybe now they would cut off all ties with her, *their screw up of a daughter*. Apparently, her job preserved the remaining thread of credibility she had with them, and now that too was gone. All their hopes for her, intentionally discarded.

Lauren looked again at the flyer. *Honor Thy Mother and Father.* It had taken the job resignation for her to see her parents for who they were. Had part of her wanted to test them? Didn't she get it? They were *ashamed* of her! But as cruel as they could be, they *were* her parents. Maybe the rabbi's seminar would give her some insight on how she could fix, or at the least *improve* relations with them. She looked at the address at the bottom of the sheet. The lecture was being held in Arden Station, at a place called "The Arden Station Jewish Learning Center". She had never heard of it before, but it would be easy enough to get to, a quick twenty-minute drive without traffic.

The night of the lecture, an attractive woman Lauren's age welcomed her at the door. She was petite—barely over five feet, even with the wedge boots she wore under a long denim skirt and fitted red blazer. Her hair was strawberry blond, long and pulled back in a low ponytail. Fair skinned, she had a splattering of ruddy freckles around her nose and wore very little makeup. The woman introduced herself as Janine Miller, the rabbi's assistant. She took Lauren's coat and handed her an informational brochure about The Jewish Learning Center along with a list of weekly classes and special lectures.

Though the subject matter of *Honor Thy Mother and Father* turned out to be different than what Lauren had expected (it dealt primarily with the Jewish laws of caring for sick or elderly parents), Lauren enjoyed the lecture nonetheless. The rabbi was knowledgeable, entertaining and most importantly, had a great sense of humor, which he demonstrated by incorporating several funny anecdotes into his talk. It had been far too long, Lauren realized, since she had laughed.

"I always make it a point to say hello to a new face," the rabbi said, approaching her after the class. "I'm Yehuda Orenstein." He was an attractive man, probably in his late thirties to early forties, Lauren estimated, tall and well dressed in a gray suit and tie. His dark beard had flecks of gray and was trimmed neatly. He wore a black velvet yarmulke and smelled faintly of old spice.

"It's nice to meet you, Rabbi Orenstein," she said, shaking his hand. "I'm Lauren Donnelly."

His eyes smiled, emanating more warmth than she had felt in months. "Please call me Yehuda."

She nodded, feeling a lump form in her throat. "Yehuda."

"So Lauren, did you enjoy the class?"

She wiped an eye, hoping he would assume something had irritated it, rather than she was crying. "Very much. The hour practically flew by."

He smiled coyly. "So I didn't ramble? That's a relief! I try to wind down before people start fiddling with their blackberries and texting each other."

Lauren laughed. "I hope no one did that tonight!"

"No, but the young guy in the corner was snoring." He scratched his forehead. "Though I think he may be a med student, so he gets a pass."

Lauren laughed again. She hadn't known many rabbis in her life, but this one was a keeper.

"So, tell me," Yehuda said several weeks later, "what was it exactly that brought you to The Jewish Learning Center?"

Lauren had become something of a regular at the rabbi's nightly classes after quickly realizing that her entire social life had revolved around her former job. Of course it didn't help that she had been romantically involved with a co-worker. The relationship, which ended badly, had caused a huge scandal in the office, and now it felt like no one from the company had time for her. She had grown accustomed to the polite excuses whenever she called one of her former colleagues and suggested a get together. Now, Lauren treaded lightly, sharing only some of the less incriminating details of her resignation with Yehuda. Any thoughts about her recent breakup with Max, however, went unmentioned. That heartache, like all the others, she would deal with privately.

"And the interest in Jewish topics?" Yehuda asked. He understood that she was lonely, and it occurred to him that she might be looking more for companionship than an education.

"Genuine," she assured him, momentarily worried that he'd give her the boot. "I'd like to learn… Judaism is part of my heritage, after all."

She was raised on the west coast, she told him, as the eldest of three daughters born to a Jewish mother and Catholic father.

Yehuda laughed. "I was curious about the name *Donnelly*," he said. "It's not exactly Goldberg now is it?"

Lauren laughed. She and her sisters received what she called *religion ala carte*, she told him, Christmas trees and *dreidles*, Easter baskets and chocolate *matzah*. For some reason that she couldn't recall, she *had* attended Hebrew School—though only briefly—when she was very young. Sadly, she retained very little of what she learned.

Nothing Lauren said seemed to faze the rabbi, not even when she confessed that before taking his classes, she had no idea what a "mitzvah" was, or that "Hashem" meant *The Name*—a respectful reference to God. Yehuda didn't so much as raise an eyebrow; he simply nodded his head and smiled. "I can one up that," he said.

She braced herself for a funny punch line.

"Believe it or not, I didn't even know I was a Jew until I was nearly twelve years old!"

She waited, but it was clear he wasn't joking.

"But how are you... I mean, how were you able to become a rabbi?" Lauren asked.

"Rabbi Akiva, one of the greatest Jewish sages of all time did not start learning until he was forty. It is said that a man need only make the smallest effort; God will take care of the results." He leaned toward her and smiled. "I'm living proof of that, I guess."

The next Friday evening, Lauren arrived at the rabbi's cape cod style home, welcomed with open arms by Yehuda's wife Hannah, as if the two were old friends.

"Thank you for inviting me," Lauren said, handing her a bottle of *Shiraz* and carefully stepping over a wooden train set. "This will be my first Shabbat dinner."

Hannah took Lauren's jacket and while she made room for it in the over-stuffed closet, Lauren studied her closely, curious as to what kind of woman Yehuda would marry. She would never say so, but she had expected someone who may have at one time been attractive, but had let herself go. After all, Hannah was pregnant with her fifth child, so it was a reasonable assumption that she would be fat and unkempt—frumpy, even. But other than the normal pregnancy bulge, Hannah was actually quite beautiful. About 5'5", she was fashionably dressed in a long black skirt, and gold sequined sweater. She had huge eyes and gorgeous long hair, perfectly styled, that fell below her shoulders.

"Well, I'm glad you finally said *yes* to Yehuda. I know he's been after you for a few weeks," Hannah said. "You must have quite a social life."

Lauren smiled. Apparently Yehuda hadn't shared details of their conversations with his wife. If he had, Hannah would have known that other than the classes at The Jewish Learning Center and an occasional visit with her eighty-year-old neighbor, Mrs. Sills, Lauren *had* no social life. Hannah would also know that Lauren's idea of "having plans" was doing a load of laundry, eating cereal in bed, and watching TV with her cat.

Lauren followed Hannah into the living room which appeared to double as a playroom. Toys and games littered the beige carpet. A plastic fisher price workbench lay on its side in front of a well-worn couch. A wood coffee table was covered with children's books, a mix of religious and secular.

"Lauren, I'd like you to meet Sonia Lyman," Hannah said, gesturing to an attractive woman sitting on the couch.

Tall, slim and blonde, Sonia wore black leather pants, which reminded Lauren of Olivia Newton John in the movie *Grease*. Sonia didn't look a day older than eighteen.

"It's nice to meet you," Lauren said. It occurred to her that Hannah must be completely secure in her relationship with Yehuda to bring such a hottie into her home. "That's a beautiful sweater."

Sonia's eyes welled up as she touched the sleeve of her red mohair cardigan. "My mother... she made it for me before I leave to come to America."

Sonia's accent was subtle and vaguely familiar, Lauren thought, probably Eastern European, where Lauren's grandmother on her mother's side was from. Suddenly Sonia was more than just a pretty face.

"Sonia's from Ukraine," Hannah said, gesturing for Lauren to sit down.

"Kiev," Sonia said, very businesslike.

Lauren nodded politely and sat next to Sonia who smelled faintly of lilac. She had doe shaped blue eyes and her complexion was perfect, like a human Barbie doll.

"I hope you don't mind me saying so, but you speak English very well."

Sonia nodded again, but still maintained a serious demeanor. "Thank you. I study English in school."

"What brought you to the United States?" Lauren asked wondering if the girl ever smiled.

"I get married and my husband—we first move to LA."

Lauren almost laughed at Sonia trendy choice of saying *LA*, instead of Los Angeles. She pictured Sonia with a young John Travolta look alike.

"Sonia's husband Gary wasn't able to join us tonight," Hannah said, matter-of-factly.

Sonia looked down. "He travels now for work."

After a few more minutes of conversation, Hannah excused herself to tend to things in the kitchen, and Lauren struggled to make small talk with Sonia. Her cell phone rang and Sonia stood up and pointed to the receiver. "Is Gary, my husband calling. Excuse me." Sonia's face strained as she spoke into the phone. "No, Gary. I can't know that would happen. I'm sorry. I fix tomorrow!" The poor girl looked unnerved. "Please don't be angry! I promise I fix!"

Lauren was startled by Sonia's dramatic change in demeanor. She stood up quickly, not sure whether to stay or leave. She knew how it felt to be the object of eves-dropping and petty gossip, so she wanted to give Sonia some privacy, show her some decency.

Lauren motioned to Sonia to sit back down. "I'm going to see if Hannah needs a hand in the kitchen," she whispered. Sonia now looked both miserable and confused, probably at the expression *hand in the kitchen*, but eased herself back down on the couch.

As she followed her nose to the kitchen, Lauren now wondered if she appeared insensitive by leaving Sonia so abruptly. Maybe she should she have stayed to comfort her? Well it was too late now.

"It smells so good!" she told Hannah in the kitchen. "Can I help you with anything?"

"Oh, you are so sweet to offer," Hannah said, untying her apron, "but everything's ready—just keeping warm in the oven."

"This room is so beautiful," Lauren said, putting Sonia out of her mind. Her gaze passed over the tall cherry wood cabinets and stainless steel appliances. The countertops, now covered with empty serving plates, were Corian, specked with browns and reds. For an older home, the kitchen was quite modern, most likely having been gutted and completely remodeled. "But, if you don't mind me asking, why do you have two sinks and two dishwashers?"

Hannah hung up her apron and motioned Lauren to the butcher-block table where they both sat down. "Are you familiar with the laws of *kashrus*?"

"Kashrus?"

Hannah shook her head. "I'm sorry. The laws of keeping kosher."

Lauren thought for a moment, tracing her fingers along some ridges on the tabletop.

"They're rules from the Torah about what we can and cannot eat," she said, looking up, expectantly.

"Right," Hannah said. "For example, we only eat meat that comes from animals that have hooves and chew their cud…"

"And no shellfish," added Lauren, suddenly recalling this long forgotten piece of information.

"Right again," Hannah said. "No shellfish. In fact, any fish we eat must have fins and scales."

"And the reason for doing this is health based, right?" Lauren asked.

"Actually, *no*," Hannah said. "It's not. Sadly, many people believe that, and they also think that because our food handling practices are more sanitary nowadays, these laws are obsolete."

Lauren scrunched her forehead, "So if they're not health based, what exactly *is* the reason for them?"

"Well," said Hannah, "in the Torah, there are three types of Jewish commandments: *Mishpatim, Edos,* and *Chukim.* The laws of Kashrus fall into the last category. No explicit reason is given for them. We can't assume to know God's intent, or that we're even capable of comprehending something that likely happens on a strictly spiritual level."

"But in Mishpatim and Edos, explanations *are* given?" Lauren asked.

Hannah nodded. "Mishpatim translated means *judgment.* Moral laws such as 'don't steal or murder' fall into this category."

"Oh, I see... they're for the good of humanity," Lauren said.

"Exactly!" Hannah said, clearly impressed. "Rules for a civilized and moral society."

"And Edos?"

"Edos means *witnesses.* Commandments falling under this category serve to remind us of God's presence. They include rituals and festivals as well as the laws involving *tefillin* and the *mezuzah.*"

"But as far as Chick..."

Hannah smiled. "Chukim... translated it means *decrees.* These are God's decrees—whether or not we understand them, we must abide by them."

Lauren glanced at the two sinks. "Meat foods and dairy foods are kept separate, right?"

Hannah nodded. "Yes, and we have two separate sets of dishes and pots."

Lauren thought about the idea. Even if she did ever decide to keep kosher, there was no way two sets of dishes could possibly fit in her tiny apartment kitchen.

"Not everyone has separate sinks and dishwashers though," Hannah said. "Most people use rubber mats in the sink—one for meat, one for dairy—and they designate the dishwasher for one or the other."

"I guess it makes it easier to have two," Lauren said.

"Oh, yes! It's *much* easier this way," Hannah said, admiring her kitchen. "I didn't always have it so easy," she added.

"How long have you lived here?" Lauren asked.

"We bought the house about three and a half years ago," Hannah said. "Another religious family lived here before us. They had just redone their kitchen when the husband got transferred to Baltimore."

"That was lucky for you," Lauren said.

Hannah smiled. "We were living in a twin on Primrose Street at the time, but were outgrowing it by the second," She thought for a moment. "I was eight months pregnant with Yitzi. The former owners did what they could to make it work, but the house was still priced out of our range."

"But somehow you were able to buy it?" Lauren asked. She couldn't imagine a family as large as the Orensteins squeezing into a twin.

Hannah smiled. "Thank God for family! My mother in law—Yehuda's mother—saw it and insisted we buy it. She helped us with the down payment. Honestly, we couldn't have done it without her."

Lauren was surprised at Hannah's candor. Most people would be embarrassed to admit they needed financial help, but Hannah looked at it from a position of appreciation and blessing.

Hannah suddenly looked at her watch and jumped up. "Oh my, where did the time go? We have to light!" she announced, tapping her wristwatch. "I'll get Sonia."

Hannah returned a minute later. "It looks like it'll just be the two of us," she said, a bit deflated and with obvious concern in her voice. She led Lauren into a large dining room. The table was set for ten, beautifully laid out with white china and heavy flatware. In the center of the table stood a glass vase with yellow mums. A distressed wood sideboard along the furthest wall held two silver candelabras. Several shorter candlesticks stood in front.

"Would you like me to help you with the blessing?"

"Yes, It's embarrassing to admit this, but my grandmother is orthodox, and yet I don't know the blessing."

"Your mom's mother is orthodox?"

Lauren nodded. "But I haven't seen her since I was a three or four. She and my grandfather weren't happy when my mom married a Catholic."

Hannah squeezed her hand. "Well, it'll be my honor to help you with the blessing. Just repeat what I say."

Lauren lit her candle and waited while Hannah lit six. Each one, Hannah told her, represented a member of one's immediate family. She covered her eyes with both hands and began reciting a few words at a time. *Baruch ata Hashem Elohainu melech haolam, asher kiddshanu bemitvotav, vitzivanu, lahadlikner, shel shabbat,* which Lauren dutifully repeated.

"Shabbat Shalom!" Hannah said when they finished. Her smile lit up her entire face as she pulled Lauren toward her and gave her a warm hug.

Twenty minutes later, Yehuda returned from the evening prayer service with the four Orenstein children trailing behind. Nine-year old Rachel was impeccably dressed in a velvet blue dress, white tights and dress shoes. Her spirally brown hair was pulled into a low ponytail. David and Eli, at five and six respectively, looked practically like twins in their dark suits and white shirts. Yitzi, meanwhile, looked like a typical three year old in mud stained corduroys and a blue un-tucked dress shirt. A single brown hair stuck straight up on the top of his head. Yehuda removed his suit jacket and hoisted Yitzi up into the air, revealing two mismatched shoes. "Who put your shoes on?" Yehuda admonished playfully as he tickled his son's tummy.

Yitzi giggled. "I did it Abba!" He spoke in a funny husky voice, bracing himself for another round of tickling. "I put my own shoes on!"

The front door opened and Janine Miller, Yehuda's assistant, walked in, followed by two men Lauren immediately recognized from classes at the center. But before introductions could be made, Yehuda was ushering his guests to the table. Hannah took Sonia's hand and led her slowly to a seat next to her own. Lauren searched for her name card and discovered to her surprise that she was seated between the two men. When she looked up, Hannah was winking at her. Lauren looked away quickly before she started to laugh. *Was Hannah trying to fix her up?* But before she could give the question much thought, there was a hush in the room as each of the Orenstein children lined up in front of their father. One by one, starting with the oldest, he placed a hand on each child's head and uttered a blessing. Little Yitzi was the last to receive his, but didn't seem to mind in the least, as he marched back to his chair, a wide smile on his face. Yehuda then got the singing started with *Shalom Aleichem*. It was a beautiful song, but one that Lauren had never heard before, so she was relieved to pick up her prayer book and discover that the words were transliterated above the Hebrew.

"We're singing to the angels," Rachel announced proudly after the last stanza had been sung. "The angels walk home with us from *shul* and protect us from harm." Lauren found the idea of invisible bodyguards comforting, especially as a single woman living in a city where crime was rampant.

Following *Eishes Chayal*, a beautiful melody honoring the woman of the household, there was the blessing for the wine, the ritual washing of the hands, and lastly, the blessing over the challah—two home baked braided loaves covered by a beautiful gold-fringed cloth.

"The cover shields the challah from seeing that the wine is receiving the first blessing," Hannah explained to her guests, as they all tasted what to Lauren was the best bread she had ever eaten. "Imagine—if we are this sensitive to the feelings of something *inanimate…* how sensitive we are—or should strive to be—with one another!"

Now that the pre-meal rituals were finished, proper introductions could be made. Howard Freed and Jonathon Bauer, the two men who had come in with Janine, acknowledged that they recognized Lauren from The Jewish Learning Center. To her embarrassment, each seemed genuinely eager to talk to her. *They must know Sonia the hottie is married,* Lauren thought. She glanced in Sonia's direction and was startled to see her downing shots of vodka, one after the other. Her mascara was smeared and she was slumped in her chair. Lauren looked away. She couldn't handle any more drama right now. With her parents' rejection, she had enough problems of her own. Besides, dinner was being served and she was starved. Apparently, being five months pregnant with her fifth child didn't impede Hannah's preparation of an array of salads, chicken soup, sweet and sour brisket, garlic chicken, potato kugel, and roasted vegetables.

Lauren dug in to her food as Howard—sitting to her left—proceeded to tell her about his year in Israel, a trip encouraged by Rabbi Orenstein. He had studied at a yeshiva in Jerusalem, he said, hiked in the Negev desert, and planned to return in a few years. Lauren told Howard a bit about herself, but after a few minutes, he excused himself to use the bathroom. Lauren turned to her right where Jonathon had been waiting patiently. He was thirty-two, "not too religious", he said, but starting to eat more kosher food. Lauren's eyes started drooping and she discreetly glanced down at her watch. It was after 10:00 already; she was usually home in bed at this time. Jonathon droned on, sounding more and more like a talking personal ad, but she quickly perked up when he mentioned that he was a chiropractor. Her neck was tight—probably from all the back and forth she'd been doing between Howard and Jonathon. She considered asking Jonathon for some pain relief, but hesitated when it occurred to her that the request could be easily misconstrued as a come on. The last thing she wanted to do was give either of these guys even an *inkling* that she was interested.

"The poor girl must have been devastated when you left," Howard said suddenly as he returned to the table. "You know… Penelope Wright, the president of your PR firm," he added upon seeing her confounded expression. "That woman whose face is plastered on every billboard on 1-95? From her photo, she looks like she'd be one tough cookie to work for."

"Oh, right… Penelope." Lauren relaxed, sinking back into her seat. She and Howard had been talking about her old job. Just before he excused himself, she was about to tell him about her former boss; he must have assumed she meant Penelope. "Penelope's the firm's president, but I didn't see her much; she was based out of the New York office. My boss was a man." She laughed. "A very colorful character in his own right."

"Well, I'd like to hear all about him and the story you were about to tell me… about the day you walked out."

Lauren sighed, remembering the drama of that twenty-four hour period vividly. "Maybe another time," she said, despite the look of anticipation on Howard's face. She craned her neck toward the Orenstein kids. "Some content may not be suitable for young children."

Howard smiled. "Okay, so I'll have to hear the details another time, but at least tell me this: Do you have any regrets about leaving?"

The table suddenly went quiet, as if on cue. Feeling the pressure of so many attentive listeners, Lauren took a moment to collect her thoughts. She heard the voice of her father and his harsh words: *It's not like you'll ever have a man to support you...*

For sure her parents had regrets about her leaving her job. But did she? Lauren sat up and spoke calmly. "I knew I wanted to do something else with my life, but I was afraid for so long... Afraid of change, I suppose." She shrugged. This was the part she had to tiptoe over; the affair at work was not something she was particularly proud of. "Then one day I just did it. I guess it was the right time... though, I have to admit, there were a few sleepless nights after that." She hesitated, then looked up and smiled at Yehuda. "But, I'm happy to report that I did finally stop second guessing myself thanks to that exercise we did last week in class." Howard and Jonathon nodded knowingly.

"What is this exercise you do?" Sonia whispered from across the table looking directly at Lauren. Besides a bit of hush-toned conversing with Hannah, these were the only words she had spoken out loud during the entire meal.

"Yehuda had us write own obituary," Lauren said, speaking directly to Sonia. "It sounded morbid to me at first, but it made me really think: What would I want it to say? When I'm gone, what do I want to be remembered for? What will my legacy be?"

Sonia's face dropped. Lauren's words were having some kind of effect on her, though not necessarily a good one.

"We all want meaning in our lives—not regrets," Lauren added.

# Seventeen

"Um, my friend's sitting there," a blond, bug-eyed woman told Lauren. The woman grabbed the chair and pulled it closer. Then she plopped her bag on it, marking her territory like a dog.

Lauren sighed. Like Sonia, she must have had too much to drink at the Orenstein's home last month. Why else would she have promised to attend one of Hannah's daytime classes at The Jewish Learning Center? Especially today. She should have known things would not go well *today*. First Rosie had gotten into some curling ribbon and thrown up on the carpet, then her car wouldn't start—*again*—and she ended up taking the train and getting stuck sitting next to a man who smelled like he had slept in a dumpster. Lauren was further dismayed to walk into the center and find no sign of Janine, who was always around during Yehuda's evening classes.

"Sorry," Lauren said, backing away. She quickly found another seat around the giant square that had been formed from four long tables, and watched as the bug woman warmly greeted her friend minutes later. *So much for Loving Thy Neighbor* Lauren thought dryly. She picked a couple of cookies from a plate that happened to be within arms reach, watching intently as more and more women, ranging in age from twenty-five to forty came in and took their seats. They were an attractive group—*well maintained,* Lauren would call it—physically fit with long manicured nails, perfectly waxed eyebrows and bouncy highlighted hair. Some wore workout spandex; others waltzed in wearing tailored slacks and fitted blouses. They all had the same self-assuredness she lacked, and not just because of the jeans and sweatshirt she had chosen to wear today. The bug-eyed woman stood up to get a cup of coffee. She wore low cut designer jeans with an oversized buckled belt, probably intended to draw attention to a pilates-toned midriff. Funny, surrounded by this group, Lauren couldn't help but feel like she didn't belong. In a way, it felt like high school all over.

Ten minutes passed and still, Hannah had not yet arrived. But the women didn't seem to mind. Around the table, they chatted away like they were at a cocktail party; several animated conversations taking place all at once. Lauren overheard pieces of them—about clothing, jewelry, diets, vacation plans, restaurants, finding a good nanny or housekeeper or personal trainer. She glanced around expectantly, wondering if Hannah was *ever* going to show up, and met the gaze of the bug woman's friend, a tall brunette, freshly pedicured with leather flip-flops on her feet. The woman returned Lauren's smile by giving her a once over and abruptly turning her head and whispering something to her friend who glanced Lauren's way and nodded. Lauren swallowed and tugged on her braids. Max always liked her in braids—said she looked cute—but here, with these women, she felt like an idiot. *Nice group* she thought, and considered getting up and leaving. If only she could walk out without drawing attention to herself! But she had promised Hannah she would come to a class, she reminded herself, and took a deep breath. She reached for her purse and rummaged through it, looking for her palm pilot. Until Hannah arrived, she decided, she would use the time to update her electronic calendar, deleting the tasks that had been scheduled in her former life as a fully employed woman. Weekly breakfast meetings with Chip—*delete.* Monthly print media forecast session—*delete.* Three day convention in Aspen? Damn… she had forgotten about that one! Oh well—*delete.*

To Lauren's relief, Hannah came flying in minutes later, handbag swinging and blurting her sincere apologies. Her prenatal checkup had gone on longer than expected, she told them, placing her hand over her pregnancy bulge. According to the doctor, this baby was much more active than the others had been. Nothing to worry about though, everything was fine. After polite acknowledgments, the room quieted and Hannah took her position at the head of the table. The topic for the day? *Tzniut.* Modesty in action and appearance. Humility in our dealings with others. Lauren nearly choked on her cookie.

An hour later, the women collected their designer handbags, and filtered out the door. Hannah gathered up her notes and to Lauren's astonishment, headed straight toward Bug Eyes.

"How did the surgery go?" she heard Hannah ask.

"Fine, fine. He'll be home tonight," Bug Eyes replied so sweetly it made Lauren want to puke.

"Baruch Hashem," Hannah said, giving her a squeeze of the hand and smiling warmly into her eyes.

*Totally clueless,* Lauren couldn't help but think. Hannah might be knowledgeable as far as religion went, but she obviously couldn't see through people at all. After a minute, Bug Eyes left with her friend, and Hannah headed toward Lauren, but was intercepted by a tall woman who must have come in late and taken a seat in the back. The woman had an odd gait, walking with her shoulders hunched like she was either in pain or wanted to make herself smaller. Lauren studied the woman's face carefully—she looked so familiar—and was shocked when she suddenly realized who it was. *Sonia Lyman.* Sonia wore a shiny tracksuit and had tucked her long hair into a black baseball cap. Her face was free of makeup and her eyes looked puffy, like she had been crying for hours. Lauren swore she saw Sonia flinch when Hannah knowingly placed a gentle hand on her back and led her to a private office.

Lauren plopped down in her chair, completely shocked by Sonia's transformation. Last month at the Orenstein's home she had been beautifully dressed and confident. Confident in *appearance,* anyway. Lauren recalled how quiet Sonia had been during the meal. The only time she spoke up was when the discussion turned philosophical. *We all want meaning in our lives, not regrets.* Did Sonia need vocational guidance? Did she miss her family? Her country? Lauren sighed. That was probably it. She understood too well how it felt to be uprooted. It wasn't easy to start fresh. But Sonia had done it by choice. She had *willingly* married an American; certainly she had to understand that doing so would mean leaving her family behind. Lauren recalled the way Sonia spoke on the phone to her husband—apologizing for some mistake she had apparently made—she sounded so afraid. A bad marriage would explain Sonia's homesickness, and it didn't take a genius to see that the honeymoon, if there had ever been one, was long over.

Lauren folded her arms, disgusted as she glanced around the table. Most of the women had left their mess for someone else to clean up. What was that all about? They couldn't spare a minute to throw away their paper cups? Bug Eyes even left used tissues behind! Spoiled, that's what they were! These women were used to living perfect lives and getting waited on hand and foot.

"Hey there! How was class?" Janine Miller hustled in, weighted down by a brown grocery bag. She flew past Lauren toward a small kitchenette in the back, returning seconds later with a spray bottle and a roll of paper towels. "Did Hannah leave? She usually hangs out for a while after her class."

Lauren was still annoyed, thinking about the women from class. She lifted her chin, gesturing toward the closed office door. "She's in there with Sonia Lyman."

"Oh... Okay," Janine said, studying Lauren. "Uh, everything all right?"

"Peachy."

Janine grimaced. "Was class *that* bad?"

Lauren couldn't help but laugh at Janine's exaggerated expression. "Class was fine. It's a few of the *students* I wasn't so thrilled with."

Janine nodded knowingly. "Let me guess, was it Cynthia?"

Lauren shrugged. "I don't know her name."

"Did she have eyes that kind of stuck out from her face?"

Lauren laughed again. "That's the one."

"Cynthia Bergerman... yeah, she can be tough... but you shouldn't let her get to you," Janine said, waving her hand.

"Easier said than done," Lauren muttered. "What's her deal, anyway?"

"You mean why is she such a *witch*?" Janine asked, making a funny face.

Lauren nodded, covering her mouth to stifle what felt like an explosive laugh.

"Well first of all, she married money," Janine said, no longer joking. "Cynthia's father-in-law owns the Bergerman Bagel Company. Hubby works in the business, though he had a brief falling out with his dad a year or so ago..."

"How do you know all this?" Lauren asked.

Janine smiled coyly. "I have the scoop on everyone who comes through those doors. I suppose it's a benefit of my natural attention to detail. I don't miss *anything*."

"Well, I've known a lot of wealthy people," Lauren said, shaking her head in disgust, "and they're not all like that."

"I know," Janine said. "I guess it has to do with upbringing."

"In other words, her parents probably spoiled her," Lauren said.

Janine shrugged. "Maybe… Hey, want to hear something funny?"

Lauren lifted her eyebrows and leaned in. "Sure."

"Cynthia makes her housekeeper wear an actual *maid's* uniform."

Lauren scrunched her forehead doubtfully. "Come on… *really?*" she asked skeptically.

"I swear!" Janine insisted. "One time I had to drop something off at her house… or should I say *mansion*… and I saw it firsthand."

Lauren laughed. "Let me guess… was it a *French* maid costume? Her husband must love that."

"Not quite. Cynthia's the jealous type. She doesn't hire anyone unless they're at least thirty pounds overweight. The maid I saw was even heavier."

"You're kidding. Cynthia's really *that* insecure?"

"Uh huh."

For a split second Lauren felt a pang of sympathy for Cynthia; after all, she knew firsthand what it felt like to be unsure in love. But one look at the pile of snotty tissues and she snapped right out of it.

"Does she live around here?" What Lauren really wanted to know was *will I be bumping into her often?*

"Cynthia? Are you kidding? No way!" Janine could tell from Lauren's expression that she had no idea what she was talking about, so she elaborated. "Most of Hannah's students live further out in the *wealthier* areas. Cynthia lives in Wynnford."

Lauren had heard of it. "Pretty swanky."

Janine nodded. "You can't find a house for under a million, two out there."

Lauren gestured toward the table. "Let me give you a hand with this."

"Great," Janine said, tossing her the roll of towels. "I'll clear, you wipe."

Lauren picked up a tray of cake and sighed. "I don't know why you even bother putting this stuff out! Not one of those women ate more than a bite."

"Well, they're excused for being on perpetual diets," Janine said, "since they *are* paying my salary."

It took Lauren a minute to realize what Janine was saying. The Jewish Learning Center relied on contributions. These women—or their husbands—apparently gave *big*.

Just then, the office phone rang and Janine jogged off toward the front desk to answer it. Two minutes later she returned, her cheeks flushed.

"What is it?" Lauren asked. "What just happened? You're practically glowing."

"Remember Howard from the Orenstein's Shabbat dinner?"

"Of course."

"He wants to get together for coffee."

"Oh…Well, he seems like a nice enough guy," Lauren said without looking up. She was busy brushing some crumbs into her hand.

"Oh my gosh," Janine said, "You were talking to him too… I hope you weren't…"

"I wasn't *what*?" Lauren asked as Janine bit her lip nervously. Suddenly Lauren understood. She held up both hands in protest. "Oh, no! Not at all. Trust me Janine, Howard's all yours."

Janine exhaled.

"So you agreed to meet him for coffee?" Lauren asked, trying to steer the conversation back on track.

"Yep. Tomorrow." Janine laughed. "Wait until I tell Hannah that her strategy worked!"

Lauren tilted her head. "*Strategy?*"

Janine nodded. "Hannah seated me next to Howard at dinner to try and—you know—fix us up." She wagged her finger playfully. "Be forewarned Lauren; Hannah's into matchmaking—big time!" Janine carefully covered a plate of bobka with plastic wrap, but not before popping a small piece in her mouth. "I don't know what her secret is, but I have to admit, she has quite a knack for it."

Lauren grabbed a cookie off another tray before Janine could cover it. "Then why did she put me on Howard's other side?" she asked, before realizing the question made it sound like she was actually interested in the guy after all.

"Oh, I don't know," Janine said. "Maybe in case it didn't work out with Howard and me. I guess even matchmakers have to cover their bases."

"They do?" asked Lauren, chomping on her cookie.

"Sure," Janine said. "She seated you between Howard and Jonathon probably because she doesn't know you so well yet—she doesn't know your *type*." Janine laughed. "Well anyway, as soon as Jonathon tracks you down, the four of us can go on a double date!"

"What if I told you neither one is my type?" Lauren asked.

Janine thought for a moment. "Then I'd say, 'it's not me you should be telling this to, it's Hannah."

"Impossible. There might be a conflict of interest."

"What do you mean by *conflict of interest*?" Janine asked, narrowing her eyes.

Lauren scratched her head. "Haven't you ever been interested in the wrong person?"

"Wrong person?"

"Yeah, like someone who wasn't *available*?"

"As in someone who was married?"

"Sure, like someone who was married," Lauren said, looking away.

"I admit, I've been attracted to married men before," Janine said. "But I would never go after them."

"Why not?"

Janine looked completely surprised by the question. "Because they're off limits; that's why!" she said adamantly.

"But suppose it wasn't a happy marriage..."

"I still think it's wrong," Janine insisted. "Besides... how could you know for sure they weren't happy? People lie you know... to get what they want."

Lauren took a deep breath. Janine was right. People did lie. She thought of Max and how she had been completely misled into believing the two of them had a future together. Deciding she no longer wanted to talk about relationships, Lauren grabbed a folding chair from under the table. "Where do these go?" she asked Janine.

"Oh, I leave them set up for the evening class," Janine said. "It saves me time later. You *are* coming tonight, right? Yehuda's topic is *Pirkei Avos*—Ethics of our Fathers."

Lauren shrugged. "I'd like to, but first I have to check the train schedule."

"I thought you had a car."

"I do, but it's old and unreliable. I never know when it's going to start."

"Well, at least the train's just a quick ten minutes or so..."

*Which feels more like ten hours if you're sitting next to a homeless guy.*

"Right," Lauren said. She finished wiping the table and plopped down in a chair. "Does your job require that you be here for every single class, Janine?"

"How else would I get dates?" Janine said, laughing. "No, in all seriousness, I knew when I took this job, that I'd be a one woman show."

"I thought you were Yehuda's assistant," Lauren said.

"*And* office manager *and* receptionist *and* event planner *and* errand runner *and* custodian..."

Lauren held up her hand. "Stop! I get it! Whew! I'm getting tired just listening to you! Your hours sound worse than mine used to be."

"But I'm *happy!*" Janine said. "I'm sure working in P.R. you made five times what I'm paid, but I feel like I'm making a difference here. Yehuda is good to me, and I know he appreciates me—I'm treated like part of his family."

Listening to her words, Lauren was overcome. She could only imagine what it would feel like to be part of Yehuda's family. She saw the way he related to his children, his wife.

Janine was caught off guard at Lauren's sudden display of emotion. She grabbed a box of tissues. "Lauren, I'm so sorry. I didn't mean to imply..."

Lauren waved her off. "You didn't imply anything. I've just had a lot of upheaval lately." She wiped her nose. "I've felt pretty alone this last month or so."

Janine leaned in. "Look, if you ever want to talk... or if there's anything I can do for you... anything at all..."

"Thank you," Lauren said, forcing a smile.

"And listen," Janine continued, "I live less than a mile from here on Oak Lane. You're more than welcome to stay over at my apartment. You know—if the weather's bad, or you have car trouble, or even if you just want company." Janine ran to get her purse. She sat down and rummaged through it. "In fact…"—she smiled and pulled out a single key—"this is a key to my place. Feel free to use it, whether I'm home or not."

Lauren looked at her, doubtfully.

"Honestly, anytime."

Lauren took the key, touched by the display of kindness. Janine barely knew her, yet she was willing to extend herself in this way. Lauren thanked Janine again and excused herself to use the bathroom. She returned minutes later, her face washed clean of makeup smudges. She glanced at her watch and pointed toward the closed office door. "Hannah and Sonia have been in there a while."

Janine checked her own watch. "They don't usually speak for more than a half hour, so they should be out any minute."

"So this is a regular thing?"

Janine nodded. "With this kind of arrangement, I would imagine the first year is hard."

Lauren scrunched her forehead. "What *arrangement?*"

"Oh, I thought you knew."

"You thought I knew *what?*"

"About Sonia coming from Russia."

"I do, but…" She paused and her eyes widened. "Are you saying Sonia's a *mail order bride?*" She asked this in a tone louder than she would have liked.

"Shhh!" Janine held her finger against her lips. "You make it sound like she was ordered from a Sears catalog."

"Well, isn't that what it basically is?"

"It's not like the men just look at pictures and have their wife *FedEx*-ed overnight—they actually spend time together before they get married."

"Really?" Lauren asked skeptically. "How *much* time?"

Janine thought for a moment. "Hmm, I don't actually know. It varies, I guess. But the point is, they *do* get to know each other before the wedding ceremony."

Lauren considered this. "Well, for whatever reason, Sonia doesn't seem very happy."

Janine shrugged. "It's not fair to assume a person's unhappy just because they don't smile," she said. "Sometimes it's a cultural thing. Russian women aren't as demonstrative as American women. Besides, in all fairness, what couple *doesn't* have problems once in a while?"

"True, but Sonia's only been married a year..."

"Less than that," Janine admitted. "It's been more like ten months, I think."

"Then that makes it even worse," Lauren said.

"So, what did you think?" Hannah's voice boomed from behind them before Lauren could say anything more on the subject. With her head down, Sonia slunk toward the front door. Lauren prayed she hadn't heard them talking, though she was still curious about the entire mail order bride business. It didn't make sense that someone as gorgeous as Sonia had to sell herself into marriage.

Hannah continued looking at Lauren expectantly.

"Oh...sorry..." Lauren said, snapping to attention. I really liked it—your class, that is." But her eyes remained fixed on Sonia as she slipped out. Was that a bruise on Sonia's right cheek?

"What did you learn?" Hannah asked, moving a couple of steps to the left—enough to block Lauren's view of the front door.

"Oh... Right..." Lauren muttered. "What did I learn? Well, for one thing, I never really thought about the idea that clothes could be so empowering to women."

Hannah nodded her approval. "Modesty in dress allows a woman to be seen for who she is spiritually, not who she is physically."

"And the idea of covering up what is most precious," Lauren added, "like jewels protected by a velvet cloth… that point was very profound."

Hannah smiled, apparently pleased with Lauren's retention of the subject matter. "There is a saying," Hannah said, placing her hand to her chest. "'The daughter of the king is dignified within'."

Lauren nodded respectfully, though she found it ironic that Hannah spoke about modesty to an audience of spandex-clad, materialistic women. She wondered if it came naturally to Hannah to see only the good in people and overlook their flaws.

"So, you'll be back for the next class?" Hannah asked eagerly.

"I'll try," Lauren said, though she knew it wasn't true.

"Great… and on a separate note, how about spending this Shabbat with us?"

"Friday night dinner?"

"No. I want you to experience an *entire* Shabbat—Friday night to Saturday night."

"You're inviting me for a sleep over?"

Hannah laughed. "There's no reason to drive on Shabbat if you can avoid it," she said. "Besides, we have a very nice guest room."

Lauren was still a bit surprised. "Uh, sure. That sounds great," she said.

"Oh and just so you know," Hannah added, swinging her bag over her shoulder, "a few very nice young men will be joining us for meals." Then she looked at Janine and winked, like this was a private joke.

Lauren's face dropped.

Janine bit her lip, containing her smile.

# Eighteen

"It was absolute destiny that you came into our lives when you did—completely *beshert!*" Hannah told Lauren repeatedly after an early labor scare had confined her to bed rest. Though she didn't necessarily agree with Hannah's theory of divine intervention, Lauren was more than happy to help. Ever since that first *sleep-over* Shabbat four months earlier, she had practically become an extension of the family, dropping by several times each week to run errands, help Hannah cook, or pick up the kids from school. At Yehuda's insistence, Lauren had become a regular overnight Shabbat guest too, much to the delight of the Orenstein boys. Not everyone liked to play their favorite games of *stratego* or *tap tap trio*, but Lauren did; so each Saturday morning, she would routinely awaken to the feel of Eli and David's warm breath against her face, and sounds of their muffled giggles as they hovered beside her bed, awaiting her tickles.

It was mid June and school had recently ended; the Orenstein kids were still adjusting to their summer schedules. The plan was for Lauren to arrive each morning to help Yehuda wake the kids, give them breakfast, and see them off to their respective camps. David and Eli rode the bus to *Camp Rafael,* a full day sports camp about forty-five minutes away. Rachel walked Yitzi three houses down to the Goldman's house, where she helped some local high school girls run a backyard toddler camp. While the kids were at camp and their father at The Jewish Learning Center, Lauren made the beds, folded laundry, straightened up the house, and tended to Hannah, who was permitted out of bed only to use the bathroom and join her family—legs propped—at the Shabbat table.

"I still cannot believe you aren't married!" Hannah exclaimed one afternoon to Lauren who was sitting on the rocker beside Hannah's bed, which was cluttered with books and magazines. "You're beautiful, smart, funny, great with kids, and you are an *amazing* cook!" As if on cue, she bit into a piece of the apple cake Lauren had baked the day before. "And, as if that wasn't enough… you're *traditional* too!"

Lauren looked down at the four rows of yellow garter stitch on her knitting needles and laughed, embarrassed by so many compliments. "Well, in all fairness, credit for this has to go to Sonia Lyman. She's the one who taught me."

Hannah smiled. "Sonia's been spending a lot of time with you lately… I'm glad. I think she's lonely."

Since she had no job, no children and lived close by, it was easy enough for Sonia to pop over; and from what Lauren could tell, she seemed to relish her time with the Orensteins. Lauren often wondered why Sonia didn't just move in with the family altogether. It would be better than staying with that husband of hers. Lauren had met Gary Lyman recently. So much for a John Travolta look alike! Gary was at least twenty years older; he was an inch or so shorter than Sonia, had thinning hair, and instead of walking, he *shuffled*, like an old man.

"She's a sweet girl, but very reserved," Lauren said. She had tried repeatedly to coax Sonia out of her shell, but had been only mildly successful. Sonia spoke openly about her family back in Kharkov and her old job as a hostess at the Hotel Kiev; but when it came to her husband, Sonia either welled up with tears or clammed up altogether.

Lauren groaned as she removed a row of stitches from the knitting needle. "Apparently, I can't yet talk and knit at the same time."

"God willing, you'll have those booties done before this baby is born!" Hannah said, laughing. She placed an open hand on her enormous abdomen. "Now about a husband..."

Lauren quickened the pace of her knitting. "Things aren't so simple in the real world, Hannah," she said without looking up.

Hannah tucked a few stray hairs under her blue *snood.* During the warmer months, she favored this type of head covering to her *sheital;* it made the summer heat much more bearable. Besides, now that she was on bed rest, there was no need to dress as she did when she was up and about. Lauren remembered the first time she had been in Hannah's bedroom and noticed the wig resting atop its Styrofoam head. "Oh, you didn't know?" Hannah had asked. The truth was, Lauren, like most people, had no idea that married orthodox women typically covered their hair. Now it made perfect sense! All the women in the community with their precision cuts, always professionally styled—what were the odds of so many women within a two mile radius *never* having a bad hair day? An added advantage to wearing a sheital, Lauren learned, was that a woman could select any color and style she wanted. Hannah had opted to keep her natural brown shade, but she had exchanged her curls for a sleek, straight cut.

Hannah lifted her cup of tea and took a slow sip as she studied Lauren, now carefully counting her stitches. Sitting cross-legged in her tan cargo pants and white T-shirt, Lauren was adorable. She was the same height as Hannah, but slimmer and with the long straight hair that Hannah—with her unruly spirals—had always yearned for. *She's twenty-six! Surely she must want a man in her life!* Hannah suspected that Lauren was pining over someone from her past—someone named Max, specifically—but there was no reason to let that small complication get in the way. Besides, it was best for any woman to put past hurts behind them and move forward.

"Well, you're in *my* world now, and I have someone I'd like you to meet," Hannah said, with the enthusiasm of a cruise director. "His name is Benjamin. He's visiting from Chicago. His mother's friend is married to someone my husband went to yeshiva with." Hannah struggled to get all the words out. The combination of her size and enthusiasm for the subject matter left her breathless after each sentence, and she paused before making her final point: "He'd make a wonderful husband."

Lauren stared blankly at Hannah. As much as she had come to admire and maybe even envy Hannah's perfect life, there was no getting around the fact that no matter how much she learned in class, or how many *mitzvahs* she performed, Lauren could *never* be part of Hannah's world. Unfortunately, Hannah was extremely stubborn and wouldn't take *no* for an answer. Admittedly, Lauren had been mildly amused at that very first Shabbat dinner when Hannah had seated her between Howard and Jonathon. She even found it funny when the same thing happened with two different men during the subsequent overnight visit. And then Jonathon had stopped by for lunch the next day. "He lives half a mile away," was Hannah's explanation for the "surprise" visit. "Naturally, it's convenient for him to stop by since he lives in the *eruv*."

The novelty of Hannah playing cupid had worn off and had ceased being even mildly entertaining; yet, she persisted. Last week another single man *just happened* to drop by claiming to have an important letter for the rabbi. It was obvious to Lauren what his visit was really about when he asked for a glass of water, all the while checking her out. For all Lauren knew, the envelope was empty. But she was still polite; he was a nice guy; and it wasn't his fault—not if Hannah had put him up to it. Yes, Hannah could be quite pushy when it came to this matchmaking business. How in the world could Lauren make the woman understand that she didn't want to be set up? At least not like this. Hannah waved her off whenever she tried to broach the subject politely. "Just give me time," Hannah would say. "You just haven't met the *one*." Hannah had no idea how wrong she was. In fact, lately, the whole production had gone from mildly annoying to grating on Lauren's nerves, and she had come dangerously close to letting Hannah have it. The most recent instance was after Hannah's comment that Lauren, at twenty-six, was "getting up there" in age. "I was barely nineteen when I met Yehuda!" Hannah added smugly.

*Yehuda.* Did Hannah even consider that maybe Yehuda was different than most men?

For the past several weeks, each evening, before Lauren went home, she had been joining Yehuda and the kids at the park. He was such a great father, so loving and compassionate—the complete opposite of what her own father had been. Yehuda kissed *boo boos* and said *I love you* often and without flinching. Lauren couldn't help but be drawn to him, his openness, his sensitivity. Lauren knew he was a child of divorce, raised by a single mom. Though she didn't know much about Yehuda's sister Sunny, chances were, being raised in a house full of women had softened him.

Lauren didn't say a word as Hannah droned on about finding a man for Lauren, but inside she seethed. It was obvious Hannah had no clue how lucky she was to have Yehuda—lucky to have someone like him to share her home, her life, her future—as opposed to Lauren who was utterly, completely alone.

When she returned to her empty apartment that night, the first thing Lauren did was the exact same thing she did every night: check her phone messages, in the hopes that Max had called. *Just in case you decide it's time to leave Michelle and come back to me,* Lauren thought wistfully. And like those other nights, there was nothing. Not a word. *How long did it take for heartache to go away?* she wondered, pouring herself a stiff drink. She downed it in record time and poured a second. She put on a CD and collapsed on the couch, her location of choice for these nightly pity parties.

Reminiscing about her childhood, Lauren recalled the passionate dreams she'd once had. Yet even then, part of her knew she was deluding herself; a husband, two kids and a white picket fence were not in the cards for her. Even the proverbial dog hadn't happened. Just then, as if on cue, Rosie skittered by as if saying *a cat of my caliber is an obvious upgrade from any dog, thank you very much.* In grade school, Lauren and her girlfriends liked to plot their futures. "I'll marry Bobbie Kenya and you marry Stevie Addison and we'll live on the same block and our kids will go to the same school and..."

Ha! So much for that fairytale! Lauren refilled her glass and stretched out on her couch. Oh, if only miracles happened and she could change things! She knew her parents would suddenly be bragging to everyone about their beautiful, successful and *married* daughter. But for that to happen, she'd need a husband. "Let's see," she said out loud to Rosie who was sitting, bowling pin-like, on top of the couch, "who would make me a good husband?" She laughed at both the absurdity of her question, and the serious expression on Rosie's face, but continued anyway. "How about Yehuda? What do you think, Rosie? Would you like a *rabbi* to be your daddy?"

To Lauren's chagrin, Hannah spent her final weeks of pregnancy in bed compiling a list of untapped prospects and making reference calls. *Who is his rabbi? Where does he learn? Has he been married before? What type of work does he do?* Hannah would speak into her hands-free phone like a telemarketer while scribbling diligently onto a notepad. New faces appeared for dinner each Friday night—men in their thirties and forties wearing suits or jeans, *yarmulkes* or baseball caps. On the rare occasion when Lauren wasn't annoyed at all this nonsense, she found the whole concept fascinating, this complex process of betrothal in the orthodox world.

# Nineteen

The three Orenstein boys were engulfed in a sea of black Legos when Lauren arrived at the Orenstein home late Thursday afternoon.

"Lawen!" The nervousness Lauren had felt during the entire ride dissipated at the sound of the three year old. Yitzi always wore his heart on his sleeve. Excited to see her, he popped up and ran over, sliding into her open arms.

Lauren squeezed him tightly. "Yitzi! I missed you so much!" She peered cautiously over his head, almost expecting Hannah to come flying into the room and yank him away from her.

"Uh, hi guys."

Yitzi's brothers hadn't seemed to notice her. Were they giving her the cold shoulder intentionally? "Hi guys," she repeated, a bit louder and waving an open hand.

"Oh, hi Lauren," David and Eli said in unison, without looking up from their creation.

*They were just concentrating, that's all.* "What are you building?" she asked.

"Come see!" Yitzi said. He tugged at her sleeve.

"It's a *Star Wars* ship," Eli said with obvious pride.

"Hmm, looks challenging..."

Eli smiled. "It's not hard for me. I'm good at these." He held up a colorful booklet with a picture of the finished model on its cover. "See? This is what it'll look like when it's all done."

David panned the floor, ever the reliable assistant, searching for a particular piece. "Are you sleeping over?" he asked.

"Uh huh. I'm staying for a few days," she said.

David found the piece he was looking for and handed it to Eli.

"Your Abba asked me to come." For some reason, Lauren felt inclined to add this piece of information.

"Mommy's in the hospital," Eli said, in the same way a person might say *it looks like rain*.

"She's sick!" added Yitzi, puckering his lips and showing more concern than his older brother.

"Yes, your Abba told me..."

"Hey!" interrupted David. "If you're staying with us for more than one night, does that mean..."

Lauren smiled. "It sure does! In fact, I'm going outside to get her right now."

Yitzi ran to the bay window and pressed his hands and face against the glass, watching as Lauren retrieved Rosie from her car.

"Rosie!" they all shouted, running over to the cage. Rosie cringed at the far end, nearly tipping the carrier out of Lauren's grasp.

"Hold on guys. Back up, we don't want to scare her."

Yitzi tugged on Lauren's sleeve. "She wemembas us, wight Lawen?" he whispered. He had a concerned look on his face. Lauren tried not to laugh, which was difficult since he looked especially adorable when he was being serious. "Yitz, after Rosie has a chance to look at you and smell you, she'll remember."

Yitzi looked doubtful. Lauren got down on her knees to look him in the eyes. "I promise," she said.

At that moment, Yehuda walked in holding a cell phone against his ear. Lauren popped up and he acknowledged her with a little wave. She forced a polite smile in response, while avoiding his eyes. Her heart pounded a mile a minute, she felt so exposed. *He doesn't know,* she told herself. *Remember, he doesn't know.*

"Yes, okay, I understand… I'll be leaving in a few minutes. Thank you doctor." Yehuda shoved the phone into his pocket and smiled wearily at her. Lauren was startled at his thin and haggard looking appearance. She wanted to reach out to him at that moment—give him a hug, or at least a reassuring squeeze of the hand—but she knew the rules. Orthodox men did not touch women who weren't their wives, mothers or daughters. Hannah had explained that since our society had become so desensitized to touch, this was a way of preserving that special physical bond between husband and wife.

Then why had he shaken her hand at The Jewish Learning Center that first night? Lauren had wondered about this before Janine explained that Yehuda made an exception when meeting women who were not familiar with the custom.

Yitzi hopped up and down excitedly. "Abba, look, it's Wosie!"

Yehuda stared at him like he was speaking a different language.

"You said it would be all right if I brought her," Lauren said, more for Yitzi's benefit since he seemed startled by his father's lack of response.

Yehuda snapped out of his trance. "Yes, right. Thank you for coming, Lauren." He turned to his son, "And yes, I see… Rosie's here."

"Abba, can Mendel come over?" Eli interrupted.

Yehuda struggled to switch gears. "Uh, sure, how about after lunch?"

He turned to Lauren. "Lauren, Eli can invite Mendel over after lunch."

"Oh... okay, sure," Lauren said, carrying on as though she had not heard him say the exact same thing less than five seconds before.

Suddenly Sonia Lyman appeared, making her way quietly down the stairs. "Baby is sleep now," she told Yehuda.

"Thank you Sonia. You've been a tremendous help."

Sonia looked at Lauren, avoiding her eyes. "Hello," she said, curtly.

Lauren forced a smile and gave her a little wave. Yehuda did not appear to notice the tension between the two women. Instead, he turned to his sons. "Boys, I have to speak privately with Lauren now, and in a few minutes I'm going to go visit Mommy in the hospital."

"I go now?" Sonia asked. She cast her eyes downward. "I'm sorry I cannot stay... Gary... He wants me home..."

"It's okay, Sonia... Lauren's able to help us." He turned to her for confirmation. "You *are* planning on staying over, right?"

Lauren nodded. "I can stay through the whole weekend if you need me."

Sonia hastily grabbed her coat from the closet and said her goodbyes—which included a long hug from Yitzi—before slipping out the front door.

Lauren followed Yehuda to the kitchen, dodging tiny game pieces, which were sprinkled along the hallway like breadcrumbs. They passed the rabbi's small study, with it's sturdy desk and built in bookcases, each brimming with scholarly texts. When they reached the kitchen, Lauren was taken aback at the sight. Matchbox cars, puzzle pieces, books, and—Lauren wouldn't have thought it possible if she was wasn't seeing it with her own two eyes—*more* Legos were scattered everywhere. The counter was cluttered with plastic containers, open cereal boxes, and paper plates with half eaten sandwiches. One look at the garbage pail and Lauren understood why. The lid was resting high above the container, balanced on a two-inch layer of garbage that clearly exceeded its intended capacity. The thing probably hadn't been emptied in two days. Evidently Sonia hadn't been here long enough to start cleaning.

*Forty-eight hours without Hannah and the place was in shambles.* Lauren might have joked out loud about this if only Hannah was away at a spa, rather than in intensive care.

As if reading her mind Yehuda said, "Hannah always keeps this place together. I'm afraid I haven't been able to measure up."

They were about to sit when Yehuda noticed a long smear of peanut butter on the table. He grabbed a wet paper towel and began wiping.

"Looks like Yitzi was doing some finger painting," Lauren said, lightheartedly. She expected at least a smile from Yehuda, who normally saw creative potential in just about everything his kids did. But he seemed not to have heard her and continued wiping the mess in a dazed and automatic manner. Lauren smiled sympathetically as she watched him. It was clear she had made the right decision by coming. He was in no condition to keep things together by himself.

"Uh, it looks like you got it all, Yehuda." She reached out her hand. For a moment he just stared at it, as if he wasn't sure what it was or what he was supposed to do.

"I'll take that now," she said.

He stared down at his own hand, gripping the crushed paper towel. "Right… Thanks Lauren." He took a seat, leaned his elbows on the table and rubbed his temples while Lauren carried the sticky towel to the garbage pail. She took one look at the volcanic eruption about to happen, and instead, shoved it inside an empty milk carton, which lay sideways on the counter. Lauren washed her hands, then joined Yehuda at the table. She hadn't noticed just how gaunt his face was until now. It reminded her of how he looked on Yom Kippur, when after twenty-four hours of fasting, he appeared to have dropped a significant amount of weight.

"I suppose you want to know what happened," he said.

She couldn't help but notice how red his eyes were. He looked exhausted—probably hadn't had a good night's sleep since God knows when. "Well, only if…"

He didn't wait for her to finish. "On Monday night, Hannah was at the *mikvah*…"

Lauren's heart sped up.

"She and Estelle Ginsberg—the *mikvah* attendant—were attacked," Yehuda continued, looking down at the table.

Lauren braced herself.

"Estelle didn't make it," Yehuda said.

Lauren's hand dropped away. "Are you saying…?"

He nodded. "She was *nifter*—she died," he said softly, his eyes wet.

Lauren stared at him, shocked.

"She was…" But he started sobbing before he could get the words out. Lauren had never seen Yehuda cry before. For a split second she forgot herself and instinctively took his hand. It seemed like time stood still at that moment while he stared at their joined hands, tears falling from his eyes. Suddenly, she realized what she had done, and pulled back, embarrassed. "And what about Hannah?"

He shook his head. "Hannah's been in a coma ever since."

"A coma?" Lauren repeated in disbelief.

He swallowed and nodded. "The doctors say it could be days, weeks—even longer before she wakes up."

Lauren chose her words carefully. "If she's been asleep the whole time, then she hasn't been able to tell you anything that happened that night."

He grabbed a tissue, and wiped his eyes. "No. She hasn't spoken a single word."

Lauren leaned back and exhaled. Why did she need reassurance? They hadn't spoken. *He didn't know.*

"How did it?... I mean, does anyone know *anything?*" she asked after a moment of contemplation.

Yehuda looked away. This was so hard to talk about. Thankfully, the police were adamant about keeping details of the incident quiet— at least for now.

"There aren't a lot of details yet," he said. This was the canned response he had adopted.

*What about memory loss? Was it possible that Hannah would have no recollection of what happened?*

"But they must know *something* about that night!" Lauren insisted.

Yehuda just stared at her for a moment. It was odd; he had never known Lauren to be so pushy. She probably just wanted answers, like he did.

"They have someone in custody," Yehuda said. "That's all I can tell you... Now you said something on the phone earlier..."

She cut him off. "Sorry... did you just say they have someone in custody?"

He nodded.

"Who?"

"A man... from the church... they just identified him... but he's not talking."

Lauren leaned back, taking this information in.

"The police may want to speak to you, Lauren," Yehuda said suddenly. "It's just a formality," he added, noting her concern. "They're interviewing everyone who came in contact with Hannah and Estelle that day."

He stood and walked slowly to the sink. "Water?" he asked, filling a plastic cup.

She held up her hand. "No. I'm fine, thanks."

*"Baruch ata Hashem Eloheinu melech..."*

Lauren listened respectfully as Yehuda sanctified the water before lifting the cup to his lips. Orthodox Jews always recited blessings before consuming food or drink. Even little Yitzi knew the blessings for each category of food.

*The police... What would they ask? More importantly, how much would she tell them?*

"It's odd. I tried to call you that night," Yehuda said, "the night it happened...but there was no answer."

"Oh, I... uh...I must not have heard it ring," Lauren replied, shifting uncomfortably in her seat.

Yehuda set his cup down on the counter and scanned the disarray around him. He shook his head, as if answering his own personal question. Was he suspicious about her not answering the phone that night? No, she reminded herself, he was probably just thinking about Hannah, or the chaos right here in the kitchen... Whichever it was, it saddened her to see him so troubled. *If only she hadn't gone to the mikvah that night and confronted Hannah!* What would have happened if she had just driven straight home instead? Would things have turned out differently? Poor Yehuda. He didn't deserve to suffer like this! That was the last thing she would ever want. But at the same time, he didn't deserve to be deceived either. Should she just tell him? Just blurt it out right here in the kitchen and wait for his reaction? Or maybe not say anything and just take off—grab her bags, grab Rosie and head for the door. *Something suddenly came up... Sorry Yehuda, I can't stay.* No, it was too late for that. He needed her now. Was it possible she could redeem herself by taking care of him and the kids during this difficult time? Maybe then he wouldn't hate her. At the very least, he would know she wasn't a terrible person, that she never meant to lie...

One thing she was absolutely certain of—she didn't have much time. She had to prove herself before it was too late. Before Hannah woke up and made sure she never saw any of them again.

# Twenty

Tova slid the last tray of almond *mandelbrot* out of the oven, removed her oven mitts, and took a seat at the kitchen table. The chicken and kugel were ready, and the challah had been braided and baked earlier in the week. There wasn't much else to do except maybe make a salad, and since Shabbat dinner would just be the two of them, she wasn't concerned with tidying up. She knew Saul would have liked having guests tonight—he said it might lift her spirits—but the truth was, ever since Estelle's funeral, the *last* thing Tova felt much like doing was socializing.

She grabbed a pair of scissors and opened the box that had been delivered earlier from the printer. They were the new brochures ordered last month—she had nearly forgotten. Well, socializing could be put on hold, but work certainly couldn't. She pulled on her reading glasses to get a closer look. On the glossy front page was a photo of a peach tree next to a beautiful pond. Tiny flecks of light shining on the water gave the appearance of daybreak. A white life ring with rounded lettering *J.W.- S.O.S.* bobbed lazily in the water. Inside, along the entire top of the tri-fold, *Jewish Women-Supporting our Sisters* was printed in bold lettering. *One out of every ten Jewish women is, or has been a victim of domestic abuse. Most never come forward, and spend years suffering silently..."*

Tova's thoughts turned to one woman in particular. It had taken several months of bi-weekly calls, but the woman had finally started opening up about her husband. Verbal put-downs, threats, withholding of money. Initially she had felt embarrassed about calling and Tova had to convince her that even without physical scars, this was in fact abuse. Hopefully it would never *turn* physical, but Tova knew better. These things almost always escalated. It was just a matter of time. In the meantime, she advised the woman to document *everything*. This information would be vital if and when she finally decided to leave.

Tova always found it difficult to understand the young woman— and was constantly asking her to repeat herself—but during the last call, nearly two weeks ago, she had found it virtually impossible. The woman could barely speak, she was hyperventilating so much. Her husband had threatened to kill her, she said, admitting that it wasn't the first time. Tova told her to get out immediately, *insisted* that she get out immediately. In fact, Tova was suddenly so concerned for this woman's safety, she did something her training advised her never to do—she gave the woman her full name and home address. "You always have a place to stay... come right now... come any time," Tova told her, right before the line went dead. If only Tova knew who she was, where to find her. But these women always punched in a certain two-digit code before calling, a fail proof method of concealing their identities.

After that call, Tova had waited up nearly all night, finally falling asleep on the couch after 4 AM. But the woman never came. And she hadn't called since. Did that mean something had happened? Had her husband actually done it? Had he killed her? Tova's heart sped up. *Has*

*Vashalom. God forbid.* She remembered the woman once saying that her husband traveled often on business. Maybe he was away and the abuse had stopped, at least for now. If it had, then the woman would have no reason to call. Tova prayed this was the case. She prayed the woman was okay.

Tova sighed and reached for a tissue to wipe her eyes. It had always sickened her to think that there were men out there who would willingly hurt their wives, but she had once been naïve enough to believe it wasn't a problem within the orthodox community. That is, until it happened to her own child, the eldest of her three daughters.

It started with verbal jabs: *The house wasn't clean enough, the soup was cold.* Thank God Mira had the sense to get out the first time he smacked her. Who would have guessed that a Torah educated, God fearing man could so easily raise a hand to his wife? It was then that Tova began broaching the subject with other religious women. She was shocked to find that if not directly affected, most knew of *someone* who had been abused by a boyfriend or husband. Investigating a little further, Tova learned that abuse in the Jewish community, including child abuse, was routinely swept under the rug. People were reluctant to speak out for several reasons. Foremost, they wanted to distance themselves from any involvement with such matters. Many feared repercussions within the community itself such as difficulty obtaining a proper *shidduch* or marriage partner for their sons or daughters. Then there was the fact that the abuse was viewed as inherently shameful—a personal or communal failure that would be a stain on Judaism if the larger public were to find out. Lastly, many people were concerned about the Jewish Laws involving *Loshon Hora*, or improper speech. There were strict prohibitions against speaking about any individual in a way that could damage their reputation or impact their livelihood. Strange as it seemed, these people were more concerned with the potential *aveyra* of speaking improperly than with the safety and well being of others.

Tova believed that abused women would be less reluctant to come forward if they had a safe place to speak anonymously. This was her motivation for starting up a local *S.O.S.* chapter. Along with a small group of volunteers, she posted flyers around the community and took out several ads in local newspapers. The phone started ringing almost immediately. Women called from Jewish communities in Pennsylvania, New Jersey and Delaware. They were orthodox, conservative, reformed, and reconstructionist. Tova was surprised at how many callers were not Jewish; one woman explained that she was afraid to call her church hotline for fear that someone might recognize her voice. There were some that considered themselves atheists, and even a few men. Tova tried to help them all. She was armed with lists of resources: recommendations for safely leaving an abusive relationship, locations of women's shelters, lawyers who were willing to represent abused women and their children *pro bono*. But despite the extensive training she received at the national *S.O.S.* headquarters in Georgia, Tova quickly learned that above all, most callers simply wanted someone to *listen*. Initially the phone lines would be manned from Tova's home. Fortunately, David Tuttle had heard about the project and had generously offered to provide a space for *S.O.S.* in his new Jewish Life Center. The entrance would be in the back, discreetly placed next to the mikvah, so as not to attract attention. The new facility was slated to be ready by early summer.

*Was.* That was the definitive word. With the recent attack at the mikvah, Tova doubted that she would ever see that day. Really, no one could blame Mr. Tuttle if he just sold the property and wiped his hands clean of all its problems once and for all. There had been so many stops and starts on the project, she wondered if Mr. Tuttle had ever considered, like her, that it just wasn't meant to be. Of course this would mean *S.O.S.* would remain homeless until a new opportunity presented itself. But none of that was important. What mattered was that Hannah Orenstein pulled through, and that the man responsible got the punishment he deserved. Tova sighed. That was the *only* bright side to this whole ordeal. *They had the man in custody!* No one else would be hurt—at least not by *that* lunatic! Tova had learned that the attacker had been a homeless alcoholic wandering the streets of Philadelphia. The story went that some years ago, the priest of St. Agassi—Herbert McCormick—had offered him a job at the rectory. That was nearly fifteen years ago and the man had remained with the priest ever since.

Though it was Tova's nature to feel compassion for any individual facing tough times—especially addiction—given the circumstances of this particular case, it was simply impossible. In fact, it was Tova's opinion that compassion may have played an unfortunate roll in the crime itself. After all, wasn't it feelings of empathy that had induced David Tuttle to keep the rectory open during construction? Ha! So much for being a *mensch*! Tuttle's intention was to appease church parishioners by accommodating their priest. Instead, it looked as though having a bird's eye view of St. Agassi's transformation is what fueled a criminal's growing animosity.

Tova grabbed a tissue and blew her nose. Poor, poor Estelle! Surviving the holocaust only to be killed by yet another anti-Semite! The senselessness of it all was just one more thing for Tova to ponder as she lay awake at night. She had known anti-Semitism all her life, was all too familiar with the faces it took. She had seen it as a girl, watching her father, a salesman from Chicago struggle to make ends meet because people wouldn't do business with a Jew. Tova remembered the way people stared when she and Saul first settled in Arden Station twenty years ago. They were one of the first religious families to move to the area. In all fairness, some people were simply curious—they had never seen an orthodox family up close before—but others had disgust on their faces as they drove by, gawking from car windows at the Katz family walking to *shul* on Saturday morning. Even shopping at the supermarket with her large brood of six children provoked attention, her three young sons traipsing through the aisles in their unusual garb of *kipas* and *tzi tzi's*. But now, Tova was well over sixty years of age. Her children were grown and she was a Bubbe. How was it that ignorance and intolerance still persisted in the world? What had happened at the mikvah was pure evil as far as she was concerned. As much as she tried, she couldn't fathom a level of hatred so deep that a man would attack two innocent women.

*It could have been me.*

*If Esti hadn't gone into labor that night, I might not be standing here today.*

The thoughts haunted Tova. But her relief at being unharmed was coupled with guilt. She was the one who had called Estelle to fill in at the mikvah; and now Estelle was dead.

*It could have been me.*

She stood up and went in search of her book of psalms; lately the words of *David HaMelech* had been a daily source of comfort.

Maybe her husband was right; maybe she needed to get out of Arden Station, spend some time in Monsey with Esti and the grandkids. Either that or she would have to make an appointment with a professional, find someone to listen to *her* for a change.

# Twenty-one

The heavy door made an unsettling screech as John Collins and Ron Smith stepped out of the morning light and into the dark vestibule of the St. Agassi church rectory. It was still early enough that a light October frost lingered on the boxwoods outside, a reminder that winter was just around the corner. John had not been looking forward to this visit, the first with Father McCormick since his rectory employee, Peter Stem had been officially identified as the man arrested at the mikvah. John had no idea what the priest's condition would be.

Father McCormick greeted them at the door wearing black dress pants and a Penn State sweatshirt. It was then that John remembered that Father McCormick was a Nittany Lion fan. *Odd*. If the priest was getting ready to watch a football game, how troubled could he be about Peter's situation?

"That door's solid cherry from the original carriage house," Father McCormick said. He chuckled, "been making that same noise since the day I moved in, over thirty-five years ago. Enough to drive a person batty!"

"Well, it does add character to the place," John said, relieved to hear the priest joking. He took a moment to admire the intricate carvings on the door. Over the years, he had come to learn a thing or two about old homes and character.

"And at least you never have to worry about surprise visitors," Ron added, wiping his feet on the rubber mat.

"Father, I'd like to introduce you to Detective Ron Smith," John said.

Ron shook the priest's hand, and then reached into his overcoat. "I have the warrant right here, Father."

The priest waved him away. "Even if I *could* read it, Detective, it wouldn't be necessary," You needn't have gone to such trouble. I would have allowed you to pick your way through the entire rectory—even my own possessions—to your heart's content. All you need do was ask."

"Well, as much as I appreciate that," Ron said, a hint of superiority in his voice, "in order for anything we discover to be admissible in court, I need one of these." He waved the paper in the air and tucked it back inside his coat pocket.

Father McCormick shrugged and led the men into the foyer. "You can hang your coats here," he said, indicating a wrought iron coat rack, bare except for a red windbreaker and checkered derby cap. "Can I offer you gentlemen something to drink? Something to warm you up? Hot cocoa perhaps?"

"No, thanks, we're good," Ron said, answering for both of them. His eyes darted about the room in anticipation. "It's best we get started right away."

"Of course," Father McCormick said. "Shall I show you around then?"

"No need. We'll be fine," Ron said immediately.

"As you wish."

John detected a hint of disappointment in the priest's voice. It didn't take a genius to see that Father McCormick was lonely. St. Agassi had been long closed and many of the former parishioners had died off or moved away. Those remaining were old themselves, and unlikely to venture out for a visit, especially during the colder months.

"I must warn you, finding your way around the rectory can get confusing—especially with the two staircases."

"I'm sure we'll manage," Ron said, rolling his eyes.

"Well, if you have any questions…"

Ron sighed. "We'll be sure to let you know, Father."

As John glanced around, it occurred to him that in all the years he had known Father McCormick, not once had he set foot inside the rectory. After Jay died, nearly all of their personal meetings were held at Windmere, perhaps one or two in the church office on those rare days when John agreed to take communion and offer confession.

The first thing to occur to John was that the rectory shared the same beautiful wood floors as St. Agassi Church. But sadly, the similarities ended there. The rectory felt cramped and stuffy, like it needed a good shake and airing out. It's ceilings were low, it's walls dark and depressing. This was a startling contrast to the forty-foot ceiling and multi-colored stained glass windows which once adorned St. Agassi Chapel. John couldn't help but compare Father McCormick's modest living conditions with his own sizeable dwelling. Few would expect a cop to be living in a place like Windmere; in much the same way, John would never have imagined that a man of God could be living so unremarkably. But beyond essentials, John reminded himself, housing details probably didn't matter much to Father McCormick. He was a simple man, more interested in people than objects. He preferred gestures to aesthetics. Small things like homemade pie or a kind letter touched his heart, brought tears to his eyes. Even more remarkable to John was the priest's unremittingly acceptance of his lot in life. What wasn't a blessing, Father McCormick considered a challenge, an opportunity to grow closer to God. It was unfathomable to John that the priest had shown no anger when the archdiocese elected to shut down St. Agassi, nor was he the slightest bit resentful over his ever-debilitating physical handicap. John recalled one time in particular when he asked Father outright whether he considered his blindness a divine punishment. It was just a few weeks after Jay's death and John was feeling brazen. But Father McCormick remained stoic and simply reiterated his long-suffering faith: If God saw fit that he no longer have vision, then how could he be angry or frightened? "Jesus never said it would be easy... our troubles are what bring us closer to the Lord." At the time, John thought this last statement was a bunch of *B.S.,* and if the person saying it had been anyone other than a blind priest, he might have told him as much. Instead, he continued prodding Father McCormick, trying to get him to admit that he *was* angry at God—that he had a *right* to be angry at God. But the priest wouldn't budge. "I'm like *Didymus the Blind,*" he said, "I pray not for physical eyesight, but for illumination of the heart." It didn't matter. At that time, with the loss of Jay so raw, John had enough rage in him for the both of them.

Father McCormick made his way to the living room. He moved confidently, slipping around a coffee table without the use of a cane or the help of Samson, his companion dog, who was nowhere in sight. Paneled in dark wood, the room was modestly decorated. A worn couch and two high back chairs were set caddy corner to a blackened stone fireplace, a stack of wood piled neatly to the side. Tucked away in the far corner of the room, a single reading chair and pedestal table stood next to a built in bookshelf. John stepped aside to take a closer look. There was the usual array of bibles, catechisms and psalms, but

John was surprised to see a wide variety of non-religious titles as well, including Agatha Christie, John Grisham and James Patterson—all in Braille.

"Isn't that something?" John fingered a few of the spines. "Who knew they printed all those books in Braille?"

"Peter found them on the world wide web for me," Father McCormick said. "I also listen to books on tape; Peter gets them from the library."

John couldn't get a mental image of it—the same disheveled man arrested at the mikvah with soiled pants carefully selecting *books for the blind* from the public library. No; John just couldn't see it.

"Hey; how about we get this show on the road already!" Ron interrupted from the stairs. His voice conveyed his growing impatience at what must have appeared to be some kind of sentimental reunion between John and Father McCormick.

"You go on ahead," John said, motioning with his arm. "I'll meet up with you in a few."

Ron shrugged and headed up the steps, while John and Father McCormick took a seat by the fireplace. The priest placed a green crocheted blanket over his legs. Neither one spoke for a minute.

"I'm sorry," John said, finally breaking the silence.

"No need to apologize," Father McCormick replied immediately. "You're just doing your job."

John rubbed his knuckles. Clearly, Father McCormick didn't understand.

"What is it, John? What's troubling you?" the priest asked. "If you're worried about inconveniencing me with this search, I assure you, it's no trouble..."

John shook his head. "No; it's not that..."

"Then what is it?" the priest asked, his forehead creased.

"I was rough on him," John blurted out. "When I arrested him… I sprained Peter's arm, Father."

Father McCormick took a deep breath and leaned back. "I see." Then to John's surprise, he smiled. "Well, I'm certain it was unintentional, John,—an unfortunate error."

In truth, John shouldn't have been surprised by the priest's complete understanding and patience. After all, Father McCormick had spent a lifetime listening to people bare their souls. But John wasn't so sure the roughness had been unintentional. Throughout his entire career in law enforcement, he had always kept his cool. He prided himself for never once using unnecessary force on the job, and now suddenly *this*—nearly breaking the wrist of an unarmed man! Maybe he needed to return to therapy.

"There's more?" Father McCormick asked when John didn't respond.

"Maybe if I realized who he was I wouldn't have… I mean, I should have at least recognized him!"

"Oh, so that's what this is all about," Father McCormick said, leaning back. "You mustn't be so hard on yourself, John. Peter kept to himself most of the time, and if my memory serves me, the two of you were never formally introduced."

"That's true… we weren't," John agreed, feeling slightly vindicated. Father had a knack for that too.

The priest sighed. "I hear Peter's not doing so well."

John shook his head. "He's still not talking."

The priest frowned. "That's what Rose Downey told me."

Rose was the daughter of a former parishioner who ran the *Books Behind Bars* program. When Peter had been taken into custody, he had been carrying no identification on him. It was Rose's recognition of him two days later that enabled police to ID him as Peter Stem.

"Well, Peter has always been on the quiet side," Father McCormick said. "Perhaps in time…"

John couldn't believe his ears. Did Father McCormick think Peter was simply being shy? "Actually, Father, the public defender assigned to Peter wants to have him evaluated for competence to stand trial," he said.

"Competence? Trial?"

Had John been meeting the priest for the first time, he might have questioned *his* mental health, but he knew Father McCormick was sharper than others half his age; besides, the priest had done all the appropriate things—called Estelle Ginsberg's brother to offer condolences, contacted Rabbi Orenstein to inquire about his wife Hannah's condition.

"Father," John said gently, "Peter has been arraigned on murder charges. He may be looking at time in prison." John purposely substituted the word "time" for "life". He was about to say something else when Samson suddenly ran into the room, her tail wagging happily, despite a short bandage on her front left paw.

"Must be ten," Father McCormick said, patting her head.

John instinctively checked his watch. It was ten on the dot. "Father, did you hear what I said? Peter is in serious trouble…"

The priest ignored him and stood up. "Samson eats a late breakfast… Come on John, I'll get you something hot to drink." He paused and gestured toward the hall stairs. "By the way, that other detective…what is it he's looking for exactly?"

"Anything that would help explain what Peter was doing at a Jewish mikvah," John said, again choosing his words carefully. Given the priest's questionable mental state, the last thing he wanted to do was admit to Father McCormick that they were looking specifically for weapons and white supremacist materials.

Samson, in the meantime, had run ahead and was waiting eagerly by her food bowl in the kitchen, her tail slapping into a pantry door with each hardy wag.

"All right, my girl, I know you're hungry!" Father McCormick chuckled as he leaned over to give her a pat. He scooped a cupful of dry kibble from a Rubbermaid container and poured it into her bowl with practiced accuracy. While the priest filled a second bowl with water from the sink, John glanced around the room. The decor was drab and looked like it hadn't been updated in years. The floors were covered in yellow linoleum and overhead, harsh, industrial looking fluorescent bulbs flickered and clicked. A stainless steel counter held a deeply set sink and several appliances, including a chrome toaster and a *Proctor-Silex* coffee maker, each at least thirty years old.

"Did you have a break-in Father?" John asked, his eyes fixing immediately on a back door partly boarded up with plywood and strips of black duct tape.

"No, nothing like that," Father McCormick said as he laid a filter in the coffee maker with surprising ease. "Samson went and put her paw through the glass storm door. Saw a squirrel or something outside." He scratched his head. "Strangest thing, completely out of character for her! Dr. Wentz says she has to wear her bandage for two weeks—the poor girl—but I bet she's learned her lesson!"

Samson looked up from her food bowl. John would have sworn he saw remorse on her face. Sometimes he thought dogs had more sense than humans. He had always wanted a dog, but could never talk Patty into it.

"When did it happen? When did she put her paw through the glass?" John asked.

"The night of the storm."

*The night Peter was arrested.* The hairs on John's arms stood up. A primitive response, but one that had always served him well. "And you say it was an animal she saw?" John asked.

"Well, yes," Father McCormick said. "I just assumed... Ever since the construction began on the old high school, we've had everything from groundhogs to rabbits to chipmunks hanging around. I suppose they want to get away from the ruckus. Peter spotted a red fox the size of a dog a couple of weeks ago; the rascal was having a grand old time, digging through our garbage cans."

John furrowed his brow and examined the boarded up door. "But Samson's never gone after any of those other animals before?"

"Never."

"Well, whatever it was, it's not a good idea to leave it like that," John said.

"Is it that much of an eyesore?" Father McCormick asked. "The patch job was supposed to be temporary. Peter was going to fix it the next day."

"Wait a second," John said, holding up a hand. "You're telling me this damage happened while Peter was still *here* in the rectory?" For some reason, perhaps because the priest didn't suggest otherwise, John assumed it had occurred much later in the evening.

Father McCormick nodded. "Well, yes. I was in bed at the time. I came down when I heard some noise."

"What kind of noise?"

"Mainly a crashing sound."

"So you went downstairs to investigate?"

"That's right. Peter was pulling glass shards out of Samson's paw."

"What time was that?"

"Hmm. Well, let's see... I headed up at 8:00, listened to one chapter of the new Andrew Greely book—He's terrific John, have you read him?"

"I think Patty has."

The priest tapped his chin. "One chapter wouldn't have taken more than fifteen minutes, so I'd estimate it was about 8:15 when I came down."

"8:15," John repeated. "And Peter was here, in the house with you the whole time?"

Father McCormick nodded. "He bandaged up Samson as best he could; unfortunately the phone lines were down so we couldn't call Dr. Wentz... Peter said he would call him in the morning. Then he boarded up the door."

"And where were you at this time?"

Father McCormick shrugged. "There was no reason for me to stay up. Peter had everything under control, so I went back to bed."

"And that would have been what time?"

"Maybe 9:00, but I can't be certain."

John stared at the door, processing this information. "I'd be happy to see that the door gets taken care of," he said after a minute.

"Thank you, John, but that won't be necessary," Father McCormick said, lifting the coffee pot off its burner. "Peter will be home soon, and he'll see that it gets fixed." He spoke casually, as if Peter was out of town on business.

John cringed as Father McCormick poured two mugs full of scalding hot coffee and handed one to John. Surprisingly, he didn't spill a drop. "Please, make yourself comfortable," he said, indicating a retro chrome table and four chairs, each padded in red vinyl. "This is where Peter and I eat most of our meals."

A small black and white TV perched unsteadily on a nearby tray table, its rabbit ears pointing like outstretched arms forming an "L".

They sat quietly drinking their coffee.

"Will I be able to see him soon?" Father McCormick asked after a minute.

"Probably not until his family is contacted," John said.

Father McCormick nodded. He'd expected as much.

"Maybe it's best that you hold off on your visit anyway," John added. "He's really not doing so well."

"I thought a visit from a friend might help lift his spirits," the priest said. Now he sounded as though Peter had just had his appendix removed. It was apparent that Father McCormick didn't have a clue how bad the situation with Peter was, though he would certainly find out soon enough.

"It might, but not until after his family is located," John said again, "And who knows how they're going to want to handle all this? I'm sorry Father, but how can I say this politely? Don't hold your breath."

# Twenty-two

The rabbi's mother arrived on Shabbat three hours before *mincha*, the afternoon prayer service. Striking as usual in a tan pantsuit and white silk blouse, Judith Orenstein prided herself on being stylish without being over-the-top sexual in her presentation. Actually Judith pitied women who clung to youth like it was the last life raft off the *titanic*—women in their fifties, sixties and seventies who wore short skirts to work and strapless dresses to weddings. Didn't they realize how ridiculous they looked? Judith thought they were pathetic; women with aged spots and sagging breasts trying to look like their daughters; women desperate to convince the world (or was it themselves?) of their eternal youth and desirability. Did they need a man's approval that badly? Did they really believe relinquishing their self-respect could somehow shelter them from adultery, sickness, even death?

"Nana?"

Yitzi shuffled hesitantly past Lauren, then bounded at once into his grandmother's arms, nuzzling his face into her silver hair. Styled in a sleek chin length bob, it gave her an air of friendly credibility, a presence not unlike the distinguished look of an evening news anchor.

"Yitzi! I can't believe it! Look how big you are! Growing like a little weed!" She squeezed him tightly, yet still managed to hold on to her suede clutch. Yitzi arched his back and stared at her in disbelief. If she hadn't just visited a mere six weeks earlier, chances were, he would not have recognized her.

"Nana? How come you came?"

It was a reasonable question since Judith always planned her visits well in advance. Never before had she dropped by unexpectedly, not even when Hannah had gone into premature labor with Nehama last summer. Judith tried to visit at least once every few months or so; but her schedule was so full that despite good intentions, her plans didn't always work out.

"It's a surprise Yitzi," she told him. "Your Abba doesn't even know I'm here." She lowered him to the ground and stood up quickly, extending her hand. "You must be Lauren. I've heard wonderful things about you." Her smile dropped away as she studied Lauren's face.

"Uh, thank you," Lauren said, nervously tugging on her two braids. "We've actually met—in September—when the baby was born."

"Ah, that must be why you look so familiar to me," Judith said. She pursed her lips and tapped her chin trying to remember the cases she was working on back in September. She found that her recall of events was much sharper when she used this technique. "Oh, yes. Now I remember! I could only stay for a few hours in the morning. I had to be in court at 2 PM." She winked at Lauren. "But my son told me not to worry. He said the new babysitter had everything under control."

Yitzi beamed. "You're face is all wed Lawen!"

Lauren patted him on the head, knocking his baseball-patterned *kippa* slightly askew. "Yitz, go tell Rachel and your brothers that your Nana is here."

The two women watched silently as Yitzi shuffled down the hall. "Wachel... Eli... David...!"

Rosie bounded around the corner and flew up the steps in a flash of orange at the sound of Yitzi's voice.

"What in God's name was that?" Judith shouted, her hand flying over her chest.

"Oh, sorry... that's just Rosie, my cat," Lauren said. "I couldn't leave her home alone."

"Well, I certainly hope you found a suitable place for its litter box! The last thing this family needs right now is the stench of a cat."

Lauren's face dropped, but Judith didn't seem to notice. Her attention had shifted to the mantle where several picture frames were prominently displayed. Hannah updated them frequently, so chances were, there were some new ones she hadn't seen before. She slipped on her reading glasses and carefully examined each one. *The entire family in their Purim costumes—Rachel as Queen Esther... Yehuda accepting a community award... Hannah in the hospital with newborn Nehama... Hannah's father in the nursing home in Israel, looking frailer than ever.*

"Mrs. Orenstein, do you have any bags I can help you with?" Lauren asked.

Judith ignored her and leaned in toward the final picture. It was Lauren playing *Connect Four* with David and Eli, her long braids spun in two buns on top of her head like Princess Leah.

"Mrs. Orenstein?"

Judith turned around and removed her reading glasses. "Bags? No, I just have the one. I'll have Yehuda carry it upstairs after Shabbat."

"*Motzei* Shabbat," Lauren said, smiling.

Judith shrugged. "If you say so dear."

"It means *after Shabbat*," Lauren said. "It has a pretty sound to it doesn't it? Hebrew is such a beautiful language."

Judith tossed her clutch on to the couch but continued standing, gazing around the room like she was sizing it up. "If you ask me, the best thing about those two words—*Moochie Shabbat*—or whatever it was you just said, is their meaning... *after, the end, kaput!* Our lives are our own once again!"

As Lauren watched in astonishment, Judith raised her arms and looked up toward the ceiling. "Hallelujah! Thank you Lord!" she shouted, sounding more like an evangelical preacher, than a rabbi's mother. She dropped her arms, pushed aside a couple of children's books and plopped down on the couch with a sigh. "Honestly, I couldn't survive being so restricted! Don't get me wrong; I can understand wanting a day of rest. I see the value of turning off the TV, even the computer for a few hours; but to say I can't cook for twenty-four hours? I can't make a phone call? Write a letter? It makes absolutely no sense!" She made a *tsking* sound and shook her head. "And to think they impose this on themselves every single week! I'm sorry, but it's just not my cup of tea."

"Yes... well... I suppose it *does* take some getting used to," Lauren said. It was a neutral enough response to an obviously opinionated woman.

Judith ignored her. Her attention had shifted and she was scanning the room with a critical eye. "When Yehuda and Hannah first looked at this house, this room was much more formal. The previous owners had a breakfront right here and a baby grand piano in that corner," she said, gesturing with her hands. Suddenly she paused, shifted slightly, and examined the couch she was sitting on. "Would you believe they've had this couch for over ten years!" She leaned back, crossed her legs and extended her arms across the cushions on either side. "I said 'why not donate it to charity and let me buy you a new one?' I must have told them a million times I'd be happy to help them redecorate. All they have to do is give me the go ahead,"—she snapped her fingers—"and it'll be done."

"I think the furniture is fine," Lauren said, "I mean, they do have young children, so I don't know how practical redecorating would be right now."

Judith shrugged. "That's what Yehuda says also. Maybe he's right. Well, I'm not one to interfere with any of my son's choices, including his religious ones. I try to respect his beliefs... *usually*. Of course, there are exceptions—like today." She sighed. "Visiting on the Sabbath is a big no-no!—mainly because Yehuda doesn't like me driving. Apparently it's another prohibition!" She rolled her eyes. "There are so many, I can't keep track! Well, Sabbath or no Sabbath, today, there was no room for debate, I had to come!"

"Yes, of course."

"I flew in from London this morning... made a slight change in my plans and landed in Philadelphia instead of Newark," Judith said. "I had the cab drop me off around the corner so the kids wouldn't see that I rode in a car."

"But won't they wonder how you got here?" Lauren asked, immediately regretting the question since it had a sarcastic ring to it.

But Judith was busy adjusting a small pillow behind her back and showed no sign of being offended. "Well, I'm sure Rachel will figure it out. That girl does not miss a beat.... She's intuitive too, obviously takes after her Nana!"

Judith smoothed her hair. "I've always been perceptive—especially when it comes to people. It's a gift, really—keeps me from getting burned." For a moment her gaze lingered on Lauren's face.

Lauren smiled politely and shifted uncomfortably in her seat. "Uh, I'm sure you're wondering where Yehuda is..."

Judith snapped out of her trance. "What? Oh Yehuda... I just assumed he was at shul."

"No, he's making a *shiva* call at Estelle Ginsberg's brother's home."

Judith sighed. "How could I forget? The funeral was Wednesday, wasn't it?"

Lauren nodded.

"That poor dear. Her life was so difficult... Well, at least they have the bastard! I hope he hangs!"

Lauren swallowed. "Well, as far as Yehuda goes... I'm sure if he had known you were coming..."

Judith waved her off. "I'll have plenty of time with him tonight."

"Actually, he mentioned that he'll be going to the hospital tonight," Lauren said gently. "And I don't think Hannah's allowed any other visitors."

"Oh, there's no need for that."

"No need for *what*?"

"No need for him to go to the hospital," Judith said. "I'm sorry to report there's been no change in Hannah's condition since yesterday."

Lauren narrowed her eyes. "How can you know that?" she asked.

"I spoke to her doctor—Doctor Patel—as soon as I landed," Judith said, pulling a compact out of her bag.

"But... I thought doctors were only allowed to speak to immediate family," Lauren said.

Judith didn't answer until she had powdered her nose and closed her compact. "Oh they are, but I convinced him to bend the rules. Did I mention that I can be quite persuasive when I want to be?"

"See! I told you it was Nana!" Yitzi's excited words were followed by a thundering of approaching feet. Lauren leaned back as the rabbi's mother plastered a smile on her face and embraced her grandchildren.

# Twenty-three

The meals started arriving almost immediately once word of Hannah's condition got out. Deep pans of breaded chicken, hearty beef stews, sweet and sour brisket, and stuffed cabbage. There were pans of *kugels*—potato, asparagus, apple, and peach—carrot *tzimmis* and broccoli soufflé. Tupperware containers of salad, and stacks of homemade *rugeluch*. Shortly thereafter came the tentative knocks on the door, the phone calls and e-mails, friends, neighbors—nearly the entire community—offering their support. Being that she was no stranger to the workings of an insular society, Judith was not the least bit surprised. In fact, she couldn't help but be touched by a bit of nostalgia at the outpouring of love for her son's family. Without question, the support of the community was the most positive element of Yehuda's lifestyle, and witnessing it firsthand brought back a rush of long buried memories.

Judith had been barely twenty-one when she and her husband Larry joined the commune in New Mexico. Aptly named *Peace Farm* by its founders, it's non-written by-laws required members to live off the land in the spirit of communal love and shared ownership. Fueled by the political and social turbulence of the sixties, there was huge interest in this type of lifestyle, and at one point, there were nearly one hundred members living on the farm. Chores were divided and all income from the organic crops pooled. Each family occupied two private bedrooms and a single bathroom in one of five two-story residential buildings. Within each building, multiple families shared a modest kitchen and common recreational area. Yehuda and Sunny were schooled with the other children, taught by the women of the commune, usually mothers of one or more of the students. The climate in Santa Fe was generally warm and dry so the majority of the children's lessons could be taught outside. Judith still remembered Yehuda's favorite spot to read: it was on the southernmost border of the compound, under a grove of quaking aspen trees, away from the steady whirrs of farm equipment.

For years, Judith convinced herself that her abrupt departure from commune life was simply fallout from the end of her marriage. She couldn't very well stick around while her husband started a new life with his pregnant girlfriend, now could she? But the truth was, commune life, like most things, had its downside. Lack of privacy. Rampant drug use. Judith often felt more smothered than alive. With her self-identity slowly eroding away, it became increasingly difficult to distinguish her own opinions from those of the larger community. As a young girl she had been considered strong and spirited, yet as a member of her new extended "family" found herself hesitant to speak up, even when things were blatantly unfair, like the inequitable division of labor. It wasn't the fact that the women handled the domestic responsibilities, while the men ran the farm. This she understood as a biological reality. What bothered her was that while the men always had daily down time—periods when they would go off in a pack to make music and smoke pot— the women did not. Even with large numbers of them working together, the chores never seemed to end. With the growing number of children and their need for constant attention, the women rarely, if ever, got a break.

In this same way, the orthodox community to which her son and daughter-in-law belonged reminded Judith of her life on the commune. In both worlds, the women got the raw end of the deal. Just like the women of Peace Farm, the women of the orthodox community were overworked and undervalued—even if they didn't know it. This was especially glaring on the Sabbath. Most women felt pressured to have guests each Friday and Saturday, which meant there was additional shopping, cooking and cleaning to do in the preceding days, all while taking care of their large broods. Then, throughout the entire Sabbath, or supposed "period of rest", the women were *still* hustling: setting the table, serving meals, clearing dishes, taking care of children. Their men, meanwhile, were socializing, learning, and napping. Judith wouldn't exactly call herself a diehard feminist, but fair is fair.

# Twenty-four

"Shouldn't the boys be doing that?"

Judith sat upright on the couch feeding Nehama her bottle; but her eyes remained fixed on Lauren as she crawled about the floor, corralling small pieces of toys.

"Oh I don't mind straightening up once in a while," Lauren said. The truth was she had spent all of Friday picking up toys and getting the house back in order. Thank God there was plenty of prepared food to see them through Shabbat, because there had been no time to cook; Lauren had been too busy doing laundry, scrubbing the kitchen floor and disinfecting the bathrooms. Her arms were weak and her lower back ached, but it was well worth a bit of discomfort, especially after Yehuda had taken her aside and thanked her so profusely. He had been surprised to arrive home and find his mother there; Lauren guessed he would not have liked her to see the house in such disarray.

Lauren tossed several *Thomas the Tank Engine* pieces in a large plastic bucket.

"The kids are so happy you're here," she said, smiling up at

Judith, who was finally able to exhale after several hours of wound up grandchildren vying for her attention. Yehuda had hauled them all off to shul and the noise level had dropped back to normal.

Judith set the bottle down and adjusted her position. Nehama grunted unhappily and moved her head around, rooting against Judith's blouse. Judith quickly popped the bottle back into the baby's mouth. "It would be nice if I could see them more often," she said, "during better times."

"Well maybe you could start," Lauren suggested.

Judith shook her head. "I'm afraid that's impossible. My schedule doesn't allow it."

"Really? That's too bad." Lauren thought of her own father whose work schedule was so hectic he rarely made it home for dinner or to his daughters' soft ball games.

Judith shrugged. "Anyway, it doesn't matter much. The truth is you can spend all your time with someone and not really love them at all. Kids aren't dumb. They know when they're cared about." Judith remembered all the hours she was forced to spend away from Yehuda and Sunny, first while attending law school and then while working full time. They always knew she loved them. At least she assumed they knew.

"That's true, but don't you want to *be* with them?" Lauren asked. "You know, share their lives? Watch them grow?"

Judith stared blankly at Lauren. She was doing better than merely sharing their lives—she was *financing* them! But this girl couldn't possibly know that. Nor could Lauren have a clue that it was because of her that the family didn't have to live cramped in a two-bedroom twin. That it was because of her that the kids could attend summer camp. Lauren couldn't possibly know that she had put money aside for their college educations.

169

"What is it that you *do* exactly, Lauren?"

"I'm not working right now," Lauren said. *What did this have to do with Judith spending time with her grandkids?* "But I'm taking classes at Rosedale College; I want to get my teaching certification."

*Teaching certification?* For some reason Judith thought of Marigold, the bitch that had stolen her husband from her years ago. Barely twenty-one, Marigold had moved onto the commune as a single woman, an exception that was made because she was certified to teach in New Mexico. The state was cracking down; the kids could be home schooled by volunteers, officials said, as long as there was at least one certified teacher on board. Marigold was that teacher, except her real name was *Mary*. She arrived at Peace Farm wearing prim buttoned up blouses and polyester slacks, but quickly re-outfitted herself in bellbottoms and Indian tunics. The name change came soon after. She claimed it suited her free spirit better.

Nehama's sucking slowed until the plastic nipple fell out of her mouth. Judith was still thinking of Marigold—funny, she hadn't thought of her in so long—and she didn't notice.

"Uh, Mrs. Orenstein?"

Judith sat up and carefully eased the bottle away and placed it upright on the floor. The baby's eyes fluttered as she slept contently. Judith lifted her up and placed her against her chest.

"Mmm! What a delicious baby girl!" she said, rubbing Nehama's tiny back.

"That formula stains; be careful," Lauren said. "Your suit looks expensive."

Judith literally jumped out of her seat. "Oh God, you're right." She extended the still sleeping Nehama at arms length to Lauren. "Hold her a minute while I go change."

Judith returned minutes later wearing a blue sweatshirt that hung nearly to her knees. "Wouldn't you know, I didn't bring anything suitable; I guess that's what happens when you don't plan ahead." She yanked at the bottom of the shirt. "This is my son's. Hannah only had *maternity* clothes in her closet," she added, rolling her eyes.

Lauren couldn't believe her ears. How could Judith be so nonchalant about going through her son and daughter-in-law's things? "Well, it looks very comfortable," Lauren said.

Judith eyed Lauren's faded overalls as she took Nehama from her. "You would know, wouldn't you dear? It looks like *comfort* is something you're very familiar with."

Lauren wasn't sure if this was a compliment or a put down. She took a mental inventory of the clothes she had packed for the visit. They were more of the same—mostly sweat suits and jeans. "Well," Lauren said somewhat defensively, "I've never been a big fan of skirts. I only wear them if I absolutely have to."

"Overalls suit you, Lauren. It's funny; I wouldn't usually expect that a tall woman like yourself would look good in them, but you actually do."

"Thank you," Lauren mumbled, forcing a smile.

"What are you, about 5'5"?" Judith continued.

Lauren nodded. "I never considered myself *tall* though."

"You're Hannah's height exactly," Judith said. "Height is one of those things that is completely relative I suppose. I'm barely 5'3"so to me, you're a giant, but my son is over six feet, so compared to him, neither one of us is so tall anymore."

Lauren hadn't realized Judith was so short. It must be that her dynamic personality added several inches. "Yehuda's father must be tall."

Judith's face dropped. "I really wouldn't know," she said, suddenly interested in Nehama's *onessie* collar.

"Excuse me?"

Judith stared at her blankly. "I haven't seen Yehuda's father in over thirty years, so maybe he's shrunk since then."

"Oh, I didn't realize…"

Judith shrugged. "His loss entirely. Just look at this gorgeous baby! See what he's missing! I never imagined myself as a grandmother—a *Nana*—but here I am holding my fifth grand baby! It's remarkable!"

Lauren gazed at Nehama, her full cheek now plumped like a pillow on Judith's shoulder. It was the perfect photo-op, but snapping pictures was another "no-no" on Shabbat. "All five of them are wonderful. Yehuda is a great father."

Judith smiled. She couldn't agree more. Her son was a good man. Hannah had hit the jackpot as far as she was concerned. "Yes, he is," she said. "And it's nice to slow down and remind myself how blessed I am. And to take time to—as they say—smell the roses. Or better yet—smell the babies!" Judith pressed her nose against Nehama's head. "Mmm! I simply adore the scent of freshly powdered baby!"

"It's true. They all have that same great smell, don't they?" Lauren said, smiling.

"I wish I could bottle it and carry it around with me," Judith said. "It's not a substitute for the real thing, but since I can't get here as often as I'd like…"

"Right. You said that before," Lauren murmured. "What is it exactly that keeps you away?"

"Work," Judith said. "The divorce rate is unbelievable—especially in the higher income brackets. When there's that much at stake, it's understandable that people want the very best representation. The problem is, it's usually the husband who gets it. The wife usually hasn't a clue."

"That's depressing," Lauren said.

"It could be, but that's where I come in. I represent the wives of those spineless pigs."

Lauren's face flushed. She held up a hand. "I'm sorry, but I don't see how you can call Thomas Buchanan a *pig*. I'm sure you know he heads two of the largest cosmetic companies in the world."

Judith sat up. "I'm impressed you remember that case Lauren. That was over two years ago! You must read a lot of tabloids."

"I don't read *any* tabloids. I'm familiar with the case because I worked on his business campaign," Lauren said. "I used to work in public relations."

"Oh... I see..." Judith said, momentarily amused. "You worked on the campaign for Buchanon that *just happened to* coincide with his divorce?"

"Well, yes."

"So you're familiar with the old 'affecting public opinion' strategy."

Lauren felt like she was being led to the slaughter. She opened her mouth to speak, but Judith cut her off. "Isn't it fascinating how these philanthropic sides of people suddenly reveal themselves at the most advantageous time?"

"Thomas Buchanan was donating money and cosmetics to women's shelters all over the country," Lauren said quickly, before Judith could interrupt again. "I thought he was extremely generous."

"Generous, my ass!" Judith shouted. "Buchanan was more interested in saving his own skin and protecting his shareholders!"

Nehama stirred and let out a startled cry. Judith patted her back, and she immediately settled back down.

"No wonder you're no longer working. You just don't get it!" Judith said, shaking her head scornfully.

Lauren swallowed. It *wasn't* the reason, but she wouldn't tell Judith that.

"It's the oldest trick in the book," Judith continued as she placed Nehama in her infant seat. "The guy was simply manipulating the media the same way he had manipulated his wife and business partners for years! It's all about influencing public opinion—garnering sympathy among the masses! Where do you think our judges and juries come from? You better believe Mr. Buchanan was well aware the power of public opinion! Tell me, do you really think it was a coincidence that he just *happened* to go on a philanthropy binge at the same time he was at risk of losing millions to his estranged wife?"

Again Judith didn't give Lauren a chance to answer. "Trust me Lauren, he wouldn't have so much as *blinked* if his wife ended up in one of those women's shelters!" She rolled her eyes. "Oh, but of course, she would have had plenty of lip liner and mascara!"

"So it was better for his wife to get everything?"

Judith crinkled her forehead, to the surprise of Lauren who would have expected it to be botoxed. "Is that what you think happened? You think we took him to the cleaners?" She burst into laughter. "How cliché!"

Lauren looked away. Suddenly she remembered. After his divorce, Thomas Buchanan had moved to Monte Carlo. There were photos printed of him in *People* partying with Prince Albert and romping in the ocean with some very beautiful—and young—European models.

But Judith didn't wait for an answer. She stood up and began pacing in front of the couch as she spoke, stopping every so often to emphasize a point. "It wasn't like that Lauren! It rarely ever is. In my line of work I do what's right—what's *ethical*. I give these women good representation so they get what they're entitled to—nothing more, nothing less." She pursed her lips and looked quizzingly into Lauren's eyes, as if something just occurred to her. "Let me ask you something Lauren: how old are you?"

"Twenty-six. Why do you ask?"

Judith nodded. "Hmm. Twenty-six. That explains a lot. See, women of your generation have very little appreciation for what women of my generation—and older—experienced. You take your rights for granted." She shrugged. "You've always had them, so you can't possibly fathom any other way. But trust me Lauren, things were not always so peachy. For starters, did you have any idea that when I was raising Yehuda and his sister, I couldn't have my own bank account?"

"What do mean?" Lauren asked, a puzzled expression on her face.

"I'm telling you that my husband's name had to be on the account! It couldn't be in my name only! I couldn't have my own credit card either for that matter—not without a male co-signer." Judith didn't stop. "And another thing: my name couldn't be on a property deed either. Only my husband's could—even if the property was purchased jointly."

"You're kidding, right?" Lauren hadn't expected a history lesson in women's studies, but she was spell bound.

"Sadly, I'm not. Most women were utterly dependent on men… on their husbands or fathers. They were completely vulnerable—like pets or children. Most of the time they looked the other way if their husband cheated on them. They even covered up their bruises when their husbands knocked them around. The mere *prospect* of being on their own was often scarier than the abuse."

Lauren suddenly felt very ignorant. "It sounds like the dark ages… I had no idea."

"Of course you didn't," Judith said, softening her voice. "How could you? You weren't there. But I was…" She sighed. "I've been scared, dependent, vulnerable… you name it! And you know what?

There's no way in *hell* I'll ever allow myself to go back! Sure, times are different now—women have ownership rights, more opportunities in their education and careers—still, whatever I can do to protect them, empower them, I'm happy to do." She paused. "That's why I have such a hard time with…"—she waved her free hand back and forth, showcasing the room around them—"with all this!"

Lauren scanned the room, not sure what Judith had a problem with. Was she bringing up the decorating issue again?

"It seems so *backward* to me," Judith continued.

Lauren understood now. "Being religious?"

Judith dropped her arm and nodded.

"But people *choose* a religious lifestyle," Lauren said. "It's not like they have no say. God grants everyone free will."

Judith smiled. "Ah, I see you've attended my son's classes."

Lauren blushed.

"The fact that we have free will," Judith continued, "almost makes it worse! Today, women have a choice! It's no longer the cultural status quo, and yet… *yet* they choose to subject themselves to this kind of life! All I can say is thank God my son is a good man or Hannah might really be in trouble…"

Nehama started fussing, her tiny fists clenching as she bore down. Lauren was actually happy for the distraction. The conversation was getting a bit intense, and it was becoming increasingly clear to Lauren just how Judith felt about men.

"This is a long and complicated discussion," Judith said, "perhaps one best left for another day."

*Or not,* thought Lauren, but she smiled politely and scooped up the baby. While upstairs, she took her time changing Nehama's diaper; she had no desire to listen to more of Judith's sexist dialogue. But she couldn't help pondering Judith's words. *Not having control of her own money?* Lauren couldn't imagine it! Okay, so women had, at one time, been at the mercy of men—that was a sad, historical fact. But when it came to Judith's assertion that orthodox women were subjecting themselves to the same dependency of the past, Lauren wasn't sure what to believe. It was true that most of the orthodox women Lauren had met from the community were home with four or five, even six children. Most believed that the use of birth control was prohibited without a rabbi's consent, so it wasn't unusual to see the same women pregnant year after year. It followed that if they were home with their children, then they were dependent on their husbands for financial support. But wasn't that okay? Hannah often spoke about the inherent differences between men and women. She said that Jewish law provided for those differences by way of the marital contract. Going as far back as biblical times, it was understood that once the *Ketubah,* the marriage contract, was signed, a man was not only obligated to support his wife financially, but also emotionally and sexually. As ancient as Judaism was, one had to admit, these tenets were pretty darn progressive.

Lauren placed Nehama in her crib and sat in the rocker. She thought more about the orthodox families she had met this past year. The women often looked harried—understandable given all their responsibilities—but most seemed content and maintained strong community ties. Actually, now that Lauren thought about it, most of the women had college degrees; and many had had careers prior to getting married. Maybe that was what made the difference—a woman being *capable* of financial independence.

But then Lauren's thoughts turned to Sonia Lyman. For some reason, Sonia preferred to keep to herself. She felt sorry for the young woman, living on the fringe of the community like that... Sonia seemed so alone. Lauren thought back to the summer—just a few months ago—when Sonia had been spending more time at the Orenstein home. She was her most relaxed then, happily teaching Lauren how to knit, cooking up some of her family's traditional recipes of *borsht* and *golubtsi*. Sonia probably would have opened up eventually... if only Lauren hadn't messed up... if only she hadn't been so *stupid*!

Lauren sighed, still regretting that day. She had immediately apologized, and Sonia had accepted, but it was obvious from Sonia's curt "hello's" that she was still angry. Once again, Lauren replayed the scene in her mind: It couldn't have been more than a week after Hannah had come home with baby Nehama. Most women would have enough to do with a newborn and four other children to take care of. *Most*, but not *Hannah*. No, Hannah jumped right back into her usual routine of planning elaborate Shabbat meals and playing matchmaker. Without missing a beat, she started up again with Lauren about finding a husband, even going so far as to imply that younger wives made happier wives.

"Really? Well, Sonia doesn't seem so happy, does she?" Lauren had fired back impulsively. How could she have known that one of the boys had let Sonia into the house just seconds before? How could she have known that Sonia was making her way up the steps and had heard every word? But as wrong as she was for saying it, Lauren still believed it was the truth. Sonia *didn't* seem happily married! Besides, it wasn't as though Hannah disagreed! If Hannah saw things differently, shouldn't she have spoken up? Immediately come to Sonia and Gary's defense?

According to Janine, Sonia's husband made a good living as a C.P.A. They lived in a beautiful new house on one of the nicer streets in Arden Station—in a development called Trinity Lane Estates—not far from where the new Jewish Life Center was being built. And Lauren remembered Sonia mentioning that she had worked in a hotel before getting married: *The Hotel Kiev*. This meant she had skills to fall back on if she ever needed to support herself. So why did she seem so sad? Was it a simple cultural difference like Janine said? Was she homesick? Or was it what Lauren suspected: Was Sonia stuck in a miserable marriage? And if so, why didn't she just *leave*?

But now that Sonia was offended and not speaking to her, Lauren realized she might never find out the answer. Beyond speculation, people never really knew for certain what went on inside another's head—or in their home, behind closed doors. Lauren knew how easy it was to fool others into thinking you were something you were not. After all, she had been doing it most of her life. In fact, she had been hiding her own secret for so long that she sometimes forgot who she really was. To Lauren, public personas were as comfortable as an oversized shirt, hiding well the unsightly marks underneath.

# Twenty-five

"So tell me what's going on," Lewis began, settling into an oversized chair in his daughter's cozy family room. Elise handed him a coaster and he carefully set his coffee on the glass table in front of him. "You said there was something very important you needed to talk to me about."

Still a bit jet lagged after his return to the states two days earlier, Lewis had taken an early afternoon train in from Boston, sleeping for most of the six hour trip, and arriving an hour before dinner. He was greeted at the door by a squealing three year old holding an enormous helium balloon with the words "HAPPY BIRTHDAY!"

"Ben picked it out," Becca explained, standing behind him and rolling her eyes. "Even though it's not even your birthday!" She pointed a finger at herself. "*I* wanted to get the one that said "WELCOME HOME", but Ben had a fit in the store."

As with all of his visits, the kids dominated their Pop-Pop's attention throughout dinner, yapping excitedly about everything that had happened while Lewis was away. For a special dessert, Becca proudly presented the cupcakes she helped make in his honor—vanilla with chocolate frosting.

Since it was a school night, the kids were now in bed. Evan was in his study watching the 11:00 PM news.

Elise took a deep breath. "A woman in the community—Estelle Ginsberg—is dead."

Elise placed an open hand on her heaving chest.

Lewis leaned toward her, concerned. Elise had suffered an occasional asthma attack as a child, but had outgrown the condition.

She waved him away. "I'm okay. Just give me a minute."

Lewis waited while Elise dabbed her eyes and blew her nose.

"I'm fine now," she said, her breathing regulated.

Lewis spoke gently. "Estelle Ginsberg has died..." he prompted her.

Elise nodded. "And Yehuda Orenstein's wife is in the hospital—in a coma."

Lewis sat up. "Yehuda Orenstein? The rabbi from The Jewish Learning Center?"

"Yes."

He leaned back in his chair, rhythmically stroking his clean-shaven chin in a stereotypically Freudian kind of way. "What happened?"

"Estelle and Hannah were at the *mikvah*—last Monday night. When the police found them... Estelle was already dead."

"She was close to ninety, right?" Lewis asked. Already he was forming a scenario in his mind: an elderly woman getting overly excited by some unforeseen event—maybe something having to do with the construction—and her heart giving out.

"Eighty-six, I think."

"And Hannah?" Lewis hadn't come up with a scenario for Hannah yet. What possibly could have happened to land a young, vibrant woman in a coma?

Elise sighed. "Hannah was alive—barely." She shook her head back and forth and covered her face as the tears flowed.

Lewis handed her a box of tissues. "Sweetheart, we can continue this tomorrow if you want."

Under normal circumstances, Lewis would *never*, during a dialogue so entrenched with emotion, offer an out for the patient. For a psychiatrist, tears were like striking oil. Sometimes you could drill for months, years even, before hitting anything. But once that nerve center was hit, and the flow started, it was fascinating to see just how much had been pooled below the surface, and watch as it was carefully dredged up. Lewis suspected his daughter's strong reaction was a display of some latent, unresolved grief; therefore he reasonably concluded that there was no need to force the issue tonight.

"No, it's okay, Dad...Really, I'm alright." She placed the tissue box on the coffee table beside her and continued. "By the time they pulled him off her..."

Lewis held up his hands. "Wait a second... pulled *who* off her?"

Elise stared at him blankly. "The guy who attacked them... he was on top of Hannah."

Lewis stared back at his daughter, silent, stunned. He hadn't expected the story to unfold like this. So much for his theory of unresolved grief.

Elise repeated herself, figuring her father had not heard her. "Dad, this man... from the church across the street... he was on top of Hannah." She paused and lowered her voice. "Dad, Hannah was completely naked."

"Did he...?"

Elise shook her head fervently. "No! No... Oh God, no! The police think he would have… that he probably planned to… but they got there before that could happen."

"And this man, you say he's from a church…"

"He's from the church next door to the mikvah—St. Agassi."

"I thought St. Agassi was closed."

"It is, but apparently the priest still lives in the rectory, and this guy—the one they arrested— he lives there too. He's the custodian or something."

Lewis took a minute to organize his thoughts. "You said Estelle was found dead…"

Elise nodded.

"What was the cause of death?"

"Blunt force injury to the back of her head," Elise said. "He hit her with a vase. Nearly cracked her skull open."

Lewis closed his eyes and took a deep breath. "He confessed?"

"No."

"Then how did he explain his being there?"

"He didn't."

"He didn't give a statement to the police?"

Elise shook her head. "Not one word."

"They were able to keep him locked up without a confession?"

"Yehuda's mother says that given the circumstances of his arrest there was never an issue."

"The rabbi's mother said this?"

Elise nodded. "Judith Orenstein. I don't think you've met her dad; she doesn't come in too often. Well, she didn't until now. Until this."

"I take it she's a lawyer," Lewis said.

Elise nodded. "She practices in New York. Pretty high powered, specializes in divorce, I think."

Lewis sat quietly for a minute processing all that he had just heard. "And Hannah Orenstein? What is her prognosis?"

Elise exhaled loudly. "She still hasn't come out of the coma. *Head trauma.*"

He shook his head empathetically. "What a difficult time for the family," Lewis said, shaking his head. "All they can do is wait…"

Elise nodded. "That's exactly what the doctors told Yehuda. They said she had water in her lungs, but the police aren't sure how long he held her under."

Lewis shook his head in astonishment. *How long he held her under.* The facts were getting more and more shocking. Maybe Arden Station wasn't the best place for his daughter and her family to live.

"Dad," Elise said softly, interrupting Lewis's private growing annoyance at his son in law for bringing Elise to this area, "I know I don't have to tell *you* of all people about confidentiality, but the general public does not know certain details about what happened."

"Nothing's been published about this?" Lewis asked, surprised. "Doesn't your paper have a police blotter?"

"Yes of course, but something of this magnitude would be more likely to show up as a front page story. Given the nature of the crime— and the fact that the guy they're holding isn't talking, let alone actually confessing—they're trying their best to maintain a low profile, at least for now."

Lewis wondered how many other area crimes the public didn't know about.

"They might also be concerned about the *motive*," Elise continued.

Lewis knew what she was going to say even before she said it.

"Specifically that it might have been a hate crime," Elise continued.

"There are people who aren't very happy about a Jewish Life Center being built on church land."

Lewis recalled hearing that the site had been vandalized on several occasions, but those events had taken place years earlier. *Why the sudden resurgence?* "And this guy—the church custodian—he's unhappy about it?"

Elise shrugged. "Apparently he was about to lose everything—his job, his home. I guess he blamed us."

By *us*, Lewis knew Elise meant *us Jews.*

"And if it *was* anti-Semitic in nature," Lewis said, "the police are probably concerned about copy-cat crimes."

"They are. In fact, they're so worried that they've closed the mikvah and posted a security guard to watch the property at night," Elise said.

"But hasn't that drawn public suspicion?"

"Not at all. The only ones who even know the mikvah is there are members of the orthodox Jewish community. And as far as the security guard being at the building, well, it's not at all unusual see security at construction sites."

"That's true," Lewis said. "And I suppose Yehuda is relieved that it's being kept quiet."

"Yes, he is… for the children's sake."

Lewis was silent for a moment. "Tell me Elise, how *are* the children coping with their mother being in the hospital? There are four of them, right?"

"The baby makes five."

Lewis smiled. "Ah, yes, baby Nehama, the one who gave her parents quite a scare… the other children are all boys?"

"They have three boys and an older daughter. The boys have been doing very well according to their grandmother."

"Yehuda's mother—the lawyer?"

Elise nodded. "I brought over a meal this afternoon. Judith told me the boys seem perfectly fine. She said only Rachel seems to be suffering. At nine years old, Rachel can more fully grasp the magnitude of the situation. Unfortunately, I think she suspects that there is more to the story than what she's been told."

Lewis nodded. He agreed with Elise's assessment. Before she stopped working to be a stay at home mom, she had been a wonderful social worker. Lewis was certain she would have made an even better psychiatrist.

"Do you happen to know what exactly Rachel's been told?"

"I know *exactly* what she's been told. That somehow her mother and Estelle Ginsberg slipped on the wet floor and hit their heads."

Lewis crinkled his forehead. "Sounds sketchy to me; no wonder the child doesn't believe it."

# Twenty-six

John didn't like Ron's office. It was a reminder of life *before*. Before
Jay died. Before Ron Smith's dad—John's former partner—was forced
into retirement.

During the last five years and through six phases of construction, the
township had consolidated all of its municipal offices into one central
facility, built around the original eighty-year-old police headquarters.
The result: the Arden Station municipal complex that housed every
department from *Building and Planning* to *Refuse and Recycling*. But
while every other office had been tastefully refurbished with Berber
carpet, neutral walls and functional workstations, Ron's remained
stuck in a time warp. With its metal desk, shag orange carpet and circa-
1950 wood paneled walls, the office was a total eyesore, a disturbing
contrast to the rest of the department. John understood *why* he did it,
but *how* Ron managed to convince the higher-ups to leave the single
office untouched was a complete mystery.

"You might want to consider some new carpet, buddy," John said,
though he suspected that Ron would ignore the comment.

"John?" Ron sat at his desk, a tall glass of water in his hand, and about seven different vitamin bottles lined up in front of him. He squinted in disbelief. "What the heck are you doing up here?" Before John could answer, Ron was gesturing with his free hand for him to take a seat. Ron then proceeded to open each vitamin bottle, pop a pill or two in his mouth, and follow it with a quick swig of water.

Actually, John wasn't sure *why* he was there. In the last four years he hadn't been the least bit interested in Ron's office—or the younger man's work for that matter—so he was calling the visit something of a courtesy call on behalf of Father McCormick.

"I think you should canvas the area, talk to the neighbors around the old high school," John blurted out.

Ron stared at him blankly then shook his head. "No. No way." He unscrewed the cap from a bottle marked *Omega 3 Fish Oil* and shook a capsule in his hand. "Think about it, John. Why should I send guys out to canvas the neighborhood? You damn well know what will happen if I do! People will start asking questions! You heard the D.A.; the last thing we need is a wave of panic running through Arden Station. Besides, this thing's open and shut, John, you even said so yourself."

Admittedly, John *had* said as much, and more than once. The night of the arrest. On the ride over to the rectory. The facts were indisputable: Peter Stem had been arrested at the scene, his DNA recovered from Estelle Ginsberg's clothing. Not to mention that he had been pulled off the naked body of Hannah Orenstein. Ron's point was valid. Why should they go knocking on doors as though they were searching for their killer?

John rubbed his temples. Despite the incriminating physical evidence, there were a few things that concerned him. Most significantly was the fact that Peter's fingerprints hadn't turned up a match in the system. Statistics showed that a felony of this nature was almost always preceded by other, smaller offenses; yet no fingerprint match meant Peter had never had a prior arrest. And then there was Father McCormick's casual response to the entire situation, his constant intimations that Peter would be home soon. *As if this was all a big mistake. Some kind of misunderstanding.* Was Father McCormick simply deluding himself? Or was there more to this story? John couldn't help but wonder: *was it even remotely possible they were holding the wrong man?*

"Look, John, I know you and this priest are close," Ron said, as if reading John's mind. "But I have to tell you, you're starting to get some strange ideas."

John waited as Ron gathered the vitamin bottles and dumped them with one fell swoop into his desk drawer.

"I just think you need to gather as much information as you can," John said. "There's been no confession. We have no idea what actually happened at the scene. All we *do* know are there are two victims, neither of which can help us out. Meanwhile our alleged perp's not talking either... So, all I'm saying is, don't you think you should find someone who *is* talking?"

For some reason the word *alleged* felt like a cheap shot to Ron. He shook his head solemnly. "I don't get it John; you haven't been interested in investigations in *years*, and now, suddenly you get all worked up and try to tell me how to do my job?"

"Look, Ron..."

But Ron cut him off. "No! *You* look, John! Peter Stem's a loner. He's basically been a shut in with a Catholic priest for the past fifteen years... tell me, how normal is that?"

John didn't respond. He felt a sense of loyalty to Father McCormick and he didn't want to belittle an individual the priest held in high regard, even if it *appeared* that individual was undeserving of such sentiment. Instead, John thought back to the night of the arrest, trying to recall something, *anything* that he might have missed. He and Robert had arrived on the scene before midnight. There had been some candles burning in windowsills in a few neighboring houses. Surely someone must have seen or heard *something*. That's when it occurred to John: he didn't need Ron's blessing to go door to door! He and Robert would go about it quietly. They would ask only general questions so as not to let on... *Tonight during their shift*. They would be discreet. Besides, it would be good experience for Robert.

Ron sat up abruptly and clapped. *Earth to John.* "Here's how it is," he said dramatically, his palms out. "Our perp's been living in the church for his entire adult life and now, he's about to be evicted. Every day he watches the construction continue at the high school. Life as he knows it is drawing closer and closer to an end! Then he starts noticing the women. Each night they parade unchaperoned into the back of the building. They're small and vulnerable... the perfect victims."

John sighed. Ron was barely half his age, yet he was so sure he had it all figured out. He was so much like his father, Ron Sr.; both could be a bit dramatic at times. But admittedly, it was as likely a scenario as any John could think up. It was definitely better than Ron's initial theory that Peter was a latent homosexual who hated women, an idea quickly discarded when Ron found an old *Penthouse* shoved under Peter's mattress. That magazine was the extent of Ron's discovery from his search of Peter's room. Bottom line was there was nothing found in the rectory indicating either homosexual or misogynist tendencies. And there hadn't been any anti-Semitic evidence either. That should have been a relief since it took the religion card off the table. Nevertheless, it was obvious the guy was wound pretty tight, Ron insisted, seeing how meticulous he kept his room. Too bad he didn't feel the same commitment to his closet. According to Ron, the three-foot space looked like a tornado had hit it. But what about a weapon? Ron had expected to find one, but had come up empty handed. What kind of criminal didn't have a gun, a knife... something! And then there was Ron's theoretical motive. Could it possibly be true? Was it simply Peter's pending eviction from the rectory that instigated the whole tragic event? It was such a ridiculous thing to set someone off, yet it didn't bode well for Peter that he *did* possess all the qualities of someone who would commit such a senseless sort of crime—he was a former addict, a loner, seemingly uneducated. Yet John couldn't get past the fact that his actions did not appear to be *pre-planned*. It was puzzling: Why that particular night? Had something unusual happened or had Peter just seized what appeared to be the perfect opportunity? That was the million-dollar question. The more John thought about it, the stronger his belief in the former. *None of it was pre-planned. Something happened that night to set Peter off.* It was the only way he could reconcile Father McCormick's stellar opinion of the man with the crime he was accused of committing. But he would feel a lot better if he knew *what* exactly that "something" was.

"So you still believe Peter's goal was to shut down construction at the high school?" John asked.

"Desperate men do desperate things," Ron said. He reached into his fridge for a yogurt and offered John one.

John laughed. "Don't you ever get tired of all of it, buddy?"

Ron didn't seem to understand the question.

"You know the health food, the vitamins..." John laughed. "I'd go nuts without my meat and potatoes..."

Ron narrowed his eyes. "Not all of us are born with perfect genes, John; but I guess you wouldn't know anything about that."

John immediately regretted his comment. He ignored Ron's remark and looked away while the younger man dug in to his yogurt. After a moment, he spoke up, getting back on point. "You say Peter wanted to do something that would halt construction," John continued, his tone a bit softer. "But would shutting down construction bring back the church? Or prevent Father McCormick from moving out of state?"

But before Ron could respond, John shook his head and answered his own question. "No, those things—all of them—were a done deal."

Now Ron looked more annoyed than ever. "You forget; we're talking about a *crackpot*, John, *not* someone who's thinking rationally."

"But how do we know he's a crackpot if he hasn't given a statement?" John asked.

"You know what I think? I think it's all *bullshit!*" Ron said, throwing his spoon down. "This whole *not talking* thing is an act! I think he's just a psychopath trying to pass himself off as criminally insane. Life in a mental institution sure beats life in the state pen. The food's better; I hear even the pillows are fluffier."

John didn't say a thing. If what Ron was implying was true… if Peter *was* faking it, then he was brighter than the detective gave him credit for… which meant he was smart enough to know that halting construction would do nothing to keep him in the rectory.

John shrugged. "I don't know Ronnie…"

Ron pounded his right fist on the desk. "It's *Ron!* Damn it, John, I haven't been *Ronnie* since I was ten!" He leaned back, clasping his hands behind his head. "Oh, whatever… The only thing I want to think about right now is closing the file on this case. The sooner we get this thing wrapped up, the better."

"Your dad?" John asked gently.

Ron avoided his eyes. "Yep."

"What's going on?"

Ron took a minute to answer. "I have to get him settled in his new place."

John nodded. He had asked only to be courteous. He really didn't want to start taking about Ron Sr.; it was just one more reminder of God's cruelty. "Well, it shouldn't be long now," John said, pushing away his own nudging doubts. "With the case I mean. You're just waiting on the CODIS report, right?"

Ron took a gulp of his drink. "Yeah, that's right," he said, all business. "We should have it in a few days, and then we'll know what this son of a bitch Peter Stem has really been up to."

# Twenty-seven

Rachel sat cross-legged at the kitchen table, her white blouse sleeves rolled neatly up to her elbows as she peeled her way through a mountain of braeburn apples. Her Nana had promised to bake them into a pie for tonight's dessert. It was her daddy's favorite; maybe it would make him happy. It seemed to Rachel that she barely saw her Abba anymore. He was either working or visiting Mommy at the hospital. When he arrived home, he would plaster a smile on his face and say things to the children like "I told Mommy about David losing his front tooth" or "Mommy heard all about Nana spending a few days with us!" Her brothers were satisfied with these nuggets of information, but Rachel had her doubts. She didn't want to accuse him of being dishonest, but she didn't understand how it was possible to talk to someone who was asleep all the time. She often wished she could go to the hospital and see for herself, but her Abba had not offered to take her, and she had not asked, partly because she was frightened of what she might find. Last year her class had gone to visit a nursing home. "Some of the men and women you will meet are very sick," her teacher whispered before they went in. But these words did not prepare them for what they saw. Most of the residents looked like walking skeletons. The skin on their hands was pulled tight, revealing uneven purple ridges. Their vacant eyes stared into space as their young visitors sang *Purim* songs. Some residents were slumped, sound asleep in wheelchairs with breathing tubes under their noses. Two of Rachel's classmates cried.

Rachel wished someone would assure her that her mommy wasn't as sick as the people in the nursing home. She wanted to hear that even after nearly a month, her mommy still looked beautiful, that she had the same big smile, the same bright eyes. But Rachel couldn't ask her Abba; what if her questions caused him more distress? He had dropped a significant amount of weight, and had taken to wearing suspenders to hold his pants up. She knew he wasn't sleeping well; the floorboards gave him away each night. Behind the smile he wore for the benefit of her and her brothers, his face looked different somehow. There were deep creases along his forehead and white hairs in his beard that Rachel was certain had not been there before.

Rachel put the peeler down on the table and tucked a long curl behind her ear. "Nana, why isn't Mommy waking up?"

She gazed patiently up at Judith who was standing at the stove, tending to a big pot of chicken soup that Lauren had put up earlier. The soup smelled delicious, Rachel thought. Lauren was a good cook, but not nearly as good as Mommy. Of course she would never say this out loud—she wouldn't want to hurt Lauren's feelings. The Torah said hurting someone's feelings, or embarrassing them was equivalent to murder! Besides, Lauren was trying so hard to be helpful—cooking the family's favorite things, helping her and her brothers with their homework, and just yesterday, had volunteered to help out with the school's Chanukah production. Rachel knew she should be appreciative of how much Lauren was doing for all of them, so why was it that she often wished Lauren wouldn't come anymore?

Rachel watched as Judith untied the loose knot in the front of her apron. Mommy had a whole collection of aprons, the sillier the better, she always said. This one happened to be one of her favorites: airborne bagels with wings on a clouded sky background. Rachel thought it odd that Nana tied the apron in the front that way. Mommy always made a bow in the back as did Lauren, so Rachel assumed this was the right way, the *only* way. Now she wished Lauren would tie hers in the front too, like Nana instead of Mommy. Maybe it would make things easier for Yitzi. Even before Nehama was born, Yitzi sometimes slipped and called Lauren *Mommy*. And now it was happening more frequently. What if Yitzi kept calling Lauren *Mommy* and forgot about their *real* mommy? If he forgot about her, would God think they didn't need their real mommy anymore? Would he bring her up to heaven instead of sending her home? Rachel was deeply concerned about this. As the oldest, it was her responsibility to make sure it didn't happen.

Judith pulled the apron over her head and hung it carefully on a hook by the door. She was glad Lauren had taken the boys to the park, happy to have this time alone with her granddaughter. Private moments with *any* of her grandchildren were hard to come by. Even though Judith had been visiting every weekend now—arriving Friday afternoon, leaving Sunday—it seemed Lauren was always hovering around.

"Why, Nana?" Rachel said again. "Why isn't Mommy waking up?" This time it sounded more like a plea than a question.

Judith patted her hair down and took a seat next to Rachel. Relaxing her shoulders she said, "Well, sweetheart, it's very complicated..."

Rachel burst into tears. "I want to know why Mommy's not better and Abba won't tell me! He doesn't tell me anything!" she said, sobbing.

In a flash, she pushed back from the table, her chair legs screeching against the floor, and fell into Judith's open arms. Judith rested her chin on top of Rachel's head as she gently stroked her hair, her heart aching for her granddaughter. With Yehuda working so much, it was as if the children were missing not one but *two* parents. Admittedly, the way Yehuda had thrown himself into his work—adding classes to an already full schedule—reminded Judith of herself. Work was something he could control, a distraction from the things he couldn't.

"It's okay, sweetheart. Don't worry, everything will be fine," Judith said, actually wishing she could snap her fingers and make it so.

Rachel pulled away and looked up innocently. She wiped her wet cheek with an open palm. "*How* Nana? How will everything be fine?"

Judith gazed lovingly at her granddaughter. Rachel was the spitting image of Hannah with the same gumball eyes, full cheeks, and creamy complexion. She even had Hannah's spirally hair, though in a slightly darker shade of brown. Oh how Judith missed her daughter-in-law! She missed her contagious laugh, her warm, genuine smile, the goodness in her heart. Hannah had never been anything but welcoming and appreciative of Judith, yet Judith had always remained a bit standoffish, using all she did for the family financially as her excuse. Money, like work, Judith realized, afforded her a wall of protection. It was hard to believe that after all these years, she had never bothered to tell Hannah how much she admired her—her ability to take such wonderful care of her large family yet still find time to teach and volunteer. Like most people, Judith never thought there was any urgency in conveying such sentiments. Now she wondered whether she would ever again have the opportunity.

At times, this all felt unreal, like one long, never ending nightmare. But sadly, this was no dream. After the initial shock and stalling of their lives, all they could do was forge on, resume living; all the while the fear of possible outcomes, the "what-ifs" hovering overhead like a swarm of summer gnats. *What if Hannah died? What if she pulled through but was brain dead?* It was all too much for Judith to wrap her mind around, so she continually *shoo*ed the thoughts away as quickly as she would any pest. It was usually at night when she was in bed—in that window between being awake and asleep—that the thoughts took hold, and Judith considered the possibility that Hannah might not make it. Without a doubt the kids would suffer immeasurable damage; they might need counseling for the rest of their lives. But after a year or so, Yehuda would likely remarry. After all, it was the orthodox thing to do. What was it she heard him say more than once? *In Beresheis, God says it is not good for man to be alone.*

The thought of Yehuda with anyone other than Hannah was troubling to Judith; a stranger acting as a surrogate mother to her grandchildren was incomprehensible. Baby Nehama never knowing her real mother? And what about Yitzi? How many memories would he have? As inappropriate as thinking such thoughts were, it was the idea of her son sharing his bed with another woman that sickened her more than anything. For some crazy reason, Judith imagined it would be someone younger, thinner, prettier. *Where the hell had this clichéd image come from?* Judith shook off the image. After all, her son was nothing like the men Judith had known! Nothing like his own father who had so callously traded them all in for a more youthful model. She must think positively! Hannah *would* pull through, Judith told herself. Hannah *had to* pull through!

In a way, it was ironic how strongly Judith felt about the issue, especially since she hadn't always been so fond of Hannah. She remembered how stunned she was when Yehuda announced his engagement—stunned not in a "happy, excited" way, she would later tell Hannah, (who burst into fits of laughter each time Judith recounted the story) but in a "what did I do to deserve this?" kind of way. Who could blame her? After all, Judith hadn't even met the girl her son intended to spend the rest of his life with. She had never seen a picture; nor could she recall hearing the girl's name mentioned even once! Yet there he was, her twenty-two year old son, delivering this monumental news to her *over the phone* from Jerusalem; the words hitting her like a long-range scud missile. It was a good thing she didn't have a heart condition she told Yehuda years later, or she would have dropped dead from the impact.

Yehuda had assured his mother that a well-respected Israeli matchmaker had made the introduction—a *shadchan* he called her— and that he was absolutely certain that he had met his intended, his *beshert*. Judith had only been speechless on one prior occasion—walking in on her husband and best friend twelve years earlier. And just like then, she had no words. *Using a matchmaker? Having only three dates before proposing?* She didn't understand any of it. It was bad enough that Yehuda had taken off for Israel so soon after graduation. At the time, Judith wasn't concerned; she assumed he was merely postponing his entry into the real world and the inevitable responsibility of getting a job. In hindsight, it should have been obvious to her that Yehuda had a plan for himself. If only she had paid more attention while he was living at home, he might have even mapped it out for her.

Yehuda started showing interest in Judaism at the age of twelve, the year he and Sunny, then nine, enrolled in Jewish Day School. From day one, Sunny made her dissatisfaction known. *Why couldn't she go back to her old school? She didn't understand anything the Hebrew teacher said!* Sunny whined and carried on until Judith finally gave in and pulled her out. Yehuda, on the other hand, was drawn in almost immediately; he would later say that the new school felt like a second home. He was mesmerized by Jewish history and took solace in the daily prayer sessions. He heard the Hebrew language as music, saw the beauty of each Hebrew letter as an art form originating from God's very own canvas. Judith was perplexed. She didn't understand how a religious day school could have such a transformative effect on her son; but she was pleased to see him go from being a boy who was sad and introspective to one who was enthusiastic and vocal. Ever since the move to Florida, Judith had to practically drag her son out of bed each morning, but now he was the first one up, eager to get to school. At home, Yehuda peppered his grandpop with questions about the Orenstein family history, and pressed him to share stories of his descendents' lives in Romania. Yehuda's teachers marveled at his enthusiasm, but pointed out that without additional tutoring, it was unlikely he would catch up to his peers. He began working every afternoon with a young rabbi from the school, and to everyone's astonishment, his Hebrew reading and comprehension was soon on par with that of his classmates.

Yehuda's enthusiasm for religion didn't end there. By the end of that first year, he had convinced his grandparents to have a traditional Friday night dinner each week, when he would stand at the head of the table—a black yarmulke on his head—and recite *Kiddish* over grape juice and *Hamotzi* over two loaves of store bought *challah*.

Judith accepted full responsibility for her son's fanaticism. Okay, so it was her father who had suggested religious school, but *she* was the one who went along with it, telling herself that a public school education wasn't good enough for her kids. Besides, religious school would keep them out of trouble. Clearly, the fanaticism Yehuda was showing was the result of his prior lack of *any* Jewish identity. Her father, in fact, had an excellent theory: Yehuda was experiencing Judaism much like someone who hadn't eaten for a month, and then went to an *all you can eat* buffet—he was gorging himself, not on food, but on *Torah*.

Before long he would vomit it all up, or at the very least, reach a point of satiation. Then he would calm down.

But Harvey was wrong. The changes continued and it became clear that Yehuda's religious zeal was not something he would simply outgrow like an old pair of sneakers. Judith couldn't help but feel a sense of loss as she witnessed her son's transformation. These were supposed to be carefree years; Yehuda should have been out having fun instead of praying three times a day! He should have been playing basketball like other teenagers, not studying *Gemorah* at the local orthodox shul. At a time when boys his age blew their money on comic books or arcade games, her nutty son used *his* savings to pay for new dishes and pots for the kitchen. But the true point of no return came the day he called them all together to make an important announcement: He was no longer "Ira", he told his family. He was now using *his real name,* his *Hebrew name*—"Yehuda".

Later, when Judith privately voiced her objection, he respectfully reminded her that after her divorce she had reclaimed her maiden name, and not only for herself but for he and Sunny as well.

"But that's completely different!" she said.

"*How* is it different?"

"Your father's name—Richman—is no longer who I am," Judith said firmly. "It isn't who *any* of us are."

Yehuda looked squarely into his mother's eyes and nodded. "Our name defines us—not only to ourselves, but to the world," he said.

Judith couldn't argue. Her son had made his point, and he had somehow managed to do it while sounding more like a *man* than a fifteen-year-old adolescent.

When Yehuda flew home from Israel to introduce his bride to be, Judith welcomed her with a polite smile, while Yehuda's grandparents looked like they were about to burst from happiness. Their grandson was a yeshiva *bachur*! He was studying to be a rabbi! And now, he was engaged to a nice Jewish girl! Judith knew her parents took pride in having a hand in Yehuda's upbringing, in knowing they had helped him successfully navigate through adolescence—without his eloping and running off to some crazy commune like his mother.

Nineteen-year-old Hannah Borsky was tall and slim and had a head full of spirally brown hair that bounced like a hundred coiled *Slinkies* each time she turned her head. At dinner that first night, Judith studied Hannah carefully, listened to what she said, looking for something, *anything* to find fault with. But the girl was intelligent, witty, and refreshingly open. She was born in Tennessee ("yes there are Jews there!"), and had moved to Israel with her parents at age ten. Hannah worked as a pre-school teacher. She loved children, she said, and wanted a large family.

Throughout the evening, Judith noticed Hannah and Yehuda sending private glances to one another. Was it possible that Yehuda had been right, that he had found his match? Even Sunny, who could always be counted on for a critical assessment, gave a rare seal of approval of her brother's wife to be.

The next day Sunny took Hannah to the farmers market and Judith seized the opportunity to sit her son down for a heart to heart. Something had occurred to her that might make him want to reconsider his marriage plans.

"See, it comes down to compatibility," Judith said, speaking like someone who was an expert in the field. Whereas Hannah had grown up in a religious family, she told him, *he* had not. It wouldn't be easy being married to someone so religious; in fact, it was equivalent to marrying someone from a foreign country, someone who barely spoke English! The cultural differences would most certainly strain the marriage—it was just a matter of time. But it wasn't too late; they weren't married yet. Yehuda could call off the wedding. It would be the honorable thing to do. Hannah would thank him later. She would be grateful that one of them had come to their senses before they made such a foolish mistake!

But even as the rehearsed words fell out of her mouth, Judith realized she was firing rounds at an invisible target; her words were pointless, directionless. The truth was Judith didn't trust her own judgment any more than she trusted her son's. Who was she to say what made a good marriage, especially when she herself had failed so miserably at it? She had no way of knowing if Yehuda was making a mistake, so her efforts to protect him were futile.

Judith stopped talking and took in the image of her son as he stood across from her, his six-foot body towering over hers. Though she didn't deserve it, he had been completely respectful as she lectured him, never interrupting or counter arguing, as she undoubtedly would have done in his position. As always, he was dressed in his yeshiva clothes—black pants and white dress shirt. His black velvet yarmulke was perched obediently atop his head and the thin white strings of his tzi tzi's hung down his legs. Judith studied him carefully. Even with his height, he had a boyish face that made him look deceptively young. He always looked silly to her—penguin-like actually—as though he were in costume. But now studying him, there was something different, and not at all funny. He wasn't a child. He was a man making his way in the world, creating the life he envisioned for himself. One day, he would be a rabbi. Even before then, he would be a husband, possibly a father. Judith took a deep breath. She felt utterly ashamed. How could she not have noticed it before? How could she have missed it? Somewhere along the way, her Ira had truly become Yehuda.

"Why isn't she waking up, Nana?" Rachel asked again, snapping Judith abruptly from her daydream. At once, the *what if's* returned, spring boarding off her granddaughter's question.

Judith considered her words carefully before speaking. She knew firsthand that Hannah's prognosis was *fair* at best. The doctor had said it was improbable that Hannah would come out of this thing unscathed. There *would* be damage—how much, and to what degree, he did not know. When Hannah woke up—*if* she woke up—there would be months, maybe years of rehabilitation. Judith knew of a woman—a former client— who had to learn how to feed herself all over again. But how could she explain any of this to a nine-year-old? *Even if* her son permitted her to speak truthfully, how could she tell Rachel that her mother was probably brain damaged? That she might not be able to speak, walk, or hold a fork. That there was a chance her mother might even *die*. Judith was thankful not to have to contemplate that one. Yehuda had given her—had given *everyone*—strict instructions with regard to the children. No details were to be spoken about what had actually transpired at the mikvah; it was to be referred to as "an accident." The children were to be told that their mother had slipped and hit her head. And most importantly, *not a single word* was to be uttered about the extent of Hannah's condition or medical prognosis. Judith disagreed with her son's decision to withhold information from the kids. She believed that the children should be given some semblance of the truth, or at least as much information as they were capable of processing. Yehuda knew how she felt, but still insisted that the children were to be told that their mother was getting better and would come home soon.

*Soon.*

How long could they keep saying that? Didn't "soon" have an expiration date? Judith looked into Rachel's expectant eyes and sighed.

"Sweetheart, the doctors say that when your mommy hit her head, there was some damage which needs time to heal. Did you know that our bodies heal and grow when we're asleep?"

Rachel shook her head and sniffled. "They do?"

Judith averted her eyes. "Yes, that's right, honey. Your mommy's body is sleeping now and repairing itself. And when she wakes up, she'll be better."

Rachel sat up and wiped her eyes with the palms of her hands. A smile slowly made it's way across her face. She was pleased with this new information.

"Then before you know it, she'll be home," Judith said.

# Twenty-eight

"Janine's here!" Eli bellowed from the bottom of the stairs to nobody in particular.

Judith was upstairs packing her bag while speaking with a client on her cell phone. It was Sunday afternoon and she would be heading back to New York in a few hours.

"Janine's here!"

With this second announcement, Judith quickly ended her call. "Okay David, I'm coming!" she hollered in the direction of the stairs.

"I'm not David! I'm Eli!"

Judith shook her head, admonishing herself. After spending the last three weekends with the kids, she should recognize their voices by now.

"Sorry Eli!" She gripped the railing and made her way down the stairs, taking care not to lose her footing.

"Mrs. Orenstein! How great to see you!" Janine said, eyeing her sleek black pantsuit and red *Manolo* pumps. "You look stunning!"

Judith reached for Janine's hand and gave it a quick squeeze. "I keep telling you to call me Judith, dear. Now, come, I'll make us some tea."

Janine waved her hands. "Oh, no. I don't want to put you out."

"It's no trouble at all. I was about to have some myself."

"Well, okay, but I can only stay for a minute," Janine said, then lowered her voice to a whisper. "I have a date."

In the kitchen, Judith filled the teakettle and Janine took a seat at the kitchen table. This was her first time in the house since the accident and she was stunned at how clean and orderly everything looked. There were no crumbs in the seat cushions. Even the toaster oven shined. She knew it was Lauren who deserved full credit.

"So you have a date?" Judith said pointedly. "Anyone I know?"

"No, I don't think so. His name is Howard—Howard Freed. We've been seeing each other for about two months now."

"I see… and where is this Howard taking you?"

"To a coffee house down town," Janine said, feeling like a teenager being interrogated. "It's Jazz *open mic* night."

Judith sighed dramatically. "Have a wonderful time," she said. "But remember Janine, an independent woman is a free woman."

"Oh I wasn't… we weren't…."

Judith raised her eyebrows in amusement. "In other words, don't quit your day job." She held up her hand, putting an end to the discussion. "Now, as far as Yehuda, I expect he'll be back any time now; he's been at the hospital all afternoon."

"Actually I was looking for Lauren," Janine said.

Judith made no effort to conceal her surprise. Apparently the two women had forged a friendship through the Jewish Learning Center. But other than being the same age, Judith couldn't see any compatibility. Janine was sweet, dependable, and consistent—a true asset to the Learning Center. Lauren, on the other hand was something of a mystery. Certainly, she was a help to Yehuda and the kids, but there was something about her that rubbed Judith the wrong way. The more time she spent with Lauren, the more she felt it. Judith couldn't quite put her finger on it, but there was definitely something strange about the girl. Even Rachel sensed it, and was uncomfortable. Rachel never actually *told* Judith this, but there was no need. Judith had seen it with her own eyes; like just that morning, when Lauren nonchalantly put her hand on Rachel's shoulder. The way Rachel flinched, you would have thought a spider was crawling on her! She nearly jumped out of her skin!

"Lauren's out running some errands, but she should be back any time now," Judith said.

Janine glanced at her watch. "I don't have a lot of time... Instead of waiting, would it be all right if I left this with you?" She reached into her bag and pulled out two sheets of printer paper. "What I am about to present you with is the triple confirmed volunteer schedule for the next two weeks," Janine said, grinning proudly.

"*Triple confirmed?*" Judith laughed, as she took the papers. "But honestly, I thought we already had volunteers. Both freezers are packed, that's for sure."

Janine nodded her understanding. "So many people want to help and I suppose making a meal is something easy enough to do." She pointed at the paper in Judith's hand. "But that list has to do with *childcare*. Apparently, there was some miscommunication..."

"Oh?" Judith interrupted. "My son never mentioned anything."

"That doesn't surprise me," Janine said. "Lauren's not one to complain, but she did confide in me that some of the volunteers never showed up this past week, which left her in a bind. Did you know she missed several of her classes?"

"She did? Oh that's terrible!" Judith said. "The poor girl shouldn't have to miss her classes!" For some reason, she liked the idea of Lauren spending more time in school, less time with Judith's family.

Janine nodded and held the papers up for Judith to see. "I agree completely. That's why I've lined up volunteers to come while Lauren's in school: Monday, Tuesday and Thursday from 7 AM through 3 PM. Lauren's at the house by then, and she can handle things on her own until bedtime."

"No night classes then?" Judith asked. Now that she thought about it, she wasn't so keen on the idea of Lauren playing mommy to her grandchildren and tucking them in every night.

The teakettle whistled and Judith got up to turn off the stove. "Is green tea okay?"

She brought over two oversized cups of tea and a plastic bear-shaped bottle of honey. As Janine stirred her tea, Judith took another look at the schedule.

"When you see it all laid out on paper like this, you realize how much work goes into just a single day."

Janine cupped her mug with two hands and took a tentative sip. "It's quite a job taking care of such a large family. I don't know how Hannah and your son do it. They certainly are exceptional parents."

Judith sipped her tea silently. After a moment, she set it down and leaned in toward Janine. "Can I ask you something, Janine?"

"Sure."

"It's about Yehuda."

"Okay."

"Has he been coping all right at work?"

Janine felt a bit odd being taken in as a confidante by the older woman. She took a moment to consider her answer. "Well, given everything that's happened, yes, I would say he's doing surprisingly well. In fact, I think the teaching might be keeping him sane."

Judith recognized the wisdom in Janine's statement. It was true; work *was* the ultimate distraction.

"Well Janine," Judith said, scribbling on a piece of paper, "I'd like you to have my cell phone number, just in case."

"In case?"

Judith wasn't quite sure herself. "Call for any reason; if my son's behavior changes, for example." Judith raised her cup to her lips, but set it down before taking a sip. "Or perhaps if you notice Lauren…"

"If I notice Lauren *what*?" Janine asked.

Again, Judith wasn't exactly sure. "If you notice her acting oddly… from all the stress I mean."

Janine looked at the number before slipping the paper into her purse. She fought back the urge to say something else. "Sure. No problem."

"My son's very fortunate to have you, Janine. You're invaluable—the way you look after things. You keep the center running so smoothly. And, more importantly, you manage to do it with a smile on your face!"

"Thank you Mrs. Or… Thank you *Judith*. That's very kind of you, but truthfully, *I* feel like the lucky one!" She held her hand over her heart. "I love my job, I love your son…" She blushed at her poor choice of words. "What I mean is, I couldn't ask for a better boss."

"Well, then it's a win-win all around!" said Judith. Her fondness for Janine grew each time she saw her.

Judith's phone rang from the other room and she excused herself to go answer it. While she was gone, Janine looked again at the volunteer schedule. She had to admit, the list was solid and impressive. Lauren would be so surprised. Probably relieved too. Yehuda had no idea just how much Lauren was doing for his family, making it so he could come and go without worrying about matters on the home front.

"Just one of my secretaries," Judith said, returning a few minutes later.

"They work on weekends?"

"Of course," Judith said, sounding surprised at the question.

Suddenly David popped his head in the kitchen. "Nana, can you help me tie my shoes?" he asked nonchalantly.

Judith gazed critically at the long trail of white shoelace before looking up at her grandson.

"What's this? You mean to tell me you don't know how to tie your own shoes?" She narrowed her eyes and wagged her finger. "You better watch out or your baby sister will be tying hers before you!"

David's face dropped. He spun around just in time to see Lauren standing in the doorway with a look of empathy in her eyes. Instinctively, he ran toward her, burrowing his face in the crook of his arm.

Judith tapped the schedule. "It's heart warming to see so many people giving of themselves," she said to Janine, "especially when they have enough going on in their own lives. So impressive!"

But Janine's attention was on Lauren, watching as she gently stroked David's head. How could Judith not realize that she had just humiliated her grandson? Couldn't she at least see that he was crying? And what about Lauren standing in the doorway? Judith hadn't even acknowledged her! This was how Lauren was treated after all she was doing for the Orenstein family?

"Janine?"

"Wha…?"

"Are you all right, dear? I was saying how heartwarming it is to see such generosity."

Janine took a deep breath. "Well, your son and daughter-in-law are very well known and very much loved," she responded softly. "People genuinely want to help." Janine paused, her eyes remaining fixed on Lauren and David. "And then there are those few unique individuals… Individuals ready and willing to do whatever it takes to show how much they care."

# Twenty-nine

Cynthia Bergerman stood on the Orenstein's doorstep wearing a full-length fur coat and pointy high-heeled boots, cradling a giant fruit basket between her arms. The lids of her protruding eyes were painted in shades of pink and her collagen filled lips were glossed in fire engine red. An odd look for early afternoon; it reminded Lauren of the advertisements for high priced escorts she sometimes saw in the backs of magazines.

Lauren opened the door and Cynthia thrust the basket at her, before marching herself into the house.

"I'm Cynthia Bergerman," she said, extended her arm. She had to realize there was no way Lauren could balance her enormous load and shake Cynthia's hand at the same time.

"Lauren," Lauren said from behind a giant pineapple.

Apparently Cynthia didn't recognize her from Hannah's class.

Cynthia squinted. "Lauren? Lauren *what?*"

"Donnelly."

"Donnelly?" Cynthia repeated, giving her a once over. "That's Irish... I assume you're the housekeeper?"

"Uh, actually, I help with the kids."

Cynthia placed an open hand on her cheek, a flabbergasted look on her face. "You're *kidding*!" She shrugged and peeled off her leather driving gloves before slipping out of her coat. She wore a tiny leather miniskirt that barely covered her thighs and an off-the-shoulder ivory cashmere sweater. She arched her eyebrows at Lauren and then looked straight at the giant basket. "Feel free to put that down at any time."

"Right." Lauren set the basket down on the hall table, feeling oddly like she was in the middle of some kind of reality show spoof. A person couldn't *really* be this obnoxious, could they?

"Can I take your coat?" Lauren asked, after which Cynthia took a giant step back, acting as though she were afraid Lauren would snatch the fur right out of her hands and make a run for it.

"No. That won't be necessary. I can't stay long. I'm on my way to an awards luncheon at the Four Seasons Hotel. Our business is being honored by the Better Business Bureau. I'm sure you've heard of us— Bergerman Bagels."

"Yes, I have... Congratulations..."

"We send truckloads of bagels to hungry children all over the country," Cynthia continued.

"I know. I read all about it in the paper."

Cynthia perked up. "Sunday's feature story?"

Lauren nodded.

"It was picked up by the associated press," Cynthia said. "Even my parents in Sarasota saw it."

"Your family is very generous."

"Of course we are!" Cynthia said. "That's why were being honored!"

She unsnapped her clutch and started down the hall toward the kitchen. "I have something for Yehuda. Is he here?"

"Abba's at the hospital."

"Rachel! I didn't see you over there, sweetie!" Cynthia squawked, whirling around. She sauntered toward the couch, her ass swinging. Lauren wondered how Cynthia would manage to sit down in such a short skirt, but got her answer when Cynthia sat primly on the edge of the couch and draped her mink over her thighs.

"Rachel wasn't feeling well today," Lauren said, trying to meet Rachel's eyes. But as usual, Rachel wasn't interested in any form of contact. For the life of her, Lauren couldn't figure out why Rachel had become more and more distant lately. When it was just the two of them, Rachel usually stayed in her room. She was only downstairs now because Lauren was making lunch.

Cynthia scooted over an inch or so, away from Rachel. "So you had to miss school, huh?" She winked. "That's not really such a bad thing is it? Well, I hope you're feeling better now."

"I am. Thank you," Rachel said politely.

"How's your mommy doing, sweetie?" Cynthia continued. "Did she get the flowers I sent?"

Rachel's eyes welled up and Lauren stepped in. "Yehuda said they were beautiful." Lauren didn't mention that since flowers weren't permitted in intensive care patient's rooms, they had promptly been given to the nurses.

"And the bagels?" Cynthia asked. "Are you and your brothers enjoying the case of cinnamon swirl bagels I sent over?"

Lauren turned so Cynthia wouldn't see her rolling her eyes. *Was this girl for real?* "Oh good… Yehuda's pulling in now," Lauren announced from the window.

Cynthia popped up expectantly from the couch, catching her heel on the bottom of her coat and falling forward with a howl. Yehuda walked in just as she was pulling herself up on all fours. Only Lauren noticed Rachel's open-mouthed gape. She immediately ran over to Cynthia and grabbed her arm, hoisting her clumsily to her feet.

"Cynthia!" Are you all right? Did you hurt yourself?" Yehuda's eyes darted about the room in an attempt to assess the situation.

"I'm fine," Cynthia said, releasing herself from Lauren's grasp. She stood tall and brushed herself off. "I'm just not used to this full length mink!" she said dramatically. "My three quarter length fox is at the restorer. Well, I'm glad my klutziness was here, instead of at the banquet!" she laughed.

"Baruch Hashem," Yehuda said. His smile turned downward as he caught a glimpse of Rachel's horrified expression.

"I have a little something for you," Cynthia told him, extending her arm in front of his line of vision.

Yehuda blinked and took the envelope.

"Open it now!" Cynthia insisted, clapping her hands together and stamping one stiletto- heeled foot like an impatient child.

Yehuda carefully tore off an edge of the envelope and pulled out a check. He blinked and did a double take. "This is extremely generous, Cynthia."

She smiled. "It's for the center. Brad insisted."

Yehuda shook his head in disbelief. Though worth millions, Brad Bergerman had never been a big financial supporter of The Jewish Learning Center. Cynthia made small contributions here and there, but her hands were tied. It seemed Brad made all the major financial decisions in their house. "This is really extraordinary... I don't know what to say." He held the check in front of him. "I can't get over it. This is extraordinary! I'll call Brad this afternoon and thank him personally."

"That won't be necessary," Cynthia chimed in. "He's extremely busy right now anyway—some problem with the west coast distributor." She turned, headed for the door, then stopped in her tracks and spun around. "Oh, there's one more thing," she said. "I can't believe I almost forgot!"

"Anything," Yehuda said.

"I want to take Rachel shopping."

Yehuda scratched his head. "It's nice of you to offer, but I don't think this is a good time."

At first Cynthia looked completely confused. Then her mouth opened and she took a big gulp of air. "Oh, right!" she mouthed. "Because of… yes… of course." She shrugged. "Well then maybe I'll just send over a few things. What size are you, sweetie?"

Rachel looked at her father who nodded, then back at Cynthia. "Size 8."

Cynthia clapped her hands together. "Wonderful! I'm going to buy you the most adorable little things!" She slipped into her coat and sashayed out the door without looking back.

Within seconds of the door shutting, Rachel burst into tears.

"What's the matter, Racheli?" Yehuda asked, rushing to her side.

"I'm… I'm worried about Mrs. Bergerman!" Rachel sobbed.

He took her hand. "Tell me honey, what has you worried?"

Rachel took a deep breath. She shook her head. "I don't want her to buy me presents."

"Why is that?" he asked softly.

"Because she's *poor*!" Rachel said, wiping her nose with her sleeve.

"Poor?" Yehuda repeated. He looked to Lauren for an explanation, but she just shook her head and shrugged.

"What makes you think she's poor?"

"Because…." But Rachel wouldn't finish her thought.

Yehuda waited.

"...Because she doesn't have enough money for underwear," Rachel finally blurted out, wide eyed.

Yehuda's face went white. But he cleared his throat and regrouped quickly, his color returning. "Maybe she just forgot today Racheli," he said, trying to keep his voice steady. "It sounds like Mrs. Bergerman was very busy this morning... she probably forgot to put them on," he said in a more convincing voice. He looked over to Lauren who was hugging herself and looking at the floor. "She's fine, Rachel," Yehuda continued. "I promise you, no one has to worry about Cynthia Bergerman!"

A half-hour later Yehuda was sitting at the table spreading some leftover tuna onto a bagel, a quick lunch before heading back to the center.

"You're sure you don't need me to pick up the boys after school?" Lauren asked as she entered the kitchen holding a sleepy Nehama in her arms.

Yehuda dropped his knife and reached for his daughter. "No," he replied, kissing Nehama gently on top of her fuzzy head. "I spoke to my mother. She'll get them on her way in."

Lauren went to that sink to prepare Nehama's bottle. "The kids will be surprised to see her a day early," she said, trying to sound enthusiastic.

"She has a client she's seeing today in Trenton," Yehuda said dryly. "She was half way here anyway."

Lauren didn't respond. She knew Yehuda was disappointed in his mother; disappointed that despite the Orenstein state of emergency, Judith continued to put work before family.

Yehuda handed Nehama back to Lauren, then picked up his bagel and took a bite.

"Rachel's okay now?"

Lauren settled in to a chair across from him and began feeding the baby. "Seems to be. I just checked on her. She's under her covers reading… didn't mention Cynthia at all." *Didn't mention anything since she's practically not speaking to me.*

Yehuda stared down at his bagel in contemplation, then looked up at her. "I realize several of the women from Hannah's classes have signed up to help with the kids…"

"That's right. They seem to be the most flexible." *Probably because they all have live in help.* "When I'm done feeding Nehama, I can go get the schedule if you want to see it."

He waved his hands. "No, that won't be necessary. I glanced at it while Janine was finalizing it. Anyway, it looks like Hannah's women will be here most mornings with Nehama and then all day Wednesday."

"That's right," Lauren said, "I have a full class schedule on Wednesday, remember?"

"How are your classes going, anyway?" It occurred to him that he had never asked before.

She smiled. "Great…"

He stared down at his food, thinking. It was obvious he was grappling with something.

Lauren set the bottle down and propped Nehama up to be burped. "Is something wrong Yehuda?"

"No, nothing at all," he said immediately, as if suddenly having a change of heart. He looked at his watch and pushed his chair away from the table. "I didn't realize the time." He gestured apologetically toward his plate. "I'm sorry Lauren, would you mind?"

"No problem. I'll take care of it," Lauren said. He gave Nehama a quick peck on the forehead and rushed out of the kitchen, leaving his uneaten lunch on the table.

"Mom, where are you?"

Judith turned off the radio and adjusted her blue tooth earpiece. For some reason, Yehuda sounded concerned. She braced herself for bad news involving Hannah. "I'm waiting for the boys," she said tentatively. "You said 3:00, right?"

"3:00 at the school."

"I *am* at the school, Yehuda—in the parking lot. They must be running late, because none of the kids have come out yet."

"Are you sure? Because the principal just called me, asking why the boys hadn't been picked up."

Judith looked toward the front of the brick building. The doors were closed and all was quiet. "He doesn't know what he's talking about!" Judith said. She didn't have much patience for ineptitude. "I've been sitting here for twenty minutes!"

"It's okay, Mom. Just tell me where you are exactly."

"I just told you! I'm sitting in the parking lot of the school!"

"*Which* school?"

"Eli and David's school!"

"No, I mean what's the *name* of the school?"

*What kind of question was that?* "The name of the school, Yehuda, is *Little Sinai*."

Yehuda sighed. "Mom, Little Sinai is a pre-school. The kids attend Goldberg Academy."

"Goldberg Academy?"

"On the corner of Winston and Oak."

"What?" Judith stammered. "When did they start going there?"

"Rachel's been a student there for four years."

"But not the boys." It was more of a statement then a question.

"Actually, Eli started two years ago," Yehuda said. "This is David's first year."

Judith rubbed her temples, racking her brain, trying to picture Goldberg Academy. She couldn't.

Yehuda seemed to read her mind. "Mom," he began gently, "have you ever been to Goldberg Academy? Wait... hold on a second; Lauren's calling me."

"I'm pulling out now, Yehuda." Judith said when he returned to the call. "Tell me, do I make a left or right on Clemson?"

"Don't worry about it, Mom," he said. "Lauren's on her way to the school. She'll get them."

Judith swallowed. "But you said Rachel's was home..."

"One of the neighbors is staying with her until Lauren gets back."

"I'm sorry Yehuda."

"It's okay... Just go to the house... I'll see you there later."

"Yehuda... I...."

"The kids will be fine, Mom. Lauren has everything under control."

*Of course she does*, Judith thought, gritting her teeth.

# Thirty

The lobby was huge, over a thousand square feet. Father McCormick knew this because of the sounds. It was more than voices; it was the *tap tap tap* of fingers on keyboards, the whistles and toots of e-mail being sent and received, the cracking of knuckles, the scraping of chairs—typical background noises that human brains noted and filtered within nanoseconds. But for Father Herbert McCormick, insignificant sounds felt like an ambush; and now, as he sat across from the detective, struggling to focus on the younger man's words, the sounds bombarded him, sprung away, then bounced along the walls, ceiling and floor like rubber balls. Disconcerting as the rush of sounds could be, Father McCormick often welcomed them like a group of old friends. His sight had deteriorated to the point where he could only make out shadows, so he relied on the ricocheting sound waves to lay out the parameters of unfamiliar territory. Though he couldn't explain exactly how he did it, he did know that there was nothing at all supernatural about the process. Bats used the technique—like a sort of sonar—to navigate their own dark worlds.

They sat on wide cushioned chairs tucked far off in a corner, about fifty feet from a group of cubicles that housed secretaries and lower level administrators of the various township departments.

The detective spoke first. "Thanks again for coming down, Father," Ron said, as he regarded the priest. From the waist up, Father McCormick was pristinely dressed, his crisp priest's collar peeking out from a black overcoat; but below the knees, his dark trousers were flecked with gold dog hairs. The culprit—a golden retriever companion dog—lay patiently at his feet. Ron remembered Samson from his search of the rectory. Today the dog looked like he could use a good brushing. The priest's dress shoes were in need of some attention too. Scuffed up and dirty, they practically begged for a polishing.

"No trouble at all," Father McCormick said, although the truth was he rarely left the rectory without Peter. "We took a cab."

"Good. Well, let's get started."

"Shouldn't we wait for John?"

"John?" Ron was momentarily confused. Then he remembered that John and the priest had known each other a long time. "Oh, you mean John *Collins?*"

"Yes, he'll be joining us, right?"

"No. I'm afraid he *won't* be."

The priest furrowed his brow. "John was at the rectory with you during the search; I assumed you worked together."

"Sorry to disappoint you," Ron said. "But nowadays John's specialty is patrolling Arden Station at odd hours of the night."

"Oh? And why is that?"

"Couldn't tell you," Ron said. "Had enough, I guess."

"Since when?"

Ron did a quick calculation. "It's been five years or so."

Father McCormick sat quietly for a moment, trying to make sense of it. *Five years*. He had been counseling John regularly back then—after Jay died—but John never mentioned a thing about switching departments. Why would he? John *loved* investigative work. He had paid his dues, he told the priest more than once, and was now living every cop's dream. He was a *detective*!

Besides, John was an *alpha*. He liked to take charge, especially when it came to the more challenging cases, though admittedly these were rare in a town like Arden Station. The *John Collins* Father McCormick knew was a real star, naturally gifted, and had a wall full of awards and certificates of recognition to prove it. During the priest's very first visit to Windmere, Patty had led him to John's study where she proudly read each one to him, frame by frame. No, it just didn't make sense. John was not someone who would *willingly* take a back seat, especially when it came to a job he not only loved, but also excelled at.

"Does your dog need water, Father? He's panting up a storm."

Father McCormick snapped out of his private thoughts and made a mental note to speak to John directly. He held up his hand. "No, no. Thank you for the thought, but Samson's fine. She's a working dog you see—never been in a police station before; I imagine it's quite exciting for her."

"Oh, so, Samson's a *she* huh?" Ron asked. Somehow that possibility hadn't occurred to him. He laughed. "Then I bet she's catching a whiff of the male canine unit downstairs and…" He stopped speaking mid-sentence when he caught sight of one of the secretaries—a young woman who had recently returned from maternity leave. She was glaring at him from her cubicle. He held his hand up and gave her a little salute. *Sorry*. She shook her head disparagingly and turned back to her desk. Ron scratched the bridge of his nose and sighed. He didn't know why he said such stupid, inappropriate things sometimes. It was like he regressed to his idiotic frat boy days. It didn't happen often, but still it concerned him. Maybe something was seriously wrong with him. Maybe he should see a neurologist. Well, he would have to remember to apologize to the woman. Even if it was intended in dog context only, the last thing he needed was to be accused of sexual harassment.

"You said I would be able to see Peter," Father McCormick said, ignoring the detective's last remark. "I assumed that was the reason you asked me to come down?"

"Yes, well, about that..." Ron said, quickly regaining his composure. "It seems there's a bit of a problem."

"Problem? What problem?"

"As you know we couldn't get a match on Peter's fingerprints."

"Yes, you mentioned that to me on the phone," Father McCormick said. "And I told you I wasn't surprised. Peter has never been arrested."

Ron wondered how the priest could be certain of this, but he didn't ask. "Well, that's not all," he said.

"Then what is it?"

"This is where it gets complicated," Ron said. "Seems we couldn't get a positive I.D. on Peter Stem the *individual* either."

"I don't follow."

"Let me give it to you straight, Father," Ron said. "Peter may not be who you think he is."

Father McCormick furrowed his brow. "I still don't understand."

"Peter Stem may not be Peter Stem."

Father McCormick shook his head and waved his hands. "No. You're mistaken. Peter has family upstate... You just need to contact them."

Ron sighed. "Have you personally met any of Peter Stem's family?" he asked.

"Well, no."

"Spoken to them on the phone?"

"No."

"But surely they've called the rectory?"

"Not that I'm aware of," Father McCormick admitted.

Ron paused and then responded, accentuating each word as if the priest was deaf as well as blind. "They. Don't. Exist." He immediately regretted speaking this way. *Impulse control.* Impulse control was another symptom for the neurologist.

Father McCormick leaned back in his chair. "This doesn't make sense," he said softly.

"I don't know what to make of it either," Ron said. "I thought you could help."

"But how can I could possibly be of help?" Father McCormick asked. "You've already looked through Peter's things."

"Yes, and found nothing of value," Ron admitted, more to himself than the priest. "No birth certificate, no passport, not even a damn driver's license…"

Father McCormick drew in a deep breath which Ron mistook for a shocked response to his use of the word *damn.* But what the priest was actually thinking was: *All this time, Peter had been driving illegally, without a license!*

"After living together for so many years, you and Peter must have developed a close relationship," Ron continued.

Father McCormick nodded his affirmation.

"You probably trusted him completely."

"I still do." Father McCormick said.

Ron studied the priest carefully. With the exception of his eyesight, he appeared to have all his faculties intact. But his choice of words spoke volumes. The fact was, someone his age would be easy to take advantage of, especially by a former addict. Addicts were known to be manipulative.

Father McCormick knew what the detective must be thinking—that he was a religious fool who had been taken for a ride. Of course he would think that! After all, the man believed Peter had committed murder. And while it was not unusual for someone to accept assistance from the church while getting back on his feet, a fifteen year retreat was something else altogether. How could Father McCormick possibly describe Peter to someone who had never met him? How could he explain that the alcoholism, the life on the street, was *not* the true man, but a mere cloak that he had worn until he'd been saved? Maybe Father McCormick could start by telling the detective about the time Peter had performed the *Heimlich maneuver* on him while choking on a chicken bone, literally saving his life! Maybe he should mention the time Peter nursed that baby rabbit back to health…

Ron cleared his throat. "You had a close relationship and trusted Peter completely, yet somehow he never told you his *real* name? Or where he was *actually* from?" Ron spoke with a hint of sarcasm in his voice. "With all due respect Father, are you certain Peter Stem was the only name he gave you? Is it possible you might have forgotten?"

"Forgotten? No, Detective, I haven't forgotten," Father McCormick said. "I knew him only as *Peter*. Peter Stem."

Father McCormick placed his trembling hands in his lap. He tried not to show it, but he was troubled by what the detective was suggesting. How *could* he have lived with someone for over fifteen years and not known who they were? Granted, he respected Peter's—or anyone's—right to privacy, but still, shouldn't he have known the true identity of the man sharing his home? For a split second, he felt panic surge through his body. Ever since he found out about Peter's arrest, he had remained completely at ease, certain there was a simple mix up that would be sorted out quickly. But time continued to pass. Peter was still behind bars. And now, after learning the news that Peter might not be who he claimed to be, it was difficult to remain confident. Had Peter been manipulating him? Had he been using the church as a place to hide? The worst of it—something the detective was likely already aware of—was that for the past fifteen years he had paid Peter's salary out of his own pocket. Now he wondered, by paying Peter in *cash*, had he unwittingly helped a fugitive stay hidden?

"I expect Peter will need a lawyer," Father McCormick said. For the first time, he was beginning to process the reality of Peter's situation.

"There's no need. We've assigned a public defender to him," Ron said. "But seeing that Peter hasn't spoken a single coherent word since he got here, the attorney hasn't gotten very far with his client. Now, if you have someone else in mind... "

A woman from the cubicles approached them. "Excuse me, Detective, but Elise Danzig just called. She'll be a few minutes late."

Ron thanked her and glanced at his watch. "If you're still interested Father, I'll take you to see Peter now." *Take you down to the Peter-stem-cell.*

"Something funny?" Father McCormick asked.

Ron hadn't realized he'd been guffawing out loud at his private joke. He cleared his throat. *God! What the hell was wrong with him?* "No, nothing; nothing at all," he said, trying to conceal his momentary panic. "Are you ready?"

Father McCormick stood and gripped Samson's leash firmly in his hand. *Danzig. Danzig.* The name was familiar but he couldn't place it. He pushed the thought aside for the time being, and followed the detective down a freshly carpeted hall to the interrogation room. The room was little more than a cinderblock square, approximately twenty feet by twenty feet, with a heavy metal table and four folding chairs.

There were no windows, but the space was lit brightly from overhead by long fluorescent bulbs housed in plexiglass encasements. An elaborate audio-visual recording system was tucked away, high above and out of reach, in a far corner of the ceiling.

As soon as Father McCormick sat down there was a low boom— unexpected, but not frightening. Samson did little more than perk up her ears a bit. Evidently the air had kicked on, because a steady hum began, followed by the flow of cool air from flat vents on the ceiling. Father McCormick hugged himself as the cold stream hit his face. Air conditioning in November? Was this part of the interrogation process? Physical discomfort as a way to obtain information? He suddenly felt protective of Peter. Any fleeting doubts about Peter's innocence were fading quickly into the background and logic was returning. He *knew* Peter. Peter was no murderer! The fact that Peter had been found at a crime scene didn't make him guilty, just unlucky. Peter was in the wrong place at the wrong time, as the saying went. But admittedly, what Father McCormick couldn't explain was what the heck Peter was *doing* there in the first place.

"Damn it!" Ron shouted. He immediately lowered his voice. "I apologize, Father, but ever since the renovations, we go through this same bullshit every fall!" He took a deep breath. "Once you're all settled, I'll see what I can do about getting the air turned off."

There was a light tap on the door and two men shuffled in; one of them was Peter—Father McCormick recognized his distinct smell. It was remarkable how every individual, even families, had unique identifying scents. As with his hearing, Father McCormick's sense of smell had strengthened when his vision began failing.

Peter was led to the table where he slumped into a chair across from the priest, placed both elbows on the table, and buried his face in his hands, one which had an ace bandage on it.

"Hello Peter," Father McCormick said gently. *Peter.* For the first time in fifteen years, the priest felt unsure saying the man's name. *Was Peter really Peter?*

It didn't help that there was no response.

Ron shook his head in frustration. On the phone he had broached the possibility that Peter might be retarded or mute, but Father McCormick had quickly refuted that suggestion, insisting that Peter had all his faculties in place and functioned just as well as the next guy.

"Could I have a private moment with him?" Father McCormick asked. He figured if Peter was scared, then perhaps being alone with him, one on one, would make a difference.

Ron furrowed his brow. "It might be safer if the guard stays in here with you."

"I assure you detective, I am in no danger."

"Suit yourself," Ron said. He paused and looked at his watch. "How about ten minutes?"

He reached up to the audiovisual recorder and switched it on. Then he walked out, pausing to look back through the small glass pane at the unusual scene behind him: an aging blind priest, a seeing-eye dog, and an alleged—seemingly retarded—killer. "Keep an eye on them," he instructed the guard.

Father McCormick waited to hear the click of the door before moving his seat closer to Peter. Samson too seemed ready to make her move. She sat up promptly and wagged her tail enthusiastically. Tentatively, she hunkered over to Peter and nudged him with her nose. After a minute of no reciprocation, she gave up, returned to Father McCormick's side, and lay down with a sigh.

"Peter, my boy, this must all be so frightening…"

*No answer.*

"Peter, I'm here for you..." Father McCormick said slowly. "I want to help."

"Ahhhhhhhhhhhhh! The moan from Peter's mouth came just as the steady hum of air shut off with a low groan, giving it an animal-like quality. Then Peter began thrashing his head back and forth in his hands. It was as though he was consumed by despair, but totally disconnected from reality.

Father McCormick's heart skipped a beat. "Peter!" he snapped, taking care to keep his voice low. He didn't want to attract the guard's attention.

"Ahhhhhhhhhhhhhhhh!"

Peter began flailing his limbs around, stopping only when he fell with a thud from his chair on to the floor.

Father McCormick stood up and made the sign of the cross. He reached down, and touching the crown of Peter's head, recited a quiet prayer to Saint Benedict Joseph Labre, the patron saint of mental illness. Instantly Peter quieted. Willing himself to see past the general shadows before him, Father McCormick wondered: was Peter on drugs? Was he drinking again? Could the tests have missed something?

"Peter?"

But even if he were on drugs, he would be able to speak, to say *something*.

The guard poked his head in. His brow furrowed as he glanced at Peter sitting motionless on the floor. "Everything okay in here, Father?"

"Yes... fine. I need just another minute or two."

"I'll be right here if you need me," the guard said, pulling the door closed.

Father McCormick sat back down.

"I hate you! I hate you!... I'll kill you!"

The words came out of nowhere and startled the priest. He had never known Peter to use threatening language. Samson sat up and started whimpering.

"Peter…"

Peter jumped up, unclenched his fists, and lunged toward Father McCormick. "I'll kill you… I'll kill you…!"

Instantly the guard bounded through the door and intercepted Peter, shoving him off course. Peter screamed in agony as the guard yanked his arms behind his back, twisting his already injured wrist.

Ron appeared in the doorway seconds later. "That's enough one on one time, Father, don't you think?" he said breathlessly.

But Father McCormick was too shocked to respond. He reached into his pocket for his rosary beads. "*Hail Mary, Mother of Mercy… Hail Mary Mother of Mercy…*" The severity of Peter's situation was now shockingly clear. Not only was Peter being held for murder, but his behavior was irrational, his speech unintelligible. Father McCormick thought again of the question he couldn't answer: *what was Peter doing at the crime scene?* Suddenly an even larger issue came to mind: If Peter *himself* couldn't tell them what he was doing there that night, then how could he—how could any of them—offer a credible defense? Father McCormick rubbed his temples. He couldn't fathom what business Peter would have at a Jewish mikvah. Actually, as far as he knew, Peter hadn't even *known* it was a mikvah! Or what a mikvah was for that matter!

Maybe Father McCormick *had* been duped. Maybe Peter *had* played a part in this terrible, terrible crime. But how was that possible? Peter wasn't a killer! Or *was* he? Father McCormick's head was spinning; he didn't know *what* to think anymore. The only thing he knew for certain was that he couldn't turn his back, couldn't look the other way. The fact was, Peter—or whoever he really was—had no one. There were no lifelong friends; there was no family upstate. Peter was completely and utterly alone. Father McCormick understood what was at stake. A man's life was on the line. It was up to him to save Peter, or at the very least, discover the truth.

# Thirty-one

Judith marched into the kitchen and tossed her keys on the counter. "My granddaughter tells me we're having guests tonight," she said in Lauren's general direction. She plopped down at the table without bothering to remove her coat. "So, tell me... who's coming?"

Lauren sighed. *Hello to you too Mrs. Orenstein.* "The Henners," she said, forcing a polite smile. "Have you met them?"

It was an innocent enough question, but still one that yielded the slightest prick, like a paper cut. Judith didn't visit frequently, so Lauren probably assumed she didn't know many of the local families.

"As a matter of fact, I have," Judith said, smoothing her wool slacks. Then she looked up, unhappy at the sight of Lauren's apron. It was Hannah's of course—rainbow colored with deep pockets. "Elise and Evan have three children... such a lovely family!" She smiled smugly at Lauren. *There!*

"Elise's father, Lewis Danzig is also coming," Lauren said, taking no notice. "He just returned from overseas. Something to do with the military, I think."

*Damn.*

"I wouldn't know anything about that," Judith said, studying her fingernails. "Because I haven't had the pleasure of meeting him yet," she added.

But Lauren didn't seem to care either way.

"Whose idea was it to have guests anyway?" Judith asked. The question was posed in a neutral tone, but Lauren didn't want to take any chances. It seemed Judith was so darn critical of everything she did lately, why set herself up?

"I don't know," Lauren said, looking away. The truth was that it *had* been her idea—part of a larger suggestion she made to Yehuda a few days ago. She was no expert, she told him, but wasn't it important that the kids maintain as much of a regular routine as possible? Before Hannah's hospitalization, Lauren couldn't recall one Shabbat that went by without the family having guests at their table. If he ever decided to resume that weekly ritual, she assured Yehuda, she was more than willing to take care of all the necessary preparations.

Judith closed her eyes and leaned back. "What an exhausting day. I could really use a cup of coffee."

Lauren took this as her cue to put the kettle on. She pulled a jar of *Folgers* from the cabinet.

"Oh... don't tell me there's only instant," Judith moaned.

"Sorry, that's all we have."

"Well that just won't do..."

Lauren just shrugged and turned off the kettle. *Whatever.*

"Would you be a dear and run out to *Starbucks* for me?" Judith asked. Without missing a beat, she stood up and pulled off her coat, making it clear *she* wasn't the one going. "Oh and maybe you could hang this up on your way out."

Lauren took the coat in disbelief. The woman actually expected her to drop everything and drive to Starbucks? For God's sake, she was in the middle of cooking tonight's dinner! The chicken was roasting in the oven; the soup was simmering on the stove, not to mention the five-pound bag of potatoes needing to be peeled, and the colander of vegetables draining in the sink waiting to be chopped.

"The chicken still has another fifteen minutes," Lauren said.

"If you hurry, you'll be back by then," Judith said, grimacing. "And if you're not, I'd be happy to take it out for you."

*Gee thanks.* "Great," Lauren muttered. She slipped the apron over her head and smiled faintly. "I'll be right back."

"Cream, no sugar," Judith called after her.

Five minutes later Lauren returned to the kitchen to find Judith standing at the sink. The colander full of vegetables was on the counter and she was chomping mindlessly on some raw broccoli.

"That was fast," Judith said, before noticing Lauren's empty hands.

"I didn't go," Lauren said. "My car wouldn't start."

Judith sighed dramatically. "Well, I suppose I could go myself..." She tapped her fingers rhythmically on the counter. "Oh, why bother? Instant's not so terrible, is it?" She crossed the kitchen to retrieve a mug for herself. Glaring into the cabinet, she asked, "What in the world are these plates doing here?" She turned and stared accusingly at Lauren. "This is where Hannah keeps the coffee cups!"

"Oh, I just... I rearranged a few things," Lauren said, biting her lip.

Judith marched from cabinet to cabinet, opening and slamming doors. Cans of soup filled the space where the meat plates had been. Both the meat and dairy dishes were now stacked on the far side of the kitchen, closer to the table, formerly home to the Tupperware and paper products. With some effort, Judith finally located the mugs in a short cabinet above the sink. "And where, pray tell, are the dairy spoons?" she demanded, staring blankly into an empty drawer where they should have been.

"Over here," Lauren said, waving a spoon like it was a flag of surrender.

Judith shook her head and mumbled something under her breath. The room became uncomfortably silent for a few minutes. Even the soup seemed to have stopped simmering.

"So, uh, is there enough closet space in your room?" Lauren burst out suddenly. She was eager to break the silence.

Judith had a look of total disgust on her face. "Closet space? What are you talking about?"

"In your room—the guest room," Lauren clarified. "I guess you haven't been upstairs yet... so, uh, when you do... take a look and let me know."

Judith grabbed a carrot from the colander and started munching, still confused, as Lauren continued.

"I moved most of my clothes into Rachel's room," she said, "but I did leave a few items hanging in the guest room closet."

"You stayed over last night?" Judith asked, still trying to figure out what Lauren was talking about.

Lauren crinkled her forehead. "Well, yes..."

"I hope you changed the sheets," Judith said.

Lauren felt like she had been punched in the stomach. The kettle whistled and she turned to pour the hot water.

Judith shrugged. "I assume your cat sleeps with you, that's all."

"Oh, they're changed," Lauren said. *Don't worry you can't catch what I have.*

"I'm sure it's fun for the children... having overnight guests," Judith continued as she grabbed the cream from the refrigerator. "Of course, no overnight guest could possibly replace their *mother*." She took a seat at the table. "So how often exactly do you stay overnight?" Judith asked as Lauren set down her cup of coffee, "here in my son's house?"

Lauren stepped away from the table. "Wait," she said, holding up a hand.

Judith daintily spooned sugar into her cup. "Something the matter?" she asked nonchalantly.

Lauren shook her head. "I'm sorry… it's just that I thought you knew."

"Knew what?"

"About the move."

"What move?"

Lauren touched a finger to her chest. "Mine."

"What in the world are you talking about Lauren?" Judith demanded. She was losing patience.

"I moved in three days ago," Lauren said in one breath.

Judith looked stricken, as though she'd been shot. "Moved in? *Why?*" She straightened up and cleared her throat. "I thought my son had plenty of help from the community," she said, folding her arms. "I *did* see Janine's spreadsheet after all."

Lauren slipped on a pair of rubber gloves at the sink. "Yeah, well, Janine did a great job organizing the volunteers, especially getting so many women from Hannah's classes to pitch in."

"Then what was the problem?" Judith stammered. She watched as Lauren reached under the sink for the dish soap. Apparently this was the one item the girl hadn't relocated.

"The problem was having different people in the house all the time! It was stressing the kids out."

"Really?" Judith looked and sounded doubtful. "How can you say that? The volunteers were from the community, friends of the family, students of The Jewish Learning Center! There weren't any strangers in this house!"

Lauren began scrubbing a broiling pan, avoiding Judith's eyes. She couldn't very well say what was on her mind, and—though he hadn't said so outright—what she believed to be on Yehuda's as well. *Some of the volunteers weren't the best influence on the children.* "I don't want to sound disrespectful Mrs. Orenstein, but I think Yehuda and I have a good idea what the kids need."

Judith couldn't believe her ears. Did Lauren just use the phrase *Yehuda and I?* She laughed mockingly. "Well, Lauren, it goes without saying that *my son* would know what his children need. But *you*? How could you possibly have a clue? You're not their mother."

"I know that," Lauren said softly.

"Do you?" Judith demanded. She threw her arms out as if to point out the changes in the kitchen. "Then stop acting like you are!"

Lauren felt her face flush and her pulse quicken. How could Judith spew insults out so casually? After all she had done—was doing—for her family! If the woman had any decency, she would have taken a leave from that all-important job of hers to look after them herself. Lauren couldn't believe this was Yehuda's mother! So much for "the apple doesn't fall far from the tree"! As far as Lauren could tell, Yehuda had fallen to a completely different *orchard*! Maybe the best thing to do was to respond to Judith in her own language—assertive bordering on bitchy. Lauren shut off the water with a thud and looked up.

"With all due respect Mrs. Orenstein," Lauren said firmly, "I've spent more time with your grandkids this past year than you have during their entire lives."

Judith's eyes widened. "And what the hell is that supposed to mean?" she retorted, hands on her hips.

Lauren sighed. "Look, Mrs. Orenstein… I'm sorry. I know that sounded harsh… it's just that I think I'm a better judge of their emotional states right now."

"Oh, is that so?" Judith said, obviously still angry.

Lauren had no choice but to spell it out for her. She removed her rubber gloves, placed them on the counter, and took a deep breath. "Let me ask you something: By any chance did you know that Yitzi's been having accidents?"

Judith stared at her like she had a few screws loose. "What on earth are you talking about? He's been potty trained for over six months!"

"Yes, well he *was* potty trained, but now he's having accidents."

Judith narrowed her eyes and was about to say something when Lauren cut her off. "And Eli… did you know Eli has night terrors?"

Judith looked down at her hands but didn't say anything as Lauren continued. "He wakes up, almost every night drenched in sweat."

At that point, Judith looked up and shook her head. "No. You're wrong! I've been here every single weekend and not once have I heard him…"

"Could that be because either Yehuda or I have gotten to him before you woke up?" Lauren suggested gently.

Judith stood up and moved to the window, her back to Lauren, she hugged herself tightly. She wasn't sure if it was anger or shame that she felt, but whichever it was, it was humiliating. And to hear all of this from a complete stranger! She would not let Lauren get to her. She would not show vulnerability.

"And then there's David," Lauren continued. She had purposely saved this one for last, but seeing that Judith was already getting the point, softened her voice. "David worries himself sick about getting your approval."

Judith swung around and pointed at herself in disbelief. "*My* approval?"

Lauren nodded. "Yes! Don't you see it? He thinks you hate him!"

Judith stared at Lauren accusingly. "And where would he get a crazy idea like that?"

"He says you think he's a baby because he can't tie his own shoes."

"But why? Why would he think…" But suddenly she remembered. The comment she had made to him about needing help with his shoes—something about Nehama learning to tie hers before he could do his. But it was meant as a *joke*.

Judith placed both elbows on the table and rested her head against her open palms. How foolish she had been! David was exactly like Yehuda was as a young boy—extremely sensitive. She should have known better! Known that he would take her comment to heart! What could she do to make it up to him? She would apologize and make sure to never make that same mistake again. Sadly, it was all she could do. She was powerless to change the past.

"The well-being of the children is the reason Yehuda suggested that I move in," Lauren said, pulling Judith back from her private thoughts.

Judith swallowed. *Yehuda suggested it?* "But… But what about your classes?" she stammered.

"I took a leave of absence from school," Lauren said, "to help Yehuda."

Judith stood up fast, scraping the bottom of her chair against the floor. "Do you think that's wise for your future?" she asked, changing her tactic to one of concern.

"We can't always put our own interests first," Lauren said pointedly. "The fact is the kids need someone they can lean on—someone who's here for them everyday, someone who can provide more stability."

*But how could a non-family member provide stability?* Judith wondered. Wasn't she—the blood relative—the better candidate?

"Nana! Your phone's ringing!" a boy's voice boomed from the living room.

Judith glanced at her watch, happy for the interruption. "Thank you Eli," she called. Without saying a word to Lauren she hurried from the kitchen to retrieve her purse from the hall closet.

"Hello, Judith Orenstein speaking... Yes, that's right. He agreed to joint custody... No that's not correct... he keeps the 401K and everything else is a 50/50 split...What? Are you kidding me? That bast..." Her gaze fell upon Eli who was watching her over his book, an alarmed look on his face. For a second she had forgotten where she was, she had entered the all-familiar work zone, the one that had protected her and nourished her for so many years. Looking at her sweet grandson, Judith wondered if she had it in her to put her job on hold. She, a woman who could barely survive a three-day weekend away from the office... Would she willingly place her own interests on the back burner?

*Maybe she wasn't the better candidate.*

"Uh, Marla, I apologize, but I can't talk now. I'm in the middle of something that demands my full attention. Can I call you later?"

Judith shoved her phone back into her purse.

"Nana!" Eli said, "you *can't* call her back later!"

"Oh? Why is that, Eli?"

He grinned slyly, certain that she must be making a joke. "Because it'll be Shabbat! You can't talk on the phone when it's Shabbat! You're being silly, Nana!"

Judith smiled and slapped her cheeks. "Oh my! You're right, Eli! Silly me! Silly, silly Nana!"

# Thirty-two

Yehuda's face lit up as he scanned the dining room.

"Lauren," he began, "when you said you would take care of everything, I never imagined this…" He took a deep breath. "Thank you."

Lauren returned his smile then touched Rachel on the shoulder. "I couldn't have done it without Rachel's help."

Rachel flinched.

"You did a beautiful job, sweetheart," Yehuda said, squatting down to give her a hug.

Judith, who stood unnoticed in the doorway had to agree that the table looked beautiful. It was set with the family's best linens, bone china and stemware. A festive bouquet of Gerber daisies in yellows and reds stood at the center of the table, flanked on either side by tapered blue candles.

Judith's gaze moved past the table to Yehuda. Fortunately, in the past week his appetite had returned and he no longer needed to wear the suspenders she had given him. And today his face seemed to have much more color. Just then, Judith did a double take. She would have sworn she saw him wink at Lauren as she repositioned a wine glass. Surely Lauren couldn't have something to do with him feeling and looking better, could she?

Yitzi ran in and giggled as Yehuda hoisted him up. "I know one little boy who's excited about having guests tonight!"

Rachel smiled up at the two of them and nodded. "Mommy always says it isn't Shabbat without guests."

"And it isn't Shabbat if we're not joyful—isn't that right Yitzi?"

"Shabbat is a happy time, Abba!" Yitzi said, wrapping his arms around Yehuda's neck.

Yehuda pulled his son closer and blinked away some wetness. He was ashamed of his behavior these last few weeks. When he wasn't at Hannah's bedside, he was either walking sullenly around the house as if in mourning, or at the center doing what his mother had always done—burying himself in work. This all would have been fine if five kids weren't looking to him for guidance, counting on him to keep things sane. Thank God Lauren had brought him to his senses. It was agreed; the children had suffered enough; they didn't need their father falling off the deep end too. Lauren had made him look at the facts—Yitzi's accidents, Eli's night terrors, David's depression—What choice was there? He needed to get a grip and pull himself together. *Fast.* Lauren moving in was a big step in the right direction. A shift in his own attitude was another. Lauren was right. Having guests on Shabbat would be good for everyone; it would *normalize* things. As far as all the other days of the week went, he had to remain strong! It was up to him to keep everyone's spirits up, even if it meant hiding his own fears.

Standing in the shadows, Judith was starting to feel like a voyeur, and after the earlier conversation she had with Lauren, like an outsider too. Avoiding Lauren's eyes, she willed herself to enter the dining room anyway, and was relieved when Yitzi immediately ran to her, a huge smile plastered on his face.

*Was Lauren right? Did she really not know this child?*

Yitzi giggled but after a minute, released himself from her grip so he could look up at her face. "I like having Shabbat with you, Nana. Will you always come? Please?"

Judith took a deep breath. "I like having Shabbat with you too, sweetheart," she said, "and all your brothers and sisters… and of course your Abba…"

Yehuda jumped in. "Sometimes Nana is busy in New York," he told Yitzi, gently. "But we know she loves us very much and visits whenever she can."

# Thirty-three

It was after ten when Lauren took Nehama up to her crib. The baby had drifted off in her bouncy seat during the fish course, and had managed to sleep through the entire two-hour dinner, despite all of the loud talking and fork clanging.

In the kitchen, Judith stood in front of the sink fanning herself with a paper plate. The counters were loaded with dirty dishes and serving platters of leftover food. She had warned Lauren that she was preparing too much, but the girl just wouldn't listen. And now Judith would have to find room for even *more* Tupperware containers in the already stuffed refrigerator.

"Are you all right, Mom?" Yehuda asked.

"I guess after spending all day in the kitchen, I'm a bit overheated," Judith told him. Ten years earlier, she would have assumed it was a menopausal hot flash, but, never much of a drinker, she knew tonight the culprit was the three glasses of red wine she'd put away during dinner. Her attempt at drowning her sorrows, possibly. Trying to numb the menagerie of emotions that had overtaken her—anger, annoyance, and guilt. How could Yehuda have allowed Lauren to move in? Didn't he see that she was carrying on like a surrogate wife and mother? Complicating matters was the guilt Lauren had somehow evoked in her. According to Lauren, Judith didn't know her grandchildren, didn't spend enough time with them, had *never* spent enough time with them.

*Will you always come Nana?*

How could she explain to a three year old that despite the horrible tragedy that had befallen the family, the answer was still "no"?

*Sorry Yitzi, Nana has to work.*

It sounded so selfish, even as a thought form. But honestly, who could blame her? If only they understood that reinventing herself twenty-five years earlier had been her *salvation*, a life raft in rough seas. Thanks to her brains and pure gumption, she was no longer the passive woman her husband had walked out on. That pathetic persona had been tossed aside, like an old pair of socks. But she had no regrets. What she *did* have was a million dollar apartment on the upper east side and a client register that read like a Hollywood party list. It was her work—advocating for others—that made Judith who she was. It was the work that kept her *sane*. God only knew what would happen if she slowed down.

Now she felt drowsy and warm, and definitely resenting Lauren's decision to use china instead of paper plates.

"Where would you like this?" Lewis Danzig asked as he walked in with a platter of chicken. Lewis was tall and distinguished looking with a head of thick white hair. He was neatly dressed in blue slacks and a sweater vest. He had been seated directly across from Judith at dinner, but other than polite introductions, the two were unable to speak to one another. When Judith wasn't serving and Lewis wasn't either eating or bouncing one of his grandchildren on his knee, he was engrossed in a quiet conversation with Yehuda.

"Thank you Dr. Danzig, I'll take that," Yehuda said, extending his hand.

Lewis turned to Judith. "I want to thank you for a lovely dinner, Judith. Everything was delicious! Especially the chicken. What a flavorful sauce!" His eyes smiled as he spoke, the wrinkles around them conveying a mixture of warmth and sincerity.

Judith did a quick visual scan for Lauren who was apparently still upstairs with the baby. "You're very welcome. I'm glad you enjoyed it." Then she lowered her voice. "Old family recipe," she whispered.

"I was thinking about getting some fresh air if you'd care to join me," Lewis said.

Judith's heart did a little jump, but she looked around at the mess. "I better not."

"Oh, I'd be more than happy to take care of all this for you, Mrs. Orenstein; the baby's sound asleep," Lauren said, popping in out of nowhere.

Judith noticed Yehuda smiling at her appreciatively, like she just had everything under control, didn't she? "But I told you I would clean up."

Lauren waved her away. "Really, it's not a problem. Besides, it'll be quicker for me."

*Quicker only because you rearranged my daughter-in-law's entire kitchen.*

Judith gestured toward the crowded countertops. "But if you're taking care of this, then you'll need my help with the boys," she said.

Yehuda shook his head. "David and Eli are fine. They're busy playing *Sorry* with Elise's sons."

"Where's Rachel?" Judith asked.

"In her room with Becca," Lauren said. "I just checked."

"Yitzi?"

Yehuda scratched his head. "Yitzi's fast asleep on the couch. He just needs to be carried up to bed."

"I'll make sure he has an extra blanket," Lauren added quickly. It was a thoughtful statement, but nonetheless, irritated Judith.

"Well, I... "

"Mom! Go! We're all fine... Lauren's got everything under control!"

Judith yanked off her rubber gloves and plopped them down next to the sink. "Well then, seeing that my help is no longer needed here, I guess some fresh air *would* be nice." She pulled the apron over her head and caught the amused expression on Lewis Danzig's face. She turned on her heel. "Just let me get my coat."


Judith felt invigorated almost immediately after stepping outside. The dry cool air was just what she needed to counteract the dulling effects of the wine. She and Lewis started along the sidewalk, crunching hard bits of snow under their feet. An occasional flurry fell.

"Last I heard, it was still coming down pretty hard in Boston," Lewis said, looking up at the sky. "I'll probably have a foot of snow to shovel when I get home on Sunday."

"Correction," Judith said. "The person you *hire* will have a foot of snow to shovel."

Lewis laughed. "Hire someone? To *shovel*? No, I've always done it myself."

"You're kidding."

"Not at all. Does that surprise you?"

"Well, don't you have better things to do with your time?"

"Better things?"

"Of course you do!" Judith said, more than a hint of agitation in her voice. "You have a medical degree for heaven's sake!"

"What does a medical degree have to do with shoveling?"

*Why does he keep answering my questions with questions?* "Plenty," she snapped. "Your time is worth ten times what the cost of *hiring* someone to shovel is!"

"It's not about the money, Judith; You may find this hard to believe, but I actually enjoy the process." Lewis was more amused than offended by the rabbi's mother, which is probably why he winked before adding, "In fact, I rake and bag my own leaves too."

Judith rolled her eyes and arched her back. "Ugh. I'm in pain just thinking about it."

He smiled at her, again with that amused expression. "Fortunately I don't have back problems. I lift weights three times a week with a trainer. Keeps the bones strong."

Admittedly, Lewis's attractiveness had not been overlooked by Judith. His white hair gave him an air of wisdom and maturity, but he didn't have the mid-section paunch or sallow skin of most men his age. Suddenly she was self conscious, wondering how she appeared to him. Must be the wine she told herself, shooing away such silliness. Still, she wished she had taken a minute to freshen up before leaving the house.

"Well, if you work out, then you certainly don't need the exercise," she said dryly.

"I still don't understand why you find it strange that I enjoy tending to my property," Lewis said. "I love being outside, and in my line of work, I don't get outdoors half as much as I'd like. Besides, it's a great way to see my neighbors and do some catching up."

"Why not just throw a party?" she mumbled under her breath.

"Pardon me? I didn't hear you…"

"Oh, nothing. Forget it."

Lewis surmised that Judith's agitation was due to recent events. "Are you sure you're up to this walk Judith?" he asked, stopping in his tracks. "If you prefer, we can…"

"I wouldn't have come if I wasn't up to it, Dr. Danzig."

"*Lewis*. Please call me Lewis," he corrected her.

She lowered her voice. "I may be old *Lewis*, but I can still manage a walk around the block."

*Who said anything about being old?* Lewis didn't risk a response. He said nothing and avoided her eyes as they continued along in silence, an adult version of a time out.

Judith finally broke the silence after two minutes. "So… you live in Boston?" she asked in a much softer tone.

He nodded. "Brookline actually. I've spent my whole life there."

"Then I guess you're used to all the religious fanaticism," Judith said.

"I take it you know about Brookline's large religious community," Lewis said, laughing. "As a matter of fact, my grandparents were orthodox. Some of my most vivid childhood memories are of sitting around my Bubbe's enormous dining room table. We went every Friday night." He shook his head, laughing. "Boy, could she pile on those helpings! Between the liverwurst, the schmaltz and the fried kreplach, I don't know how she and my Zeide managed to live as long as they did!"

"And your parents? They're religious too?" Judith asked.

"Well, now that's an interesting story. Mother kept a kosher home at first, then it became kosher *style*; then we started having meat and milk together… It was so gradual, none of us kids really noticed until one day when the rabbi's kid came over for lunch and mother served cream of tomato soup and BLT's!"

Judith's hand flew over her mouth. "She didn't!"

Lewis nodded and raised his eyebrows. He was intrigued by Judith's momentary change in demeanor. She looked younger—free— as though the weight of the world had been lifted off her.

"You must have been positively mortified!" she said, laughing.

He smiled and scratched his head. "That's what you would think, but oddly I *wasn't*. I remember being more interested in how exactly the rabbi's kid would react to being served *traif* and then watching my mother run around the kitchen making substitutions once she realized her mistake." He tapped his forehead. "That's when it occurred to me that I might like studying human behavior as a *profession*."

A few more blocks and they came to an intersection where Judith suggested they turn right and head toward the park. They reached the end of Briar street; *White Rabbit Park* was nestled behind a hedge of boxwoods. More of a miniature playground than a park, *White Rabbit* had been designed for babies and toddlers. Lewis bent down and picked up what looked like a thick piece of black mulch poking out of the snow. "They're rubber chips—for safety," Judith said. "Yitzi plays here," she added, in case he wondered how she knew. She didn't mention that in her grandson's three years of life, she had accompanied him a grand total of five times.

*Will you always come Nana?*

The chips covered the entire play area: three bucket swings, a set of horses on spring coils, and a yellow bridge with a short winding slide.

Lewis led Judith to a bench at the far end of the park. Carved out of a tree trunk and set low to the ground, it was a perfect height if you were a two-foot toddler. Lewis brushed off a thin layer of snow with his glove before Judith sat down with a thud, misjudging just how low it was. The bench felt cold against the back of her thighs, causing a reflexive spasm along her spine. She shivered and inched forward toward the edge.

"I should have worn my long coat," she mumbled, bending over to hug her knees.

"Here take mine," Lewis said immediately. He tapped the excess snow off his glove, then stood up and began removing his camel overcoat.

Judith held up her hand. "No—I'm fine."

He ignored her. "Judith, I insist. You'll be more comfortable."

"I prefer my own, thank you."

"But you're shivering!"

"I said I was fine!" She emphasized each word as if reprimanding a child.

Perplexed, Lewis buttoned up his coat and sat down. "Suit yourself."

"I hope you don't mind, I have to make a call," Judith said, whipping out her cell phone. She hit the send button and had the phone up against her ear before he could answer.

"Go right ahead," Lewis mumbled. He stood up and walked away from her, in the direction of the play equipment. *She probably needs another time out,* he thought.

"…Hello, Marla? It's me… Now about the 401K… What? You're kidding me! That sneaky son of a bitch! What the hell's he doing playing with those accounts? That money's earmarked for the kids' private schools!" Judith jumped up and started pacing fervently in front of the bench.

Across the park, Lewis sat on the landing of the slide. At just under six feet in height, he looked uncomfortable, and like he might have difficulty getting himself upright again. He tucked his hands inside his pockets and sat quietly, his eyes fixed on Judith as she paced and ranted. He couldn't help but wonder how little Yitzi felt about coming to the park with his Nana, only to be ignored while she made business calls.

After a few minutes, Judith shoved her cell phone into her jacket pocket and looked in his direction. Lewis met her gaze but said nothing.

"Sorry about that," she shouted over to him, and then shrugged. "You know how it is... since it's..."—she made air quotes with her fingers—"*Shabbat*... I can't call from the house."

Lewis held up a hand. "No need to explain," he said. It occurred to him that someone like Judith would actually benefit from some of the *down time* Shabbat offered.

"Listen, about the coat..." Judith said, "it was nice of you to offer. I mean, it's refreshing to see a man who... well... I apologize if I sounded rude..."

Lewis hoisted himself up from the slide with surprising ease and walked toward her. "Something funny? I love a good joke," Judith said.

Lewis didn't realize he had been smiling. He shook his head. "No jokes."

"Then what?"

Lewis paused to gather his thoughts. "Well, tonight at dinner, your son gave a *dvar Torah* and spoke about blessings. How we all take so much for granted because our human nature is to focus on what's missing rather than what we have. So I was just thinking about my own blessings, the things I'm grateful for—my daughter, my grandchildren, good health—and right now Judith, I feel blessed to be here, honored to share this beautiful night with you."

Judith swallowed and looked away, flustered. "Well, yes, it is a beautiful night to be out," she said, jumping to her feet, wrapping her arms around herself, and looking up. "The sky is so clear..."

"Yes it is."

"But nothing like the sky in New Mexico," she said in one breath.

This comment surprised him, but he knew enough to wait and see where she went with it.

Judith kept her gaze fixed upward as she spoke. "I spent a lot of time there you know, back when I was young…"

"I see."

"My husband and I lived on a commune right outside of Santa Fe."

*Santa Fe and marriage.* Lewis now understood. What had hurt Judith in the past, now protected her in the present. Judith Orenstein had done something not uncommon; she had used her pain to build a wall to keep others from getting too close.

"A commune?" Lewis repeated. "*You?*"

"Don't be so shocked. At nineteen, I was eager to pave my own path."

Lewis smiled. "You were a typical teenager."

She shrugged. "Of course 'my own path' merely meant doing the complete opposite of whatever my parents were doing. Actually, it was more what they *weren't* doing… I was much more interested in exploring my inner self."

Lewis raised his eyebrows.

"*Beyond* drug experimentation," she added, having a fairly good idea what he was thinking.

"So you meditated and practiced yoga."

"That's right, how did you know?"

"Just a wild guess," Lewis said. "Yoga's made quite a comeback, hasn't it? Elise has taken a couple of classes."

"Yoga indoors does not compare!" Judith said, laughing. "No, not when you've experienced a *downward dog* with the Sangre de Cristo mountains as your backdrop." She took a deep breath. "The communion with nature—hiking, gardening... well, it was all wonderful, but a lifetime ago."

"You realize you can still do those things," Lewis said.

She shooed him with her hand. "Nonsense. I don't have the time."

He didn't feel like arguing. "I'm curious about something," he said instead. "How does a flower child go from living on a commune to raising an orthodox son?"

"Easy," Judith said. "The flower child gets divorced." She closed her eyes for a moment before continuing. "After my marriage ended, I moved back in with my parents and sent Yehuda to Jewish Day school."

"Oh, so *your* parents were religious?"

Judith shook her head. "Not quite. While I was growing up, we had an occasional Friday night dinner, but that was it." She paused. "Well, it was until my son talked them into *kashering* their kitchen."

"It was considerate of your parents to be so accommodating to Yehuda," Lewis said.

"His name was *Ira* back then, and even at fifteen he could be pretty persuasive," Judith said. "Besides, deep down, my father had a strong Jewish identity, even if his only *rituals* were eating bran cereal for breakfast and watching *Jeopardy* after dinner."

Lewis laughed. "There's nothing better than a good round of Jeopardy! In all seriousness though, routines are a comfort to people—they lend a sense of order to our lives. That's the reason we sit in the same seats, eat the same foods and why most people, even disorganized ones, have at least some semblance of structure to their day. That was probably one of things that attracted your son to orthodoxy—the structure."

Judith shrugged. "It's possible," she said. "After his father and I divorced, his whole world was turned upside down. We moved out of state, the kids met their grandparents for the first time, were enrolled in new schools." She leaned back, remembering. "Before the divorce, Yehuda was such a happy, carefree kid—but after, he became serious and introspective. He began having nightmares and worried constantly that something would happen to me, like I would get lost and never find my way home."

Lewis nodded. "Well, it isn't unusual for some individuals—even young children—to develop irrational fears after experiencing a loss. May I ask how old was he when you divorced?"

"Eleven," Judith said. "But at the time, I didn't consider it a *loss*, just a *change*."

"We didn't know then that divorce often has the same effect as death, especially if there is a lack of amicability between divorcing spouses," Lewis said.

"Oh we were amicable," Judith said, sarcastically. "My ex didn't give me a penny, but he *did* graciously hand over full custody of our two children! He made it crystal clear he had no interest in seeing me, or them again—something about us *smothering* him. Ha! What a joke!"

Lewis didn't respond.

"It's just that if you knew me back then," Judith explained, "you would realize I was pretty passive—certainly not the smothering type."

"I see," Lewis said. He suddenly understood the inspiration behind Judith's aggressiveness. She was compensating for a skewed self-perception. "Your kids really haven't seen their father since the divorce?" he asked.

Judith shook her head. "No."

Lewis shifted toward her on the bench. "What a major blow for them," he said, shaking his head, "not just the dissolution of the family unit, but a complete rejection by a parent!" He looked at her sympathetically. "That must have been a very difficult time for them, as well as for you, Judith."

"We got through it," she said quickly.

"Well, knowing his background, it doesn't surprise me that Yehuda took to religion the way he did," Lewis continued. "The rituals probably saved his sanity. Did you notice a decrease in his anxiety levels as he became more religious minded?"

Judith raised her eyebrows, surprised. She had never made that connection before, but Lewis was right. Yehuda *had* become happier and more relaxed as his interest in Judaism increased.

"Religion gives us stability—a sense of control over our lives," Lewis said.

*Or maybe a false sense of security,* Judith thought to herself, though she was impressed with Lewis's bulls eye evaluation of Yehuda. "Do you see a lot of that in your practice?" she asked.

"Ritualistic behavior in response to stress?" He nodded. "Oh, yes, I certainly do; and lately there's been a surge in the number of children I see."

"So it's pretty common phenomena then?"

"Yes, but too often misdiagnosed."

"How so?" Judith asked.

"To their parents and teachers—even trained counselors—these kids may look like they have attention deficit or obsessive compulsive disorders, but what the adults fail to consider is the *timing*. ADD and OCD don't just *coincidentally* appear after a parent walks out!"

Judith considered how many of her clients' children were on Ritalin or other mind-altering drugs. In her estimate, it was well above fifty percent.

"So those kids aren't getting the right help?" she asked.

Lewis shook his head. "Not if they're being medicated for something that has a situational rather than organic basis," he said. "Drugs have their place, don't get me wrong; I just think we're too quick to Band-Aid a problem, rather than heal it at its source. And this doesn't just apply when it comes to children, Judith. I've had more than a few seriously depressed adults come to me asking for Prozac or Effoxor. But once we talk a little, delve into some personal history, we're usually able to root out early disturbances that were never dealt with. Often times patients have a hard time believing it themselves—especially when they report that others were amazed at their ability to cope so well during the crisis itself."

"So you're saying that somehow they kept it together as young children, but then fell apart as adults?" Judith asked. "Sorry, but it sounds kind of backwards."

"Children cope to the best of their ability with what limited resources they have," Lewis said. "For those who appear to be the most resilient, it can take years before symptoms manifest."

"You're talking about kids whose parents have divorced?" Judith asked.

"Not just with divorce, but a whole range of traumas."

"But then aren't the symptoms—when they *do* manifest—simply appearing out of the blue? I thought you said that didn't happen."

"I guess I wasn't clear," Lewis said. "The subconscious mind is extremely powerful. Often times, it's main objective is survival—protection from situations that may be too much to deal with. When there are no effects immediately following the disturbance, it means emotions are being suppressed—tucked away and dormant in the subconscious mind— waiting for the right time and the right *trigger* before they manifest."

"What kind of *trigger*?"

Lewis thought for a moment. "Well, for example, I had one patient who one day out of the blue began compulsively cleaning."

"And this had to do with some tragedy from her past?" Judith asked skeptically.

Lewis nodded. "Her daughter was entering the 2nd grade when the compulsive cleaning began," he said. "I actually had to use hypnosis on her before she remembered that she herself had been in the 2nd grade when a favorite cousin was killed in a boating accident."

"It sounds impressive," Judith agreed. "But how can you be sure the two incidents are linked?"

"Good question," Lewis said, "The answer is that once the root trauma is exposed, the symptoms usually vanish pretty quickly."

"So in that patient's case, you're telling me the compulsive cleaning stopped?"

Lewis nodded. "Within days."

Judith rubbed her mitted hands together. "This may be unrelated to what you're talking about," she said, "but I had a strange thing happen to *me* once."

Lewis listened attentively as Judith continued.

"Years ago, while I was still married, I developed a rash on my finger—right under my wedding band," she said. "It got so bad I had to take my ring off. A friend suggested I was reacting to the gold, but that wasn't it."

"What was it then?" Lewis asked, although he already had a fairly good idea.

She looked away. "My husband was cheating on me."

"Ah, the power of the mind-body connection!" he said, trying to regain eye contact with her. "On a subconscious level you must have sensed the affair, Judith."

She shrugged, but still avoided his eyes. "I suppose there was a part of me that *did* know about it. I just didn't want to admit it, so I kept telling myself I was imagining things. I was too afraid I guess." Judith's earlier demeanor had changed. Now she seemed completely vulnerable.

"Another example of how remarkable the subconscious mind is," Lewis said. "Yours was reacting to what was happening in your life, even if you *consciously* weren't ready to face it."

"I guess the rash gave me an excuse to take off the ring when I wasn't brave enough to do it on my own," Judith said softly.

"You were young," Lewis said, gently. "We're all young once, and ideally we become wiser and more capable with age. You strike me as an extremely intelligent and courageous woman, Judith—especially with the challenges you faced."

Judith felt her face flush. He was so kind, maybe *too* kind, because suddenly she felt vulnerable, exposed. It wasn't a good feeling. She stood up and walked several feet away from the bench before suddenly turning to face him.

"Do you think my son's in denial?"

"Denial?" Lewis was again surprised by her sudden shift in conversation. It was the second time tonight. Both times were when he had gotten too close.

Judith nodded. "Yehuda thinks everything will be okay, that Hannah will come home,"—she snapped her fingers—"as good as new."

Lewis took a few seconds to regroup. "And Yehuda has expressed this belief to you directly?"

"No, not directly. But his entire demeanor is... well, I just think he's happier than he should be. It's *odd*."

"Perhaps he's keeping up a brave face for the kids," Lewis suggested, knowing it was in fact true since Yehuda had told him as much at dinner. *Just like you keep your brave face on for the world, Judith.*

Judith shrugged. "Well I don't know about that, but would you believe he's recruited people across the world to pray for her!" Judith made a *tsking* sound and shook her head. "As if *prayer* will make Hannah better! It's a bit naïve don't you think?"

"In all fairness Judith," Lewis said gently, "there *have* been studies showing a correlation between prayer and improved physical health. A few cases are so baffling, the experts have called them *miracles.*"

"Well my son can believe in miracles all he wants... but the kids... well, things don't always work out the way we want them too. It's a bit deceiving to believe that if we act decently, follow the rules, that we'll get our 'happily ever after'," Judith continued, throwing up her arms in disgust. "Besides, if God didn't respond to the prayers of the Jews who died in the holocaust, how can we assume he hears us at all?"

"There's nothing I'd like better than to have some one on one time with God and find out the answers," Lewis said. "I even have a few personal questions I'd throw in..." He paused. "But getting back to your concerns about Yehuda: Let me ask you something: Do you believe Hannah is receiving the best medical care possible?"

"Yes, she's receiving excellent care," Judith said.

Lewis nodded. "Good. Then, in my opinion, Yehuda's method of coping is perfectly appropriate. Assuming they are doing all they can do for her medically—and you just said you believe they are—the outcome is out of our hands. And *because* it's out of our hands, a little prayer can't hurt, and actually may help."

Judith cocked her head playfully. "You sound like my son. How much did he give you to say this to me?"

Lewis smiled. "You and Yehuda seem very close."

"I'd like to think so," Judith said, settling herself back on the bench. "Even though I can't visit too often, we do speak on the phone frequently."

"I was wondering why you and I hadn't met before," Lewis said. "Elise has been living in Arden Station for several years now, and I usually spend one weekend a month with them."

"That amount of visitation isn't feasible for me," Judith said. She sounded like one of her clients.

"Why is that?"

"Work, work and more work," Judith said, tensing up again.

"Well you managed to make it here for *this* weekend, didn't you?" he asked gently.

"Actually it's been the last five weekends," she said, "since the…"

"I see," Lewis said, sparing her from saying the word. "Then you recognize that you *are* able to find the time in certain situations. It *is* possible to modify your work schedule—when you are motivated to do so."

*Motivated?* "Motivation has nothing to do with it! No, this situation is different," Judith said. The conversation was beginning to sound familiar and she really didn't feel like getting into it again.

"How so?"

"I *have* to be here—for my son and grandchildren. They *need* me."

He sighed. "I understand Judith. The belief that *they need you here on weekends* is your motivation. So my question to you is: why not make time on a more regular basis—even without a crisis—for the people you love, for sheer personal enjoyment?"

"Personal enjoyment?" she repeated. "Work is what gives me personal enjoyment."

"What about yoga and hiking?"

"I'm not into those things anymore."

"I thought you said you don't have the time for those things."

"What I meant was I don't have the time or the *interest*."

"Oh, I see."

Judith detected a hint of sarcasm in his voice. "Honestly, I don't see how this is any of your business anyway."

He held up his hands, palms out. "Judith, there's no need to get defensive."

"Defensive?" She pointed at herself. "Let me get this straight. You think *I'm* getting defensive?"

He sighed. "If you take an honest look at your actions, I think you'll agree that you're employing typical avoidance strategies as a way of denying your own fears and guilt..."

Judith thrust her hands on her hips. She glared at him. Her lips were pursed tightly together, as if holding back a spew of insults just raring to break free.

"Look," Lewis said, "all I'm suggesting is that there is a reason you work as much as you do."

Judith's mouth flew open. "Just who the HELL do you think you are psychoanalyzing me?" she barked. "Let me tell you something, *Doctor*—I bill $300.00 an hour! If I had any interest whatsoever in any of this psycho-*bullshit*, I would hire someone who actually had something useful to say to me!"

A nearby porch light went on; a man opened his front door and craned his neck in their direction. Lewis took a few steps forward. "Excuse us... sorry for the noise!" he shouted.

The door closed. Lewis stared silently at Judith, not sure if she was finished ranting. Her eyes were fixed on him with such rage that he could see the veins in her neck. Her fists were clenched tightly, and for a second he thought she might sock him. But she didn't do or say anything more, so he nodded and looked at his watch. "Maybe we should head back."

"Now, that's the most intelligent thing you've said all night!" Judith said through clenched teeth. She tilted her arm dramatically—almost hitting him in the chest with her elbow—to get a good look at her *Rolex*.

# Thirty-four

"He's *what?*" Lewis bellowed into the speakerphone of his Boston office.

"*Possessed*, Dad... they think Peter Stem is possessed by evil spirits."

Lewis picked up the receiver, not trusting his own ears. "Possessed? Like in *The Exorcist?*"

"I guess so," Elise said, "although there was no mention of Peter's head spinning around."

"Why didn't I hear about this last weekend during my visit?"

"Peter wasn't vocal then."

*Right.* Lewis remembered now. During dinner at the Orenstein's and before the walk with Judith that had ended so badly, Yehuda had given him a brief overview of the situation. The perpetrator wasn't talking, Yehuda said, though at the time, it was assumed to be by choice, a kind of defense strategy.

"But he's talking now?" Lewis asked.

"Not really *talking*. It's more like rambling incoherently."

"Rambling incoherently doesn't mean he's possessed, Elise. How did you hear about this anyway? Yehuda told you?"

"No, actually it was the priest from St. Agassi—Father McCormick—who told me."

"Father McCormick told you?"

"Yes."

"That's odd. How do you know the priest?"

"We met last month." Elise laughed. "It's not often that you see a priest and seeing eye dog walking around a police station."

It sounded like the beginning of a bad joke. *What do you get when you put a priest and a seeing eye dog in a holding cell?*

"No, I suppose not," Lewis agreed. "I had no idea he was blind."

"He wasn't always. He told me he has some sort of degenerative condition that worsens with age."

"Macular degeneration?"

"Could be, Dad. Anyway, after I introduced myself, we began talking… Nice man; he spoke a lot about Peter, about how much he had come to rely on his help around the rectory. Apparently, Peter was more than just a custodian. Besides taking care of the church property, he handled a good deal of Father McCormick's correspondence and personal affairs. I have to admit, the way he raved about the guy, it's hard to believe he's the same person who…"

"Elise?" Lewis cut her off suddenly.

"What is it, Dad?" she asked, somewhat startled.

"What were you doing at the police station?"

"Oh… I had to give a statement. It was all routine—not a big deal."

"Elise?"

"Hmm?"

"*Why* did you have to give a statement to the police?"

*There was no way around it. She had to tell him.*

"I had to give a statement to the police because… because I was *there*… at the mikvah… the night of the attack… a couple of hours before it happened."

He was silent for a moment. This was another thing she failed to mention during his visit.

"*You* were at the *mikvah*?"

"Yes."

"I see."

Elise knew what he sounded like when he was hurt and this was it. She also had a fairly good idea what he was thinking. *You could have been killed. You moved here, became more religious, and almost got yourself killed.* Exactly the sentiments she hoped to avoid by not bringing it up. She listened to the sound of her father taking deep breaths through his nose. It was something he did when he was trying to remain calm.

"So, what is Peter saying—or *rambling*?" Lewis asked after what seemed an eternity.

Elise relaxed. He was dropping the subject altogether. "I don't know, Dad, but I assume it's demonic sounding."

"It's astonishing what a difference a few days makes," Lewis said. "I can only imagine what Yehuda Orenstein thinks of all this craziness."

"Well Dad, this may come as a surprise, but he's not ruling it out."

"What? You're kidding."

"No I'm not. He says it's a possibility—a remote one, but still a possibility. Believe it or not, Judaism believes in possession too."

"I had no idea," Lewis said.

"I was surprised too."

"And?" Lewis asked eagerly, "What did Yehuda say about the matter exactly?"

"He said it's called *dibbuk*," Elise said, "same general concept as the Catholic Church—basically it's that negative spiritual forces attach themselves to the human soul. You've heard of the Ba'al Shem Tov, right?"

"He was a Jewish sage, I believe."

"Right. He lived during the 17th century," Elise said. "Anyway, he believed that when there was some sort of spiritual vacuum, it left a person open to this kind of thing—to these forces taking hold."

"Did he believe in performing exorcisms too?" Lewis asked wryly. He was not so impressed with this sage.

"No, actually he believed in simply redirecting the possessed person's behavior to more constructive activities. He thought this would ward off the evil spirits."

Lewis laughed. "Sounds familiar—a bit like behavior modification."

"You're the expert, Dad."

"And they say Freud was the father of psychotherapy," Lewis said, still amused. "It looks like the *Bal Shem Tov* had him beat by more than a hundred years!"

"They're going to do one," Elise said suddenly. She hated to dampen her father's spirits. He was certainly getting a kick out of this conversation, and she was relieved that his mind was on something other than her brush with death.

Lewis stopped laughing. "They're going to do *what*?"

"An exorcism. A colleague of Father McCormick's wants it done."

"Dad, are you still there?"

"Yes, I'm here. Tell me Elise, has Peter been evaluated?" Lewis had regrouped and was back in professional mode.

"Yes, well, that's what I was getting at; Peter *was* evaluated, but only to determine his competence to stand trial," Elise said. "By the way, the court appointed doctor said he was *not*—*competent*, that is. But beyond that, there has never been a formal psychiatric evaluation, and that's the main reason Father McCormick called me. He wants to see that it happens. In fact, he wants *you* to be the one to evaluate Peter."

"But Elise..."

"He knows your reputation, Dad. He even mentioned your work with the Boston Diocese."

"That was over six years ago, Elise," Lewis said. "Besides I wasn't really working *with* the church, it was more of an *association*. An association by default, I might add. The court ordered them to pay the costs of my counseling services."

"Well, apparently, Father McCormick doesn't have a problem with it," Elise continued. "He's also familiar with your work involving dissociative states. Bottom line, Dad, is he thinks you're the best person to look at Peter. He has some concerns."

"As well he should!" Lewis said, with more than a hint of agitation in his voice. "Performing an exorcism on a mentally unstable individual is likely to do irreparable damage; that I am certain of."

"I wanted to give you a heads up before he called. I wasn't sure if you would be uncomfortable..."

"Uncomfortable?" Lewis repeated. "Let me be clear, Elise; notwithstanding the horrendous events that led to his incarceration, I am fully capable, *as always*, of putting aside my personal feelings in order to be of professional service."

# Thirty-five

As Lauren stood at the bay window, something occurred to her. It had been weeks since she had thought about her parents. Always battling that desperate need for their approval, Lauren had been so preoccupied lately she hadn't even remembered to call them.

*Not that they would be happy to hear from me anyway.*

Somehow, the hours spent with Yehuda and the children had filled a void that until now, she hadn't realized even existed. It was true we couldn't choose our birth families, but what a gift it was that we *could* create a life for ourselves outside their dysfunction, beyond the restrictions.

"Something interesting?"

Lauren's hand flew over her chest as she whirled around and caught sight of Judith. "Oh... Mrs. Orenstein... you startled me!"

Judith stood there in winter white pants and a gold blouse, looking past Lauren toward the window. "Something exciting going on out there?"

"No, I'm just waiting for Janine," Lauren said, noting that Judith's belt and shoes matched perfectly. They looked like some kind of reptile skin. "She's picking me up."

Lauren turned back to the window at the sound of a car driving by.

"Oh? And where are the two of you ladies off to today?"

The woman was so nosy! Lauren wished she could tell her it was none of her business, but she was pretty sure that wouldn't go off very well. "Shopping."

"Where?"

"Station Square."

"What are you shopping for?"

*Was she kidding?* Thankfully, just then, there was a light toot of the horn as Janine pulled into the driveway.

Lauren slipped into her coat, but didn't bother buttoning it. "There's Janine now! Gotta run."

"Sorry I'm late," Janine said as Lauren strapped herself in to the passenger side. "I couldn't leave the center."

"Well, that's what happens when you try to do the work of four people," Lauren said.

Janine backed slowly out of the driveway as Judith continued spying from the window, her arms crossed.

"It wasn't that," Janine said. "I had to ask Yehuda something, but he was in a meeting."

"You couldn't just jot down a message and leave it for him?" Lauren asked.

"Not for this..."

It wasn't any of her business, but Lauren's interest was piqued. She knew Janine would tell her. For a rabbi's assistant, Janine could stand to be tighter lipped.

"Cynthia Bergerman's check for $20,000..."

Lauren hadn't known the amount before.

"It *bounced*."

Lauren covered her mouth. "No."

"Yep."

"Do you think the bagel company's having financial problems?" For some reason, this possibility made Lauren happy.

"Who knows?" Janine said. "Anyway, I couldn't disturb Yehuda to tell him; he was busy with someone else's drama."

"Just what he needs right now," Lauren said, shaking her head. "As if he doesn't have his own problems."

"Yeah, it was pretty intense," Janine continued. "Sonia and Gary Lyman were in there; I heard Sonia crying. A lot."

Lauren wasn't surprised to hear that Sonia was meeting with Yehuda. Obviously, Hannah wasn't available, so her husband was the next best thing. But it *did* surprise Lauren to learn that Gary was in the meeting too. Maybe he was such a chauvinist he refused counseling with Hannah, but with the rabbi—a man—he was willing. Lauren wished she could call Sonia, ask if there was anything she needed, if there was any way she could help, but she doubted Sonia would be very receptive. Not after that obnoxious comment. Lauren cringed as she relived it once again. *Sonia doesn't seem so happy.* It was a stupid thing to say, but if Hannah hadn't been droning on and on about marriage she would have never said it! If only she could explain this to Sonia, make her see that *she*, of all people, was not one to derive pleasure from someone else's pain. *It isn't what it seems*, she would say.

But she knew Sonia wouldn't give her the chance. After all, it was bad enough to have marital problems, but to know that other people knew it too... well that was beyond humiliating. There was no way Sonia would want to face her.

"I know what you're thinking," Janine said, glancing sideways at her.

Lauren stared back at her but didn't say anything.

Janine's eyes narrowed. "You think Sonia married Gary for money and citizenship."

"I didn't say that."

Janine snorted. "Oh come on, it's so obvious! She's so gorgeous and he's so… well *old*."

Lauren shrugged. "I have no idea. Besides, it's none of my business why she married him." She turned, Looked out the window, and caught sight of what looked like a dead cat on the side of the road. "I just hope she's okay," she whispered. "I just hope she's okay."

# Thirty-six

Patty Collins had absolutely forbidden any mention of Peter Stem during the main meal, but relented now that it was time for coffee and dessert. She moved her mother's candelabra to the sideboard and began clearing away the dinner plates, stricken at how lonely the Chippendale table looked with just the two men settled at one end. It was hard to believe that seven days earlier, each chair had been occupied by one of her three daughters and their families for Thanksgiving dinner.

"To tell you the truth, Father, I'm surprised you're so supportive of this psychiatrist thing," John said, handing Patty his plate.

"Well, I owe it to Peter to consider all avenues," Father McCormick replied, "especially in light of Father Pritcher's brilliant analysis."

"Father Pritcher is the priest who thinks Peter's possessed?"

"The one and only," Father McCormick said, making no effort to hide his disgust. "The very *notion* of Peter being possessed is absolute hogwash!" He leaned toward John and lowered his voice. "Between you and me, I've never held Pritcher in such high regard. We were together at Seminary, you know—he wasn't the brightest bulb then either."

Patty entered through a heavy swinging door and placed a large serving tray of assorted cookies and cakes on the table.

"Coffee or tea, Father?"

After the death of her mother, Patty no longer retained a full time server on staff. A housekeeper to ease the upkeep demands of such a large home was not up for debate, but to be served like royalty was something else entirely. Thankfully, Patty had never been especially thrilled with the idea, because John wouldn't hear of it.

Father McCormick looked up. "Tea would be delightful, Patricia; and I must thank you for such a lovely dinner, though once again I think I'm guilty of inviting myself."

Patty gave him a loving pat on the hand. "The pleasure is entirely ours, Father," she said, and meant it. In the beginning, having Father McCormick as a weekly dinner guest felt obligatory, a belated pay back for all he had done for John after 9/11. But over the past month or so, she had come to genuinely enjoy the company of the aging priest; and though she had never been partial to dogs, Samson wasn't so bad either. She winked at her husband. "I'll put the kettle on."

"I still don't understand," John said after Patty had left the room. "Why a *psychiatrist*, Father? I mean, do you honestly believe Peter is mentally ill?" Though he knew better than to mention it, John couldn't help but recall Ron Smith's comment that Peter's behavior was all an act.

"Do I believe Peter is mentally ill," Father McCormick repeated. "Do I believe Peter is mentally ill…" He shook his head. "Truthfully, I don't know, John. However, I *am* certain that whatever has overtaken Peter is less *otherworldly*. Drugs and alcohol have been ruled out; but unless he's seen by an expert, how are we to know that what's ailing him is not a chemical imbalance?"

"Chemical imbalance?" John asked skeptically. He remembered

Dr. Hendricks using that phrase and recommending an antidepressant after Jay died. Needless to say, he'd rejected that idea. After all, wasn't it normal to feel depressed after someone died?

"Yes, misfiring of neurotransmitters," the priest continued. "That's how the psychiatrist—Dr. Danzig—described it."

"And you're not concerned that Dr. Danzig might be biased?" John asked. Patty coughed. He hadn't noticed her return to the table.

"Biased?" Father McCormick repeated. "Because of his connection to the Jewish community? No! Absolutely not!"

There was no point pursuing it, especially since John wasn't sure where he was going with the idea anyway. Sure, the psychiatrist's daughter, Elise Danzig, had been at the mikvah the night of the crime, but she had been questioned by Ron and apparently hadn't seen or heard anything of value.

"And the attorney the church hired…" John asked, switching gears, "what does he think of all this?"

Father McCormick scratched his head. He didn't like relying on church funding for Peter's defense, but he had no choice now that the Bishop had caught wind of the situation. The diocese was still in damage control mode following the pedophile priest scandal. Now they had a potential murderer in their midst, and the last thing they wanted was more public fallout. Understandably, they would do anything to protect their own long-term interests. "Let's just say, Lance Parker is spending too much time with priests like Pritcher and leave it at that," Father McCormick said.

"Well, it seems to me, Pritcher's in a position to keep Lance Parker gainfully employed, right?" John asked, although he didn't expect Father McCormick to answer. He sighed. "Peter's lucky to have you, Father… I just hope he knows it."

The priest's face dropped. "I may be all he has, John. I may be the only one who believes he's innocent. It's obvious church officials think he's guilty… why else would they look to such an outlandish defense like *possession*?" He spread his open hands on the table. "Forgive me, please. I don't want to burden either of you with this. Especially when it's not your problem."

Patty studied her husband's expression. His mouth turned down sharply, and there were deep creases in his brow. He looked so *pained*. Despite his explanation to Father McCormick about the potential conflict of interest with his being involved in the investigation, she knew there were many instances in the past few weeks when he'd considered taking a more active role in the case, *precisely* because of his relationship with the priest. But each time, he'd talked himself out of it, claiming he didn't want his personal feelings for Father McCormick to skew his objectivity.

John didn't need to look up to feel Patty's eyes on him. She had not been happy after his return to patrolling and would be thrilled to see him giving his full attention to investigating this—or any—case. Even in a suburb as quiet as Arden Station, he knew she worried, convinced that he was more safe in a suit and tie than a police issued uniform. He hadn't realized just how difficult this was for her until two months after he was back on the streets.

"Do you have a death wish?" she shrieked at him the day his foot was run over by the driver of a car he pulled over for speeding. He couldn't blame her reaction. She had gotten a call from someone at the station. There was an accident, they told her. John was hurt; she needed to get to the hospital immediately. Of course she assumed the worst.

John considered his wife's words from that day and wondered on more than a few occasions: *Did* he have a death wish? It was a ridiculous question. How could he have a death wish when he loved life too much? *His life.* Maybe that was part of the problem. Life had been *too* good. *Too* easy. *Too* perfect. Money, health, family, respect. He had it all. And what had he done to deserve it? Not a Goddamn thing as far as he was concerned. He was convinced it was fate. All of it. "I'm Teflon," he told Patty that day while being pumped with pain medication. "Nothing bad sticks to me."

*But if it was all fate, where did that leave God?*

When Jay died, John tried to drown his sorrows in booze, but each time he drank more than six beers, he got physically sick. And forget the hard stuff; for some crazy reason, his two hundred-twenty pound body couldn't stomach more than a couple of shots. So much for becoming an alcoholic like his brother Tony. There is was again. Teflon.

But there was more. John returned to work to find Ron Sr., his partner of twenty years—more like a brother to him than his *real* brothers—unraveling. Ron couldn't remember where his office was; sometimes he didn't know why he was there or what he was supposed to do. Ron would show up at the station wearing two different shoes— sometimes *no* shoes—always with that pathetic look on his face, like a lost little boy. Needless to say Ron didn't have much choice but to take an early retirement, leave with at least *some* of his dignity intact.

*Two for two,* John thought. *If there was a God, why was he taking those dearest to him? Was this some kind of divine punishment for an easy, yet undeserved, life?*

What John should have done is quit his job altogether. Leaving the force would have been equivalent to taking a knife and cutting off his own right arm. The perfect self-punishment. But then what? He'd be home driving Patty crazy. This was about hurting *himself,* not his wife. Well then, if he wasn't going to quit, he might as well make himself useful, provide a service. That's when it occurred to him: *Patrolling with rookies.* Some things they didn't teach you at the academy, like trusting your gut. Maybe, John thought, if he gave back enough, he might earn absolution from his sins. Maybe—just supposing there was a God—he wouldn't burn in hell.

"Honey?"

John jumped.

Patty cleared her throat, a bit startled herself. "I was just saying to Father McCormick that you had a few questions about the case."

Before John could respond, Father McCormick piped up. "I'd be happy to answer them," he said, "anything to help clear Peter."

John sighed. How could he break it to the priest that despite an occasional lapse in sound judgment, he too saw a guilty man?

"Honey?"

"Right," John said, relenting only for Patty's sake. "I was curious, Father, if you had given any thought as to Peter's motivation for lying."

The priest sat up. "Lying?"

"Lying about having family upstate," John said.

"Oh that. Of course," Father McCormick said, relaxing. "Peter simply wanted me to think he had family close by so I wouldn't worry about him."

"Worry about him?"

"Yes. As you know, I'm scheduled to move out of the rectory in a few months. I'm sure Peter concocted the story about moving in with family so I wouldn't concern myself with his well being."

"Then you don't believe Peter has something to *hide?*" John asked the question in a tone that suggested this was the more likely explanation.

Father McCormick leaned back in his chair. "Maybe the more relevant question in this case is: *Do I think Peter has had a difficult past?*" He paused, either to give John some time to ponder his question or to ponder it himself. "Well, if that's the question," he continued, "my answer is, *yes*, without a doubt, I do."

The teakettle whistled from the kitchen and Patty excused herself. Father McCormick leaned over and patted Samson who had been dozing contentedly on the floor, her belly full from the big bowl of chicken and rice Patty had laid out earlier. The dog looked up, gave a little yawn and gently put her head back down between her front paws.

"When I met Peter fifteen years ago," Father McCormick began, "he was living on the streets of Philadelphia." The priest straightened up in his chair before continuing. "Back then, he was consuming something like two quarts of vodka a day, sleeping in alleys. It was only by the grace of God that he was still alive. Now I *can't* tell you what his childhood was like since Peter never spoke of it, but my guess is that it was far from ideal, something he may not have been so eager to share. So I ask you: is distancing oneself from a troubled past *hiding?*" Father McCormick steepled his fingers and sighed. "I've been a priest for a very long time, John, and I've learned that leaving a part of ourselves behind is sometimes all a person can do to move forward. But do I think Peter is a criminal?" He shook his head slowly. "No, without question I *do not.*"

John understood the point Father McCormick was trying to make. To be unwittingly linked to something by chance, rather than choice was never easy. At it's best, it was challenging, at it's worst, paralyzing. He thought of his own family's expectations. Simple but firm: Collins boys grew into Collins men who then became Collins cops. In his family, a career in law enforcement was not just a tradition—it was an *obligation.*

Throughout his twenties, John met this obligation head on. He and his three brothers patrolled South Philly like their own little fiefdom, respected by neighborhood men and practically worshipped by old Italian ladies in house dresses who fed them cheese cannoli and biscotti. Fortunately for John, he genuinely liked his vocation—didn't mind the perks that went with it either. What he detested was being lumped together with his brothers, losing any semblance of a personal identity.

*Collins Cop.*

That's what some of them actually called him! The neighborhood boys who spent their afternoons playing stickball in the alleys that snaked between lines of identical row homes...

*Yo, Collins cop! Did ya' shoot anyone today?*

Kids weren't always tactful, but they were brutally honest. John knew that's how they saw him, as part of a pack—like a dog. He tried not to show it, but it gnawed at him daily—sparking fantasies of being *Officer Cooper or Clancy.* Without our individuality, who the hell were we anyway? Maybe this was why he had such empathy for his nephew. John knew once Jay made the decision not to go the academy, he was a marked man. The family had no tolerance for traitors, and John learned firsthand that there was a steep price to pay for straying from the pack. After he and Patty married, it didn't take long for his brothers to start pulling back. Was it because he didn't marry a girl from their neighborhood? Because he didn't buy a row home within blocks of his parents? His brothers acted like they didn't even know him, giving him little more than polite nods when he'd pass them at the station. "How are things in the mansion?" they'd snicker. "What time is high tea?" He heard murmurings around the neighborhood about his *marrying up*—heartless gossip fueled by his own flesh and blood. They liked Patty, his dad admitted to him one summer night after he'd put away a few too many. The *old* Patty. As if she was the one who had suddenly changed. "You'll never be able to make a girl like that happy anyways," his dad said, a feeble attempt to keep John in his place. Preconceived notions, John realized, could be as unyielding as leg irons.

Before Patty finally talked him out of it for good, John seriously contemplated changing his name. He researched it extensively, and the bottom line was that becoming a "Cooper" or "Clancy" was relatively easy. John learned that names were changed legally all the time. The way he understood it, unless a person sought the change for illegal or deceptive purposes, the process was fairly straightforward. So, yes, as painful as it was, John could empathize with someone distancing himself from his family, even severing ties altogether. But the fact that Peter Stem—or whoever the hell he really was—had taken an alias for so many years without bothering to change his name *legally* was cause for suspicion. Was Peter merely seeking refuge from a troubled past, like Father McCormick assumed? Or was he hiding from something much bigger?

"After living with the young man for so long, I think I have a pretty good sense of his character," Father McCormick continued, snapping John out of his reverie. "Maybe I don't know the name his parents gave him, or the town he was born in, but I know *him. His essence.*" He took a deep breath before continuing, speaking with even more conviction. "Peter is a decent young man. A hard worker. Caring." He shook his head. "I'll say it again: I believe his only impetus for lying about having family upstate was to spare me the burden of worrying."

"*Worrying?*" John repeated, trying not to sound condescending. "Why in the heck would you *worry* about him? It's not like he's some young kid starting out for God's sake!"

"Your point is valid," Father McCormick answered calmly. "Peter is in his thirties. For all practical purposes, he doesn't need my help, but I admit, in my heart, he feels like a child—*my child.*" He sighed. "I know it sounds silly, but he's lived with me for so long, I feel in some ways like I raised him. Needless to say, I'm not sure he's ready or even equipped to leave the nest. And now, hearing he has no family to support him, I *am* concerned. I'm fairly certain he's had no formal schooling beyond high school. Sometimes I wonder if he's even earned his diploma." Father McCormick held up an open palm. "Please don't get me wrong, John; Peter's not a dumb man—he taught himself how to use a computer—and he's remarkably good with his hands, but after all these years at St. Agassi, where will he go? What will he do? The church has been Peter's life, just as it has been mine."

John rubbed the bite mark on his arm, willing himself to reconcile the fact that the *caring young man* Father McCormick spoke of with such compassion was in fact a murderer. He looked up and noticed the dessert tray. He had completely forgotten about it. "Please Father, help yourself," he said, giving it a little push.

Father McCormick smiled, seemingly happy for the distraction. "I'd never turn down Patricia's home baked dessert!" He leaned forward against the table, squinting as he moved his head closer to the tray. "I'm afraid general shapes are all I'm able to make out."

"Oh… of course… I apologize Father. Let's see, there are cookies—sugar, chocolate chip and peanut butter, and cake—marble, pound or…"

"Lemon," said Patty, coming through the door with a shiny silver tea service. "…with tiny bits of lemon rind—a new recipe, I think you'll like it."

The priest smiled up at her. "Sounds delicious… I'll try a slice of the lemon then."

"Can I ask you something else, Father?" John asked while Patty filled three porcelain teacups, and then joined them at the table.

The priest looked pleased. "Yes, of course! Ask away, John."

"I've gone over it in my mind," John began, as Patty looked on expectantly. "We know it was Rose Downey who identified Peter at the station. But that identification took place more than *forty-eight hours* after Peter's arrest. So, my question to you is: how could two days have gone by without you noticing that Peter was missing? Or if you did by chance notice, why weren't you *concerned*? You have to understand, Father, that with most people, a day, even a few *hours* of unaccounted whereabouts, and the phones are ringing down in *missing person's*."

Patty squeezed the liquid out of her tea bag and placed it carefully on the side of the saucer. Her husband was asking an excellent question. She, herself, had wondered how Father McCormick was able to manage those few days alone without Peter's help.

Father McCormick smiled. It was a proud smile, as if John had asked something truly astounding. "That is an excellent question, John, and one that frankly, I was surprised *not* to have been asked by that young detective at the station." He paused to take a long sip of his tea, dabbed his lips with the napkin and continued. "Yes, of course, I noticed Peter's absence! As to why I didn't make anything of it: Simple. This was not the first time Peter has disappeared."

"Disappeared?" Patty and John asked in unison.

Father McCormick held up his hands. "Well, he didn't exactly *disappear*—maybe that's the wrong word. Let me put it this way: in the past, Peter has *gone away* for a few days at a time."

John was intrigued. "Did he tell you where he went?"

"No, but he didn't have to. I figured it out on my own."

"And?"

"And…" Father McCormick hesitated, then finally blurted it out. "He was off with his girlfriend."

"Girlfriend?" John nearly choked on his cookie.

"Yes, there was a young lady Peter was courting. He didn't talk about her… only mentioned her once to me, in fact. I think it was around the time of her birthday—he wanted my advice on a gift." The priest chuckled. "I told him I wasn't the best person to ask about that sort of thing—haven't had much in the way of personal experience—though I suggested he couldn't go wrong with a traditional gift of flowers and chocolate." He sipped the last of his tea and Patty promptly came around to refill his cup.

"Did he tell you her name?"

"No, and I never asked; I didn't think it was my business."

"So, you're saying that Peter would pick up and go, just like that?" Patty asked, making no attempt to hide her displeasure. "He would leave, without any consideration for you?"

Father McCormick shook his head. "Oh, I didn't mind at all, Patricia! On the contrary; I was happy for him! I'm sure he must have been terribly lonely at times. Of course he had me and Samson; and come to think of it, he did have a friendly rapport with a few of the older parishioners." He smiled coyly. "But even *I* know that it's not the same level of intimacy."

Father McCormick reached down and gave Samson a loving pat on the head. The dog didn't flinch. "Yes, my girl and I missed him, but we managed."

Just then it occurred to Patty that despite living without Peter for nearly a month, Father McCormick seemed to be getting along just fine. She wondered just how much Father McCormick actually depended on Peter, or whether he simply wanted to give Peter the impression that he did.

"So, how often exactly did he see this girlfriend of his?" John asked.

Father McCormick thought for a moment, tapping his finger against his lip. "In the beginning it was one evening a week. Peter would always be back late, or at least by the next morning when I woke up. He'd sneak in, real careful, probably thinking I wouldn't hear him." Father McCormick chuckled at the notion. "But, I always heard him—hard *not to* with my big ears!" He tugged his earlobes playfully, then resumed his serious tone. "Anyway, Not long after that, Peter started going away for a few days at a time—not too often, though. I'd say once every other month. Was with her, I assumed. But then suddenly he stopped going,"—he snapped his fingers—"just like that."

"Did you ever ask him why he stopped?" Patty asked.

"No. I didn't feel it was my place, Patricia. I thought if he needed to talk about it, he would. Went right back to life before he met her. So, naturally, when Peter disappeared this time, I assumed the two of them had worked things out."

John nodded his understanding. It was easy to see how Father McCormick would reach such a conclusion. But one thing John *didn't* understand was why this was the first he was hearing anything about it.

"And you say Ron Smith didn't ask you about any of this?" John asked tentatively.

Father McCormick shook his head. "No. Not one question." He tapped his finger on his dessert plate as if contemplating an important issue "Come to think of it, he didn't ask me about Peter's life outside the rectory at all." He looked up, his brow furrowed with concern. "How much experience does the young detective have exactly?"

John looked over at Patty who was giving him a "see, I told you so" kind of look. John leaned forward, both hands flat on the table. "Ron has worked exclusively in investigations for the past five years," he told the priest. "His father—my former partner—trained him. The man knows what he's doing." What John *didn't* add was that he suspected Ron Jr. of taking shortcuts in Peter's case. Nor did he voice his opinion that Ron was too distracted by personal matters to be working the case on his own.

"Then tell me John," father McCormick said, more than a hint of desperation in his voice, "why isn't he doing more? I get the feeling this whole episode is an inconvenience for the detective, that he'd like to lock Peter up, throw away the key and make this whole case go away."

John couldn't help but be impressed with how perceptive the priest was. Ron *was* pre-occupied. He *had* admitted his eagerness to put the case to bed.

*The sooner I get this thing wrapped up, the better.*

But Father McCormick didn't give John a chance to respond. "I can't let that happen, John! I can't stand idly by and watch an innocent man spend his life in prison for a crime he didn't commit!"

*Innocent man.*

John sighed. Okay, so Ron wasn't being thorough. He was taking shortcuts. Still, the fact remained that there was solid evidence linking Peter to the crime. What would it take for Father McCormick to stop deluding himself and face the truth? Maybe the priest needed his *own* psychiatric session with Dr. Danzig.

Father McCormick shook his head as if reading John's mind. "It was my understanding John that in this country, a man is presumed innocent until proven guilty."

John looked briefly at Patty, who had a look of absolute pity in her eyes. Was she too reading his mind? Between Ron Smith, who wanted to file this case away as soon as possible, and Peter's lawyer, who, along with the church powers-that-be, had written Peter off as guilty, Peter wasn't exactly experiencing that American ideal.

John straightened up. The whole situation was incredibly dizzying and he couldn't help but feel like he was riding a seesaw of emotion and logic. "In a court of law, a man is presumed innocent where there is *reasonable doubt*," he said finally. He couldn't let Father McCormick see him waver. The truth was, yes, in a perfect world, everyone deserved the presumption of innocence; but in this case, Peter's guilt was just so damn obvious!

"But…"

"But nothing! You're forgetting Father, I was there—I *saw* him." John was about to add *and he was on top of a naked woman* but he thought better of it. "And, I have to be honest with you, it looked pretty incriminating."

Father McCormick nodded, deflated, but appearing to accept John's words. "The attorney—Lance Parker—thinks he can get Peter a reduced sentence based on this cock-a-mamie possession defense. You know, 'the devil made me do it'." He shook his head. "This whole thing just seems like a nightmare… not mine, Peter's. But somehow, I'm the only one who can wake him up."

John couldn't help but feel even sorrier for the priest. Father McCormick had just admitted that he viewed Peter as his own son, and John understood what fatherhood felt like. He also knew what it was like to lose a child. Although preferable to death, watching a child be carted off to prison wasn't a whole lot different than burying one. It was understandable that Father McCormick would defend Peter's innocence—even if he had to remain in complete denial to do so. And this phenomenon was not uncommon. Throughout his career, John had witnessed more than his share of parents who refused to believe *their* kid was capable of the misdemeanors they were busted for—underage drinking, vandalism, petty theft. Like them, Father McCormick could not accept the truth, even when it was staring him squarely in the face. Instead, he was choosing to stand by Peter. Put in the same situation, John wondered if he might do the same.

Suddenly the priest's face lit up. "What about *evidence* John?"

"You mean *physical* evidence?" John asked in disbelief. So much for facing reality. Apparently, Father McCormick was up to his neck in a sea of denial.

"Yes, yes of course! *Physical evidence*," Father McCormick replied. "Did they gather any from the crime scene?"

What physical evidence did Father McCormick need, John wondered, when they had a hundred and fifty pounds of it in a holding cell already? John paused, and considered what he should say. Speaking in generalities was always safe. "I assure you Ron followed standard procedure collecting evidence," John said, although he privately wondered if it were true.

"And what *is* standard procedure exactly?" Father McCormick pushed.

"The crime scene was closed off; there were photos taken, measurements, that sort of thing," John said, "and any physical evidence was collected, preserved and sent to the lab." He thought about the fact that Peter's DNA was collected from Estelle Ginsberg's body, but didn't mention it. Nor did he mention that Peter's was the *only* male DNA found in the entire place.

"So there *is* a chance!" Father McCormick sounded thrilled. "There is a chance the lab might discover something—a piece of evidence to exonerate Peter!"

John shrugged. "Yeah, sure. I suppose there's always that possibility," he said, trying not to sound too cynical.

"Then you'll need to be there when it does!" Father McCormick spoke as if this was the most obvious thing in the world. "To make sure Peter is protected," he added.

John glanced over at Patty, but instead of meeting his gaze, she stared down into her cup, as if hoping to divine some wisdom from the small gathering of tealeaf sediment.

"You're a believer in *justice*, John!" Father McCormick continued. "I know you couldn't just stand by while an innocent man was punished! Besides, I trust you. I know that you of all people wouldn't do anything funny with the evidence."

John couldn't believe it. *Father McCormick was concerned with evidence tampering?* The man was beginning to sound downright paranoid! *This isn't the OJ case!* John thought, willing himself not to say it out loud.

"I still think the best course of action is to let Ron do his job," John said. "Besides, I explained the conflict of interest…"

Father McCormick waved him off. "You don't give yourself enough credit, John! You're a professional, just like this psychiatrist—Dr. Danzig. I'm sure you wouldn't allow yourself to be swayed by your personal involvement." Father McCormick took a deep breath and shook his head. "It's truly a shame, that's all."

"What's a shame?" John asked, feeling his body tense defensively.

"It's a shame to see you wasting your God given talent."

*God given talent.* The words stung. John felt his chest begin to tighten. Instinctively, he clenched his fists. "What the hell good does it do me?" he shouted. "What good does it do *any* of us? God gives us gifts… *talents* you call them! But why? What's the point? He snapped his fingers. "In a split second, our lives could be over,"—he pointed toward the ceiling— "depending on what kind of mood the big guy happens to be in."

Patty reached for her husband's hand, but he pulled back.

"John," Father McCormick said gently. "God doesn't act arbitrarily… there is a divine plan and one day it will be revealed."

"Father," Patty said softly, eyeing John out of the corner of her eye. "Please… this is not a good time."

Father McCormick sighed and pushed his chair away from the table. "Forgive me if I've offended or upset either of you." He stood, taking Samson's leash in his hand. "Too often, our emotions wreak havoc on our judgment. Perhaps I too, have been guilty of that tonight."

# Thirty-seven

To: LDanzig@newvision.com
From: judlaw@legaleagle.net
Subject: Last Friday

Lewis,

Elise gave me your personal e-mail address and assured me you wouldn't mind my contacting you in this way.

To be brief: I wish to apologize for my rude behavior last Friday night. During our time together, you were a complete gentleman, and in no way deserved to be the recipient of my venomous outburst. (You can see why I'm considered an anaconda in many legal circles!)

Please accept my sincere apology.

Yours truly,
*Judith*

Judith Orenstein, Esq.

---

To: judlaw@legaleagle.net
From: LDanzig@newvision.com
Subject: Last Friday

Dear Judith,

I was surprised and delighted to receive your e-mail of this morning.

I too have felt badly about the events of last Friday evening, and after a great deal of introspection, I have concluded that it is I who should be extending my apology to you. Clearly I was out of line in offering my opinion when you did not seek it out.

Your verbal reaction, although strong (and yes, anaconda-like) was entirely justified. I should not have spoken to you as a psychiatrist, but rather as a new friend. I regret that I did not have the wherewithal to simply enjoy our time together. I hope that you will forgive me so that I might have the privilege of seeing you again (in a strictly non-professional capacity, I assure you!)

Sincerely,
Lewis Danzig

# Thirty-eight

She stood, shaken, in front of Tova Katz's front door clutching her bag
and staring hypnotically at the ornate wood mezuzah. Tucked inside
the finger-length rectangular box was a tiny parchment containing
the words of the *Shema*. Mezuzahs, she knew, were hung from each
doorpost of a Jew's home as a reminder of the covenant with God and
as a fulfillment of the biblical commandment to place God's words
"on the doorposts of your house and upon your gates." As a sign of
devotion, many people touched a finger to their lips and brushed it
over the mezuzah as they passed through the doorway. In some circles
mezuzahs were believed to protect the inhabitants of the home. If
a child was sick, or if financial hardship befell the family, they were
advised first and foremost to examine each mezuzah. It was possible a
letter on the parchment was smudged, or the encasement damaged.

Maybe this was why things had always gone so badly in her own
home; there wasn't a single mezuzah to check. Her husband had balked
when she suggested hanging even one. *Religious bullshit* he called it.

This was what he called *anything* she learned from Hannah Orenstein at the Jewish Learning Center.

Against his wishes she had started going to the mikvah each month, but when she had suggested sleeping in separate beds during her menstrual cycle, he nearly had a fit. As far as he was concerned, being married by a rabbi, under a chuppah was enough. He had paid his religious dues. For business purposes he would give donations to Jewish causes and show up at events if the press was going to be there; but privately, behind closed doors, he couldn't care less.

Why couldn't he see that anything she did religiously was an attempt to make things right between them? She had forgiven him for his affairs, at least the two that she knew about. She begged him to come for counseling, and he did—for a single session—and promised to change. He wouldn't control all the money anymore he told her. He wouldn't forbid her to go to her classes. He even promised to stop hurting her. There were still the twists of the arm, and the occasional shove, but last night he had crossed the line. He had pushed her to the floor and kicked her in the back while she was hunched over in a ball begging him to stop. He had been high, he said later. That's all. It was a little coke. He fell off the wagon. He was sorry. Somehow "sorry" didn't cut it when you were terrified of your own husband.

She swallowed and wiped a tear from her cheek.

Her parents would be disappointed. She was sure of it. All they had wanted was a better life for her. Marrying a man with a good education and a big income would give her security. At first she had hesitated. She had a dream for herself, she told them. But they balked at the idea. After all, pursuing an acting career where she came from was beyond senseless. Sure she had played the leads in many school productions, but that wasn't the real world where her odds of succeeding were a million to one.

It was all so ironic. She had played the game so well, become the woman *he* wanted her to be. *Acting confident. Dressing sexy.* She had even changed her personality to fit her new wealthier lifestyle. She had everyone convinced. Maybe she did have a future in acting, after all. These few years had been like a run on Broadway. It had been fun for a while; but it had taken her husband's slaps to wake her up. Like so many actors, somehow she had gotten lost in the role.

Inside, a sixty-something woman bustled by the window. This must be Tova. She looked just as she had sounded on the phone—like a strong but kindly grandmother who would make chicken soup and offer an extra blanket. Hesitantly, she raised her finger to the doorbell, just as Tova called out to someone named *Saul.* A man's voice responded from another room.

She pulled her hand back, surprised. Somehow it hadn't occurred to her that Tova might not live alone, that there might be a husband. She took a deep breath. Husband or no husband, this was it. She would have to make her decision fast, before she was noticed. Ring the doorbell or go back to *him.* But she was beginning to have second thoughts. What right did she have to barge in on this woman and her husband anyway? But then Tova would not have given out her home address, she reminded herself. She wouldn't have said *come anytime, day or night* if she hadn't meant it.

# Thirty-nine

"Nana! You're early!"

It was a complete surprise to Judith to find that Rachel wasn't alone. After a warm hug, she introduced her friend Sara, a tiny girl with short hair and bangs. Sara wore an outfit identical to Rachel's—the school uniform of a white blouse and a pleated blue skirt.

"Abba just dropped us off," Rachel said. "He had to get something from the store, but he'll be right back."

"Well, it's lovely to meet you Sara," Judith said. "Will you be joining us for Shabbat?"

"I would like to, but we're going to my brother's house," Sara said. "He just had a baby."

Such a polite child, Judith thought, after congratulating Sara, and extremely well mannered too, just like all of Rachel's friends from Jewish Day School. Judith knew that a religious education wasn't perfect, but the orthodox school her grandchildren attended *did* seem to have success warding off some of the greater evils afflicting children today. This was especially pronounced with the girls. Judith had met many of them from the local community, and more than anything, she was impressed with how *stable* they were. Unlike most secular girls who dressed provocatively, were fixated on popularity, and demonstrated utter disregard for authority, these girls were a breath of fresh air. A return to innocence, Judith thought. They dressed modestly—skirts below the knees, no sleeveless tops, and no exposed midriffs—and didn't fixate so much on appearance and weight. They were healthier emotionally, much more comfortable in their own skins. Judith had always believed that "checking out" of society during the turbulent teenage years was to be expected, especially with the girls. Some of the bad behavior of today's youth made the sixties look tame. Meeting many of the composed young women of this orthodox community made her consider that maybe it wasn't inevitable.

"Can we have a snack, Nana?"

"Of course sweetheart," Judith said. "You must be starving! Your Abba told me you're getting ready for the Chanukah play."

"We had our first organizational meeting today," Rachel announced proudly. "Sara and I are in charge of scenery."

Judith led the girls to the kitchen where, to Judith's dismay, Lauren was busy at work on the evening's dinner.

"It smells so good in here," Sara said sweetly to Rachel.

To Judith's surprise, Rachel just shrugged, like she couldn't care less.

If Lauren noticed Rachel's odd reaction, she didn't let on. "It's garlic chicken with apricot glaze," she announced.

"Hmm. Yehuda's favorite," Judith said, tapping her chin. "I must tell you, I'm surprised you know that."

Lauren looked momentarily flustered. She wiped her hands on a dishtowel and excused herself to check on Nehama. When she returned a few minutes later, Judith was bent over, peering into the refrigerator.

"It's a chocolate torte."

Judith jumped. "Chocolate Torte? So fancy, Lauren! Are we having guests or are you just trying to impress my son?"

Lauren's face dropped.

"I'm kidding!" Judith said, waving her hand. "Except for the guest part, that is."

Lauren swallowed, but managed to retain her composure. "Yehuda invited Sonia Lyman and her husband, Gary."

Even after learning from Janine about Sonia and Gary's counseling meeting with Yehuda, Lauren had been reluctant to reach out to Sonia. What if she was still angry? But the last several days Sonia had been turning up in unexpected places—at White Elephant Park on Sunday, sitting inconspicuously under a tree, at the drug store on Monday where Lauren overheard her asking the pharmacist about pain medication. Then on Wednesday, Lauren had spotted Sonia on Tova Katz's front step. At first Lauren thought it odd—she hadn't realized the two even knew each other—until she remembered: S.O.S.! *Tova ran the local S.O.S. chapter!* But it wasn't until yesterday that Lauren noticed the *sling.* Maybe it was because she was seeing Sonia for the first time all week with her coat off. Sonia was sitting by herself in the back corner of Starbucks. Lauren wanted so badly to walk over to her and give her a hug. *You're not alone... I'm your friend,* she would say. But she couldn't pretend not to notice Sonia's arm; she would have to ask her what happened; and Lauren didn't have a good feeling about that at all. Just supposing Gary *did* have something to do with it—would Sonia even admit the truth? Lauren had her doubts. So she chickened out—grabbed her coffee and fled—before Sonia noticed her. If Lauren knew anything for sure, it was that confronting someone, especially in public, was never a good idea. No, it would be much better to approach her casually, in a more private and safe environment. In the meantime, she took comfort knowing that at least Sonia was reaching out to Tova Katz.

"Anyone else coming tonight?" Judith tried to sound nonchalant, though she was secretly hoping to hear Lewis Danzig's name. What was the matter with her? She never fixated on a person like this—not unless they owed her money.

"No," Lauren said, "…just Sonia and Gary."

Judith shrugged it off as not a big deal, mumbled something to the effect of, "Well, it should be a very nice evening," and went back to rummaging in the fridge. "Okay girls, about your snack—how about some Jell-O?"

"Oh… a snack. Is that what you're looking for?" Lauren asked. "Don't bother; I have it all ready." Lauren slid past Judith and pulled a plate of cut up fruits and vegetables and a container of ranch dressing. "This is much healthier," she told Judith, then turned to the girls and smiled coyly. "But don't worry, I also made you a special treat for all your hard work on the scenery."

"Brownies!" Sara exclaimed. "But we didn't do any work yet, Lauren!"

"Okay, then this is for all your *future* hard work!"

"Sara doesn't like nuts," Rachel said, dryly.

Lauren forced a smile. "Don't worry. I remembered. No nuts! Now who wants milk?"

*Who does she think she is,* Judith thought, *Martha Stewart?* She studied Lauren carefully while she poured the girls their drinks. As usual, she was wearing her hair in two braids… one of Hannah's aprons. But there was something else… *Something* was different. What the heck was it?

Lauren returned the milk carton to the fridge and smoothed the sides of her cotton skirt. *Bingo.*

"Pretty skirt," Judith said.

"Oh… thanks."

"I thought you didn't like wearing skirts. In fact, I recall you specifically saying you *disliked* them."

Lauren's face reddened at the accusation. "I… uh…"

"I think she looks great, don't you?" Yehuda said, as he entered the kitchen. He winked—though Judith couldn't tell if it was intended for her or Lauren—and set a heavy grocery bag down on the counter. "Here you go, Lauren," he said. "I hope it's enough."

Rachel ran over to greet him, gave him a quick hug, and then she and Sara went up to her room.

Lauren couldn't have been more thankful for the interruption. Okay, so she told Judith she didn't like skirts. Big deal. It wasn't like she took an oath never to wear them! Besides, the situation had changed. She had a legitimate reason to dress this way—not that she'd ever share it with Judith.

"This is more than enough," Lauren told Yehuda, peeking in the bag. She looked at Judith, who continued to eye her suspiciously. "It's potatoes and onions. I'm making potato *kugel.*"

"Potato kugel?" Judith waved her hand and marched past Yehuda on her way to the basement door. "That's silly… There are some frozen ones in the freezer downstairs; I'll go grab…"

Lauren watched with amazement. *Yehuda shows up and all of a sudden the woman wants to help me?* "No, that's okay; really… I like my own recipe," Lauren said, fighting back her annoyance.

Judith stopped in her tracks and spun around. "But it would save you so much time," Judith said sweetly. She waited for Yehuda to second the idea, but he didn't.

"Oh, it's no problem," Lauren said. "I'm not worried about saving time." She pulled a carton of eggs from the fridge. "I've got all the time in the world."

"It must be nice having no one expecting you, no place to be," Judith said, studying her fingernail. "Of course, I wouldn't know anything about that."

Before Lauren could decide whether this was intended as a put down, Judith continued. "Oh... I just remembered; while you were upstairs with Nehama, a man called."

Lauren's first reaction was to shudder and close her eyes in disbelief. *Oh God... Even a coma can't slow Hannah down.*

"His name was Jon something," Judith said as she went to retrieve the message.

At the sound of the name, Lauren knew exactly who it was. Jonathon Bauer had already left a dozen messages on her cell phone this past month. Maybe if she had bothered calling him back at least once, he wouldn't have felt the need to track her down to the Orenstein's home.

Judith shuffled through a small pile of papers. "Let's see... I have his number here somewhere... He mentioned something about seeing a show downtown, after Shabbat."

Yehuda placed an open hand on the notepad. "Don't bother... I have the number, Mom."

"Good. So, you'll give it to Lauren."

Yehuda scratched his head. He glanced from Lauren to Judith and back to Lauren. "Lauren," he said, "this doesn't seem like a good time... I mean you're pretty busy around here."

Lauren nodded, looking almost as surprised as Judith. "Well, yes, that's true."

Judith tilted her head and narrowed her eyes at her son. "What are you doing, Yehuda?"

Yehuda ignored her and continued speaking directly to Lauren. "I have to talk to Jonathon about something else anyway," he said. "I'll let him know it won't work out for the two of you."

"Oh… okay. Great," Lauren said, with what sounded like a combination of delight and relief. "Please tell him, thank you, but…" She paused, studying Yehuda's face quizzingly. "Like you said, this isn't a good time."

Judith just stared at the two of them. They sounded like they were speaking in some kind of private code. Finally, she spoke up. "Lauren," Judith said, with the voice of authority, "a young girl like yourself should get out and date… have fun for goodness sake! Now if your commitments to my son and grandchildren are interfering…"

"No!" Lauren snapped, a bit annoyed that Judith's harsh opinion of men would suddenly relax. Just what she needed—another Hannah! "I'm not interested in Jonathon!"

Yehuda held up his hand. "Enough, Mom! Lauren's made it perfectly clear… she's not interested!"

Lauren could feel Judith's eyes penetrating her, but she refused to meet her gaze. She felt almost giddy with confidence having Yehuda by her side. "Well," she said, wiping her hands on her apron and checking her watch. "I better get moving on this kugel!"

"But…" Judith started to object, but Yehuda cut her off. "I think we should leave Lauren to her cooking." When he said *we*, Judith knew he meant *her*. "…among other things," he added.

"Well, I want to help!" Judith demanded and before he could object she had rolled up her sleeves and marched over to the sink.

Lauren smiled weakly and tried to think quickly as Judith soaped up her hands. She had learned from Judith's previous visits that it was best to give her simple jobs. Anything requiring too much of a commitment would end up either undone or done incorrectly. Last week, Judith promised Rachel she would bake an apple pie, but had gotten only as far as slicing the apples; it was Lauren who ended up doing the rest. And then, after all that rushing to get it done in time for dinner, Rachel decided she was sick of apple pie and refused to eat any. Maybe at one time Judith had been competent in the kitchen, but it was apparent the woman hadn't cooked in ages; Judith was a little rusty and a lot disinterested. Even worse was that she was often interrupted by "urgent" work matters.

"Uh sure," Lauren said. "Why don't you make a salad?"

Yehuda brought his hands together. "Great idea! You'll make the salad, Mom." He checked his watch. "I've got to run back to the center. I'll see everyone in a few hours, okay?"

Rachel ran in just as he was about to leave. "Is it okay if we play outside, Abba?"

"Yes, just stay in the back where Nana and Lauren can see you from the window."

The girls went to retrieve their coats while Lauren gathered ingredients for Judith's salad. She pulled out a couple heads of lettuce, some cucumbers and cherry tomatoes from the fridge, intentionally passing on anything too complicated like avocado or bean sprouts. Judith rinsed off the lettuce and felt Lauren's eyes on her as she began chopping it with a knife.

"Something the matter?" Judith asked.

"No. Nothing."

"You were about to say something Lauren, so say it."

Lauren pointed to the lettuce. "It's better to shred it with your hands."

"Pardon me?" Judith had expected something else.

"The lettuce—ripping it preserves more of the nutrients than cutting does."

Judith vaguely remembered hearing this piece of information years ago on a television ad.

"The *lean and green* campaign," Lauren said as if reading Judith's mind. "I helped run it for the California growers association."

"That job of yours certainly gave you quite an array of information, didn't it?"

"I'm a walking *Trivial Pursuit* game, I guess," Lauren said.

Judith considered the lettuce. Then, she picked up the knife and without giving it a second thought, resumed her chopping.

# Forty

That particular Shabbat dinner would not go down in Orenstein history as one of the family's more festive meals. To start things off, Sonia and Gary had arrived late with sour faces and appeared not to be speaking to each other. Sonia still wore her sling and judging from her body language, it was apparent that she wanted to be as far away from her husband as physically possible. When he approached her from behind to help her off with her coat, she flinched. And before the food had even been served, she kept inching her chair further and further to the right, until she was practically sitting on poor Rachel's lap. Baby Nehama, as if picking up on all the negative energy, cried the minute the blessings were recited, and despite being passed around the table, would not stop fussing.

"Maybe she's tired," Judith said from the other end of the table. It took Lauren a minute to realize that Judith was actually saying: *put my granddaughter to bed.*

"I come with help," Sonia told Lauren, standing up abruptly. At that, Gary shot her a disapproving look, which only Lauren seemed to notice.

Upstairs in the baby's room, Sonia stood next to Lauren while she changed Nehama's diaper. The baby continued her fussing while Lauren slipped her out of her tiny velvet dress and white tights and into some fleecy feet pajamas. The change in clothing seemed to trigger some recognition in Nehama, and she finally began to settle down.

"Beautiful baby," Sonia said soothingly stroking Nehama's cheek with her uninjured arm, "such beautiful baby... "

Lauren gestured for Sonia to take a seat on the footstool while she sat in the rocking chair patting Nehama's back. Usually it only took five minutes of slow rocking before Nehama conked out completely.

Lauren gazed at Sonia. Even in the dimmed light of the nursery, Sonia's hair looked brittle, and her complexion pale. She had dark circles under her eyes as if she was either sleep deprived or crying too much. It was hard to believe that Lauren had once viewed Sonia as a living Barbie doll. Now she looked as though she had been mishandled, thrown against a wall even.

Lauren let her gaze move to Sonia's arm. She had to know how it happened... maybe the darkened room would offer a veil of protection, make it easier for Sonia to open up.

"Is everything okay, Sonia?" Lauren asked gently.

Sonia bit her lip and shook her head.

Lauren's heart sped up. "Is it Gary?"

Sonia nodded. "Yes." She took a deep breath. "Gary is not a bad man. He loves me..."

Lauren was shocked at how quickly Sonia admitted the source of the problem. This wouldn't be so difficult after all. "Do you want to talk about it?" she asked.

Sonia wiped away a tear. "In my country, these things—between husband and wife—they are private."

*Maybe this wouldn't be so easy after all.* But now, Lauren finally understood. *It was cultural pressures that kept Sonia from leaving her abusive husband!*

"Sonia," Lauren pleaded, "even though it feels uncomfortable, sometimes we *need* to confide in someone." Lauren would have preferred saying what was really on her mind: *Don't take his abuse! You deserve better! You must leave him immediately!!* But Sonia didn't give the go ahead, so Lauren kept these sentiments to herself. She stood up to put the now sleeping Nehama into her crib. Her back to Sonia, she thought about all those wasted sessions with Hannah. Hannah probably had *no clue* what was actually going on between Sonia and Gary.

"Sonia," Lauren said, returning to her seat, "if you ever decided you wanted to… is there *anyone* you can… is there someone you feel comfortable *really* opening up to?" More than anything, she was looking for confirmation that Sonia was in fact confiding in Tova Katz from S.O.S.

Sonia thought for a moment, as if determining if what she was about to say was self-incriminating. "Yes," she said, blotting her nose, "there is someone."

# Forty-one

Lewis wasn't sure if he was expecting Abe Vigoda or the guy from Hawaii 5-0, but it was the much younger, well-groomed Detective Ron Smith Jr. who met them in the lobby of the police station. Ron was the antithesis of the overworked, unkempt T.V. persona of Lewis's generation. The detective couldn't have been more than thirty-five; and dressed in suit pants, a pressed shirt and tie, he looked more wall street than forty-second street. Though average height and build, he was exceptionally lean and buff, the picture of health. His dark hair was slightly damp; his face was cleanly shaven, but flushed—like he had just come from the gym—and he smelled of expensive cologne.

Lewis introduced himself, and then Elise, who had driven him to the station.

Ron smiled politely. "Yes, it's nice to see you again Ms. Danzig."

"Remember, Dad—I had to give a statement," she whispered to Lewis in response to his confused expression.

"Oh, yes; of course… how could I forget? The *routine statement,*"

Lewis said. Now he gave her a look like she should know better than to frequent places where murders were committed.

Elise sighed. "Call me on my cell when you're ready," she said, then gave him a quick peck on the cheek.

Lewis followed Ron down a narrow corridor lined with tasteful black and white photos of local rail stations. As they rounded the corner, a glittery handmade sign with the words *Happy Thanksgiving!* written in orange and black marker came into view. A few turkey cut outs sat on the floor, propped against the wall.

"Out with the old, in with the new," Ron said. "By next week the snowmen and reindeer will be up. The office girls get a kick out of decorating."

They reached Ron's office and the instant Ron pulled open the door, Lewis was overtaken by the heavy air. He grimaced at what smelled like a stale combination of sweat and tobacco, and instinctively scanned the room for the source of the odor. The furnishings looked old and worn: a couple of ripped leather chairs and an old metal desk, bare except for some picture frames and a pencil holder filled with sharpened pencils and pens. To the side was a stack of puzzle books—word search, crossword puzzles, *Suduko,* and hidden pictures. These must be for the detective's children, Lewis thought. He remembered the countless hours Elise had spent at *his* office. She especially liked to tidy up his waiting area, stacking magazines into neat piles, rearranging the furniture, watering the ferns. Sometimes she sat next to the receptionist and sketched, usually pictures of the family—seven year old Elise in the middle of Lewis and Iris, all three of them with huge melon rind smiles. There were other drawings too—Lewis in his office with a floppy eared dog sitting on the couch; in his hand a sign with the words *Dr. Danzig, Pet Psychiatrist.* That was one of his favorites, drawn just a month or so before everything changed.

Though he and Iris wanted and planned for a large family, Elise was their only child. Those were the days before in-vitro was an option. But, it was probably for the best since Lewis couldn't imagine loving another child as much as he loved his daughter. The feeling was mutual. Elise idolized him. *I want to be just like you Daddy* she would tell him. *I want to help people.* He assumed she would go to medical school. She certainly had the brains for it, graduating in the top ten of her high school class. But that plan got scrapped fast enough when she met Evan her junior year of college. *I never really wanted to get my medical degree* is what she told him right after she announced her engagement. Maybe it was because Elise was his daughter—his baby—he never quite figured out why, but he never felt Evan deserved her. Even after they were married, Lewis never corrected his son in law when he called him "Dr. Danzig". He couldn't bring himself to be called "Dad" by the man who had led his daughter so far off course.

"Dr. Danzig, I'd like you to meet Father Herbert McCormick and Attorney Lance Parker. I understand you've spoken already."

Ron Smith's words snapped Lewis out of his reverie, and he focused on the occupants of the room. Two men—one in a plain brown suit, the other in all black with a priest's collar—stood up. A harnessed golden retriever lay contently by the priest's feet on a shag carpet of limp orange worms.

"Yes, that's right," Father McCormick said. "Doctor Danzig and I had a private telephone conversation a few days ago." He extended his arm. "It's a pleasure to finally meet you, Dr. Danzig."

"Likewise," Lewis said. Elise had mentioned that Father McCormick was blind, but somehow it hadn't completely registered until now.

"Gentlemen, Ron said, "let's move this meeting to the conference room. It's a little crowded in here."

Lewis couldn't help but notice that the detective had been eyeing his office uncomfortably, as if just noticing it's dated condition for the first time. *What was an office like this doing in a newly renovated building?* Lewis wondered. But whatever the reason, he was relieved to be relocating the meeting. The stench was making him nauseous. He wondered how the young, seemingly hygienic-minded detective could stand it.

Minutes later, they were all comfortably settled and breathing easy around a large table in the conference room. Ron opened a thick notebook and perused a few pages before speaking. "All right then… Dr. Danzig, as you know, Mr. Parker is representing Peter Stem."

"Yes, yes we all know each other," Lance Parker said, impatiently. He turned to Lewis. "Let's get right to the point, shall we? I'm allowing you two hours to analyze my client for the sole purpose of ruling out a psychiatric condition."

Lewis tried hard not to stare at Lance Parker's ridiculous comb-over. "*Ruling out?*"

Lance folded his hands on the table. "Correct."

Lewis's feathers weren't so easily ruffled. "Oh? Are you a psychiatrist, Mr. Parker?"

"No," Lance said, "but I have worked closely with the church for nearly a decade now… I've heard about these cases."

"Heard about what cases?"

Lance rolled his eyes as if this whole conversation was a waste of his time. "Cases of *demonic possession.*"

"You've heard about such cases," Lewis said, "but have you actually *seen* one?"

"Well, no, of course not," Lance stammered. A long black hair fell forward in his eyes and he immediately pasted it back in place. "It wouldn't have been safe—especially during the exorcism."

"I see. So it must be a pretty intense undertaking—an exorcism."

Lance crossed his arms defiantly. "Yes, that's right."

"Then before you perform something as intense as an exorcism," Lewis said, "is it really so much to ask for a non-invasive evaluation, maybe even some therapy?"

Lance shrugged. "As far as I'm concerned, the exorcism *is* the therapy."

Father McCormick shifted uncomfortably in his seat.

"With all due respect Mr. Parker," Lewis said, "the two are polar opposites."

Lance held up a finger. "Hold on just a second," he said. "What exactly makes you qualified to say that? As far as I know you have no church affiliation."

"I'm board certified and licensed to practice psychiatry in six states, including Pennsylvania," Lewis said, looking him straight in the eye. "During the course of my forty-year career, I've published over a hundred papers in all areas of neuropsychiatry and human behavior. And no, Mr. Parker, I have no church affiliation. I had my Bar Mitzvah probably around the time you were born; but, as you can probably guess, it wasn't in a church."

Father McCormick chuckled and Lance rolled his eyes but didn't say anything, so Lewis continued. "Now, as I was about to say: psychotherapy, whether directed toward the conscious or the *un*conscious mind—and I am presuming that in an exorcism we are talking about the *unconscious* mind since the idea is that a separate entity has overtaken the person's consciousness…"

Lance stared at him like he was crazy. "Would you mind speaking in English?" he asked dryly.

Lewis sighed. "Bottom line—psychotherapy on any level requires years of intensive study, training and clinical experience," he said, then turned to Father McCormick. "I admit I don't know what type of training is involved with the performance of religious exorcisms…"

"Not much," mumbled Father McCormick.

Lewis reached into his briefcase. "I brought some data on the subject which you gentlemen may find interesting." He placed a thin manila folder in front of him on the table. "This is from a published study which concluded less than five years ago." He pulled a pair of reading glasses from his shirt pocket, opened the file, and began reading. "Over a fifteen year period, twenty-two individuals with alleged demonic possession were examined. What was found was that these individuals were actually suffering from disorders ranging from mania and schizophrenia to epilepsy—there was even one case of Tourette's syndrome!" Lewis removed his glasses and looked up at the men. "Without exception, each person in the study was found to have a DMS-III defined condition."

Lance raised a finger in opposition. He had thought long and hard about the evidence in this case. A jury would be hard pressed to reconcile Peter's arrest at the crime scene, and pleading insanity was a risk, a risk Lance figured he could avoid if it was proven— or at the very least *suggested*—that Peter was possessed. As far as Lance Parker knew, 'the devil made me do it' defense had never been tested in criminal court. But surely, any reasonable jury would agree that resisting Satan was beyond the control of any mortal being.

"To play devil's advocate…" Lance began. Pleased with himself, he turned to Father McCormick—"no pun intended Father!"—then back to Lewis: "How do you explain cases where the behavior can be described as nothing else *but* demonic? Do these studies of yours offer an explanation for cases where the person behaves in ways that are completely out of character?"

Lewis removed his glasses and nodded his head thoughtfully.

"Actually yes, there is an explanation provided. Foremost, it is important to understand that the behaviors of the so-called 'possessed' show a marked resemblance to the behaviors of those with electrochemical, neurochemical, or other physical and emotional disorders. The research has also shown that often times the individual is influenced—actually encouraged—to exhibit the 'possessed' behavior expected. Although the studies I mentioned were all instances where other medical conditions were present, I think we can safely assume that in cases where *none* are present, the behaviors are being reinforced."

Lance scrunched his forehead, obviously unhappy with the doctor's extensive knowledge on the subject.

"Now, if this man, Peter is *levitating...*" Lewis began. It was a partial attempt to diffuse the palpable tension in the room.

Father McCormick laughed. "Dr. Danzig, I assure you, he is not."

"Well good. I want it to be clear from the start that I am in complete opposition to exorcisms in general, and the prospect of one being performed in this case specifically," Lewis said. "So I must tell you up front: if your plan is to conduct one, then my involvement here ends."

Lance Parker smirked. "Well, then we have a problem." He turned to Father McCormick. "Father Pritcher has stipulated that an exorcism be conducted..."

"Yes, Lance," Father McCormick spoke over him. "I'm fully aware of what Father Pritcher has said. If you recall, I assured Father Pritcher that once we exhausted all other avenues, I would give him my full support in that area."

"And he was satisfied with that?" Lewis asked. "Frankly I'm surprised that this priest—Father Pritcher—could be so adamant about an exorcism, yet give the go ahead for a psychological evaluation."

Father McCormick smiled and patted his dog. "Yes, well, lucky for us, Pritcher's always had a soft spot for animals. He spent some time with Samson and she won him over." He glanced sideways at Lance, who was slumped in his chair pouting. "With all due respect to Father Pritcher—who has been kind enough to see to it that Peter has the legal representation he needs—I think it's reasonable that we let Dr. Danzig examine Peter, evaluate him *before* we go and start sprinkling holy water around."

# Forty-two

Ron Smith was preoccupied with one of his puzzle books, rhythmically tapping his pencil on the page, when Lewis appeared at his office door. Ron motioned blindly toward one of the chairs. It wasn't until Lewis had taken a seat, that the detective looked up and stared directly into the psychiatrist's eyes. "You wouldn't happen to know a six letter word for *obstinate*, would you?" he asked.

Lewis didn't immediately respond. The question sounded like a joke. After all, he had just spent over an hour with the alleged killer, Peter Stem. Surely, the detective would be eager to hear what he'd discovered!

"Any thoughts, Doctor Danzig? The word is *obstinate*."

Lewis leaned back and scratched his head. So it wasn't a joke. "Obstinate," he repeated, then thought for a moment. "Have you tried *mulish?*"

"Mulish?" Ron asked, skeptically, "Is that even a real word?"

Lewis closed his eyes and nodded. He was feeling a bit punchy after his session with Peter. It was only about 4:00 PM, but felt much later—probably because of the darkening sky.

"Yes, I'm certain you'll find *mulish* in Webster's dictionary, Detective."

"I would never have thought of it," Ron said, shaking his head as he scribbled it in. His eyes lit up. "That's it… *mulish* works! Man, that one's been bugging me for days!"

"My pleasure," Lewis said, fighting back a yawn. The mustiness of the room wasn't helping. "Could we get some fresh air in here?"

"Oh yeah, sure thing." Ron set his puzzle book aside and unlatched the one window in the room. The sudden noise from the street below was abrasive to Lewis, but the crisp December breeze more than made up for it.

Ron returned to his desk and leaned down into his fridge. "Water? Pomegranate juice?" he offered.

"Water would be great, thanks."

"I'm eager to hear how it went with Peter," Ron said, not sounding eager at all. At the moment, he seemed more interested in reading the nutrition label on his juice. "This stuff has enough antioxidants for an entire football team!" he announced happily.

Lewis smiled politely. "Yes, that's good stuff—a bit tart for my taste though."

The detective took a giant swig and wiped his mouth with the back of his hand. "So, you had your session with Peter… "

Lewis nodded and leaned over, reaching into his briefcase. He pulled out a thin stack of stapled papers and handed them to the detective. "This is a report of my observations. If you like, I can summarize what I've found."

"Be my guest," Ron said.

Lewis took a swig of his water and then began. "If you recall,

Detective, my objective in meeting with Peter was to determine if his present state is indicative of a psychiatric condition or something more."

"Right. Go on."

"Foremost, I've concluded that there is absolutely nothing to support the theory of demonic possession. During our time together, Peter's affect remained stable, he made no threats to me, said nothing about the church or God, displayed no extraordinary physical abilities…"

"So you think he's faking the whole thing?" Ron asked eagerly.

Lewis raised his eyebrows, surprised. "*Faking*? No, I wouldn't say that."

Ron puffed up his cheeks and blew air toward the ceiling. "Don't tell me you think he's actually *insane* then?"

Lewis sat back and frowned. "Insane is not a term I like to use." He held up his hand at Ron's attempt to interrupt, then continued. "I *will* say with all confidence that Peter is indeed suffering from a psychiatric condition. Something has caused him to temporarily disassociate from reality."

"So it's not an *act*?" Ron asked, genuinely perplexed.

"No," Lewis said, shaking his head adamantly. "*Again*, his condition is definitely not an act. Peter is in the actual throes of a stress induced state of acute psychosis."

"Stress induced, you say?" Ron made no effort to conceal his annoyance. He finished what was left of his drink and shrugged. "Murder's a stressful job all right; I'd say it's up there with air traffic controllers," he mumbled.

"Unfortunately, I have no way of knowing what triggered the psychosis," Lewis continued, ignoring Ron's statement, "but whatever the event was, it happened in close proximity to his arrest."

Ron remembered Father McCormick's claim that Peter's behavior was completely normal all morning and throughout the day of the crime. This actually gave some credence to Dr. Danzig's suggestion that a specific *trigger* set him off. *Damn.* They had plenty of physical evidence linking Peter to the crime. But now it looked as though Peter would be claiming temporary insanity. That type of defense would take much longer and frankly, Ron didn't have the time.

"How long do you think he's been in this state of psych..."

"Psychosis," Lewis clarified.

"Right."

"Well, again, that would depend on the time of the trigger, Detective. I wish I could tell you if Peter became psychotic before or after you found him at the crime scene,"—Lewis shook his head—"unfortunately, I can't help you there."

"How long?" Ron asked. "How long will he be like this?"

"Actually, that's the good news. He can come out of his dissociative state at any time. In fact, there are indicators that he is starting to come out of it *now.* Indeed, that is one of the reasons I advise maintaining his current living accommodations, rather than moving him to a special facility."

"*Special facility...* as in a *loony bin*," Ron mumbled, and as expected, Lewis didn't respond.

"Well, is there any way to speed things up?"

"Speed up Peter coming out of the psychosis?" Lewis pursed his lips. "Actually, there may be a way."

Ron made a rolling motion with his hands. "Good... What is it?"

"Hypnosis."

"Hypnosis?" Ron repeated, surprised. He had expected to hear about some kind of prescribed drug—a shot in the ass, maybe.

Lewis nodded.

"Hypnosis would bring him out of his fog sooner?" Ron asked.

"Psychosis," Lewis corrected. "And it *may* help. There's a good chance, but there are no guarantees," Lewis said.

Ron shrugged. "It's worth a shot, I guess. I'll call Father McCormick and let him know." He picked up the phone, and almost as an after thought asked, "Was there anything else in your report?"

"Well, Peter said something that might be of interest."

Ron stopped dialing and nearly dropped the phone. "Hold on. You're telling me Peter *spoke* to you?"

"Yes. Like I said, he's showing signs of recovery."

"What did he say?" Ron asked, his eyes wide. "Did you ask him about the murder?"

Lewis shook his head. "No, we didn't have a dialogue, as you'll see when you watch the tape. He was too agitated; he wouldn't have responded to my questions anyway. But what I found interesting was he kept repeating one particular name—*Suzanne*."

Ron scratched his forehead. "Suzanne?"

Lewis nodded.

"That's all he said? Or was there more?"

"There were other mumblings—completely incoherent—but *Suzanne* was loud and clear. I thought the name might mean something to you."

Ron shook his head. "I'd be happy just knowing who *Peter* is." He whacked his pencil against his desk. "*Suzanne... Suzanne...* I don't know. She could be a girlfriend, an ex-wife, even another victim... Wait!" he said suddenly, then reached over and grabbed the case file. He rummaged through it until he found the paper he was looking for. He scanned it intently, all the while holding up a single finger so Lewis would stand by quietly. After a few minutes, he looked up at Lewis, shook his head and let out a big sigh. "Apparently, mikvah use is such a private matter, they don't keep official records, but this is a list of married orthodox women from the community who might *potentially* use the mikvah. I thought maybe the name *Suzanne* would be… well, you would think with over a hundred names there would be at least *one* Suzanne!" His shoulders dropped and he laughed out loud. "But *no*, that would be too easy, right?…Well, it was worth a shot." He shook his head, pulled out his clipboard and scribbled something on a blank page. He would need to run the name Suzanne through the national missing persons database, though single name searches usually took days to sift through. More time that he didn't have.

*Suzanne.*

He suddenly remembered what Father McCormick had told John Collins. *Peter had a girlfriend. He would disappear for a couple of days at a time…* John had nudged him about it, told him it might be worth looking into, but truthfully, Ron hadn't given it any consideration until now. Was Suzanne this elusive girlfriend's of Peter's? If so, could she help unravel the mystery of Peter's identity? He looked at his watch. It was nearly 4:40 PM. He picked up the phone, then remembered: Violet was expecting him by 5:15 and he promised he wouldn't be late.

# Forty-three

*Giovanni's* on Crescent Avenue was a third generation family owned barbershop. It was run by Marco Giovanni, the sixty year-old grandson of Paolo Giovanni, who had emigrated from Italy in 1918. Paolo's older brothers were skilled stonemasons who had the good fortune of finding steady work during the building boom of the 1920's, while Paolo set up a small, but profitable barber shop under the tiny apartment the family shared.

The single block stretch of Crescent Avenue had once been a thriving hub of family owned storefronts—a pharmacy, a butcher, a tailor, a baker—and in it's heyday enjoyed the bustling daily business of wealthy suburbanites. With the modernization efforts of the township—which included the building of large strip malls and the subsequent in pouring of national retail chains—the small hometown businesses began to suffer. Giovanni's managed to stay afloat, but Marco knew that once he retired, Giovanni's would be no more. He wasn't sure if he was more heart broken about losing business to places like *Hair Cuttery*, or the fact that not one of his four sons had the slightest interest in cutting hair and trimming beards.

It was nearly 8:00 PM when John Collins and Ron Smith were welcomed into Giovanni's by the crooning voice of Frank Sinatra singing "The Lady is a Tramp". The song reminded John of the shop down in South Philly, where Jacko Spinelli, at the ripe old age of eighty-four still cut John's hair each month. But the music played in Giovanni's was piped out of an I-pod speaker system, surprising for a shop that in its ambiance transported you back to the 1940's. An eight-track player would have been more fitting.

Four adjustable chairs lined one of the walls, each facing an unframed rectangular mirror. Glass bottles of *Barbisol*, combs, razors and shaving supplies adorned the counter space at each station. In a corner, three captain's chairs sat catty corner behind a table scattered with magazines and newspapers. The barbers: Marco, Lloyd, Len, and Vincent—their names were neatly stitched onto their matching blue striped smocks—showed no discomfort upon seeing a uniformed police officer enter the shop. After all, cops needed haircuts too.

John had not been surprised to learn that the psychiatrist, Dr. Danzig, believed Peter was suffering from some sort of mental trauma. Unlike Ron, John had never considered that Peter's behavior was an act. *Defecating in your pants?* Now that would have been *some* acting! John had been a bit intrigued—though not surprised—by the news that Peter had repeated a name during the psychiatric evaluation. *Suzanne.* Well, at least now Ron was giving some attention to Peter Stem's personal life. And miracle of miracles! He and Ron finally agreed on something—that Suzanne was likely the girlfriend Father McCormick spoke of during dinner at John's house.

The thing that *had* been a complete surprise to John was the CODIS report. As luck would have it, the results had just come in, and they were *negative*. Negative meant that Peter's DNA, collected in surplus from the mikvah, had not been recovered from *any* other U.S. crime scene in the past twenty plus years. Mental trauma or not, it was hard for John to believe that Peter's crime was an isolated case. This entire situation, which at first seemed so open and shut, was getting more and more bizarre. Actually, now that John thought about it, there was no way Suzanne could be Peter's girlfriend. The way things were shaping up, that would just be too easy.

*Was there anyone who would know more about this girlfriend of Peter's?* John had asked Father McCormick at Ron's request. Ron had been right in assuming the priest would be more forthcoming if John were to make the call. *As a matter-of-fact, there was someone,* Father McCormick told him. Peter had a friend—a barber named Vince Manicotti. He worked at Giovanni's. Perhaps Vince could provide some answers.

"Is there a Vince Manicotti here?" Ron asked, reaching into his coat pocket.

A couple of the barbers started snickering. The youngest looking of the group straightened up. He had a thick head of black hair, slicked back behind his ears.

"It's not *manicotti* like the noodle; it's *Mancotti,* pronounced man-cot-ee. If that's who you want, then I'm your man."

Ron flashed his badge, "I'm Detective Ron Smith,"—then pointed to John—"and this is Detective John Collins."

*Detective.* The mere sound of the word resonated through John's entire body like a shot of testosterone.

"Like it or not, you're on the case now," Ron had told John on the ride over. "I won't take *no* for an answer. Consider it a favor to Dad."

"We'd like a word with you, Mr. Mancotti," Ron continued.

"Ron *Smith*?" Marco spoke up from his station at the door.

Ron spun around.

"Are you Ron senior's son?"

Ron nodded reluctantly.

"Well, I'll be!" Marco slapped his thigh. "I used to cut your Daddy's hair! That was *years* ago when you were no higher than my knee!"—He pointed to his knee—"and boy oh boy did you love that pole outside!" He stretched his arm, proudly indicating the barber pole mounted outside the front window. "You used to lean up against the glass and watch it spin and spin… that's all it took back then to make the young ones happy—no need for videos or X Bag…"

"X *Box*!" corrected Len from two chairs down, who was meticulously trimming his customer's right sideburn.

"Yeah, that's what I said," Marco said. "Sheesh!"

Marco's attention quickly returned to the detective. "I used to tell you jokes when you came in, do you remember?" he asked, his face lit up with excitement.

"No, sorry."

"Here's one: where do sheep get their hair cut?"

"I have no idea."

Marco snickered.

"At the 'baaaa rbersop'! Get it? The baaaa rbershop!"

"Yeah, that's pretty funny," Ron said, forcing a polite smile. He turned to go.

"Wait! Here's another one. Lloyd just told me this one…"

Lloyd looked up from the beard he was trimming and gave a little salute with his finger. "Someone's gotta give Marco some decent material once in a while, or we'd be listening to sheep jokes all day!"

The others laughed.

"Ha ha… very funny," Marco said, narrowing his eyes. He turned back to Ron and rubbed his palms together. "Okay, here it is: why do barbers make the best drivers?"

Ron stretched his neck from side to side. "No idea."

Marco smiled eagerly. "Take a guess!"

"No clue."

"C'mon Guess!"

Ron looked at his watch.

"Barbers make the best drivers because they know all the short cuts! Get it? They know the *short cuts*!" Marco snorted sounds of laughter. Tears streamed down his face. "Ha! That's a good one!" He leaned forward, clutching his stomach, then grabbed on to his chair for support, subsequently spinning his customer about ninety degrees.

"Careful boss, you don't want to get yourself worked up!" Lloyd said over the sounds of Marco's hysterics.

Lloyd glanced over at John and Ron who were waiting for Marco to compose himself. "He's already had two strokes you know."

Marco slapped his knee, still laughing. His face was beet red. "... the short cuts! I love that one!" After another minute or so of knee slapping, Marco brushed himself off and exhaled loudly. "Whew!... Yep, you and your dad were attached at the hip! Hey, how's old Ron doing, anyway?"

"Fine. He's fine," Ron said, not wanting to get into it. He now regretted not sending John out here on his own.

"Well, you tell him Marco Giovanni says hello! You tell him to stop bein' such a stranger!"

"Sure. I'll tell him."

Satisfied, Marco started whistling and went back to cutting his customer's hair. The forty-year old average looking guy had been sitting perfectly still, looking down at his hands during the entire exchange. Tiny drops of sweat had slowly made their way down his forehead, picking up speed steadily as they continued along the bridge of his nose, before splashing on his black smock. The guy hadn't paid over a year's worth of outstanding parking tickets, and there was a warrant out for his arrest. It was just his luck that not one but *two* cops would show up on a Friday night in the middle of his haircut.

Vince Mancotti led the two detectives to a back room. It had a full sized retro refrigerator from the 1950's, and a brand new microwave oven.

"Have a seat," Vince said, pointing to an ugly plaid couch, piled with magazines—Good Housekeeping, Better Homes and Garden, and Oprah. "Oh, let me get those," he offered, quickly gathering them up into a neat pile. He shrugged. "Len's wife… she hangs out here… likes to keep an eye on him. What are you gonna' do?"

"You guys stay open late," John said, taking a seat across from Vince.

"Well, things are tight. The whole block's on extended hours. Marco would have us working 'round the clock if we'd go along with it."

"We have a couple of questions for you, Mr. Mancotti," Ron said, opening a folding chair that was leaning against a wall.

"You can call me Vince."

"Vince, I'll get right to the point: we're here to ask you about Peter Stem."

"Pete? Is he okay? I haven't seen him in a few weeks. Did something happen?"

"He's fine, we just have a few questions… You're a friend of his, correct?"

"Yes. We've known each other for almost ten years."

"That's a long time."

"Yeah it is. Pete and Father McCormick—from St. Agassi—get their haircuts here… uh, is Pete in trouble or something?"

"We're not at liberty to say. Just a few questions, and then you can get back to work."

"Okay..."

"What was the nature of your friendship?"

Vince leaned back. "Well, we're not gay, if that's what you're asking."

Ron eyed the Oprah Magazine. "That's not what I meant, but okay." In truth, he hadn't ruled it out.

"We hung out, like any normal guys... watched TV, had a few beers now and then—that's all."

"I thought Peter was a recovering alcoholic," John interjected.

"You're right. He is. That's why he drinks these. He pulled an empty *O'Douell's* bottle out of the trashcan. "Marco drinks them too."

Ron nodded. "Did Peter ever exhibit anger issues?"

"Pete?" Vince laughed. "Are you kidding me? Pete's one of the most mellow guys I know... and the nicest—he'd give you the shirt off his back."

"How is he with women?"

Vince shrugged. "He likes a pretty girl as much as the next guy, I guess."

"Was he ever hostile toward them?"

Vince leaned back in his chair, as if distancing himself from the question. "Never."

"Did you ever know him to express frustration or anger toward *anyone*?"

Vince crossed his arms. "No... Aren't these the same questions?"

Ron ignored him and took a deep breath. "Does the name *Suzanne* mean anything to you?"

Vince scrunched his forehead, thinking, then shook his head. "No. Should it?"

Ron looked over at John, who had been diligently taking notes. He sighed, not at all surprised that they had hit another dead end.

"You wouldn't by chance know about any girls Peter was seeing would you?"

"Seeing?"

"Father McCormick said there was someone in Peter's life. A *girlfriend.*"

"A girlfriend? " He shook his head. "No one comes to mind... unless..."

"Unless?"

"Maybe he's thinking of Lydia." He scrunched his forehead. "But that's been over for a while now."

"Doesn't matter. Any idea where we could find this Lydia?"

"Yeah, sure I do," Vince replied. "She works at the Riley's Drugs next door."

The lights were on, but Riley's pharmacy was closed. Ron looked at his watch. It was just about 8:30 PM. *So much for the whole block staying open late.* Pretty stupid business decision to close early, he thought, especially if you were a mom and pop shop competing with the likes of CVS and Rite Aid.

# Forty-four

Lauren and the kids spent the entire Sunday morning in the Goldberg Academy auditorium working on scenery. The Chanukah "play", Lauren quickly learned, was actually a full-scale production of skits and melodies, everything from a re-enactment of the Greek siege of the holy temple to a dreidel song medley, during which younger siblings would be invited up on stage to play the role of spinning Chanukah gelt. Rachel was busy at work on backdrops and stage design with her friend Sara. The job was intense—they had only a couple of weeks to prepare—but the distraction had been clearly beneficial for Rachel. The nine-year-old had thrown herself into the project, and had demonstrated a natural, creative flair for detail. She had already come up with clever, but inexpensive ways to enhance the sets. One of her ideas had been to crush the corners of empty boxes and paint them the color of boulders for the battle scene; another was to have moveable clouds on a clothesline. After several weeks of Rachel's detached attitude—at least toward her—Lauren had all but given up trying to reconnect. But today it was as though a switch had been flipped and Rachel was back to her old self. "Good job guys." That wasn't so unusual since she always encouraged her brothers; but then she actually smiled at Lauren and added, "you too, Lauren. I like the way you painted the sun. It looks really nice."

It was nearly lunchtime when Lauren headed home with the boys. Rachel opted to stay behind, happy and fully engrossed in her work, but Lauren wanted to be back before Yehuda came home with the baby. Poor Nehama had developed a bumpy rash under her chin and had been crying incessantly. Yehuda had secured her an 11:00 AM doctor's appointment.

Candle costumes in hand, Lauren was instructed by Mrs. Green, the faculty member overseeing production, to make whatever adjustments were necessary to fit them properly. Lauren was no seamstress, so her immediate inclination was to call Sonia. There was something about Russian women, Lauren realized. Somehow they were more skilled in all areas of domestic life. Sonia knit and sewed her own clothes; she could cook like a gourmet chef, and actually knew how to iron properly! Maybe that was what attracted so many American men to women like Sonia. Besides their undeniable physical beauty, they were willing to revive the lost art of domesticity. Lauren sighed. *So much for Sonia being honored and cherished!*

Now that she and Sonia were on speaking terms again, Lauren made it a point to call every other day, just to check in. Lauren hoped that Sonia would eventually open up about what was going on at home, but so far she hadn't. The more Lauren thought about Gary, the more disgusted she became. How dare he lay a hand on his wife! She had considered calling the S.O.S. line and leaving an anonymous tip: *Sonia Lyman needs help,* but then she remembered that Sonia *had* been to see Tova. Chances were that Sonia was already getting the help she needed. *Then why hadn't she left him yet?*

Well, today, like any other day, Sonia would probably jump at any opportunity to get out of the house—away from that so called husband of hers. She dialed Sonia's number, but to her horror, Gary answered. Lauren got a very bad feeling. What was he doing home from work in the middle of the day?

"Sonia doesn't feel well today," he said gruffly. "You'll have to manage on your own." Lauren felt the urge to run over to the house that instant... to do what? Confirm that Sonia was alive and well? *Relax*, she told herself, *everything's probably fine. Besides, you have children to take care of, costumes to fix, remember?*

Lauren eyed the boys as they struggled with bent arms to hold up the weight of their candle costumes. Without a seasoned seamstress like Sonia, she would just have to improvise.

"Hmm. I have an idea," Lauren told the boys. "Wait here, I'll be right back."

Lauren hugged herself against the cool dampness as she made her way down the cellar steps with Rosie following close behind. As far as unfinished basements went, this one was extremely orderly, with clearly defined areas for laundry, tools, and general storage. Perusing the tool area for materials, Lauren eyed several stuffed garbage bags that she hadn't noticed before. After a quick peek inside one of them, she remembered that Hannah had been putting together a donation for the local *gemach*. There was an assortment of old children's clothes, including several with tags still on them. Lauren knew these had been gifts from Judith. She pulled a few out to take a closer look: *A cashmere baby sweater. Toddler size silk pajamas. A boy's leather jacket.* The prices had been scratched off, but it was obvious they hadn't come from eBay. Maybe she would add the clothing Cynthia Bergerman sent over for Rachel: three miniskirts and coordinating tank tops—Yehuda had nearly gagged when he saw them. It occurred to Lauren that no orthodox parent in their right mind would outfit their daughter in such revealing clothing. No, Cynthia's gifts would have to be bagged separately and sent off to Goodwill downtown. Come to think of it, Lauren hadn't seen or heard from Cynthia since the news about the bounced check. Was *Bergerman Bagels* really having financial problems? It was hard to believe. Besides, weren't bagels recession proof?

Lauren dug further and came across a long moleskin skirt. She remembered the afternoon Hannah had dumped a pile of zippered skirts into a heap on her bedroom floor. It was just two weeks after having Nehama. "Elastic waists are not optional after five kids," she said, "or even *one* for that matter!" She had already given Lauren several pairs of shoes that day, claiming that her feet had grown a full size after the baby. And now she encouraged Lauren to sift through the skirts and pick out what she liked. "Don't take this the wrong way," Hannah said, "but you'll attract more attention if you change your wardrobe. Men like women who dress like *ladies*."

Lauren tried to remember. Who was it Hannah had been pushing on her that week? Was it the twenty-three year old, baby-faced math teacher from Brooklyn? Or the newly divorced, *he knew it was a mistake from the beginning,* accountant visiting from Vermont? Lauren declined Hannah's clothing offer; she was perfectly content wearing jeans and sweats thank you very much.

*Funny how things could change so quickly.*

Lauren looked down at the denim skirt she now wore, one of several she had picked up at Station Square last week with Janine. She had bought them a little roomy, thinking that would make them more comfortable, but it really had made no difference. *Once a pants person, always a pants person,* she thought. There had been several times— notably, when Judith gave her that special "look" of disgust she reserved just for her—that Lauren had come close to shoving her new purchases in the garbage. But each time she pulled herself together and reminded herself why she was wearing them in the first place.

*Yehuda. I'm wearing them for Yehuda.* It was obvious Yehuda preferred women who dressed modestly like Hannah. She laughed to herself remembering the visit from Cynthia. Clearly, he preferred that they wear underwear too. So what if she wasn't so comfortable? It wouldn't be forever. Just for now, she would make this tiny sacrifice to dress respectfully for Yehuda and the kids.

She looked down at her skirt and sighed. This was only the second time she wore it and it was already ruined—covered in black splotches from a minor mishap involving paint and Yitzi while mixing some colors for the miracle scene. She eyed the washing machine. Might as well toss it in the wash since she was down here anyway, and she could easily slip into one of Hannah's old skirts from the donation bag. Besides, Judith would be showing up any minute and Lauren didn't want to look like a complete slob. It would be just one more thing for her to find fault with. Thank God the woman hadn't spent this Shabbat with them and was only coming for the day! Lauren couldn't stand the feeling of Judith's eyes on her. Following her. Observing her with the kids. *With Yehuda.* It was obvious she hadn't liked Lauren from the beginning, though it seemed to have gotten worse since Lauren opened her big mouth.

*I think Yehuda and I are better judges of what the kids need.*

Lauren cringed at the memory. Why was she so damn impulsive sometimes? Why did she feel the need to be so forthright? That was the trait that always got her in trouble, most recently with Hannah. Again, that need to speak her mind! And now with Judith on her case, she was beginning to feel paranoid. Was Judith just being her normal judgmental self? Or did the woman actually *suspect* something? There had been a few instances when Lauren had come close to confessing to

Yehuda. But each time, there had been an interruption—either one of the kids needed his attention, or the phone would ring.

Lauren knew if she was going to spill the beans, it had to be soon. Although Hannah hadn't regained full consciousness, she *was* making positive strides. Dr. Patel was optimistic. It could be any time now.

Lauren brushed these thoughts away and quickly slipped out of her skirt and into Hannah's. As expected it fit almost perfectly. But the brown skirt didn't look so great with her blue turtleneck. If she remembered correctly, the skirt had a matching cardigan... Lauren rooted to the bottom of the bag. There it was! A bit wrinkly, but perfectly fine.

She returned to the kitchen minutes later holding a skein of tightly wound string. The boys had released the hold on their costumes and were dragging them around on the floor, munching meditatively on chocolate chip cookies and humming one of the songs they had practiced at school. Rosie was sleeping contentedly by the kitchen window.

"Okay guys, I have an idea for your costumes," Lauren said, clapping her hands, to get their attention. "Put the cookies down, and let's see what we can do."

She unraveled a section of the string and ran it across David's shoulder, front to back, like measuring tape. "There! Now, all we need," she said, reaching over and grabbing a pair of scissors from the table, "are two of these." She held up the measured section and then handed the end to Eli. "Hold this as straight as you can," she told him. She snipped the string, then measured and cut a second, identical piece. She motioned to David. "Now, I'm going to attach each of these to your candle and voila' you'll have instant—nearly invisible, I might add—shoulder straps!" She reached around and tickled Yitzi who had been watching the entire scene behind her, his mouth wide open in concentration, a half chewed cookie on his tongue.

"No more chicken arms for your brothers, right Yitzi?"

He giggled and resumed chewing. "No chicken arms for Eli and David!"

Lauren carefully cut holes through the laminated construction paper and slipped the straps through. David stepped into his costume and tucked his arms into the newly created straps.

"Better?" Lauren asked, pleased with the result.

"Uh huh," David said, examining himself. "I don't know why I have to be a girl candle though!"

"Just because you're pink, doesn't mean you're a girl," Eli said, handing his costume to Lauren. "Besides, candles aren't *anything*. They're just candles!"

"Then let's switch!" David said immediately. "I'll be the blue one and you be the pink one!"

"I can't switch!" Eli said, "I'm the Shamash candle!"

"How come you get to be the Shamash?" David asked, folding his arms.

"Because I'm the tallest of all the kids!" Eli said, lengthening his body to make his point.

This seemed to appease David, who sighed and mumbled something about being the Shamash candle next year.

"The Shamash candle is the middle candle, right?" Lauren asked as she worked on straps for Eli's costume.

"It doesn't have to be in the middle of the menorah," David said. He looked up at her and did a double take.

"Oh, it doesn't?" she asked, sensing a sudden change in him.

He shook his head and looked down. "No," he said softly, but didn't elaborate.

"It just has to be higher because it's the extra candle that lights all the other ones," Eli said. He didn't seem to notice that anything was wrong with his brother.

"That's right Eli! Very good!"

"Abba!" Yitzi jumped up and ran over to Yehuda, wrapping his arms around one of his legs. Yehuda patted Yitzi's head as he pressed a finger to his lips. "Shh! Nehama's sleeping."

"What did the doctor say?" Lauren asked.

"Nothing to worry about. Just early teething," Yehuda said. "The rash is from her drool."

Lauren smiled brightly. Ever since Yehuda had put Jonathon off, she felt closer to him. She often wondered if he felt the same way. "Baruch Hashem! Thank God!"

"Baruch Hashem!" Yehuda repeated, before lifting Yitzi into the air. "Now let's go help Nana. She just pulled up."

*Great*, Lauren thought. *Judge Judy is here.* Then she caught sight of David who remained seated, his knees pulled in, on the floor. Rosie sat next to him, as if to comfort him. "What is it David? What's the matter?" His face was contorted, as if he was doing everything in his power not to cry. "Are you worried about your Nana?"

"No. But you…"

"But I *what?*" she asked.

He burst into tears. "I… I…"

"What is it, David?" she pushed.

"I thought you were Mommy."

"What's going on here?" Judith boomed from the doorway. At the sight of her, Rosie gave a little screech and ran out.

Lauren gulped as she held David in her arms, trying to comfort him. David looked up at her with a "please don't tell my Nana" plea in his eyes. Even though Judith had apologized about the shoe-tying comment, he still worried about her opinion of him.

Given the circumstances, Lauren was more than happy to accommodate him. "Oh, klutzy me!" she said dramatically. "I accidentally whacked David in the arm when I was fitting his costume." Lauren stared straight into his eyes as she said this. David was a smart kid; surely he would understand what she was doing. She rubbed his arm. "All right now, sweetie?"

Momentarily confused, David forced a small smile and nodded.

Judith studied the scene suspiciously, but then said, "You really should be more careful, Lauren." She opened her arms and smiled broadly at David. "Come, David. Come give Nana a kiss!"

David obeyed and trotted over to her like a puppy. Judith glared at Lauren, even as she embraced her grandson.

"I have to practice my lines now," David said, wriggling himself from Judith's arms.

"Lines?" Judith looked around, seemingly just noticing the costumes and string in a heap on the kitchen floor.

"David's a Chanukah candle in the school play," Lauren said.

"But not the Shamash," David added, looking forlorn.

"Oh!" Judith said dramatically. "Well, that's okay. A regular candle is just as exciting as the…"

"Shamash" David said.

"Right. The *Shamash*," Judith repeated as David scurried out. Lauren tried to stifle her laughter. It was obvious that Judith Orenstein, the mother of a rabbi, had no idea what a Shamash was. Lauren expected the question to come any second, but Judith had something else on her mind, wagging her finger at Lauren's legs like she was pointing out a urine stain on the carpet. "That outfit… I've seen it before." Her eyes passed slowly up Lauren's body until she locked her gaze directly into Lauren's eyes. "But not on you."

Lauren's face flushed. Whirring sounds from the spin cycle only reminded her how foolish she had been putting on Hannah's old clothes.

"I…" Lauren began, but was interrupted by a boy's voice calling from the living room.

"Nana, Abba needs your car key!"

Judith gave Lauren a look of warning before turning on her heel and marching out of the kitchen.

Lauren waited until she heard the front door close before bolting upstairs to change.

# Forty-five

Early Monday morning, twenty-nine year old Lydia Richter walked into the police station wearing a pair of jeans and a white cable-knit sweater. About 5'4", she had light brown hair, which she wore pulled back neatly in a low ponytail. She was a plain, bottom heavy girl, probably a good candidate for liposuction, Ron thought for some unknown reason. *There I go with more stupid, irrelevant nonsense* Ron thought. *One more thing to add to the list for the neurologist.* In the meantime, he would double up on his Ginkgo Biloba intake this week.

Lydia accepted Ron's offer of a hot beverage and he took his time pouring it, hoping she would calm down a bit. It was obvious she was nervous from the way she kept shifting in her seat and biting her nails. The calmer she was, the faster they could get through this. *Just tell me Peter's real name,* thought Ron, *and be done with it.*

John joined them a minute later, introduced himself to Lydia, and took a seat off in the corner, the way he and Ron had agreed.

After asking Lydia to state her full name, address and occupation, Ron got right to the point, asking if she knew Peter Stem.

"*Peter?*" Lydia stopped nibbling her nails and crossed her arms tightly against her chest.

"Do you know him?" Ron repeated the question.

She nodded.

"Well then, I'd like to ask you a few questions if that's all right."

Lydia considered this for a minute, eyeing both men suspiciously. "I guess that would be okay."

"How do you know Peter?"

"He used to come into Riley's."

"To see you?"

"No. Mostly for Snickers bars. King size."

"I see."

"Sometimes for chips. Salt and vinegar."

"Thank you." Ron forced a polite smile. "How would you describe Peter?"

Lydia thought for a moment. "Nice but too serious."

"*Serious?* In what way?"

Lydia shrugged. "I don't know; he worries a lot."

Ron caught John's eye. "Any idea what he worries about?"

She shook her head. "About the priest mostly. He fell once."

"What happened?"

"Peter had to take him to the hospital."

"Senecca?"

"I guess."

Ron made a note to check into that later. "Was Peter ever aggressive?" he continued.

Lydia puckered her lips like she had a bad taste in her mouth. "Aggressive?" She seemed not to understand the word.

"Did he ever raise his voice, for instance?"

Lydia held up two fingers in a "V" position. "Twice"

Ron raised his eyebrows. "What happened?"

"The first time I almost got run over crossing the street and he yelled at me to be more careful and look both ways." She giggled and tapped the top of her head. "Sometimes I forget."

"And the second time?"

Lydia was about to say something, but clamped down on her lip instead. "I made a mistake. It was just the one time. He yelled at me one time."

Ron had his doubts. "Did Peter ever hit you?" he asked gently.

"You mean on purpose?"

Again, Ron eyed John out of the corner of his eye. Like a good detective, John's expression remained neutral. "On purpose or by accident... either way."

"Umm... No."

Ron leaned back in exasperation. He drew in a deep breath and exhaled it toward the ceiling.

"Peter's one of the nicest people I know!" Lydia announced with a sudden burst of energy. "He told me how once he was fishing in chocolate milk and didn't throw a fish back in time and it floated to the top and it was dead and he felt so bad he cried!"

*Huh?*

Lydia puckered her lips "What was it?" She tapped her chin. "It was called a vanilla sucky or something."

*Okay.*

Ron had to pick his jaw off the ground. "So, you're saying Peter fishes a lot?"

Lydia shook her head. "Uh uh. Nope."

Ron decided to drop the subject, especially since he hadn't seen any fishing poles or supplies at the rectory anyway.

Lydia opened her purse. "Do you want some gum?" she asked Ron.

She rifled through the contents, which Ron could see were mostly candy—M&M's, Tootsie Rolls, and a few Pez dispensers. "Peter loves Fruit Stripe gum!" she announced.

Ron shook his head and smiled politely. *Red dye # 4, No thanks, I'll pass.* Lydia turned to John and extended the pack, but he too declined. She shrugged and folded a piece into her mouth.

"How would you describe your relationship with Peter?" Ron continued.

She carefully unwrapped a second piece. "Our *relationship?*"

Ron nodded.

"We were friends. Once in a while he liked to get an ice cream sandwich from the freezer at the store. At Riley's we have the old fashioned kind—you know, the big box that sits on the floor. It's so fun! Cold air blasts you every time you open it. Did you know, I get a 10% discount on all my icecream! I saved Peter soooo much money!"

Ron realized this was going to be more difficult than it needed to be. In fact the entire conversation might just be a complete waste of time.

"Did you ever visit Peter at the rectory?"

She furrowed her brow. "I hate animals and there's a dog at the rectory."

"That's right. *Samson.*"

"Samson hates me. He tried to bite me."

"Really?" Ron asked, surprised. The dog seemed fairly laid back the couple of times he had seen her.

She nodded and clenched her jaw. "I hate animals," she said again, "including dogs."

"Fair enough," Ron said. "Tell me, when was the last time you saw Peter?"

She stopped chewing and considered the question. "I can't remember…"

"Could you give me an estimate?"

She glanced over at John, as if he could help.

"I don't know. A long time ago."

"Did you ever have a relationship with Peter Stem that could be considered 'more than friends'?"

Lydia sat up, her eyes wide. "*Who* told you that?" she demanded.

"Do you know a man named Vince Mancotti?"

She relaxed and settled back down. "Oh, Mannie? Yeah, he works at Giovonni's, next door to Riley's. He doesn't like ice-cream."

"Is that so? Well, Vince Mancotti thought you might have been Peter's girlfriend at one time."

Lydia tugged on her ponytail. "Really? Is that what Mannie told you?" She seemed pleased, even while wiping away two small tears pooling in the corners of her eyes. "No," she said shaking her head, "I *wanted* Peter to make me his girlfriend. I gave him my discount and everything! But he just wouldn't!" She blew her nose. "I'm just not pretty enough for him… Oh, wait!" she said, her mood suddenly lifting, "I just remembered something!"

Ron sat at attention, anticipating some important revelation.

"Peter likes Klondike bars the best."

First he thought it was nerves or immaturity, but now Ron considered that Lydia might have a slight to moderate mental impairment. He decided the best course of action would be to ignore her last remark about ice cream and forge ahead with the interview. "Peter actually *said* you weren't pretty enough?"

She sniffled. "Well, *no*. But I could just tell… Besides, he likes the girls at St. Agassi better."

Ron's heart sped up. "Which girls?"

"The girls that come at night—to the spa."

Ron glanced over at John. They were both thinking the same thing.

"What did Peter tell you about them exactly?"

"I don't remember," she said, scratching her head. "Oh wait... I think he said one of them was going to be his girlfriend."

"One of them was going to be his girlfriend?" Ron repeated, bracing himself. "Did he happen to say which *one*?"

"No," Lydia said, then shrugged, like it was all old news anyway. "Is it true what I've heard?"

"What have you heard?" Ron asked.

"That it closed?"

"Yes, that's true."

"I got a facial once," she said, "not there. It was at a place on Walnut Street. But I didn't like when they put the hot washcloth over my face." She fished around her purse for a tissue and spit her gum out.

"Getting back to Peter," Ron said, "did you ever call him by a different name?"

"No. He didn't like me to call him *Pete*, even though he didn't care if *Mannie* did!"

"Anything completely different, another name entirely?"

Lydia just stared at him, scratching her nose.

Ron rephrased the question. "Did he tell you he had another name besides *Peter Stem*?"

She furrowed her brow. "That's crazy. Why would Peter have two names?"

Ron let it drop. "Did Peter ever mention his family, or say where he was from originally?"

She shook her head and looked down. Suddenly, she started trembling. Mustering all her strength, she leaped out of her chair.

"Why are you asking me these questions anyway? Peter doesn't want me! He told me to stop calling and leave him alone!" She shook her head. "So why should I answer any questions about him? Why should I care what happens to him!"

# Forty-six

Lewis tapped gently on the door to Ron's office before slowly turning the knob. "Oh, pardon me. I was looking for Detective Smith."

"Well don't just stand there! C'mon in!"

The gruff words were spoken by an elderly, white haired man. He sat, hunched over Ron's desk, a blue sweatshirt hanging loosely on his bony frame. There was something familiar about him, though Lewis couldn't quite put his finger on it.

The man cocked his head and peered suspiciously at Lewis. "What are you deaf or something? Come in already! I've been waiting for you." The man had an unusual complexion—it was the same grayish white hue of a winter sky moments before it snowed—and his eyes were dark and cavernous, hollow like empty shells.

Intrigued, Lewis closed the door behind him and sat down in one of the old leather chairs.

"So have you got them for me?" The man asked impatiently thrumming his fingers on the desk.

Lewis played along. "What was it you were looking for exactly?"

The man drew a shaking fist up to chin level and then slammed it down. "Dab nab it! They told me you were a hard nut to crack. Let's stop playing games! We both know it's there!"

He was interrupted by the sound of the door opening. A weary looking Ron entered. Quickly taking in the scene in front of him, he glanced apologetically at Lewis before addressing the old man behind his desk. "Dad! What's going on? Where's Violet?"

The older man straightened up and swiped the air. "That girl? I fired her! She doesn't know where the rest of my files are for plum's sake! All I have is this one!" He shook his head. "I tell ya, every week it's something else with that girl."

Ron scratched his head, seemingly weighing the situation and considering the best way to proceed. He turned to Lewis. "I apologize Dr. Danzig; I was conducting an interview in the conference room..."

"Conference room!" the older man bellowed. "I didn't get any memo about there being a conference! See what I told you about that girl! Unreliable is what she is!"

"Excuse me a second," Ron mouthed to Lewis. He moved toward the desk where several papers were strewn about.

"What do you think you're doing there young fella? I was working on that case!"

"Well, this case is closed," Ron said, obviously losing patience.

The old man stared down Lewis while Ron gathered the papers and shoved them into an empty accordion folder. "This file is useless anyhow without the blueprints!" he said. "I want to see those blueprints! I know you have them!"

Ron sighed and unclipped his cell phone before stepping out into the hallway. A minute later a middle aged black woman came trotting down the hall, panting. "I'm... sorry... Mr.... Smith... I ran out for a... quick cigarette." She spoke loudly enough to be overheard through the crack in the door. "I wasn't... gone more than... five minutes." She wiped her forehead with the back of her hand. "Your dad... he was fast asleep. Honest."

She sounded genuinely remorseful, though Lewis knew for a fact she had been gone for longer than five minutes.

"What are you doing back here?" The old man yelled as Violet walked in. "I told you you're fired!"

"Dad... Violet didn't lose the files, I did."

The old man's eyes popped and he looked like he was going to burst a vein in his forehead.

"But, good news! I found them," Ron added quickly. He pulled out a stack of empty folders from his briefcase. "I'm sorry, Dad. It wasn't Violet's fault."

The old man eyed Violet suspiciously. "Well, all right then. Be more careful son."

Ron lit up at the word *son*. "I will Dad."

The old man turned to Lewis and extended his arm as if seeing him for the first time. "Oh hello. I don't believe we've met. I'm Detective Ronald Smith."

Lewis shook his arm gently. He was afraid he would break it, the man was so frail.

"It's an honor to meet you, sir."

Ron Smith Sr. looked blankly at his son. "And who are you? What are you doing in my office?"

Ron's face dropped.

"Dad, it's me..."

"Who?"

He lowered a voice to nearly a whisper. "Your son—*Ronnie.*" He glanced at Lewis out of the corner of his eye.

The older man squinted at him suspiciously. "Ronnie? I don't know any Ronnie! What do you take me for, some kind of fool?"

Violet stood up. "I think now's a good time to get you back home," she said.

He looked at her dazed. "Ella?"

"No honey, I'm Violet."

He spun around, panicked like a lost child. "What is all this? Where am I?"

"Visiting. You were visiting some friends," Violet said gently. "But now it's time to go." She helped him with his jacket. "I parked in the lot across the street," she said to Ron. "It might be slick because of the snow."

"Right… I'll give you a hand."

Ron wrapped his arm around his dad's waist, and guided him toward the door. He looked over his shoulder at Lewis. "I'll be back in a few minutes."

"The second half I'll show them coach!" the old man boomed as he was led out. He had a glazed but determined look in his eyes. "Once I ice this leg and get back in the game, they won't know what hit 'em!" Suddenly he began limping as though he had a sprained ankle. He sniffed the air and crinkled his nose. "You smell like an ashtray Ella! I'll tell you what; that sure is one nasty habit!... Nasty!"

# Forty-seven

Ron returned to the office several minutes later, flecks of snow in his hair. Visibly exhausted, he didn't bother removing his damp coat. Instead, he collapsed in his chair, leaned back, covered his eyes and let out a little groan.

"I hope you don't mind that I helped myself to a bottle of water." Lewis said, breaking the ensuing silence.

Ron waved him off. "Whatever," he said, putting his head down on the desk.

"Headache?" Lewis asked.

Ron closed his eyes. "Yeah, well, I don't have to tell you... that's the least of my problems."

"Stage six, I assume," Lewis said.

Ron's eyes popped open. He sat up, a questioning look on his face.

"Your father. His Alzheimer's. It presents like stage six," Lewis said.

Ron's face visibly relaxed, as if he just remembered that psychiatrists were medical doctors first. He took his time rolling up each shirtsleeve, avoiding Lewis's eyes. "Yeah. That's right. Stage six."

"It's very difficult to see a loved one change so dramatically," Lewis said.

Ron leaned back in his chair and cast his gaze toward the window. The snow was slowing down. "Change? It's more like *deteriorate!* Half the time he doesn't know who he is… doesn't know who *I* am."

A fly buzzed by in a panic, looking for a way out.

"Who'd have thought a whisky drinking, chain smoking bull of a man could turn into…"

"Chain smoking?" Lewis interrupted. "After his remark to Violet I wouldn't have thought he was a smoker."

Ron laughed, rolling forward in his chair. "Oh, he was a chain smoker all right—at one point smoking two packs a day—tried to quit a million times, but never could. Mom couldn't stand it; she made him smoke in the garage, threatened to leave him if he didn't quit. I think that was part of the reason he worked such long hours—at least he could smoke in his office without her barking down his throat." He shook his head. "Isn't it crazy how things turn out? For years Mom was worried about him getting lung cancer—and what does he end up with instead? *Old Timers!*" Ron gave an exaggerated shrug. "Sorry, that's slang for Alzheimer's. You know what they say, if you can't laugh…" He sighed loudly. "Well, anyway, at least he finally quit smoking, right?"

Lewis nodded sympathetically. "How did he manage to do it?"

"Quit? Oh, it was easy. One day, about three years ago he forgot he was a smoker and just quit cold turkey."

Lewis smiled. "It reminds me of a colleague of mine who worked with a patient with multiple personalities," he said. "Two of the personalities smoked, the third was a health nut—exercised every day and was repulsed by the mere thought of lighting up. Shows the power of the subconscious mind, doesn't it?"

"To hell with the subconscious," Ron said, puckering his lips and blowing air toward the ceiling, "I'd take my chain smoking dad back in a heartbeat. Even if he got lung cancer or emphysema, at least he would remember who the hell he was!" Ron rested his elbows on the desk and sighed. "The way he is now… well, I'm sorry to say it, but he can be a real pain in the ass—even when he's lucid! Don't ask me how Violet does it. The crap that woman puts up with…"

"Violet is his full time nurse?"

"Uh huh."

"Does your father still live at home?"

Ron nodded. "Mom took care of him up until six months ago when she died. *Stroke.*"

"I'm sorry…"

"Caring for him really took a lot out of her," Ron continued. "In hindsight, I probably should have… maybe if I had… well, it's too late for *shoulda coulda woulda's* now, isn't it?"

"Does your father know about her death?" Lewis asked gently.

Ron shook his head and sighed. "His doctor thought it might be better this way." He rolled back in his chair and reached down into his fridge. "Vitamin water?"

Lewis held up his half full water bottle. "I'm good."

"The doctor also thought it would be best if I moved back home—you know, to help."

They sat in silence, watching the fly whack itself repeatedly against the window, buzzing in frustration.

"So much for trial and error, huh Doc?" Ron said, gesturing toward the window with his chin. "Don't know why the little bugger wants out so bad anyway, not with the snow coming down like it is."

Lewis wouldn't let the detective change the subject. Everyone could use a bit of talk therapy now and then.

"How long has your father had the disease?"

Ron thought for a moment. "It's hard to say when it began. I can tell you when I started *noticing*, though. It was about seven years ago—Dad was only sixty."

Lewis was surprised at the disclosure of Ron Sr.'s age. He appeared to be at least a decade older.

"And what were the initial signs?"

"Well, for one thing, he started slipping mentally... couldn't remember names, cases. It wasn't a big deal at first. His partner and I were able to watch his back for some time but then it got so bad, he had to go."

"And you've run things in this department since then?"

"Not at first, but then when John—Dad's partner—left, I just naturally took over. That surprises a lot of people. They think because I'm younger, I don't have as much experience... But to those skeptics I say this: Arden Station isn't exactly a huge metropolis, is it? Besides, I grew up with a father whose idea of small talk was *postmortem dental identification.*" He laughed. "You can imagine what our dinner conversations were like. Mom said all the talk about dead bodies is what kept her a size six!"

Lewis suddenly remembered his own self-absorption at the dinner table, talking about the latest research, the newest meds. He'd give Elise five minutes to talk about her day before the floor was his and he'd be off, talking human behavior for the remainder of the meal. At the time he didn't think there was anything so terrible about it; after all, he was educating his daughter, giving her a leg up on information she would need in medical school!

"Besides," Ron continued, "I worked six years under Collins and my dad. On the job training doesn't get much better than that."

"Do you mind if I ask you a question about this office?" Lewis asked, gesturing with his hands.

Ron gazed at the window where the fly had all but given up, standing quietly on the thin ledge. "I asked them to leave it this way," he said. "On Dad's good days, I like to bring him here. See, this office was Dad's second home. At first, I thought maybe it would help him… maybe even cure the Alzheimer's." Ron laughed. "It's obvious I was pretty darn naïve about the disease back then! In any event, visiting this old place *has to be* a comfort to him." Ron shrugged. "Or maybe I just like believing that it is—I don't know. But, bottom line is he was a great dad and I owe him at least this much. Besides, it won't be much longer. He's moving soon. After that, the office will get a complete overhaul."

"Moving?"

"There's a facility in Florida—not far from Miami. Mom found it a year before she… Anyway, he was on the waiting list. Well, wouldn't you know, his name came up and I got the call last month, a couple days before this Peter Stem case took over my life…" He sighed. "They only give you ninety days to move in or you forfeit your slot…"

Lewis understood the situation. "Do you have any siblings, or other family members who can help?"

Ron shook his head. "Nope. The only family is my father's brother, but trust me, he has his own problems. Besides, it's not an issue now that John's working the case with me. It'll be over soon and I'll be able to get Dad squared away in no time."

Lewis was struck by how much the detective had gone through in the past several years. He had seen plenty of people crack under milder circumstances. It was a wonder the man was able to get out of bed in the morning. "Why don't you go with him?" Lewis asked.

Ron looked at Lewis like he was crazy. "I *am*. I'm the one moving him into his new home… I just told you."

"No; what I meant was, why not *stay* once you're there?"

"Stay?" Ron repeated. "What's the point?"

"The point is simply to *be* with him," Lewis said. "I'm sure I don't have to tell you the life expectancy of Alzheimer's patients, especially at stage six… It's not very long. In the meantime, your dad still has his lucid moments, why not take advantage of them before it's too late?"

"Just like that," Ron said, snapping his fingers, "just like that I should move permanently to Florida?"

Lewis sighed. "Look, I'm not telling you what to do. And I don't have to tell you what it's like to lose someone unexpectedly since you've been through that recently, but what I will tell you is that I've counseled many people in my career—individuals who knew they were going to die—and it's true what they say: in the end, very few things matter. The physical things are meaningless, as are our worldly accomplishments, how much money we've made, how many hours we've clocked at work…" Lewis lowered his voice. "What's important are our relationships, being surrounded by loved ones, spending time with those we hold dear."

# Forty-eight

It took the custodial staff nearly an hour to transform the conference room to meet Lewis's specifications. He wanted a more comfortable environment, he had explained to Ron, one more conducive to relaxation than the stark interrogation room where he first met with Peter. So, as directed, the Formica table and five of the six chairs were removed from the room, as were all wall hangings, holiday decorations, township maps and whiteboards. In addition to a single armchair—which Lewis would be using—a long side table was spared. It was needed to set up the camera and sound equipment for taping. A tan upholstered couch was brought in, along with a couple of throw pillows, blankets and a tall floor lamp. Lewis decided it would be best to forgo the harsh fluorescent bulbs and keep the lighting subdued.

The door to the room opened, and Peter entered with a guard close behind. Thanks to Father McCormick's more frequent visits, Peter was well stocked with clean clothes and toiletries. Today he wore tan khaki pants and a long sleeved black polo shirt, and appeared to be better groomed than the heavy set guard in his faded brown uniform. Had it not been for the fact that Peter was incarcerated, or his inability to communicate coupled with the glazed, far off look in his eyes, one would hardly suspect the man was troubled.

"Hello, Peter," Lewis began, "I'm Dr. Danzig. We met a few days ago... Do you remember?"

Peter didn't respond, but did appear to be processing the doctor's words on some level. He allowed Lewis to take his arm and lead him slowly to the couch. "Peter, if it's all right, I'd like to remove your shoes and have you lay down. There are pillows and blankets... try to make yourself as comfortable as possible."

After Peter was settled, Lewis pulled his chair up close to the couch. He did a final review of the list of questions Ron had given him, then signaled for the guard to go.

"Peter," Lewis began, speaking very slowly and deliberately, "I want to use a technique called hypnosis on you. I'm sure you've heard of it in cases where people are trying to quit smoking or lose weight. Father McCormick told me that years ago you had a successful session with a hypnotherapist as part of your AA program to stop drinking. Is that right?"

Peter stared straight ahead, unresponsive, yet with a twinkle of understanding in his eyes.

"You were asked to concentrate on the therapists voice," Lewis continued. "Do you remember that?"

It could have been Lewis's imagination, but Peter appeared to nod slightly.

"With your permission, Peter, I'd like to get started. You will never lose control. With hypnosis, you will merely be entering a deep state of relaxation..."

Peter closed his eyes and placed his folded hands on his chest, which Lewis took as a non-verbal consent to proceed. He lowered his voice to just above a whisper and began. "Peter I want you to concentrate on your breathing... I want you to breathe deeply. Inhaling deep breaths... with each breath, your lungs are filling. Imagine a balloon inflating... good... and with each exhale, the air is released... the balloon is emptied... good..."

Peter shoulders relaxed. His lips parted slightly as he took steady breaths.

"Now I want you to imagine you are in a forest. A beautiful, soothing forest. There are trees all around you. Tall trees that stretch high into the sky. *Breathe*... Good. It's a cool day, not too cool... the temperature is perfect. The sun's rays are shining through the trees. The sun feels warm and comforting against your skin... keep breathing... deep breath in... good.. and out.... good. You are happy in these woods, Peter... There is a lovely smell around you. The smell of fresh clean air, the smell of pine. And there are beautiful sounds... the soothing chirps of birds high in their nests. You are so happy and peaceful here. *Breathe*... good... You are safe here... completely safe... Good... keep breathing deeply... deep breaths in... good... and out..."

Peter's chest rhythmically rose and fell with each breath. His eye lids fluttered.

"Now I'm going to count to five and you are going to be in state of complete relaxation," Lewis continued. "Your body and mind will be completely relaxed. I will ask you questions and you will answer them... One... Two... Three... Four... Five... *Good*."

Lewis looked over at the camera. It had been turned on before Peter was brought to the room. The green light was flashing. *Here we go.*

"I'm going to continue calling you *Peter*, is that all right?"

Peter nodded.

"Peter could you tell me how old you are?"

"Thirty-six." Peter's speaking voice had a pleasant sound. Not especially deep and manly, but certainly not effeminate. It was the voice of a neighbor, or husband or dad.

"Thirty-six. Good. Peter, could you tell me where you live?"

"I live at St. Agassi. 524 Trinity Lane in Arden Station."

"Do you live alone?"

"No. I live with Father Herbert McCormick."

Lewis was tempted to probe in to Peter's true identity, but was concerned that Peter might have developed a strong identification with the assumed name, *Peter Stem*. If so, it would be risky—on a psychological level—to challenge it. It was better to wait and get that information later.

"Peter I want to take you back… back six weeks, to October. Is that okay?"

"Yes."

"It's Sunday, October 23rd. It's 7:00 PM at night. What do you see?"

"I'm eating dinner."

"What are you eating?"

"Chicken parmesan."

"Are you alone?"

"No. I'm with Father McCormick. We always eat together."

"Is there anything else happening at this time?"

"We're watching *Wheel of Fortune*. I'm telling Father the spaces and the letters. He just reminded me to buy dog food tomorrow."

"All right. Good. Very good. Now I want to move ahead twenty-four hours. It's now Monday, October 24th, 7:00 PM, what do you see?"

"We're eating dinner. Pork chops and apple sauce… watching Wheel of Fortune."

Lewis couldn't help but smile at the homey image Peter painted. "Good. It's now 7:30 PM. Where are you? What are you doing?"

"I'm in the kitchen washing dishes and then I have to check all the windows."

"Why do you have to check the windows?"

"The storm… some of the windows have weak latches. They might blow open."

"I'd like you to move ahead now Peter. The dishes are finished. You're checking the windows."

"I'm upstairs at the windows now. I see a car over at the high school… It's one of the old ladies. They come at night before the others."

"Who are the *others?*"

"The girls. *Women.* They show up every night. They didn't always, but now they do. Sometimes two of them, sometimes more. It's different every night."

"Do you watch them often?"

Peter nodded.

"How long have you been watching them?"

"Since the summer when they started coming. I use binoculars."

Lewis glanced at his notes. "Tell me about the van. What color is it?"

"It's red. There's a dent in the back."

"Are there any other vehicles?"

"Besides the backhoe? No, not yet. One of the old ladies always comes first, a few minutes before the others—wait, I see one coming now."

"Another car? What kind is it?"

"A Volvo. I think it's white."

*Elise.*

Lewis took a deep breath and fought to keep his objectivity, even as he imagined Peter watching his daughter without her knowledge. He swallowed. "Tell me what you see."

"She's getting out and walking to the back. She's wearing a long raincoat; her hood's on... I can't see her anymore..."

*Elise was inside.* Lewis felt a wave of panic. Presently, he knew his daughter was safe and sound; but there was no denying that hearing a play by play by the alleged perpetrator of a murder was unsettling. Things could have ended very differently.

"Now what do you see, Peter?"

"Nothing. No one else is coming."

"Okay, let's move ahead fifteen minutes."

"Here comes someone. It's the lady from the Volvo. She's getting back in her car and pulling out."

*Elise going home.*

"It's 8:30 now," Lewis said. "What do you see?"

"Nothing... But I hear Samson whining. I should go check...Oh; here comes another car."

"What kind is it?"

"A Lexus... a blond lady is driving... she's crying... now she's getting out... carrying a huge bag...Wait!" Peter's voice conveyed his sudden concern. "There's someone else..."

"Who is it Peter? Who do you see?"

"A man."

"Was he in the car with the woman?"

"No."

"A different car?"

"No... I don't see another car."

"Can you tell me what this man looks like?"

"Tall. He's wearing jeans and a ski jacket. It's hard for me to see..." Peter squinted then sat up abruptly. "No! NO!..."

"What's happening, Peter?"

"He grabbed her!"

"Grabbed who?"

"The lady from the Lexus... She's trying to pull away from him, she's trying to break free... but he pushed her down...He's hurting her!" Peter was hugging himself now. "I can't watch. I don't want to see..." Suddenly, Peter dropped his arms and tilted his head, as if listening intently to something.

"What is it, Peter?"

"It's Samson! Something's wrong."

"Where is Father McCormick?"

"Sleeping. I have to check on Samson. I'm going downstairs now... I'm in the kitchen."

A single tear formed in the corner of Peter's eye and trickled down his face.

"Is Samson okay?"

"No! Her paw is bleeding! There's glass everywhere! It's from the door... Father McCormick is here now. He's saying something but I don't pay attention... I'm busy bandaging up Samson's paw."

"I'd like to move ahead in time, Peter," Lewis suggested gently, "You're now finished bandaging Samson's paw. Where are you? What do you see?"

"I'm getting some supplies from the basement to board up the door."

"What time is it?"

"10:00."

"Are you alone?"

"Yes. Father McCormick went back to bed."

"What do you do next?"

"Check and make sure she's okay."

At first, Lewis thought he was talking about Samson. "How will you do that?" he asked.

"Go back to the window and look."

So it wasn't Samson at all. Peter was concerned about the woman from the Lexus.

"Did you ever talk to any of the women you watched, Peter?" Lewis asked as an aside.

"No, but I went over once and hid to see them close up." Peter shook his head remorsefully. "It's gone. The Lexus isn't there."

"Are there any other cars in the lot?"

He nodded. "There's a blue van."

"Do you see anyone?"

"No... they're all gone. Wait... here comes someone."

"Another car?"

"A black SUV." Peter suddenly became agitated. "It's him... He's *back*!"

"The same man?"

Peter furrowed his brow. "Uh huh. He's getting out of the car."

"Do you know this man?"

"No."

"Can you describe him?"

Peter squinted. "He's middle aged. Maybe forty-five or fifty."

"How can you tell?"

"The way he walks. He's kind of stiff. *Shuffling*."

"What else can you tell me about him?"

Peter's agitation was obvious. He was now taking short, shallow breaths. "He's wearing a long coat and a hat with strings. Boots."

"Can you see his face?"

Peter ignored the question. "He's looking for a way in! He's going around. He's going inside the gate! Oh no!... He did it! He went inside!" Peter was squirming now. He pulled his legs in and hugged his knees toward his chest. "He's going to hurt them... I know who he is!... I know what he's going to do! He's going to hurt them!"

Lewis was somewhat confused. Peter had just stated that he *didn't* know who the man was.

"Are you saying you *recognize* this man, Peter?"

Peter clenched his fists. Tears trickled down his cheeks as he nodded. "Uh huh. It's her old boyfriend!"

Lewis sat up. "*Whose* old boyfriend?"

Peter's lips trembled. "I hate him! I hate him!"

"Peter, listen to me! Whose old boyfriend is he?"

Peter burrowing his head between his knees as if trying to hide. He began rocking back and forth, crying hysterically.

"Whose old boyfriend is he, Peter?" Lewis pushed.

Peter had stopped moving. He peeked his head out like a turtle coming out of its shell. And now, it was no longer a grown man Lewis saw, but a frightened little boy.

"Momma's!"


Thirty minutes later, the guard came in to return Peter to his cell. Lewis leaned back in his chair, his hands behind his head, staring at the video equipment. It was moments like these that he was immensely grateful for technology. He closed his eyes and exhaled, still amazed at what he had just witnessed, what had been documented in it's entirety on video tape. Without the recording, he doubted the detective—or anyone else for that matter—would believe it; he was having a hard time swallowing it himself. He would review the tape later, perhaps even consult with a few of his colleagues. Lewis understood there would need to be an investigation to validate Peter's claims before anything got out; but as far as publication went, there was no rush. This case was so sensational, it was practically *screaming* to be memorialized in print.

Assuming the facts checked out, the case of Peter Stem just might be one of the most dramatic examples of posttraumatic stress Lewis had ever seen. Who would have ever guessed that Peter was simply a man with a tragic past? So he happened to have a bit of voyeurism in him—what man didn't? Sadly, it was his voyeurism that triggered the event. Seeing that man—whoever he was—in the mikvah parking lot reminded Peter of someone from his past, someone who had harmed his mother. Without a doubt, the tape would help exonerate Peter. Unfortunately it still wouldn't answer the question of who attacked two innocent women.

# Forty-nine

From her position at the sink, Judith watched as Lauren trudged around the backyard with Yitzi and David. The boys were bundled up in hand-me-down snowsuits, David in Eli's old pants, which fit him perfectly, while Yitzi swam in David's bib overalls. Lauren had done her best to roll up the bottoms, but they continued to unravel and drag in the slush. There was less than two inches on the ground, and the rising temperature and rain forecasted for that evening would surely liquefy any snowman they managed to build. Still, they persisted happily, taking occasional breaks from their efforts to pound each other with watery snowballs.

"She's great with them, isn't she?"

Judith spun around, "Yehuda! I didn't hear you! How long have you been standing there?"

Yehuda gave his mother a peck on the cheek. "I just walked in a minute ago."

She recoiled at his touch. "You're freezing! Let me get you some tea." She promptly filled the kettle and placed it on the stove. "Roads okay?"

"Fine."

"And Hannah?"

Yehuda smiled. "Great."

Judith studied her son's face. He looked refreshed, genuinely happy.

"Dr. Patel says her vitals are stronger than ever," he said, "and the fact that she's been stable for this long is an excellent sign."

Judith sighed. "Are you're sure he knows what he's talking about?"

Yehuda's smile fell away. "Mom…"

She shrugged. "I just wonder how competent he is, that's all."

"What do you mean?"

"For starters, he's impossible to track down, and then he doesn't have anything new to say about Hannah's condition anyway."

"Maybe if you didn't call him so much, he'd have more to tell you," Yehuda said. He regretted giving Dr. Patel permission to keep his mother updated; with all the upheaval he hadn't considered her general tendency to be a nuisance. "Besides, I've never had a problem reaching him; and when he's not at the hospital his service has him call me right back…"

"That's my point!" Judith interrupted, clapping each word. "Why should you have to speak to his answering service at all? If you ask me, he should have given you his cell phone number!"

"The man is entitled to a private life, Mom."

"Oh really? Even when people are counting on him? When actual lives are on the line?" She placed her hands on her hips and stood taller. "I wouldn't *dream* of doing that to one of my clients!"

"Well, maybe you *should*," Yehuda snapped.

She stared at him, surprised at his tone. "My clients need me,

Yehuda," she said calmly. "They have the right to reach me without the aid of a third party."

Yehuda sighed. "But at such a high cost…"

"I'm worth every penny," she said immediately.

"You know what I mean."

She shrugged and turned away from him.

He placed a hand on each of her shoulders, coaxing her to turn and face him. "Do you have any idea how stubborn and opinionated you are?" he asked.

She turned away from him. "I have high standards. Is that such a bad thing?"

"Only when it keeps you apart from others," he said.

"I'm here now, aren't I? I promised the kids I would stay an extra day and that's what I intend to do!"

"Yes… and I thank you for that. But…"

"But *what?*" she pushed.

"What happens when this is all over?"

*All over.* In one way or another, Judith knew, it would be all over. *Would Hannah pull through or would Yehuda find a replacement?* She pulled away from him. "I have responsibilities to my clients, Yehuda."

"Yes, but you also have a family who loves you. The kids deserve to see more of you. Visiting four times a year just isn't acceptable anymore."

Judith walked to the window and gazed out. Lauren and Yitzi were on their backs making snow angels. Judith felt a lump in her throat. "And you're just realizing this now?" she asked, her back to him.

"I think I've always known it," Yehuda said. "I just didn't say anything before—out of respect for you." He sighed. "I was wrong. I should have spoken up sooner."

She turned to face him. "So what am I supposed to do?" she asked, a look of exasperation on her face, "roll around in the slush like *her*? Will that satisfy you?"

"Mom...."

"I'm not twenty anymore Yehuda. I can't do certain things..."

Yehuda held up his hand. "I'm not asking you to ... "

Judith looked out the window again, hugging herself tightly. "Good, because you couldn't pay me a million dollars to be that age again... such stupidity!"

Yehuda didn't understand any of her ranting. "Mom, please, just listen to what I'm telling you."

Judith hadn't said anything about it before—partly because she was ashamed that she hadn't known about her grandkids' problems. But now, suddenly, she was determined to see Lauren removed from the house. If only Yehuda could see through her facade! She swung around to face her son. "Do you know what she told me?"

"Do I know what *who* told you?"

"*Lauren!*" Judith spewed. "You know—the one who's so *great with the kids*... as you, yourself put it."

Yehuda didn't say a word. He just stared at her, completely perplexed.

"That girl," Judith continued, pointing toward the window, "had the *audacity* to tell me... to tell me I didn't know my own grandchildren!" Somehow the words didn't *sound* as terrible as they felt.

Yehuda shoved his hands in his pockets. "I see."

Judith waited, palms out, but he said nothing more. What happened to the respect he just talked about a second ago? Why didn't he seem offended at Lauren's slight? Why wasn't he at least disputing what she had said? Judith rubbed her hands together in an attempt to warm herself from the sudden chill in the air as she remembered Yehuda's reaction when that man—Jonathon—had called for Lauren. *I'll let him know it won't work out for the two of you.*

"Well?" Judith's voice cracked. "Can you believe her nerve? Speaking to me so disrespectfully!"

He sighed, but said nothing.

She threw her arms up in exasperation. "Don't tell me!... No!... I can't believe it! You *agree* with her!"

He didn't say a word.

"Is this because I didn't know where the kids school was? Look, you know how busy I am, Yehuda! I can't be expected to know as much about them as someone who..."

"As someone who spends as much time with them as Lauren does?" Yehuda said, suddenly finding his voice.

Judith felt a lump in her throat. She couldn't believe this was happening, couldn't believe he was favoring Lauren—practically a *stranger*—to his own mother!

"Lauren's not your wife, Yehuda!" Judith shouted.

Yehuda narrowed his eyes. "My wife?"

"That's right! In fact, somebody should remind that girl that she's a paid employee for God's sake!"

Yehuda shook his head. "Technically, she's a volunteer."

"What?"

"Lauren's refused to take a cent from me."

Judith crinkled her forehead. "And you don't find it *odd* that she would work for nothing? You don't question her *motives?*"

"*Motives?*" Yehuda parroted. "What motives? Lauren's been a lifesaver for us! The kids love her. I can't say enough about how much she's helped them get through this..."

"Well, it's obvious you're in complete *denial!*" Judith mumbled.

Yehuda sighed. "I don't know what kind of crazy ideas you're getting about Lauren, but they're *wrong*."

Judith turned away. Obviously Yehuda was blind to the reality of the situation. Or maybe he wasn't. Maybe something was going on between the two of them! Suddenly, Judith felt like she might be sick. "I don't feel well," she said. "I have to go… I need some fresh air." She moved toward the front door, but Yehuda followed close behind.

"Where, exactly, are you going?"

"Where I can think," she said, grabbing her coat and bag from the closet.

"Mom, wait… sit down, I want to talk to you."

"There's nothing more to talk about. Everything's been said."

Yehuda sighed. "Fortunate is the generation in which the elders listen to the youth."

She stared at him blankly.

"It's from the *Talmud*," he said.

"Figures," Judith said. She walked to the door and put her hand on the knob just as the teakettle whistled from the kitchen.

"Let me guess, I'm the elder and Lauren is the youth."

# Fifty

It was odd that as Lewis made his way down the township building steps, he thought more about the burden carried by Ron Smith, than the revelations that had come out of his session with Peter Stem. The news that Peter Stem was likely *not* guilty of the crimes for which he was being held meant freedom for an innocent man, yet would require from Ron a considerable amount of time and attention—attention that should have been directed toward his father who needed to settle, ASAP, into his new facility in Florida.

"Can I give you a lift?"

Lewis was surprised to see Judith Orenstein parked in front of the building. With a flick of her fingers, and before he could answer, she unlocked the Jaguar's doors.

"Hop in," she said, tossing her briefcase onto the back seat. "It's going to start pouring any second."

As if on cue, there was a crack of thunder. Judith immediately thought of Yitzi and David and hoped they were safe and dry inside.

Lauren, on the other hand could be locked out of the house in a torrential down pour as far as she was concerned.

"Look at that! You certainly have perfect timing Judith!" Lewis ducked inside and settled himself in the passenger seat. "I didn't realize there would be a storm today," he said, unbuttoning the collar of his coat.

With a gloved hand, she flipped on the windshield wipers. "Well, I'm glad *someone* appreciates me," she mumbled under her breath.

"What were you doing here anyway?" Lewis asked.

"If you must know, I was on my way to the expressway. As luck would have it, I was driving by just as you were coming out of the township building… When I saw you, I just *knew* I had to pull over." Judith felt her face flush. Was it her imagination or did she just sound like someone with a schoolgirl crush? She cleared her throat. "I thought it would be a good opportunity to apologize again for my atrocious behavior. Call me old fashioned, but e-mails just don't hold the same weight."

"That's very kind," Lewis said, "but there's no need. What's done is done; it's all in the past."

Outside, a man in an overcoat rushed by, fighting to keep a grip on his umbrella.

"You had business in the township building?" Judith asked, gesturing that way.

"Business? Well, in a way, *yes*," he said. "I was working with Peter Stem."

Judith raised her eyebrows. "Really? And you weren't concerned?"

"*Concerned?*"

"That he might attack you."

"No; that possibility never occurred to me. Probably because there was a guard posted right outside the door."

"So, what did you find out? Is he just your typical nut job?" Judith asked, contempt in her voice.

Lewis sighed. "I don't like to refer to anyone that way Judith. And as far as what I found… well, it's all confidential. Certainly you can understand that."

Judith tucked a loose hair behind her ear. She liked a man who wasn't intimidated by her. Lewis was direct, he gave it to her straight. "Understood," she said.

They sat in silence, listening to the rain patter against the windshield. Lewis expected Judith to start the engine at any moment, but the minutes continued to pass.

"Aren't you going to ask why I was headed toward the expressway?" she finally said.

He closed his eyes and leaned back. "Do you *want* me to ask you?"

She looked at her hands. "I was heading back to New York."

"I see."

She lifted her eyebrows suggestively. "Aren't you going to ask me *why* I was heading back to New York?"

They stared at each for a few seconds before he burst out laughing.

"What's so funny?" she demanded.

He opened his eyes, sat up, and threw out his arms. "I don't know what you want from me, Judith! The last time I started questioning you, you nearly punched me!"

Her impulse would have been to feel insulted, or at the very least *slighted*, but she didn't. Instead, she felt a wave of sadness wash over her. "I don't know, Lewis. I just don't know."

He was struck by the change in her voice. It was softer, vulnerable.

A fat tear skipped down her cheek. "I'm so confused. I don't know what's happening to me... I don't know what I want."

Lewis pulled a tissue out of his pocket and gently wiped away her tear. The gesture touched something inside her. A stream of tears fell from her eyes just as the sky opened and water slammed onto the windshield. Within seconds the rain was so heavy, they couldn't see out in front of them. It was like being in the middle of a carwash. He instinctively reached for her and she leaned in to him.

"Shhh. It's all right. Everything will be all right," he said, stroking her head. She felt like a child being soothed by a loving parent. Her eyes fluttered.

Ten minutes later she awoke with a start. "How long was I asleep?"

"Not very long," he said. "Do you feel better?"

She shook her head. "Not really."

He waited.

"I don't know where I belong anymore," she said.

"You belong with your *family*, Judith."

She rubbed her forehead. "I've messed up, Lewis. I've been a terrible mother... a terrible grandmother..."

"Come now, Judith; do you really believe that?"

"I didn't always," she sniffed, "but now... I think I do."

He waited while she dabbed her eyes.

"I had a fight with Yehuda... You're going to think this is crazy Lewis, but I think he's falling for Lauren."

The statement *did* sound a bit crazy. Maybe the stress of Hannah's hospitalization was affecting her more than anyone realized. Lewis sat up and shook his head. "Judith..."

But she cut him off. "No, honestly, you should see the way they look at each other. I'm positive there's something going on between them! Sometimes they even speak to one another in private code."

"Judith, trust me, you're *wrong*. Yehuda would *never*!... He's a committed family man. He loves Hannah."

"If love was enough, I wouldn't have been a single mother!"

"Yehuda's different," Lewis said. "You raised him to be a good man. He would never do to Hannah what your husband did to you. Not all men are like that."

"Oh, so I can assume adultery played no part whatsoever in you and your wife splitting up?"

"*Splitting up?*"

She shrugged. "Your wife's never with you when you visit, so naturally I assumed you were divorced."

"Divorced? No, Judith, I'm not divorced."

"Separated?"

"Try again."

She closed her eyes tightly, shutting out the one remaining possibility. "Oh God. I'm so sorry Lewis... *When?*... When did it happen?"

"A long time ago," Lewis said. "Elise was eight."

*Younger than Rachel,* Judith thought.

"Drunk driver."

"I'm so sorry..."

"It was November 1st, 1979; so long ago, yet I still remember it like it was yesterday. It was a Thursday night. I had a professional dinner at the Copley Hotel. Who the hell schedules a professional dinner on a *Thursday* night? The thing is, Iris—my wife—didn't want to go. God knows I dragged her to enough of those things over the years! That night she was feeling run down. She had been out trick or treating with Elise the night before." Lewis paused, as if recapturing a private memory. "Elise went as a Smurf..." He smiled and looked into Judith's eyes. "Iris was a wonderful woman. You would have liked her, Judith. *Everyone* liked Iris! She was a great mother. You know, one of these parents who always volunteers to bake cupcakes or help with the school play... she even sewed Elise's Smurf costume herself."

Judith fought off an image of Lauren fixing the boys' Chanukah play costumes.

"Iris was a Brownie troop leader too," Lewis continued. "They were getting ready for their big weekend camp out. Poor Iris was exhausted from all the planning. But stubborn me, I wouldn't let up! I just kept nagging her about how important the dinner was." He sighed. "The truth was I didn't even know who the speaker was that night, but I told her to take a couple of aspirins and she'd feel better." Lewis shook his head remorsefully. "She should have gone straight to bed and either I went alone, or not at all. But that's not what happened. Like the trooper that she was, she took the aspirin, got dressed and we went. She was uncomfortable the whole night—glassy eyed, her head was pounding. The aspirin hadn't helped at all. By the end of the main course she was burning up. It was obvious she was more than just a bit rundown and should have never been out to begin with."

Lewis's regret was palpable.

"You know what they say, Lewis, *hindsight is 20/20*," Judith said, though she doubted it would help.

But it was obvious he wasn't finished. Judith wasn't sure if he felt obligated to tell her the entire story, or if it was simply a relief to let it all out. She wondered if psychiatrists ever sought the counsel of other psychiatrists. Something was telling her in this case at least, Lewis had not.

"We left before dessert and Iris fell asleep in the passenger seat," Lewis continued. "I remember looking at her all curled up, feeling terribly guilty and thinking that I would make it up to her. There was a cruise she had her heart set on. For months she had been showing me pictures of the ship, and the islands it stopped at—Puerto Rico, Bermuda... but I kept putting her off—I was too busy with work, I said. *It was always about the work.* Looking back, she was probably doing it for me. She knew I needed a vacation. I should have never put it off—should have never put *her* off. We never know how much time we have with those we love.... The guy—the drunk driver—he came right at me. It all happened so fast, yet everything seemed to be happening frame by frame, in slow motion. He was driving on the wrong side of the road without his headlights on... coming straight at me! I veered and he side swiped me on the passenger side." Lewis snapped his fingers. "And then, just like that, my Iris was gone."

"I'm so sorry, Lewis..." Judith took a deep breath, willing herself to find the right words. "You must forgive yourself and focus on what you and Iris had for so many years... the love you shared. The wonderful marriage that would be continuing today if she were..."

Lewis nodded. He recognized the sincerity in Judith's eyes and appreciated what she was trying to do.

"Not everyone is as fortunate as you and Iris," Judith continued. "Most people never experience that kind of love and commitment. Trust me, in my work I've seen plenty of the opposite." She shook her head. "I guess some of us spend too much time screwing up our lives—making mistakes that can't be fixed."

"The only mistake you made was choosing a man not worthy of you," Lewis said pointedly. His words, though impassioned, seemed to come out of nowhere and left Judith speechless. With her last remark, she had actually been referring to her relationship with Yehuda and the kids. But before she could clarify this point, Lewis had taken her hand and was now looking directly into her eyes. "Your life is far from over, Judith. You mustn't let your bad marriage taint the way you feel about men. There are plenty of decent ones out there. Men who aren't afraid of love. Men who know how to treat a woman."

Judith's heart skipped at the word *woman*. Is that how he saw her? As a *woman*? Judith was so busy running around being a strong voice for so many *other* women, she couldn't remember the last time she thought of herself this way.

*Really? Show me one decent man besides my son.* This might have been her witty, *Judith Orenstein style* comeback line, had the answer not been staring her squarely in the face.

# Fifty-one

It was understandable that the hospital staff would have concerns about fires being lit in patients' rooms, but Yehuda was adamant that his wife should witness, albeit unconsciously, the mitzvah of lighting Chanukah candles. With the help of some homemade jelly donuts, a traditional treat served during the holiday, he persuaded hospital administrators to make an exception—just this once—assuring them that he would remain inches from the flames until every single candle had burned down to the quick and extinguished itself.

As with the last three nights, Yehuda had driven to Senecca Hospital in total darkness. Each year, Chanukah fell during the shortest days of the year, and the moon offered little more than a sliver of illumination against the charcoal black sky. There had been potato latkes at dinner and multiple rounds of dreidle spinning, with Yitzi somehow managing to win the lion's share of chocolate gelt. Eli and David had gotten into their pajamas early. The Chanukah production was less than a week away, and they wanted to be well rested. Rachel, on the other hand, wasn't quite as eager. Working on the stage sets had consumed most of her time lately; and the labors of all her hard work would soon be coming to fruition. Yehuda couldn't help but be concerned. He expected that there would be the anticipated "let down" that comes after any big event, but whereas the other children would return to some semblance of normalcy, for Rachel, there would be no normal until Hannah returned home.

Yehuda settled into the recliner and leaned back. The flames danced happily atop their colorful wax candles, moving and burning as if they had personalities and ambitions all their own. But directly behind the silver menorah, the reflection of machines monitoring Hannah kept Yehuda firmly planted in the present.

To Yehuda's relief, things had been relatively calm on the home front this past week. Fortunately, his mother had a change of heart and returned to the house within a few hours of storming out after their fight. To his surprise, she even rearranged her schedule and extended her visit by three days. Judith had been much nicer to Lauren too, come to think of it. The bottom line was *someone* had knocked some sense into her, and Yehuda suspected it was a certain psychiatrist. His mother had been mentioning the name *Lewis Danzig* a lot lately. He laughed out loud as he thought about it. *Did Judith Orenstein, Esquire actually have a romantic interest?* All those years after his parents divorce, Yehuda had only known his mother to date one man. "Uncle Dan" they called him. It lasted only a couple of months, but Uncle Dan made his mother laugh and taught Yehuda and Sunny how to build card houses… Yes, it was refreshing to see his mother happy like that again.

"Yehu…da?"

It was the faraway sound of Hannah's voice. Yehuda's heart skipped and he sat up. He must have dozed off and been dreaming of her again. He immediately checked the menorah, relieved that the candles were nearly burnt out. How could he have fallen asleep after his promise to the hospital staff? He felt a sense of shame, like the time he had fallen asleep feeding Nehama. Thank God he hadn't dropped her.

"Yehu...da?"

This time he jumped clear out of his chair, his heart racing.

"Hannah?... Oh my God, Hannah!" It *wasn't* a dream! He ran to her side, staring in disbelief as she blinked her eyes into focus. Tears streamed down his face, blurring his vision as he raised her hand to his mouth and kissed it tenderly. "Baruch Hashem." *Thank you merciful God.*

A nurse peeked in. "I saw you on the monitor, Rabbi Orenstein; is everything all right?" The concern on her face gave way to delight as she realized what she was seeing. She quickly backed out of the room, nearly tripping. "Dr. Martin! Dr. Martin!" she called urgently down the hallway. Within seconds, the doctor flew in.

"She said my name!" Yehuda sputtered, barely containing himself. Part of him still wasn't convinced any of this was really happening.

"Call Dr. Patel!" the doctor ordered the nurse.

Hannah smiled weakly, a throaty sound came from her, as if she was trying to either cough or laugh.

Dr. Martin was busy checking her vitals. He held a bright light inches from her eyes and she winced in pain. "No!" she said, her voice scratchy. She tried to lift her hand to shield her eyes, but it fell down with a thud. She stared at it, a look of absolute horror on her face.

"Your muscles have atrophied," Dr. Martin said slowly. "It's best if you don't force any movement just yet."

She stared at the doctor as if trying to place him. After a few seconds, she let her eyes drift to the equipment surrounding her.

"Wh... Where...?"

"You're in the hospital, darling," Yehuda said.

"Why?" she asked with some difficulty. Suddenly her lips turned up into a sly smile and her eyes glimmered like her old self.

"Did I... have... another... baby?"

"It is nothing short of a miracle... I have no other explanation," Dr. Patel told Yehuda as he paced in front of his office desk an hour later. Dr. Patel wore a tuxedo, apparently having been paged in the middle of some black tie event. Finally, there was a light tap on the door and a tech entered with a large folder, which he handed to Dr. Patel. The doctor removed his jacket and tossed it aside. "Let's see what we have..." he said. He rubbed his hands together eagerly, then slipped three MRI films from the folder, and slapped them against a backlit screen on the wall.

"Hmm...remarkable...just remarkable!"

The doctor made several calculations and kept referencing a large file that was splayed open on his desk. Then, he dropped his pencil and smiled up at Yehuda.

Yehuda's heart raced through the blur of the next few minutes as Dr. Patel took his pointer to the scans and indicated the frontal and temporal lobes of Hannah's brain, comparing and contrasting shaded areas of white and gray, all the while interspersing the words "miracle" and "remarkable" in practically every other sentence.

Finally, Dr. Patel spoke the word that Yehuda had once feared he might *never* hear.

*Home.*

Once Hannah could hold down solid food, he said, she would be transferred to the rehabilitation unit of the hospital. Dr. Patel was happy to report that if all went well, Hannah could be back home—with the help of a full time aid, of course—within a month.

Chills ran through Yehuda's body. *His Hannah... home!*

"What about her memory of the event?" Yehuda asked, trying to stay focused. Two things occurred to him. One, her memories were likely to be traumatic. Two, the police would be very interested in speaking with her.

Dr. Patel sighed. "Many individuals remember nothing. *Ever.* Others recall fragments—small pieces over time." Just then, the doctor's phone rang. "Excuse me please, Rabbi… yes, I see. I'll be right up."

Yehuda stood up, his eyes wide. "Is it Hannah?"

Dr. Patel waved his hands. "No… no. Another patient needs my attention." He smiled warmly. "It appears I was not meant to eat shrimp cocktail tonight after all."

# Fifty-two

Between his accelerated speech and the fact that he was standing outside a noisy hospital cafeteria, Lauren could barely make out what Yehuda was saying.

"Hold on a second," he told her, breathlessly, "I'll go where it's quieter."

Thirty seconds later and she was able to hear each word perfectly: *Hannah was off of the ventilator... she had spoken... even moved her arm!... The doctors were running some tests now and preparing her for another brain scan. Baruch Hashem, it was nothing short of a miracle!*

Yehuda told Lauren he would be staying by Hannah's side throughout the night. Oh, and he had called his mother. She was on her way.

*Great.*

After Lauren hung up, she went up to her room, flung herself on her bed and burst into tears. She hadn't expected this to be happening so soon. In fact, there was a part of her that thought it would *never* happen. Shameful, yes. But true. All along there had been that lingering, yet unspoken possibility that Hannah wouldn't pull through. Lauren grabbed a tissue and wiped her eyes. Any *decent* person would be ecstatic hearing the news. Of course, Lauren *had* been thinking about Hannah too, just not about her *recovery*. For some reason her thoughts came at night while she rocked Nehama to sleep, nuzzling against her tiny scalp and inhaling that clean baby scent. She couldn't get past what had taken place between the two of them at the mikvah. No matter how she tried, Lauren just couldn't get Hannah's harsh words out of her head.

But despite the animosity between herself and Hannah, Lauren had to admit, she was crazy about Hannah's five children. And she knew they loved her too. Lauren would never confess this to anyone, but it warmed her heart when Yitzi accidentally called her *mommy*. Lauren had always wanted her own kids—maybe that would still happen one day—but in the meantime, in taking care of Rachel, Eli, David, Yitzi and Nehama, she had come to appreciate just how strong her maternal instincts actually were. Sure she had helped Hannah all those months while she was on bed rest, but there was something about being *the* woman of the house… It made her see just what a great mother she could be. Despite what her parents might think, she *was* a real woman, capable of a leading a normal, fulfilling life.

Lauren looked around the room and couldn't believe how much she had accumulated over the last month. Besides furniture, was there anything left in her apartment? She realized she had been carrying on as though she would be staying here with Yehuda and the kids indefinitely. In a way, it did seem only natural; her apartment lease was up in a couple of months, anyway. The cat, too, had acclimated to their new life. Rosie no longer ran from Nehama's squeals of excitement, and had learned to tactfully avoid getting her tail yanked. Rosie had grown accustomed to the larger living space, the big sunny bay window. It seemed cruel to downsize her again.

Lauren blew her nose. What was she getting herself all worked up about anyway? Hadn't she known it would eventually come to this? Here she was back at the same crossroads: either come clean and confess, or leave in peace. Either avenue had its own set of consequences.

Suddenly, the phone rang, Lauren looked at the caller ID. It was a familiar name, one of the neighbors, but she didn't answer it. *Good news travels fast.* Soon, the phone would be ringing off the hook. People in the community wanting to know: *was it true what they heard about Hannah? God forbid,* they would say. *God forbid someone would be cruel enough to start such a rumor if it wasn't!*

Lauren tiptoed into Nehama's room. The baby was on her back, cooing at her *Hey diddle diddle* mobile. After a minute she noticed Lauren and smiled. Did Nehama think Lauren was her *mother?* Hannah hadn't been gone so long, but proportional to Nehama's short life, it probably seemed like forever. Would the baby even *recognize* Hannah?

Lauren wound up the mobile and watched Nehama flail her legs in excitement as the familiar tune started up and the dog, cat and moon shapes began their rounds.

How could she leave this beautiful baby? How could she *never* see any of them again? It was her own damn fault for letting this happen, for getting so attached! What she was facing was nothing new; she had known it all along! She and Hannah could not coexist in this house. It was either one or the other.

Lauren sat in the rocking chair, feeling more drained by the minute. Then it dawned on her: *there was still time.* Not much, but *some.* It might be days before Hannah regained her memories of that night, and was able to articulate them to Yehuda. Lauren could get to Yehuda first! She wouldn't hold back; she would tell him *everything.* He was going to find out sooner or later anyway, so wouldn't it be better to come from her?—explained in her own words without Hannah turning it into something *ugly?* Hannah was some matchmaker, but there was one thing she would never understand: love couldn't always be planned or controlled. Sometimes it simply overtook us.

Lauren felt a shiver go down her spine in nervous anticipation. Did she have the guts to tell Yehuda? But the bigger question was: how would he respond? Would it be like the time Cynthia didn't have on underwear? Lauren had never seen a man's face get so red! And what Lauren had to tell him was just as titillating! To discover that Lauren had these secret thoughts… a secret *life!* Without a doubt, he would be shocked. Okay, *shocked,* she could handle. But then, what? Would he reject her completely? Or had she misjudged him? After all, he had stuck up for her lately—defended her against Judith, not to mention getting Jonathon off her back! Ever since Yehuda had spoken to him, he hadn't left her a single phone message. *Hmm,* Lauren thought, Had she missed the signs all along? Had she misjudged Yehuda's feelings? A smile forming on her lips. *Perhaps the rabbi would be able to handle the news after all.*

# Fifty-three

John awoke to the sound of his wife's voice. Patty stood in the doorway, the cordless phone in her hand. Dressed in jeans and a turtleneck, she looked like a woman closer to forty than sixty. He sighed. Apparently, Patty had worried more than he realized. Now that he had left patrolling and returned to investigations full time, twenty years had come off her appearance, virtually overnight.

"It's Ron Smith," she said, handing him the phone.

Light filtered through the plates of stained glass. The sun appeared to be just coming up. John rubbed his eyes and took a quick look at his watch. *4:33.* He looked again at his wife. Why was she dressed so early? Then it dawned on him. The sun was *setting.* It wasn't 4:30 AM, it was 4:30 PM.

Patty saw the confusion in his eyes. "It's okay," she said. "You were off today."

Right. He was off today. But how could he have fallen asleep? He wracked his brain. The last he remembered, he had come in to the chess room this morning with a cup of tea. That was about 9:00 AM or so. He glanced around, eager for confirmation. Sure enough, the mug was resting on the table beside him, nearly half full. He must have been exhausted. John pushed himself to an upright position, feeling the cumulative effects of several hours spent hunched in a chair. The left side of his neck had cramped into a tight knot. He groaned and placed the phone against his ear. Pain pulsed down his arm, sending a shock wave only matched by the news Ron Smith delivered.

"You know that Familial CODIS search...?"

"Of course," John said, taking a sip of the coffee Patty handed him. "The *Familial* report," he laughed, "if I remember correctly, you didn't see the point of running it."

Ron should have expected the ribbing. He deserved it. "Yeah, well, I thought after the first report... anyway, as luck would have it, they found someone with Peter's family DNA."

John leapt to his feet, nearly spilling his coffee. "I'll be right down."

John drove on autopilot, and by the time he arrived at the station, there was a bustle of activity. Two huge events had occurred within the last twelve hours, while he was sound asleep in the chess room. The first involved Hannah Orenstein. She had awakened from her coma, and according to her doctor, was officially out of harms way. The second had not yet been released to the general public: the alleged killer, Peter Stem had been released—all charges dropped by the DA.

Ron spread the contents of Peter Stem's file out on his desk.

"He's in Michigan State Penitentiary serving two life sentences," Ron said, running his hands through the top of his scalp. He pushed a computer print out across his desk toward John.

John took a look; it was a rap sheet for some guy named *Roy Bunton.*

"Roy Bunton is Peter's biological father," Ron explained. "In 1976 he killed Peter's mother—Gail Michaels—along with Peter's twin sister."

"Peter had a twin?"

"Uh huh. You want to take a guess what the twin's name was?"

John didn't have to think long. "*Suzanne?*"

Ron nodded. "Peter witnessed the entire thing from under his bed. He was seven, didn't know Roy Bunton was his father. To him, the guy was just his mom's ex-boyfriend."

John closed his eyes and rubbed his temples. "Man oh man… that's gotta screw a person up."

"From the report, it was pretty gruesome too… I'll spare you the details; you can look it over yourself."

"So Peter was essentially an orphan?"

"That's right," Ron said. "After the murder, he was placed in the foster care system until he graduated school at age seventeen."

"Did you speak to any of his foster care parents?"

"*One.* Hettie Wimsdale from Flint Michigan. Peter was in her care from age fourteen to seventeen."

"And?"

Ron raised his eyebrows. "And boy, did that woman like to talk!" He read aloud from some notes he had taken. "Peter was extremely shy, didn't have many friends. He ran track in school, but was happiest when he was fishing with her husband—his foster dad—Hank. They'd fish by some dam in Genesee County—caught white sucker and channel catfish. And get this, Hettie said sometimes after a storm, the water would look like chocolate milk."

John leaned back. "Chocolate milk. Just like Lydia Richter said."

"Yep."

"So, Peter's back at the rectory now?" John asked.

"Uh huh. He's back with Father McCormick and being overseen by Dr. Danzig."

John nodded. He would call Father McCormick when he had a free minute, though he doubted that would be anytime soon. Peter exonerated meant they still had a killer to catch. "Looks like we have our work cut out for us, buddy," he said to Ron.

Ron grinned at the word *us*. He looked like he was mustering up the courage to say something, but John cut him off.

"It's going to be a long day... I hope you have enough vitamin water in there," John said, pointing with his chin.

Ron leaned back and took a look in the fridge. "Let's see... Extra Ginseng, B-Vitamins...Yeah, I'm good," he said, playing along.

# Fifty-four

"Let's go through it again," John said.

Ron took a deep breath and flipped back to page one of the transcript. This would be their third review of the same information in the past hour and a half. But Ron shouldn't have been surprised. He had watched his dad with John all those years and knew this was how John liked to work. Unlike most people whose brains shut off after staring at the same material over and over, John claimed the creative centers of his brain turned on—like lights set on a timer—the longer he pondered an unsolved case.

"Transcript of hypnotically induced deposition of Peter Stem surrounding the events of Monday, October 24th," Ron began. He hadn't slept a wink last night and was getting punchy from exhaustion. Coming up with this long, drawn out title was mostly for his own amusement.

John leaned back with his arms behind his head and stared up at the ceiling, waiting. Ron continued, serious now. "Peter and Father McCormick eat dinner at the rectory at 7:00 PM. After dinner, Peter heads upstairs to close windows. At approximately 7:30 PM, he's positioned at the second floor hall window with his binoculars and sees Tova Katz's van pull into the high school lot."

"The original mikvah attendant," John said out loud. It was more of statement than a question.

"Up until Estelle Ginsberg came to fill in later," Ron added.

"And Tova corroborated the time?"

"Yep. Tova Katz confirmed that her arrival time was about 7:30."

"But then she had to leave prematurely," John added.

"Her daughter went into labor," Ron said.

"Okay, we know Estelle Ginsberg, the back up attendant didn't drive, so how did she get to the mikvah?"

Ron flipped through his notes on a separate pad. "Hannah Orenstein picked her up."

"How do we know?"

"Tova called Hannah at approximately 9:30 PM and asked her," Ron said. "Minutes before that, she called Estelle Ginsberg, asking her to fill in. Hannah and Estelle arrived at approximately 9:50 PM; Tova left about the same time."

"The phone lines were down. How did she call them?" John was beginning to sound like a drill sergeant.

Ron shrugged. "Cell phone. Same way her husband called her to tell her about the baby."

"We have those records?"

"Right here." Ron held up a fax from the wireless carrier.

"Good," John said, smiling. He was glad to see Ron paying more attention to details. "So getting back to the time sequence…"

"Right. At 7:30, Peter sees Tova Katz's van. A few minutes later he spots a white Volvo, driven by Elise Danzig. Elise exits her car and goes into the building. Approximately twenty-five minutes later, Elise gets back in her car and exits the lot, once again leaving Tova alone in the mikvah."

"And these times were corroborated?"

"Yes, Elise Danzig confirmed the times." Ron took a deep breath and continued. "About 8:30 PM, Peter sees a black Lexus pull in."

"Do we have an ID on that?"

"No."

"A woman exits the vehicle," Ron continued. "She's alone."

"Physical description?" John asked.

Ron scanned the page. "Blond. That's all we have… Oh, but this might be important: Peter claims she was crying in her car before she got out."

"And we have a pretty good idea what she was might have been crying about," John prompted.

"Right. The Caucasian male who shows up without a car… guy just walks right on to the lot."

"Could be from *The Estates* across the field?"

Ron shrugged. "It's possible, though we don't know which direction he came from. We *do* have a physical description on him, though. Peter describes him as tall, wearing jeans and a ski jacket."

"And there's a scuffle between him and the woman?"

"That's right. But Peter doesn't stick around long enough to see what happens. He hears Samson carrying on downstairs."

"Samson put her paw through the glass door," John said. "According to Father McCormick , she was reacting to an animal outside."

Ron did a quick perusal of the transcript and shook his head. "There's nothing on the transcript to indicate that Peter actually saw the animal himself."

John recalled that Father McCormick hadn't seen an animal either, he had merely *assumed* there was one.

Ron continued, "Peter proceeds to bandage up Samson's paw, then he boards up the hole in the door and returns to the upstairs window at 10:00 PM. By this time, both Tova Katz's van and the Lexus are gone; and there's no sign of the man."

John took a deep breath. "The problem is this hour gap. While Peter was tending to Samson, we don't know who else may have come on the scene."

"True, but then Peter *does* see the man again," Ron continued, "only this time he drives up in a black SUV."

"And we have no idea who this guy could be," John said.

"No clue, but according to Peter, he tried to access the building." Ron looked up. "…And that's where we lose him…"

"The guy?"

"Yeah, him, and *Peter* too. Seeing this guy shook Peter up so much that he moved away from the window and hid in his closet."

John couldn't help but feel a twinge of guilt. According to Dr. Danzig, this point marked the official onset of Peter's psychotic episode. In fact, immediately after the rectory search, Ron had commented about how neat and orderly Peter's room was—everything but the closet, which Ron said looked like a tornado had hit it. *Unbelievable!* All along, the evidence was right there, staring them in the face! What grown man makes a protective fortress for himself inside a closet?… Burrows under a pile of shirts? If only John had paid closer attention to Ron's words! Or better yet, if he had actually gone upstairs that day instead of having coffee and a chat with Father McCormick in the kitchen! Maybe if he had seen it with his own eyes… Peter would have gotten out, gotten the help he needed, that much sooner.

"Yep," Ron continued, "he dove right into that closet—didn't even bother moving his shoes—just pulled his clothes off the hangers and *buried* himself! I didn't see it for what it was at the time... the perfect place for a little boy to hide from the bogey man."

"Well, now we know *why*," John said, rubbing the spot on his arm where Peter had bitten him. Animals, John realized, weren't the only ones who bit. Children did too. And sometimes, they even wet their pants. *It was all so darn obvious now that they understood Peter was reliving the event he witnessed as a boy!*

"The coroner put Estelle's time of death between 10:15 and 10:30," Ron said. "Where was Peter at that time?" He flipped a page and answered his own question. "Still hiding."

John reached for the transcript and took it from Ron. "According to this, he doesn't even *leave* the rectory until about 11:00 when Father McCormick hears the front door screeching," John said. "He gets to the mikvah door and it's open. There's no sight of the man, but he sees Estelle Ginsberg unconscious on the floor. Peter goes in, locks the door behind him..."

"Supposedly to lock out the bad guys..." Ron interjected.

"Just *one* guy. John said, "...or the memory of him."

"Inside, Peter tries to resuscitate Estelle," Ron said.

"...Which explains his saliva all over her face and mouth," John added.

It was pretty incredible to John to think that Peter could actually attempt pulmonary resuscitation while in a psychotic state, but Lewis had assured him that it was possible. He explained that people do things on autopilot all the time, comparing what Peter did, to 'zoning out' while driving to work; somehow you pull into your parking spot with no idea how you got there. *Sometimes the brain decides to run the show on it's own*, Lewis said.

Ron continued. "Peter runs like a wild man through the entire facility—leaving his prints on every door handle—until he comes to the ritual pool room and spots Hannah underwater. He jumps in, pulls her out, pumps water out of her lungs."

John nodded. "And by the time Robert and I barge in, he's clinging to her like a crazed lunatic."

"It's still the most unbelievable thing I've heard in my life," Ron said, shaking his head. "He saved Hannah Orenstein's life! The guy's not a murderer, he's a goddamn hero!"

# Fifty-five

By the following morning, news of Hannah's awakening had spread like wildfire throughout the community, and the phone was ringing off the hook. Flowers, balloons and cards filled the Orenstein home. It was as if the entire *kehilla* had held its breath for the past six weeks, and were now exhaling a big communal sigh of relief.

Lauren was folding clothes in the guest room when Eli wandered in. "Do you think Mommy will like my card, Lauren?" he asked, holding out a folded piece of red construction paper. In a few hours, Lauren knew, the kids would be heading over to the hospital to see their mother for the first time in almost two months.

"Lauren?"

"What? Oh, yes, Eli, I'm sure she'll love it."

"But you didn't even look at it!"

Lauren forced a smile. "I didn't have to. I saw you working on it downstairs, remember?"

He shrugged. "What are you doing?" he asked, noticing her suitcase splayed open on the floor.

Yehuda hadn't come home yet—ever since Hannah's awakening, he had remained at the hospital keeping vigil by her bed—so Lauren had not had an opportunity to speak to him. In a way, she was relieved to have the extra time to prepare herself, but the more time she spent ruminating, the closer she got to chickening out altogether. "Oh, well, since your mommy's almost better, I'll be going home soon," she told him.

Eli looked concerned. "But aren't you coming with us to the hospital?"

She tossed some t-shirts into the suitcase. "No, I'll see your mommy another time, okay?"

"What about Rosie?" he asked. "Can she stay?"

"No, Eli. I'm afraid Rosie has to come home with me."

"But she'll be back, right?"

Lauren didn't want to lie. "We'll have to see, okay?"

He nodded.

She looked at her watch. "Now, you better go change. Your Abba will be home soon and he'll want to leave right away."

Eli scurried out of the room and bumped into Judith who must have been standing right outside the door. It figured she was listening in. Lauren pretended not to notice her.

Judith coughed.

"Hello Mrs. Orenstein," Lauren said without looking up.

Judith stood in the doorway. "I see you're packing," she said.

"Yes."

"Probably a good idea—now that the children's *mother* will be home soon."

"Is there something you wanted?" Lauren asked. She was in no mood to play games.

"Yes, as a matter-of-fact there is. Someone's here to see you."

"To see *me?*" Lauren asked doubtfully. "Who?"

"Sonia Lyman."

"Sonia!" Lauren perked up. "Well… tell her to come up!"

"I think you better come down," Judith said, her voice suddenly softened. "She has something to show you."

Lauren didn't move, almost expecting this to be some sort of trick. "Uh, sure. Okay. I'll come down."


"Lawen! Lawen! Come see! Come see!" Yitzi met Lauren at the bottom of the stairs and was now yanking her arm toward the living room.

Lauren's jaw dropped. There, on the couch, sat Sonia with an infant swaddled in her arms. But that wasn't why Lauren was suddenly speechless. It was the fact that not since that first Shabbat dinner nearly a year ago had Sonia looked so beautiful. Even in a simple pair of jeans and turtleneck sweater, the woman was *radiant.*

"Sonia?" Lauren began, hesitantly.

Sonia extended her arm, beckoning Lauren closer. She squeezed Lauren's hand, her eyes bluer than ever. "Gary and I… we are parents now!" A tear dripped down her cheek. She giggled and wiped it away with the back of her hand.

Lauren stared in disbelief at the baby girl. A tiny pink ribbon was clipped onto a single brown hair. The infant was sound asleep, inhaling and exhaling softly through her tiny mouth.

*What the hell was going on?*

Lauren dropped to the floor, kneeling at Sonia's knees. "A *baby?* … but I… aren't you… I mean…"

Sonia smiled. "Her name is *Naomi*. Named from my grandmother." She looked warmly at Lauren. "I'm sorry I didn't tell you before. I know you worried for me."

"But…but what about Gary?" Lauren noticed the stunned faces of the boys and Rachel, and realized she had just *screamed* the question. "Sonia," she said, pulling herself together and rising to her feet, "can I speak to you privately?"

An hour later Lauren was still in shock. It was hard to accept that somehow she had gotten it all wrong. Everything she had ever assumed about Sonia and her husband was flat out *incorrect*!

As Sonia explained, she and Gary had been receiving treatment for infertility since their third month of marriage. The problem was with Gary, Sonia explained. To put it in medical terms: his sperm refused to fertilize her eggs.

"Gary felt not like a man," Sonia explained. "He keep saying to me, I should leave him and find better husband." She made a fist against her chest. "But I have better husband already! I love Gary!"

At this point, Lauren interjected a question that she had been contemplating for quite some time. "But Sonia, how can you love someone you barely know?"

"Barely know?" Sonia's crinkled forehead suggested she didn't understand what Lauren was asking.

Lauren struggled with the best way to say *mail order bride*. "I thought you didn't have a lot of time between courtship and marriage, that's all."

"We date for three years! That's not enough time?"

Lauren was stunned. "Three years?"

"Yes. Gary was on work project in Kiev. He stay at my hotel. We meet there."

*But Janine said you were a mail order bride.* Lauren shook her head. Apparently Janine didn't have her facts straight either. This changed everything. "I'm so sorry," Lauren said, "I must have misunderstood."

It took a few minutes for Lauren to get her bearings. "Sonia…" she said, suddenly remembering her concern for Sonia's physical safety, "Does Gary hurt you?"

"Hurt me?" Sonia shook her head fervently. "No, of course not! He yell many times, but I know why. Because of what I say to you… he felt not like a man!"

"But your arm… you had it in a sling!" Lauren demanded.

"Yes, I slip getting out of the tub," Sonia said calmly, but Lauren was still not convinced.

"Then what were you doing at Tova Katz's house?" she prodded. "I saw you on her front porch!"

Sonia shrugged like it wasn't a big deal.

"Tova runs the S.O.S. hotline for abused women!" Lauren said pointedly.

"Yes, and Gary is S.O.S. *accountant*," Sonia replied. "I drop off tax papers."

"But… but I saw you other times!" Lauren sputtered, "and…and you looked like…"

Sonia lifted her eyebrows. "I look like *how?*"

"Injured."

"I *was* injured!" Sonia said. "Six times I have hospital procedure to get pregnant!" She shook her head remembering. "There was much pain and how do you call it? Cramps! Terrible! Then I decided, enough! I tell Gary, no more! It's not fair all this suffering of both of us! We will adopt!"

There it was in a nutshell. How could Lauren have been so blind? But there was one more thing. "How in the world did you and Gary manage to get a baby so *quickly?*" she asked Sonia.

Sonia smiled. "It wasn't so quickly. When I have fertility procedures, we also trying to adopt the whole time… *How* our baby comes, was never important for us."

# Fifty-six

A large Rottweiler wedged his nose past the man's legs, trying to get a good sniff of whoever was outside the front door.

"Mr. Katz?"

"Yes?"

"I'm Detective Ron Smith and this is Detective John Collins. We were hoping to have a word with your wife."

It was good to get out of the office, even if it *was* on official business. After fifteen non-stop hours of working the Peter Stem case, John and Ron were happy with any kind of break, including the breakfast they had just eaten—courtesy of Arden Station taxpayers—at the local diner.

Saul called out to his wife and she bustled toward the door wearing a loose fitting knit dress and white sneakers. She smiled brightly, but when she saw who it was, the smile fell away. She turned to her husband. "This is about the mikvah?"

Saul nodded solemnly and moved to the side to allow the detectives entry.

"Thank you," John said. "This should only take a few minutes." But Ron hesitated, glancing downward. "Is the dog okay?"

"You mean *Reuben*?" Saul said, and chuckled. "Oh sure! No worries, unless you're a bad guy that is. He can sniff *those* out in a second."

John laughed out loud. "Does Reuben need a job?" he asked, giving the dog a pat.

"I don't know if you've heard, but Peter Stem was released this morning," Ron began, after they had all settled on floral patterned couches in the modest living room.

Tova's hand flew over her mouth. "Oh dear God... no!"

Saul patted his wife's hand. "They're sure?"

John nodded. "We were holding the wrong guy."

Saul had a feeling he already knew the answer, but he asked the question anyway. "Do you now have the *right* guy?"

"No, I'm afraid not. That's why we're here—to go over some facts with your wife."

Saul looked at Tova, concerned. Just that morning she had been so happy... they had both been... exhilarated by the news that Hannah was out of the coma, that it looked like she was going to pull through. Saul had been married long enough to know what his wife was thinking now: *the women of Arden Station are in danger. A killer is still on the loose...* "Are you going to be all right?" Saul whispered in her ear.

She dabbed each eye with a tissue, took a deep breath, and nodded. "They need to catch him... I want to do whatever I can to help."

"On the night of Monday, October 24th," Ron began, "did you happen to notice any men in the mikvah parking lot? "

"Men generally don't drive their wives," Tova replied. "The night a woman immerses in the mikvah is an extremely private event. It would be embarrassing to be seen by another woman's husband."

"So I take it you didn't see anyone lingering?"

Tova furrowed her brow. "*Lingering?*"

"Yes," John said. "Peter Stem saw a man loitering in the parking lot around 8:30 PM."

Tova took a deep breath upon hearing the man's name spoken again. It would take some time for her to come to grips with the idea that Peter Stem was not guilty—had *not* committed a hate crime against two women from her community.

She shrugged. "I wouldn't have seen anyone. I was inside the whole time..."

"He saw the same man again after 10:00," Ron interjected, as if this information might help.

"I went out to my car at 9:45, but I'm sorry, I didn't notice anyone," Tova said.

"I know who it was," a tiny voice said suddenly.

"The detectives swung around. A thirty-something woman stood in the doorway. She wore a sweat suit that looked two sizes two big. Her blond hair was tucked in a loose bun. She wore no makeup and judging from the dark circles under her eyes, looked as though she hadn't slept in a week.

Tova stood up immediately and went to the woman. Taking her hand, she led her back to the couch.

"Cindy, these detectives are investigating the mikvah crime." Tova spoke gently, as if trying not to upset her.

"Yes, I know," the woman said, taking a seat next to Tova. "I was there, at the mikvah, that night..."

Tova's eyes widened in surprise. So many women used the mikvah—many from outside the community—that Tova didn't know them all by *name,* but she prided herself on at least *recognizing* them. Yet, last week, when Cindy knocked on her front door, she would have sworn it was the first time they had met face to face.

Cynthia looked over at Tova, as if reading her mind. "It would have only been my *third* visit to the mikvah. The last two, Estelle was the attendant. And that night... October 24th, I never actually made it inside.

"Your name is Cindy?" Ron didn't feel bad about interrupting. He wanted to move the conversation along. After all, the woman had just claimed to know who the man in the parking lot was.

"Yes. That's right. My name is Cindy. Cindy Bergerman."

"Bergerman? As in *Bergerman Bagels?*"

She nodded.

"I see. Well, Ms. Bergerman, do you recall what time you arrived at the mikvah the night of October 24th?"

"It was a little before 8:30."

"Do you drive a Lexus, by chance?" John interjected. It was a sudden hunch.

"I *did.*"

*Bingo.*

"And you saw a man in the parking lot?"

"Yes." She took a deep breath. "The man in the lot was my husband."

Tova's hand flew to her chest.

"What was he doing there?" Ron continued.

"Threatening me," Cynthia said. "I wasn't supposed to leave the house that night."

"Any particular reason?"

"No...just control. Head games. He's good at those."

"Cindy is currently separated from her husband, Brad Bergerman," Tova told the detectives. "She has a restraining order against him."

John nodded and looked at Cindy. She was around the same age as his daughters, but appeared to be carrying the weight of the world on her shoulders. "Has he given you any trouble since?"

Cynthia shook her head and smiled over at Reuben, all one hundred and twenty pounds of him splayed out in the corner. "No. I'm completely safe here."

John scribbled something on a card and handed it to her. "You call me directly if anything changes, okay?"

"Could you tell us what happened when he confronted you in the parking lot?" Ron asked.

Cynthia thought for a moment. "He just lost it because there was a scratch on the Lexus. He yanked my arm and told me to get in the car."

"And did you?"

She wiped the corner of her eye. "What choice did I have?"

Tova held Cynthia's hand as she continued. "His car was parked a couple blocks up. He stopped to get out and told me to drive home or else."

"Why didn't he drive on to the mikvah lot to begin with?" John asked.

"He was worried about his precious car," Cynthia said angrily. "His *Mercedes*. God forbid a branch should fall on it or something."

"What time did all this take place?" Ron asked.

"Between 8:30 and 8:45," Cynthia said.

"And what happened when you got home?" John asked gently.

Cynthia took a deep breath. "He slapped me around. Told me I was a worthless piece of shit, that I was lucky to have him. Then he raped me."

"Did you go to the hospital?"

Cynthia looked over at Tova. The older woman was biting her lip, staring down at her hands in her lap. "No. I know I should have, but I didn't."

"Did Brad leave the house anytime after that?"

She shook her head. "No. He passed out in our bedroom. He didn't go anywhere."

"How can you be sure?"

"Because I didn't sleep all night, that's how! I would have heard him!"

"Do you own an SUV?" Ron asked.

Cynthia nodded. "Brad owns six cars. One of them is a black Range Rover."

"Is it possible Brad could have taken the Range Rover out without you realizing?"

"No."

"Would you excuse us for a moment?" John said suddenly, gesturing Ron toward the front door.

It was understandable that Ron felt annoyed at the interruption. After all, John was interrupting his flow. "What's up?" he demanded after stepping outside. Across the street, a neighbor was standing on his porch, apparently curious about the police car parked out front.

"It's not the same guy," John said in a low voice.

"What?"

"There were two different men Peter saw that night."

"But Peter said…"

John shook his head. "I *know* what he said, but he was mistaken."

"But how can you be sure?" Ron asked, skeptically. "Cindy Bergerman may have fallen asleep without realizing it… if she had, she wouldn't have heard her husband leave."

John placed his hands on his hips. "Tell me this: why would Brad

Bergerman drive his Range Rover willingly onto the lot when he didn't want to risk scratching his Mercedes?"

Ron shrugged. "Maybe he thought the Range Rover was more rugged?" But even as he spoke the words, Ron knew John had a point. Some guys were simply nuts when it came to their cars—*all* of them, no exception.

"Excuse me, Detectives," Saul said, suddenly joining them on the front porch. "Is there a reason you're asking about that model car in particular?"

"The black SUV?"

Saul nodded.

"A man, in his mid to late forties was spotted driving a black SUV onto the mikvah parking lot sometime around 10:00 PM," John said.

"Gary Lyman drives a black SUV."

"Who?"

"Gary Lyman," Saul repeated. He does the books for my wife's non-profit organization."

"And you think Gary was the man in the SUV?" John asked.

"I don't just *think* he was. I know for a *fact* that Gary Lyman drove to the mikvah at 10:00."

# Fifty-seven

Back at the station, Ron stood at the whiteboard, writing the names *Bergerman* and *Lyman* in black. "So much for our two mystery men," he said, striking a line through the names just as quickly as he had written them.

John stared past him, tapping a pencil on the table. "Yeah, Bergerman was only interested in intimidating his wife."

"And Gary Lyman was just being *neighborly*," Ron added.

At the house, Saul had explained how he had called Gary Lyman and asked him to check on Tova. Even after leaving two voice mails about their daughter Esti going into labor, Tova still hadn't called him back. Saul was worried, and he wanted to be certain she got the message.

"It made perfect sense to call Lyman," John said. "Tova knew him, and he lived close by, just across the field in *The Estates*."

"But Tova *had* gotten the messages and by the time he got there, she was gone," Ron said. "That's why she didn't see him."

"So what's next?" Ron asked. "Peter Stem is not our killer; and

411

the two other men—Bergerman and Lyman—are accounted for. Both were on the mikvah lot, but neither set foot inside the building." He sighed. "So now what? Where do we go from here?"

For the life of him, John did not have a clue. But before he had a chance to admit this to Ron, his cell phone rang, and he stepped out to take the call. Minutes later he returned shaking his head. "What a day! Man oh man, Ron, you are *not* going to believe this…"

John had nearly forgotten that evening two weeks before when he and Robert had canvassed the neighborhoods surrounding St. Agassi. Thanks to the nor'easter, most people easily recalled the night in question—the storm and subsequent power outages—but few had noticed any activity at the old high school. One *thirty-something* woman couldn't offer any assistance, but did seize the opportunity to go off on a long-winded tirade, ranting about the disgraceful response time of the local power company, and the inefficiency of the police department. The woman's two young children were wrapped around her legs like monkeys, gaping at the two officers.

"And remember, I pay your salary!" she spat at them before slamming the door.

"Nice lady," Robert said sarcastically. "Sheesh!"

John rubbed his temples and shook his head in disgust as they trudged on to the next house. Long before, he had stopped taking these outbursts personally, but he couldn't help but feel a bit agitated about the kids standing there, looking on as their mother berated a police officer. This was the reason there was such little respect for authority anymore. But they moved on to the next house, and then the next, and in three hours time, John had distributed an entire stack of business cards, often times inserting them into mail slots or slipping them under front doors with a short note of explanation.

And now, John should have been thrilled. An unexpected eyewitness from the community coming forward was huge, but the truth was all of this, including the interview with Tova and Saul Katz, should have happened much earlier, despite the fact that they had a man in custody. Technically, Ron was responsible for the delay. From the beginning he was the one calling all the shots. Yet, John still blamed himself. Now that he thought about it, this was Ronnie's first big case—John's help was needed from the start. In hindsight, it was clear John should have put his own personal issues aside and insisted that protocol be followed. Officers should have been pounding the pavement within hours of the arrest.

"And what was this witness doing out at that time of night exactly?" Ron asked.

"Walking his dog. He says that while the dog was doing his business he got a nice long look."

Ron was interested but skeptical. One thing he had learned from his dad was that enough so-called "witnesses" had more of an interest in notoriety than providing actual information. "He had good visibility?"

"He says they were standing on the sidewalk, right outside the parking lot," John said.

"And he had enough time to take in the sights? How long does it take a dog to go anyway?"

"Long enough. It seems the dog wasn't used to going on a leash."

"So why was he that night?"

"He says he lost power at his house. The invisible fence line was out too. He didn't trust the dog to stay in the yard without it; apparently he ran away twice before."

"What kind of dog?"

"Dalmatian."

Ron snickered. "Granted, they're not the smartest breed."

John knew the joke and went along with it. "You know what they say: any dog that runs into a burning building..."

"And your guy—he remembers details?"

"Colors, tags everything... That dog of his was taking his sweet old time."

"Okay then, bring him in. Let's hear what he has to say."

# Fifty-eight

Mickey Landis was short and burly and liked to talk. He showed up at the station dressed in a button down lumberjack shirt with his undershirt showing. His faded jeans hung below his huge belly. Every few minutes he'd grab hold of his waistband and yank them up; a futile effort since they'd invariably inch down to their original position within seconds. His feet were shaped like blocks; his filthy sneakers were as long as they were wide. Originally from north Jersey, Mickey moved to Arden Station after his divorce two years before and now lived with his brother Patrick in a two-bedroom twin on Westmont Street, about six blocks west of St. Agassi.

"I always felt sorry for my big *bro*, you know, seeing that he never found anyone; but turns out he had the right idea all along," Mickey told the detectives. "Talk about being taken to the cleaners! My ex-wife never worked a day in her life, and somehow she gets half my money!" Mickey removed his glasses and rubbed his eyes. "I'm still waitin' for someone to explain that one to me!" He looked expectantly at John who merely smiled politely and held up his empty hands.

"Sorry. Can't help you there. I've been married for almost forty years."

Mickey looked down and shook his head. "Forty years! My condolences go out to you, man."

"Mr. Landis, what is your street address?" Ron asked.

"2059 Westmont."

"Your brother Patrick Landis owns that home?"

"Yep. I don't have any assets in my name. With paying alimony and all, its better this way."

"And what do you do professionally?"

Mickey stood up and reached around his back pocket for his wallet. He handed Ron a card and yanked up his pants before sitting down.

*Mickey Landis, Husband for Hire.* Ron looked up. "I don't get it."

"I'm a handyman," Mickey said, leaning back and crossing his arms proudly. "I'm not one to generalize, but the men in this town are pussies! These sons of bitches have loads of money, but somehow they're not man enough to change a light bulb in those McMansions of theirs!" He looked at John and snorted. "I'm still waitin' for someone to explain that one to me!"

Ron coughed. "So, you fix things?" he asked. He looked again at the card. The caption read: *No job too small. Mickey Lands does it all.*

"Yeah, that's right. But I do anything, really. Plumbing, electric, build an addition..."

"Build an addition?"

"Yeah. Sure. I've got a couple of guys that I work with on the bigger jobs." Mickey suddenly regretted his *pussy* remark. "Uh, if you need something done, either of you two detectives, I can set you up... give you a discount too, like the one I give the group home two miles up the road from my brother..."

Ron waved him off. "Thanks. I'll let you know. Have you always done this type of work?"

"I used to manage a hardware store. But you know, since the divorce."

"Right."

"Things are tight."

"Okay."

"Are you divorced, Detective?"

Ron rolled his eyes. "No, actually I'm not."

Mickey crossed his arms and rested them comfortably on top of his stomach. "Ha! Well, I'll tell you what: you wait! You just wait!" He wagged his finger and nodded his head, knowingly. "You wait 'til things start going sour. You'll think it's nothing, just PMS or somethin'. Then she'll start telling you some bullshit about growing apart. She'll say she wants a divorce, and before you know what hit you, you'll see money flying out of your paycheck every frickin' week! Man oh man, talk about being blindsided! Ha, you just wait til it happens!" he snorted, "you'll be knocking on my door wearing your painter's pants!"

Ron nodded slowly, mentally debating whether to point out his single status. Maybe it would shut Mickey up. "Okay then…"

"See, when you work for yourself," Mickey interrupted, "the money you bring in varies week to week. Sometimes it's good, but most of the time it's not. Thankfully, most of my customers don't mind paying in cash." He winked at John. "You know what I'm sayin' right?" But he didn't wait for an answer… "I gotta look out for me—Mickey Landis," he said, poking himself several times in the chest. "You think I feel guilty about keeping a few bucks for myself? Well, I don't and I'll tell you why…"

John and Ron looked at each other. *Great. Here we go.*

Mickey's face reddened. "You know what she did with my money?

Went and got herself a boob job! Guess she thinks she's Pam Anderson or somethin'!" he snorted.

He flicked some beads of sweat off his forehead. "Man, I'll tell you what—she got those boobs for her new boyfriend. She's old enough to be the kid's *mother* and she goes and shacks up with him! Disgusting! Ha! I'd like to see the look on his face when he finds out how old she is!" He leaned back and crossed his arms. "From what I hear, he makes a decent living though—wears a suit to work everyday. An accountant or something." Mickey sighed. "I have to hand it to the old broad; she's no dummy. She knows the second she marries him, or anyone, the alimony payments stop. So the two of them get to play house in *my* house while I foot the bill!"

John could hear the contempt in Mickey's voice. It was making his head spin. He knew that divorce brought out the worst in people, but he often wondered why couples didn't just stay together since they were going to keep right on hating each other after the split anyway.

Mickey's eyes suddenly widened and he sat up at attention. "Hold it. You're taping this right?"

John and Ron eyed each other.

"We told you earlier that we'd be recording your statement," John said.

"Uh, so this tape will be played in front of a judge or something?"

Ron didn't try to hide his annoyance. Mickey Landis should have thought of this half an hour ago; maybe then he wouldn't have wasted everyone's time with his rambling.

"The purpose of the recording is to collect information about the night in question—October 24th," John said. "Anything *not* having to do with our case will *not* be admitted as evidence."

Mickey leaned back, only slightly relieved.

Ron coughed, an indication that he wanted to get back on track.

"Okay then. You were out the night of Monday, October 24th, walking your dog. Is this correct?"

"Yes, Actually it's my brother's dog—his name's Charlie."

Ron smiled. Mickey's rambling had officially ended.

"What kind of dog is Charlie?"

"Dalmatian."

"What time was it when you walked him?"

"I left the house at 9:45 PM."

"You're sure?"

Mickey nodded. "Positive. I wanted to be back in case the power came back on before my show."

"A television show?"

"Yeah. *The Best of Divorce Court.* It's starts at 10:30."

"I see. And what route did you take?"

"We walked from Westmont to Belmont and made a left on Trinity. I noticed the power was on at the construction site next to the church and I wanted to check it out—see if they had a generator, or what."

"So you reached St. Agassi High School at what time?"

"About 10:00 PM or so. Charlie had a bunch of stops and starts along the way. He's not used to doing his business on a leash." Mickey looked over at John. "I think I told you that before."

John nodded.

"And what happened when you reached St. Agassi High?" Ron asked.

Mickey shrugged. "Nothing much. We stood on the sidewalk, right outside the parking lot. "

"You saw some vehicles?"

"That's right."

"And what do you remember about those vehicles?"

"The first one was a minivan, parked in the lot. It was a blue Honda Odyssey. The license plate was PA T894PR."

Ron looked down at his notes. *Impressive.* Mickey had just provided the exact plate number of Hannah Orenstein's van. "You have quite a memory Mr. Landis."

"Thanks, but it's only with plates. I drove a sixteen wheeler for ten years. Come to think of it, my wife was probably screwing around on me while I…"

Ron raised his eyebrows and motioned with his pencil toward the tape recorder.

Mickey grimaced. "Sorry. Anyway, as I was saying, there were days I'd be on the road twenty-four hours straight. Memorizing license plates kept me awake. I'd repeat them back to myself, sometimes ten at a time. Guess it worked. I'm still alive."

"The van was empty, I assume?" Ron asked.

Mickey shrugged. "I didn't see anyone."

"You told John there was a second vehicle."

"Yep; sure did. Flew in to the lot just as I was about to head home with Charlie. Nearly ran us over! I'm not positive about the color. It was either dark blue or black. A Toyota Camry."

"And were you able to get the plate on it?"

Mickey smiled. "Now *that*, I am sure of. *JAM 29.*"

# Fifty-nine

After leaving the office of her Princeton client, Judith flew north up the turnpike toward Manhattan, trying to drown out her own thoughts with talk radio. It wasn't something she had *planned* to say, she reminded herself, but once she saw Lauren's suitcase—still open from the day before when Sonia stopped by with her new baby—she had just blurted it out:

*It's probably best that you go now Lauren. The kids will have an easier time getting back to their old routine; you know, the one they had before you moved in.*

The girl was packing anyway, Judith reminded herself, so why then did she feel so guilty?

Judith glanced at the clock. It was a few minutes before one. Yehuda and the kids were probably leaving the hospital and heading over to school for the final Chanukah play rehearsal. Tomorrow was the big event! If all went smoothly at the office this afternoon—thankfully, Judith had only one deposition to attend—she would be back in Arden Station tonight by dinner, in time for a pre-production celebration.

Rachel was ecstatic Judith was coming. "*Nana's very first school event!*" she had announced innocently. Still, Judith cringed at those words. How could she have let this happen? How could she have wasted so much time?

Judith raised the radio volume. Mavis Murphy, the famous baby-boomer psychologist was discussing her new book *Love Don't Live Here Anymore*.

"Women have been sold a bill of goods," Mavis was saying to the interviewer. "Feminism told us that we could have it all. That we could be like men. Earn like men, *bleep* like men… Oh sorry."

"It's okay, we have a six second time delay."

"And don't I need it!" Mavis laughed. Her voice was scratchy, probably from years of smoking. "As I was saying… women were told they could do everything a man could, but what they *weren't* told was that there was a catch. That in order to reap the benefits bestowed on *man*kind, we had to bury our femininity. In essence, resurrect ourselves as men. On some unconscious level, women understood this. There was a time early in the movement when women even began dressing like men… "

The interviewer chimed in. "I remember: pin striped suits, ties and… "

"That's right," Mavis interrupted right back. "Of course that came on the heels of bra burning. Remember… how we dress on the outside tells the world what's going on in the inside. Our clothes define us."

It sounded like something Hannah would say, Judith thought. She ran a hand down one of her pant legs. It figured she had pin stripes on.

"So your advice to women is…?"

Mavis sighed dramatically. "How much time have we got?"

"Apparently not enough," the interviewer said. "But seriously, your message is what exactly? Are you suggesting that gender roles should be more clearly drawn? And, if so, wouldn't that only serve to subjugate women to the very limitations that they fought so hard to overcome?"

"The goal of my book *Love don't live here anymore*—which is available online and in bookstores nationwide—does not seek to tell women what they should or should not do with their lives," Mavis said. "The message of my book is directed to women in their fifties and sixties who were swept up in the feminist movement. Sadly, many of these women are suddenly awakening to the harsh reality that something is missing from their lives. I challenge these women to entertain the possibility that what is missing is a man! Too many of us are ashamed of our biological drives. We equate *wanting* a man with *needing* a man."

"What a *crock*," Judith mumbled. She switched off the radio but couldn't get Mavis Murphy's voice out of her head. *Women have been sold a bill of goods...* followed by the more sincere words of Lewis Danzig: *your only mistake was choosing a man not worthy of you.*

Her heart fluttered. What was the matter with her? Why couldn't she get Lewis Danzig out of her head? She missed him, that was why. After their impromptu meeting outside the township building, Lewis had been calling her every day. "Just checking in," he would say. They would chat for a few minutes and then he would end the call with "I hope you have a day as lovely as you are, Judith." Sure it was corny, but she had come to look forward to hearing his voice. A voice of reason, she called it. After all, he was the one who convinced her that even if Lauren *did* by some remote chance harbor a crush on Yehuda, it was not in his character to betray his family.

But now that Peter Stem had been released from prison, the call frequency had decreased significantly. Lewis was spending long hours at the rectory overseeing Peter's care. From what little he told her, Peter was making progress every day.

Judith gripped the wheel tightly as she contemplated the fact that a killer was still on the loose. Naturally her first concern had been for Hannah. Was she in danger? Would the guy come after her to finish the job?

An RV barreled past her, the license plate from Texas. She was just recovering from the scare when her cell phone rang, making her heart jump yet again.

"Hello?"

"Judith?"

She didn't recognize the voice at first. "Yes, this is Judith Orenstein."

A pause and then, "This is Janine Miller...."

"Janine! Yes, of course. What is it dear? Oh no... Is something the matter with Yehuda?"

"No, but I'm trying to reach him."

Judith relaxed. The call was apparently work related. "He's not with me, dear. I'm in the car—on the way to Manhattan. Did you try his cell?"

"Yes, but there was no answer."

"He probably has it turned off because of the play rehearsal," Judith said.

"Oh I forgot—the school play..."

"I can barely hear you dear. Why are you whispering?"

"I'm at the police station... in the ladies room actually..." Judith noted the growing panic in Janine's voice. "I really need to speak with Yehuda."

"The police station? What on earth are you doing at the police station, Janine?"

Janine ignored Judith's question. "Is there any way you could get in touch with him?"

"What is this all about Janine?" Judith demanded.

Janine didn't answer.

"Janine!"

"Yeah... Sorry. I'm here." She swallowed. "Two officers came into the center and asked me to come in for questioning."

"Questioning? What about?"

"They have an eye witness who saw my car at the mikvah the night Hannah was attacked..."

Judith's heart jumped at what sounded like a freight train, but was actually the horn of a tractor-trailer trying to nudge her out of the left lane. She took a deep breath and eased into the right lane, allowing the truck to pass.

Judith wasn't sure she heard correctly. "Someone saw your car at the mikvah the night Estelle was killed?"

"Yes."

Judith collected herself before she spoke. "Have you been read your rights Janine? You do realize you have a right to legal counsel?"

"Yes, I mean *no*... They told me I could call a lawyer, but I don't need one! I wasn't involved!" She paused. "You don't think I was involved do you Judith?"

"It doesn't matter what I think," Judith said, "but if an eyewitness saw your car at a crime scene, then you have some explaining to do."

"I didn't understand it either," Janine continued. "When the police showed up, I was so flustered... I didn't know what was going on... up until ten minutes ago, I couldn't figure it out..."

"Did something change in the last ten minutes?" Judith asked.

"No, nothing changed. It's just that I remembered..."

"Remembered what?"

"That someone had the keys to my apartment and access to my car."

"What?... Who?" Judith racked her brain trying to remember the name of Janine's boyfriend. Was it *Hank*?

Janine hesitated. "I should probably talk to Yehuda first. I don't want to accuse anyone of..."

"Who was it Janine?" Judith asked more urgently. *Howard*. Howard was Janine's boyfriend! *Howard* something.

"I don't know if I should..."

"Who was it?"

"Lauren."

Judith nearly dropped the phone.

"Janine, are you telling me *Lauren* drove your car to the mikvah?"

"No... I'm not saying that at all! I'm just saying that Lauren had *access* to my car."

Judith fought to retain her composure. "Is she the only one? Are you sure no one else has a key?"

"I'm positive. Lauren's the only one who could have taken my car."

Somehow Judith continued to drive even as her heart pounded violently against her chest. Could it be? Could it be that it wasn't a man, but a *woman* who had attacked Estelle and Hannah? Oh God; now it made perfect sense. Judith wasn't crazy after all! She had been right all along! It was all beginning to make perfect sense. Lauren *was* after Yehuda! In fact, she wanted him so badly, she was willing to kill for him! Judith thought of Hannah, naked and vulnerable in the mikvah water. *Lauren had tried to drown her!*

"Janine," Judith sputtered, "listen to me! You must tell the police immediately!"

Janine hesitated.

"Janine!" Judith screamed, sounding much more crazed than she would have liked. "Did you hear what I just said?"

"Yes... yes I did... Okay, I'll do it. I'll tell them right now."

Judith got off at the very next exit and turned her car around. *It wasn't Peter Stem. It wasn't any man.* She grabbed her phone and dialed directory assistance. "Arden Station, Pennsylvania. This is an emergency! I need the number for the township police!"

# Sixty

Judith hoped Yehuda and the kids would be home by now; but to her disappointment, the house appeared empty. She finally found her key and unlocked the front door, noting the time on her watch: *4:05*. She had redialed Yehuda's number during the rush back, each time being automatically dumped into his voice mail. To her frustration, the school office wasn't picking up either. Fortunately, Detective Smith at the Arden Station police headquarters had been easier to reach; especially when she mentioned that Janine Miller, their "person of interest" had called from a bathroom stall and provided her with some important information. Once the detective got on the phone, Judith practically talked his ear off. She told him *everything*: how Lauren had suddenly come into the Orenstein's lives less than a year ago. How she had cared for the children while Hannah was on bed rest (she probably developed her infatuation with Yehuda during that time, Judith speculated). The fact was that *somehow* this manipulative woman had fooled all of them, including her brilliant son the rabbi!

There was no need to barge in and disrupt the Chanukah play

rehearsal, the detective assured Judith when she suggested that he send Arden Station's version of a S.W.A.T. team. He was concerned about igniting a wave of panic around the community. She reluctantly agreed, adding that her son's family had been through enough tumult already. The only urgency seemed to be in locating Lauren and bringing her in for questioning. The Center City, Philadelphia precinct had been notified; they were dispatching a unit to Lauren Donnelly's apartment immediately.

Judith looked at her watch again. That conversation with the detective had occurred over an hour ago. Chances were good they now had Lauren in custody. What a relief! Judith kicked off her shoes and collapsed onto the couch. And now, she would just sit tight until Lewis got here. She had called him after she hung up with the detective and asked him to come over as soon as he could, promising to explain everything once he arrived.

Judith closed her eyes, trying to relax, but was jolted by a thud coming from the upstairs bedroom. Had the family been here the whole time? No, that wasn't possible; she would have heard the kids before. Besides, the car wasn't in the driveway.

Judith grabbed her cell phone and tiptoed cautiously up the steps. She reached the top of the landing and paused. There was a slight rustling coming from the master bedroom. She waited while her breathing returned to normal before continuing down the hall. She reached the master bedroom. The door was open a crack and it was easy to see the figure sitting at the base of the armoire.

*Lauren.*

"What the hell's going on here!"

Lauren jumped up. "Mrs. Orenstein... I... I didn't hear you come in! I thought you were at the rehearsal."

"No, I had business appointments." Judith tried to sound calm despite her pounding chest. Looking past Lauren, she shook her head in disgust. The bottom drawer of the armoire was pulled open and a pile of clothing was strewn about the floor. "I can't believe you would actually go through her things! But then, there isn't much you *wouldn't* do, is there?"

"What?"

"Suddenly you have a hearing problem?" Judith said sarcastically. "I said, I can't believe you have the nerve to go through Hannah's things."

"No, I… uh…"

"You what?" Judith snapped.

"I was just looking for…"

"You were just *looking*? What did you want to do? Take more of my daughter in law's things?

Lauren's face went white. "What? I never took…"

"Don't lie! I saw you wearing her clothes."

*The moleskin skirt from the basement.* "No! it's not what you think!"

"I know about girls like you Lauren! Your own life isn't good enough, so you think you can just move on in to someone else's!" Judith crossed her arms tightly against her chest. "I see the way you look at him."

"Look at who?" Lauren asked. Tears streamed down her face.

"My son… the way you look at my son, the *rabbi*."

Lauren shook her head fervently. "No! No! You don't understand!"

"Oh I understand perfectly, Lauren… it's *you* who doesn't understand! My son is a good man. There is no way in hell he would betray his wife, destroy his family for a fling with you or *anyone*!"

Lauren covered her mouth. "Oh my God… is that what you think? That I wanted to…"

"You thought it wasn't obvious?" Judith said, her hands on her hips, "the endless flirting with my son! First you act like my grandkids' *mother*, then you parade around in Hannah's clothes, and now I catch you red handed, going through Hannah's things—God only knows *what you've stolen!*"

Lauren shook her head. "Flirting? No! And I would never steal!... I can explain if you'll just give me a chance!"

"I'm not interested in your lies!" Judith shrieked. "But you know what I am interested in?"

Lauren shook her head, defeated.

"I'm interested in what *really* happened at the mikvah."

Lauren started trembling. "You think I had something to do with Estelle's death? With Hannah...?"

"You tell me."

"I didn't! I swear I had nothing to do with it!"

"Really? Then why were you there that night?"

Lauren's eyes widened.

"That's right. I know!" Judith shouted, wagging her finger at Lauren. "The police know too. And they're out looking for you as we speak."

"Oh my God...!"

"What did you think? By using Janine's car, she would be blamed for this?"

"I only borrowed hers because mine wouldn't start!"

"So you admit it!... you *were* there!"

Lauren swung her head around as if the room was closing in on her. "I have to get out of here... I have to go..." She ran toward the bedroom door, pushing past Judith. Judith fell to the ground with a thud and landed on her rear end. Meanwhile, Lauren bolted down the steps, nearly running over Lewis.

"Helloooo! Judith? Are you here?" Lewis's voice called up the steps.

"Lewis! Up here! I'm upstairs!"

Lewis bounded up the steps. "What happened?" he asked, giving Judith a hand and simultaneously eyeing the mess near Hannah's closet. "Lauren just ran past me like the house was on fire."

"I caught her going through Hannah's things!" Judith said breathlessly as she plopped on the bed. The excitement and potential danger of a confrontation with a murderer was just now catching up to her. "And then, she assaulted me!... I called 911... they're sending an officer, but maybe we can stop her..."

She stood, but Lewis grabbed her arm. "Sit! Catch your breath!" he ordered. He gave her a quick once over. "Are you hurt?"

She ignored his question and tried to pull away. "Don't you understand? We have to stop her!"

"Calm down, Judith! Whatever she took can be replaced."

Judith realized he didn't have the slightest idea what was going on. "No! It's not about that! She didn't steal anything..."

"Then what?" He took her hand, trying to calm her.

"Lauren was *there*—at the mikvah—the night of the attack!"

"Wait," he said, "You think that young girl had something to do with Estelle's death?" He looked doubtful.

"Why else would she be there and not tell anyone?"

He scratched his head. "I can't say, but there's got to be a logical explanation."

Judith yanked her hand from his and stood up. "What is it with you men? she screamed, her face red. "You see a pretty girl and your brain shuts down?"

Lewis knew no matter what he said, she would argue. Judith had never liked Lauren, that he *did* know. He just didn't realize how deep her disdain ran until this very moment. Her ranting was coming from a place of pure emotion, without one iota of logic.

Yehuda felt an uncomfortable sense of déjà vu when he saw the township police car parked in front of his house. *Oh God, what now?* He set Nehama's baby carrier down on the porch and fumbled for his house key, but soon realized the door was unlocked. Inside, his mother, Lewis Danzig, and two detectives were milling about the living room, speaking in low voices. Ron Smith—the detective who had informed him of Peter Stem's arrest, and then of his subsequent release—was scribbling something on a pad.

"Mom? What's going on?" Two words came to mind at once. *Hannah* and *relief*. Was this about Hannah? Was she all right? Had she suddenly take a turn for the worse? But he was relieved the kids weren't with him to hear whatever information would be given. Fortunately, by chance, Rachel, Eli, David and Yitzi had all decided to stay behind at school to help set up the chairs for tomorrow's performance. They would be getting a ride home with a neighbor in an hour or so.

Judith wasted no time. "These gentlemen have some news for you," she said, gesturing toward the detectives.

"Rabbi Orenstein, we have an eyewitness who saw Janine Miller's car in the high school parking lot the night of the attack," Ron said.

"Janine at the mikvah?" Yehuda had a flash of thought about what Janine—an unmarried woman—might be doing at the mikvah. There were occasions having nothing to do with family purity when women sometimes immersed in mikvah waters. Most had to do with major life changes: religious conversion, divorce, overcoming an addiction. Some women went after overcoming a bout with a serious illness. Other times, women who had never been to a mikvah simply felt curious and wanted to see what the mystery was all about. It was not unheard of for a mikvah attendant to give a personal tour, especially to newly religious women who were weighing the decision whether or not to take the monthly plunge. But so late at night?

"Miss Miller didn't drive the car that night," Ron continued. "Actually, she was out of town."

Judith stepped forward, nearly bursting. "It was Lauren! *Lauren* had Janine's car!" She delivered this additional piece of information with what sounded like victory after a bet.

John nodded. "We've confirmed that at the time, Miss Miller was in Atlantic City at Caesar's Hotel and Casino with a gentleman named Howard Freed," he said.

"Yehuda," Judith said, "it was *Lauren*."

"Lauren Donnelly drove Janine's Miller's car to the mikvah," Ron said. "She was there a little after 10:00. Your mother said she confessed this fact to her directly."

When she didn't get the anticipated shocked reaction from her son, Judith stepped forward. "Lauren was *here*, Yehuda! She attacked me!"

He stared at her for a few seconds. To Judith's dismay, there wasn't a hint of concern for her safety in his eyes. When he finally opened his mouth to speak, Judith was even more shocked. "Where is Lauren now?" he asked the officers.

It must be that Yehuda was in a state of shock, Judith told herself; how else could she explain his misplaced concern?

"She ran out," Rabbi Orenstein," Ron said. "We have two patrol cars looking for her."

Yehuda didn't respond. He kneeled down and reached into Nehama's carrier and carefully removed the sleeping baby's snowsuit.

Judith approached him. "Did you hear what the detective just said?"

"I heard him."

*Was that agitation in his voice?*

Yehuda looked past his mother at Lewis and the detectives. "Would any of you men care for a drink of water?"

Lewis held up his hand while John and Ron looked at each other, very much confused by the rabbi's calm demeanor, before verbally declining the offer. Without saying anything more, and to Judith's chagrin, Yehuda left the room. A minute later he returned a cup of water in one hand, a piece of paper in the other. "What's this?" he asked, waving the paper accusingly at Judith.

"I don't know," Judith sputtered, "I haven't been in the kitchen since…"

But Yehuda cut her off. "I'll tell you what it is, Mom. It's a note from Lauren."

"Oh?"

"It says, 'I think it would be best for everyone if I return to my apartment in the city'."

Judith shrugged. "Seems reasonable. I guess she moved out."

"You wouldn't by chance have anything to do with this, would you, Mom?"

Judith pointed to herself. "Me? Why would you think I had something to do with it?"

Yehuda took a deep breath. "Maybe because she told me you did?"

Judith folded her arms defensively. "So?… What does it matter why she left… Don't you see, Yehuda? She was *there*. At the mikvah. She was *involved!*"

He didn't respond. It was then that Judith noticed Lewis. He was standing off to the side, studying the scene intently. She had nearly forgotten he was there.

"She has something to hide, Yehuda!" Judith said, returning her attention to the matter at hand. "Why else would she be sneaking around here?"

"Sneaking around? What are you talking about?" Yehuda asked.

"For one thing, why would she move out this morning only to come back a few hours later?" Judith barked. "I'll tell you why! She knew the house would be empty… and… and I caught her going through Hannah's things!"

Yehuda leaned back on the couch, covering his eyes with his hands.

"I knew there was something *not right* about that girl!" Judith said, looking directly at John, in her opinion, the wiser looking of the two detectives. "Girls lose their minds when it comes to men… especially men they can't have!" She shook her head. "I tried to warn my son, but…"

Yehuda popped up suddenly and held up his hand. "Mom, stop! Enough!"

But Judith ignored him and continued talking. "See, even now, it's hard for him to accept…"

"I *asked* her to come back!" Yehuda blurted out. "And, I *asked* her to go through Hannah's things!"

Judith's jaw dropped. *Was it true then? Did Yehuda actually have a thing for Lauren too?*

Yehuda sighed. "She did such a terrific job organizing the kitchen, I wanted her to do the same with Hannah's clothes. I thought it would be a nice homecoming surprise for her."

Judith's felt a bit off kilter from this new information, but she wasn't about to be side tracked. "Well, okay, so she was organizing Hannah's clothes… but that still doesn't explain what she was doing at the mikvah."

"I don't believe you, Mom! Yehuda said, shaking his head. Do you honestly think Lauren would *kill* a woman?" Yehuda knew his mother could be stubborn and opinionated, but this was an entirely new level she had stooped to.

"Yes, I do," Judith said pointedly, turning her back on him. "I think that girl's capable of a lot more than you'll ever believe! Why do you think she started dolling herself up for you all of a sudden?"

"*Dolling herself up*? You mean the skirts?" He shook his head. "Lauren was wearing them as a favor to me… out of respect for the way Hannah dresses at home!"

"Bullshit!" Judith screamed. "That girl is a liar… she's manipulative, and if I were you, I'd keep her the hell away from your children!"

Yehuda shook his head in disbelief. "You have it all wrong. You have *Lauren* all wrong."

"No!" she came back at him, her finger pointed. "You're the one who…"

But what Yehuda said next stopped Judith in midsentence. "Lauren's like Sunny, Mom."

"*What?*" Judith crossed her arms. "What did you just say?" Her face had gone completely white.

Yehuda took a deep breath. "Lauren's like Sunny, Mom."

"But… but how… how do you…" Judith stammered.

"Pardon me," Ron began, glancing over at John who seemed to be thinking deeply about something. "Who is *Sunny?*"

"Her daughter," Lewis said. It was the first thing he'd said since Yehuda walked through the door.

Judith leaned back in the couch, biting her lip. "My daughter— Yehuda's sister…"

"Sunny's a lesbian," Yehuda said suddenly.

The room went silent except for the sound of Lewis taking a deep breath.

"With all due respect, Mrs. Orenstein," Ron said, "you've told us repeatedly over the past couple of hours that Lauren Donnelly had a romantic interest in your son—that she was *pursuing* him."

"No. That's not true. I wasn't pursuing Yehuda—ever."

Yehuda spun around. "Lauren!"

Judith's hand flew over her heart in surprise. Lauren had returned? No, this didn't make sense! Guilty people usually kept running!

*I'm sorry,* Yehuda mouthed to Lauren. He looked genuinely ashamed that he had disclosed something so personal.

Lauren stepped through the doorway. She straightened up and looked Judith directly in the eye. "What Yehuda said is true. I am a lesbian… I came back because I realized I have nothing to be ashamed of,"—she paused—"except, that is, for the way I spoke to Hannah." She turned to the detectives. "It's also true that I was at the mikvah the night Estelle was killed. I was. And I'm sorry…" One by one, she looked each of them in the eye. "I realize there might be some legal consequences, but I swear, I had nothing to do with what happened to either Estelle *or* Hannah!"

In the kitchen, Lauren slowly recounted everything for the detectives, with Yehuda standing by at her request. Lewis and Judith remained behind in the living room, but were able to hear every word.

"Hannah asked me to come and watch the kids for a few hours on the evening of October 24th," Lauren began. "Yehuda was teaching a class and she had to get ready for the mikvah… Hannah took her bath while I put the kids to bed. Later, she started up about Jonathon, chiding me for not giving him a chance. It seemed Hannah was *always* on my case about men! She accused me of being too picky, told me again that I wasn't getting any younger… Anyway, Yehuda came home from the center a little after 9:30 and I left. It was pouring outside and

I walked up the block to where my car was parked. It wouldn't start…
*again.* I was so upset I sat there for a minute and just bawled my eyes
out. Normally I would have just stayed over at the Orensteins, but I
didn't want to deal with Hannah when she got back from the mikvah.
I've stayed over at Janine's before—her apartment is within walking
distance—but I knew she was away with Howard for two days. Then I
remembered that I had a copy of her apartment key… I had never used
it before, but I figured I would stay there for the night. When I got
to her apartment I saw her car keys on the kitchen counter. I thought
about driving home, sleeping in my own bed, and then just returning
the keys in the morning. I really wanted to get as far away from Arden
Station as possible."

"And then what happened?" Ron asked.

"I got into Janine's car and headed for the expressway. I was thinking
about Hannah, getting more and more angry… I decided to finally put
an end to all the matchmaking business—confess the truth, *my* truth
to her—and let the chips fall where they would. Do you have any idea
how hard it is living a lie, Detective?"

"So you drove to the mikvah?" John prompted.

"Uh huh. I changed direction and drove to the mikvah. It was a
little after ten when I got there. The door was locked so I rang the bell.
Estelle Ginsberg answered. I told her I needed to see Hannah, that it
was urgent. I stood in the waiting area and Estelle tapped on one of the
bathroom doors. About a minute later, Hannah came out in her robe.
She looked very concerned. Of course she thought something must
be wrong at home or why else would I be there? She asked me if the
kids were okay. I told her everything was fine… I began having second
thoughts about being there, but it was too late. For a minute, we just
stood there in the hallway, staring at each other, and then finally, I just
blurted it out."

"What did you say exactly?" Ron asked.

"I said, 'Hannah, I have something to tell you'." Lauren shook her head, remembering. "Then it was like the levee just broke... all those years of keeping it bottled up, I guess. I just lost it! I remember speaking really loudly, really fast.... something like, 'I'm a lesbian! I've known since elementary school... I like *women*... so you can stop all the bullshit about trying to find the right guy for me... there *isn't* one!' I could see Estelle out of the corner of my eye. She was staring at me with what looked like a combination of confusion and disgust. I'm sure Hannah saw it too. She told me I should leave, something about the mikvah not being an appropriate place for this discussion. Then I left. I drove the car back to Janine's apartment and stayed there for the night, although I didn't sleep a wink. The next morning—Tuesday—I took the 6:40 train into the city and went home. I didn't learn anything about the mikvah crime, or what had happened to Estelle and Hannah until Rachel called me Thursday morning."

"October 27th was the first time you spoke to Yehuda?" Ron asked.

"Uh huh. I was totally surprised by the call. After what I told Hannah Monday night, I didn't expect to hear from any of them ever again."

Yehuda, who had been quiet during the entire discourse, finally spoke up. "You thought Hannah disapproved?"

"Of me being a lesbian?" Lauren snorted. "Of course she disapproved! She's an orthodox Jew!... It didn't even occur to her that not everyone is... that some of us are... that I could be gay."

It wasn't long before the detectives had all the information they needed. A few more questions confirmed that indeed, Hannah and Estelle were both alive and well when Lauren arrived at the mikvah. But, unfortunately, other than Mickey Landis and his Dalmatian, Charlie, she had seen no one else in the area.

"You're right. It didn't occur to her." Yehuda said after the two officers had gone. "Hannah called me that night... after you left the mikvah... and told me what you had said."

"And?"

"And to be honest, she was very surprised."

Lauren shook her head in disbelief. "I can't believe you've known the whole time."

"Yes. But only because after she found out, Hannah felt terrible about how she had carried on all those months."

"The whole husband search..."

Yehuda nodded. "All along, she thought you were hesitant because you had been hurt in a past relationship."

"Well, in a way, I was. It just wasn't the kind of relationship she assumed it was." Lauren took a deep breath. "Her name was Maxine, but everyone called her Max. She was already involved with someone—one of my supervisors at work actually. There was a commitment ceremony and everything and I kind of stole her away for a while. It was wrong, I know... and it ended up blowing up in my face."

"That was the real reason you left your job?"

"Pretty much. But I've known for a while PR wasn't for me," Lauren said. "Yehuda, can I ask you something?"

"Of course."

"You say that Hannah felt bad when she called you from the mikvah, but then why did she seem so *angry* when I told her?"

Yehuda thought for a moment. "Honestly, knowing Hannah, it was probably more that she was caught off guard. She probably didn't want Estelle—or anyone else—hearing something so private. When she called me, she told me she was going to talk to you the next morning and apologize... Unfortunately, she was never able to do that..."

Lauren shivered at the sudden realization that within minutes of leaving the mikvah, a killer had struck. For all she knew, the guy could have been hiding in the bushes, waiting for his opportunity.

"And what did *you* think when you heard?" Lauren was surprised to hear herself speak the question out loud. She couldn't deny that his opinion of her mattered. "Were you completely shocked?"

Yehuda didn't need time to contemplate his answer. "No. Actually I wasn't." He smiled. "Now when my sister Sunny came out, it was a different story. That was years ago, right around the time when I earned *shmita*—my rabbinical credentials." He smiled at the memory. "Lets just say my opinions were a bit more black and white back then. I didn't see a whole lot of gray."

"And now?"

"I'd like to think I'm a bit wiser, and a lot more accepting."

"But doesn't the Torah say that I'm an *abomination*?"

Yehuda sighed. "Yes, but it also says it's an abomination to eat non-kosher food."

He noticed that she was tearing up. "Anyway," he continued, "how could a so called *abomination* bring such light into the lives of children? He looked directly into her eyes. "Lauren, you've been a God send to us, you've helped us get through this difficult time… my children, my wife, and I… we're all tremendously grateful."

"You have to know that I would have never *chosen* to be like this," she continued "For years, I prayed that God would change me… make me normal."

"Look," he said gently, "we do not understand why God created some individuals with homosexual preferences… The Torah doesn't discuss whether sexual orientation is genetic or environmental. But what the Torah *does* assure us of is this: without exception, we are all beloved in the eyes of God."

To her surprise, he took her hand. "We're all climbing the ladder,

Lauren, trying to be better people. Isn't that the point? One step at a time, we move up. The Jewish rituals are there to help us along this path, but it's not *all or nothing*. To say that one's sexuality negates their place on the ladder to begin with… well, I don't believe that."

In the living room, Judith was shaking her head in disbelief. "How could I have been so completely wrong about everything?" She took the tissue Lewis offered and blew her nose. "I honestly thought Lauren was interested in Yehuda! But even worse… I was convinced she was a murderer! What the hell's the matter with me?" She held her palm to her forehead. "Am I losing my mind?"

Lewis took a deep breath. "Are you asking me rhetorically, Judith? Or would you like to hear what I think?"

She sniffled. "I need to know if I have some kind of mental illness! Or maybe I have a brain anuyerism?"

He smiled sympathetically. "I can assure you, your brain is functioning just fine." He was quiet then, contemplating something in his mind. "Can I get personal with you Judith?"

She nodded slowly. "I'll even promise not to attack you."

He couldn't help but smile at her attempt at levity. "Very well," he said, "I wondered about the woman who had the affair with your husband. What memories do you have? Could you describe her to me?"

Judith stared at him blankly. She couldn't fathom what something that happened over thirty years ago had to do with her delusions about Lauren, but the memory of Marigold burned so brightly in her mind, it was an easy enough question to answer. "She was a pretty girl, but kind of plain… dressed down, never wore jewelry…"

"Go on."

"She was taller than me by a few inches—maybe Hannah's height."

"Hair color?"

"Dark brown. She always wore it in braids."

"How old was she when the affair happened?"

"Oh, I don't know—twenty-five or twenty-six."

It was just as Lewis had suspected. "Judith," he began, "I'd like you to think of someone else who matches that description."

Judith shook her head. "I don't understand any of this Lewis! This is ridiculous! First you ask me about the woman who destroyed my life and now you want me to come up with someone who... " Suddenly Judith stopped speaking. Her eyes widened as she made the connection. "Oh God... Oh God, Lewis... *Lauren?* It was suddenly clear as day. "You mean I was..."

Lewis nodded.

Judith's hand flew over her mouth. "Then I *was* temporarily insane!"

Lewis wrapped his arm protectively around her. "You never finished grieving Judith. The pain has been with you all these years."

She grabbed a handful of tissues and blew her nose again. "I've been so busy... I never had the time..."

"Or perhaps you've kept yourself busy for a *reason.*"

Judith looked at him, her eyes bloodshot. "I've buried the pain, haven't I?" She took a deep breath trying to absorb what she knew to be true. After a minute she asked him, "Tell me honestly, Lewis, is it too late for me?"

"Never," Lewis said firmly. "It's never too late to reclaim a life."

# Sixty-one

"If you have something to say to me, then just say it already!"

It was a mere six-mile drive back to the township building and John had been silent the entire time. After the fiasco back at the Orenstein's house, Ron was fully aware of the long hours of work awaiting them. Okay, so if John wanted to tell him off, so be it. Ron knew he deserved it. He took full responsibility for mishandling the case. *From day one,* he had told John. *It was on me from that very first day, and I screwed it up.* And now, he would say it again, if it would get John to stop all this silent treatment bullshit.

John turned his head in Ron's direction and Ron braced himself.

"It was something the rabbi's mother said... got me thinking."

Ron could hardly believe his ears. "Judith Orenstein? You were thinking about Judith Orenstein this entire time?"

John nodded. "I remember it exactly. She said, 'Girls lose their minds when it comes to men, especially men they can't have.'"

Ron relaxed. For the moment, at least, he had caught a break. "Yeah well, so much for her theory about Lauren Donnelly, huh?"

"It got me thinking about that girlfriend of Peter's," John said.

"Lydia Richter?"

"Yeah."

"What about her?"

"There was something she said…" John tapped his forehead, clearly frustrated. "I just can't remember it…"

Ron smirked. "I don't believe it! John Collins having memory problems? With those perfect genes of yours? Who'd have *thunk* it?"

Five minutes later, they were back in Ron's office. "Here it is," John said, rummaging through the case file. He located the transcript of Lydia Richter's interview, took a seat and read through the entire conversation. "Okay, right here," John said, tapping eagerly at the paper. This is what I was looking for! One of the last things Lydia Richter told you was that Peter didn't want her as a girlfriend. She said she wasn't pretty enough." He looked up at Ron. "Then *you* asked if Peter had actually *said* she wasn't pretty enough. She told you 'no'… but then, she said something else."

Ron motioned with his hands. "Go on."

"She said, 'Peter likes the girls at St. Agassi better.'"

John looked elated, but Ron was unimpressed. "That's it?" he asked

"Almost," continued John, "You then asked Lydia specifically *which* St. Agassi girls she was referring to."

Ron nodded. "Okay. Right. I vaguely remember. Go on."

John's voice was serious. "Lydia responded, and I quote, 'the ones that came at night—to the spa.'"

John smiled, victoriously; but Ron still didn't follow. Sure, Peter was innocent of the crimes committed at the mikvah, but there was no disputing the fact that he *had* spied on the women. Therefore, it was a reasonable inference that he might have developed a crush on one or two of them. It was also possible that he had mentioned these "crushes" to Lydia Richter, especially if he wanted to get her off his back.

John threw the paper on the desk. "Don't you get it Ron?"

"Get *what?*"

"Lydia said Peter liked the women who came the *spa. The spa!* Tell me: why would she call it that? How is it that Lydia Richter would even have a *clue* what went on inside that building?"

Ron shrugged. "I don't know… Maybe she used the mikvah herself?"

John's shoulders dropped. "Come on! She's not even Jewish!… or married," he added.

"Okay, so maybe Peter *told her* it was a spa?"

John shook his head. "No. Peter didn't know what it was either. Before the night of the attack, he had never been inside."

"Hold on," Ron said. "Didn't you tell me Robert Sedgwick thought it was some kind of spa too?"

John nodded. "But only after he *saw* it. We both did actually. That's the only context a non-Jew, or anyone not familiar with a mikvah would have." He held out his hands. "You take one look at all the bathrooms and what looks like a Jacuzzi, and you automatically think *spa*. And just supposing Lydia *had* actually used the facility…"

Ron sat up. "Then she would have called it exactly what it was—a *mikvah!*"

"But she *didn't*," John said.

Ron was visibly excited. "My God, John. You're right! Lydia Richter was *inside*! She had to have been! There's no other explanation!"

"I think it's about time we see what Miss Richter has to say for herself," John said, grabbing his coat.

Ron glanced quickly at the top of the transcript. "517 Meetinghouse

Road. Hey, that's not too far from our buddy Mickey Landis," he said.

"Or the mikvah," John noted.

Ten minutes later they were pulling into the circular driveway of #517—a hardscape of red brick pavers.

"Nice house," Ron said. "Lydia must live with her parents. There's no way Riley's Drugs pays for something as nice as this!"

*Though sometimes that has nothing to do with it,* John thought to himself.

They stepped out of the car and admired the expansive plantation style house. Tall French windows adorned the front entranceway and white columns stretched to the second floor. A forty-something woman in black leggings sat in a rocker on the wrap around porch.

"Mrs. Richter?" John asked as they approached. It was just above freezing but the woman only wore a t-shirt.

"No. My name is Mandy Somers," the woman said, rubbing her hands together. Her teeth were chattering.

"Hello Mandy," John said. "Does Lydia Richter live here?"

Mandy nodded but didn't move.

"Is she home?"

Just then a second woman walked out, about ten years older than the first. "Mandy! You know better than to be out here without a coat! You'll freeze to death!" She ushered Mandy through the door and turned to the detectives. "Can I help you?"

John flashed his badge. "We're looking for Lydia Richter."

"Is there some kind of problem?"

"Are you her mother?"

"Mother?" The woman looked either surprised or offended. "No. I'm Connie Spellman. I run the group home."

"*Group* home?" Ron asked, looking behind him. "I don't recall seeing a sign."

Connie shrugged. "We have eight young women who live here."

Ron glanced over at Mandy as she walked inside. Connie apparently had a loose interpretation of the word *young*. Or maybe some of them had been here so long, they had grown out of young.

"The women who live here, they have special needs?" John asked.

Connie nodded. "They have mild to moderate mental retardation."

"And Lydia Richter is a resident here?"

"Yes. She's one of our more mild cases—able to function very well in the world."

"We understand she holds down a job," John said.

"Yes, it's part of our vocational placement program. She's been at Riley's for over three years now. Lydia's very friendly. The customers love her."

John glanced around the porch. "Is she here now?"

"No. She's at the market with one of the volunteers." She gestured toward some chairs. "Please have a seat. May I ask what this is about?"

"We have a few additional questions for her."

Connie narrowed her eyes. "*Additional?*"

"That's right; we interviewed her about a week or so ago…"

"You interviewed Lydia *here?*"

"No. Down at the township building."

Apparently, this information was news to Connie. "How did she get there?"

Ron shrugged. "We didn't ask."

Just then a van pulled up and Lydia and two other women jumped out. One of the women appeared as though she had a mild form of down syndrome. Lydia's smile faded away when she saw the two detectives sitting on the porch.

"Lydia?" Connie stood up, her arms crossed. "I'd like a word with you."

"I can't... I have to help bring these in," Lydia said grabbing a brown bag from the trunk.

The woman who had been driving took it from her. "It's okay, Lydia. Darla and I will unload them."

Reluctantly, Lydia made her way up the porch steps and took a seat next to Connie. Her hands in her lap, she avoided eye contact and licked her lips nervously.

Connie looked at her pointedly. "Lydia, did you meet with these detectives last week?"

Lydia nodded.

"At the township building?"

"Uh huh."

Connie shifted uncomfortably in her seat. "How did you get there?"

"I took the bus."

"The bus! By yourself?"

"Yeah. I'm old enough."

"That's not the point. We have rules here, Lydia. You know that. You are not to travel alone!"

"It's a dumb rule."

"You may think so, but you agreed to abide by it when you moved in."

"My parents agreed," Lydia mumbled.

"And how long ago was that?" John interjected.

"Five years."

Lydia looked around nervously like she wanted to make a run for it.

"Am I in trouble?"

"Well, I'll have to think about it," Connie said. "This is a very serious offense."

There was a tap on the window. It was Mandy. She was laughing and cupping her hands against the glass, saying something that they couldn't make out, but evidently Lydia could.

"Shut up Mandy!" Lydia hissed. She waved her arms. "Go away!"

Connie looked back and forth at the two women trying to discern what was going on. "Excuse me a moment," she told the officers.

Inside, Connie took Mandy by the arm and led her away from the window, deeper inside the house, and out of sight. Lydia averted her eyes from the officers and started nibbling her nails, nervously.

"We have a problem," Connie said, returning minutes later. She held a brown paper bag in the crook of her arm. "Lydia, I need you to go to your room immediately."

"She's a liar! She lies!" Lydia shouted as she ran into the house.

"These questions you have for Lydia," Connie began slowly, "they wouldn't by chance have to do with these?" She gently opened the bag and scooped out a handful of small white tubes. "Mandy says Lydia *stole* them. Is that what all this is about?"

Ron looked at them, bewildered, but John recognized them immediately: samples of the same Israeli body lotion used at the mikvah. *Exact replicas of the ones that had been scattered on the floor next to Estelle Ginsberg's dead body.*

# Sixty-two

"Nice Office."

Ron took a seat in a tall leather chair, directly across from John who sat behind a mahogany desk.

"Yeah, well Patty works fast," John said, smiling. "Once she heard that I was moving back inside, she had the furniture sent over from the house. Wallpaper's coming next week."

"Impressive," Ron said. "I'll have to get some tips from her for my office... hey, what's with the head?"

John shook his head. "It's called a *bust,* Ron. Jay made it before he..."

Ron approached the pedestal to get a closer look. "It's amazing, John—looks just like you," he said after studying it carefully.

John tapped his pencil. "Yeah, well, my nephew was a talented kid."

"He'd be glad to see you back, John."

"That's what Patty says too..."

Ron gestured with his chin. "Those are from her?"

"The flowers? No. Actually, Father McCormick sent them over. He says they're called Forget-me-not's. Says he doesn't want me to forget what *almost* happened to Peter."

Ron nodded. "How's he doing anyway?"

"Peter?" John glanced at his watch. "I'll tell you what," he said, standing up and grabbing his coat, "I'll give you a full report in about an hour. I'm on my way over to the rectory right now."

The rectory felt different this time. Warmer, cozier. Like a real home, John thought. Samson slept contentedly in front of the fireplace. In the corner, by the bookshelves, a Christmas tree stood, newly trimmed.

"So how's he doing?" John asked.

"Better," Father McCormick said with a smile. "Each day there's improvement. Dr. Danzig just left a few minutes ago— went to spend some time with his grandkids."

John handed the priest a box of Peter's belongings. The binoculars lay right on top. "Would it be okay if...?"

"Sure. Go right on up, John."

But John didn't budge and Father McCormick sensed his hesitation. "Come on," he said, placing an open hand on John's back, "we'll go together."

Peter lay in bed, propped up against two pillows, sifting through a shoebox of cards and letters. "Hello?"

"Peter, this is Detective John Collins."

"*John Collins*," Peter repeated. "You're the guy who handcuffed me."

John cringed and glanced at Peter's wrist, which, he was happy to see, was now bandage free. John wondered just how much of that night Peter remembered.

"Dr. Danzig told me," Peter said. A smile spread across his face. "He also told me it's because of you that I'm a free man."

John shoved his hands in his pockets and shifted uncomfortably. Peter seemed like a nice guy. A normal, everyday guy. "I'd say Father McCormick deserves credit for that. He never stopped believing in you, son." John had no idea why he just used the word *son*. For a split second he worried that it might cause some kind of psychological set back in Peter. "Anyway," he added quickly, "I'm glad to see you're doing better."

Peter's expression turned serious. "What's going to happen to Lydia?" he asked.

John took a deep breath. "Well, it looks like she'll be serving time for manslaughter."

Peter closed his eyes. "But it's not all her fault…"

"Well, it was her actions that killed Estelle Ginsberg," John said pointedly.

"But I'm partly to blame!" Peter said. He turned to Father McCormick. "I was inappropriate with her, Father. I misled her."

Father McCormick reacted as though he could see the despondent look on Peter's face. "What took place between you and Lydia happened a long time ago," he said.

"From what is sounds like, she wouldn't take no for an answer," John offered. "She was more than mildly obsessed with you. Did you realize she was watching you that night?"

"She was?" Peter asked, sitting up. "Oh. I get it. She was watching me watching *them*."

John nodded. "Samson saw her too. She claims the dog tried to attack her."

"Samson… her paw," Peter said. "I thought it was an animal."

"We both did," Father McCormick said.

"Lydia was watching you at the window. When you disappeared she assumed you were over there with one of them."

"She thought I was with a woman when I was actually hiding in my closet?"

John nodded.

Peter covered his eyes shook his head in disbelief. "I still don't want to see her suffer. Lydia's not a bad person…"

"Well," John said, "Hannah Orenstein will be home soon. Her doctor expects that after some physical therapy, she'll make a full recovery. Her prognosis may help Lydia get a reduced sentence."

"By you saving Hannah," Father McCormick offered, "You may have saved Lydia."

Peter nodded. He felt slightly vindicated. "What she did wasn't much different than what Roy did," he said after a moment.

John noted that Peter said "Roy" instead of "my dad". Peter probably still hadn't come to terms with the fact that Roy Bunton, killer of his mother and sister, was not only his mother's *boyfriend*, but also his and Suzanne's biological father.

"I think he loved her but she didn't love him back… and it made him crazy."

"Love sick or not," Father McCormick said firmly, "humanity cannot survive without morality. God gave us free will, Peter. It's up to us to make the right choices."

# Sixty-three

"Hey stranger!" The sight of Judith, looking both warm and glamorous in a long black poncho took Lewis's breath away. Little Yitzi, doing his best impression of a galloping pony, trailed behind.

"Sorry we're late," Judith said. "There was a last minute emergency." She pushed off her hood and tousled her hair, which she had recently decided to grow out a bit.

"Whew! That's better!" She gave Yitzi a nod and he took off in the direction of Benji Henner on the slide.

"What kind of emergency?" Lewis asked, expecting to hear about another deadbeat dad.

"I'll tell you in a second," Judith said. Her hand disappeared under her poncho and surfaced seconds later with her cell phone. She flipped it open and checked the screen. "Good. No calls, so, everything's all right."

"As expected, Judith Orenstein, Esquire has everything under control," Lewis said with a laugh.

"Try Judith Orenstein, *Nana*," she said winking. "I'll have you know, the 'last minute emergency' was Rachel getting gum stuck in her hair. She was in the middle of combing it out when I left. I told her to call if she needed me to come back." Judith smiled coyly at him. "You assumed it was work, didn't you?"

He held up his hands. "Sorry… I confess… guilty as charged."

"Well, I can't say I blame you," Judith said. "But I do want you to know that work is the furthest thing from my mind right now. In fact, I even hired a partner." She looked past him, at Yitzi who was flying headfirst down the slide. "I can't very well be a proper Nana to my grandchildren if I'm working all the time, now can I?"

She couldn't help but notice the delighted expression on Lewis's face and it made her heart flutter.

"May I?" he asked, hooking her arm and leading her toward the bench. For a few minutes they sat quietly watching Yitzi and Benji run back and forth across the bridge. Then the boys moved to the swings. They were set so low, Yitzi had to back himself up several feet just to get to a standing position.

"Jaw dominos!" he shrieked before pulling his legs up and flying forward.

Judith covered her mouth, stifling her laugh, as she leaned into Lewis. "Geronimo," she whispered. "He meant to say *Geronimo*."

Lewis shook his head. "I wouldn't have gotten that one… not in a million years."

Judith burst out laughing, finding the expression on his face incredibly funny. "What?" she asked as he stared into her eyes.

"It's nice to see you so happy, Judith," he said. "And by the way, have I ever told you what a beautiful laugh you have?"

"Hmm…" she said, narrowing her eyes. "That wouldn't be a pick up line by any chance would it?"

He scratched his chin. "I hadn't considered that."

"Maybe subconsciously you want to ask me out, but your consciousness just doesn't know it yet."

He pursed his lips and nodded slowly as if pondering a complicated matter. "You may just have something there, young lady."

She poked him with her elbow. "Young lady! Who are you calling *young?*"

"Nana! Nana! Look at me!" Yitzi shouted from the swings. Judith jumped up and waved. "Wow, Yitz! You're going so high!"

"You never gave me an update on the rectory worker," Judith said, settling back onto the bench.

"Peter."

"Yes. Peter. How is he doing?" Judith asked.

Lewis smiled. "He's going to be just fine."

"Is it true then?" Judith asked. "Did he really watch as his mother and sister were…?"

Lewis nodded. "It's a horrific thing for anyone to witness, let alone a child of seven." Lewis said nothing more, lost momentarily in his own thoughts. *The resilience of children. The complexity of the human mind.* He shuddered when the image popped into his head. A young boy cowering in his closet as his mother and sister were bludgeoned to death, not knowing if he, himself, would live or die.

"So what's next for Peter?" Judith asked gently.

"It looks like he's going to move out west with Father McCormick. The archdiocese has managed to arrange a job for him as a grounds keeper for Mt. Lemmon Village."

"So he won't be heading home to Michigan?"

Lewis shook his head. "Home? No, Michigan hasn't been his home since he was a teen, Judith."

Judith nodded.

"He asked me to visit," Lewis said. "I told him I would. In fact…"

He reached into his jacket pocket. "There's a beautiful resort about twenty miles south of Mt. Lemmon." He unfolded the brochure and handed it to her. "See? Trail rides… yoga… hiking… He stretched his legs out in front of him, and folded his arms back, behind his head. "The truth is, I could use a vacation. I'm *ready* for a vacation!"

Judith smiled politely. "It sounds great, Lewis."

"I'm glad you think so," he said, sitting up and shifting his body so he was facing her, "because I was hoping you would join me."

She opened her mouth, about to say something, when he leaned in and kissed her—literally taking her breath away—before she had a chance to object.

# The End.

SARAH SEGAL lives with her family in a suburb of Philadelphia. She can be reached at:

sarahsegal@comcast.net

LaVergne, TN USA
06 December 2009
166115LV00003B/132/P